PENGUIN

THE FOUR... KT-415-685

Debbie Taylor is editor of *Mslexia*, the fastest-growing literary magazine in the UK. She has been writing and travelling ever since she abandoned her career as a research psychologist. She has worked as editor of *New Internationalist* magazine, and has co-edited *The Virago Book of Writing for Women*. Her non-fiction book, *My Children My Gold* (Virago), was shortlisted for the Fawcett Prize for women's writing. She lives with her partner and daughter in a disused lighthouse at the mouth of the River Tyne.

The Fourth Queen

DEBBIE TAYLOR

PENGUIN BOOKS

PENGUIN BOOKS

Published by the Penguin Group
Penguin Books Ltd, 80 Strand, London WC2R 0RL, England
Penguin Group (USA) Inc., 375 Hudson Street, New York, New York 10014, USA
Penguin Books Australia Ltd, 250 Camberwell Road, Camberwell, Victoria 3124, Australia
Penguin Books Canada Ltd, 10 Alcorn Avenue, Toronto, Ontario, Canada M4V 3B2
Penguin Books India (P) Ltd, 11 Community Centre, Panchsheel Park, New Delhi – 110 017, India
Penguin Books (NZ) Ltd, Cnr Rosedale and Airborne Roads, Albany, Auckland, New Zealand
Penguin Books (South Africa) (Pty) Ltd, 24 Sturdee Avenue, Rosebank 2196, South Africa

Penguin Books Ltd, Registered Offices: 80 Strand, London WC2R 0RL, England

www.penguin.com

Published by Michael Joseph 2003
Published in Penguin Books 2004

3

Printed in England by Clays Ltd, St Ives plc

Acknowledgements

Thanks to Gillian Allnutt, Andrea Badenoch, Julia Darling, Peter Day, Elizabeth Fairbairn, Kitty Fitzgerald, Maggie Gee, Chrissie Glazebrook, Penny Smith and Margaret Wilkinson, for comments on early drafts of the manuscript; to my agent, Judith Murray, and my editor, Harriet Evans, for their input in the final stages; and to my partner, Bill Herbert, who was involved at every stage.

The Fourth Queen was supported by a Northern Arts Writers' Award.

Part I

'At a place called Mill of Steps stood a cottage, which was once the residence of the Empress of Morocco. She was the daughter of a cottager, who discorded with her parents and left them, taking nothing but what she had on.

'While crossing the Atlantic for America her vessel was captured by an African pirate and carried into Morocco. Her beauty having captivated the affections of the Emperor, she soon became Empress.

'The maiden name of the Empress was Gloag, of which several persons of that name are still living in the parish.'

Antiquities of Strathearn, with Historical and Traditionary Tales and Biographical Sketches of Celebrated Individuals belonging to the District,
by John Shearer, 1836

Mill of Steps is a hamlet just outside the village of Muthill in Perthshire, Scotland.

1

Helen hefted the bundle she was carrying on to the floor and stared round the ship's passenger cabin. It was crammed with people, blundering about in the semi-darkness, tripping over one another's belongings, laying claim to the strange cloth beds that hung like strings of onions from the walls.

She sank back against the wall. She'd imagined little round windows, splashed with salt water; perhaps a few neat partitions to separate different family groups. Not this creaking barn, with its slimy, swaying floor.

To stop herself crying, she closed her hands into fists and forced her nails into the flesh of her palms. She'd no one to blame but herself. If she hadn't run away, what was the worst that could have happened? Meg couldn't have stayed angry with her for ever. She thought of her old box bed at home; the blankets smelling of sweet hay and woodsmoke. If she left now she'd be back at Muthill in less than a fortnight.

Below water level the only daylight came from two trapdoors with ladders leading up to the main deck. She could smell rancid butter and rotting fish, and a midden stink was already seeping from the close-stools behind the screen in the corner. Vomit nudged at the back of her throat. She would have to spend the next twelve weeks in this place, buried with a hundred other souls like worms in a coffin.

She squeezed her fists tighter and her nails bit deeper. Why did she never think before she did things? Going to John Bayne's house in the middle of the night: barefoot, like a hussy. Did she expect to be treated like a lady? No wonder he'd taken her to his servants' quarters. Retching into her shawl, she staggered over to a ladder and scrambled back up towards the light.

Outside there was shouting everywhere. Men were rolling barrels towards holes in the deck or spidering high overhead in a web of ropes and poles. Others leant over the side hauling sacks up from the skiffs bobbing far below in the water. A man with porridge skin spied her standing there, young and dazed and pretty, and started towards her, grinning like a dog. Stumbling over a coil of rope, she turned and fled to the side of the ship.

There was still time. She could persuade one of the skiffs to take her back to the Greenock quay. Leaning over the railings, she looked down at the unruly flotilla nudging at the ship's belly like puppies. She thought of hailing one and scrambling down a rope ladder. Then what? She'd no money for the stage-coach to Perth, and no one to go with. Her travelling companions Betty and Dougie were still in the cabin; they'd never come back with her. There was nothing back at Muthill for them but digging neeps for a pittance for the rest of their lives: this journey to the Colonies was their only hope.

Pressed against the ship's railings, Helen felt cornered. She thought of the sturdy, well-ordered cottage she'd left behind; of her father, Muthill's blacksmith, with his big, kind hands and leather apron; of the grey kirk school; the river skipping over clean pebbles by the mill. How could she have run away from all that? And the weans; and Meg, her stepmother, for all her fierceness. Meg was right to be angry with her, sneaking home with bruised lips at five in the morning. But she'd have calmed down eventually – if Helen hadn't slammed out of the cottage. And seen Betty and Dougie in the distance, setting off on the first stage of their journey to America. Now it was too late. Now she was trapped on this ship and there was no going back. Her chest tightened and panic clogged her throat.

She needed somewhere to cry; somewhere no one could see her. Climbing over a pile of lumpy sacks, she squeezed behind a stack of hen-coops and crouched down out of sight. The hens jostled and pecked at one another in their cramped quarters. Helen watched a smashed egg ooze slowly out between the bars and began to feel calmer.

After a while she knelt up and peered cautiously out. Soon she noticed a small group of people boarding the ship. They must have come on a special boat because they were far too well dressed to have been ferried out with the pea sacks and cheese barrels like the other passengers. She counted five men; but it was the one woman, in a vivid green cloak, who caught her attention.

The woman was swaying lightly, as though she was going to swoon, holding on to one of the men's arms with a lace-gloved hand. The other men clustered anxiously around her, and one of them barked an order to a passing sailor, who ran off to fetch a small folding chair.

The woman hesitated, looking down at the chair. It was a rickety little thing, with thongs strung through it for a seat. Even at this distance, Helen could tell she'd never sat on anything so crude in her life. The woman laughed and shook her head, clearly protesting that she felt much better. Then, in a sudden change of mood, she was tugging on her husband's arm and pointing, urging him to check on the sailors who were lugging their bags on to the ship.

Kneeling in her filthy skirt, Helen watched transfixed as grown men scurried to serve the pale-haired woman in her emerald-green cloak. What must it be like to be cared for like that? After a while, the man who'd ordered the chair bowed to the group and gestured towards the upper part of the ship, offering to conduct them to their quarters. Quite forgetting her distress, Helen slipped out of her hiding-place and hurried across the deck after them.

'Helen! Thank God – we were afeared you'd gone over the side!' It was Betty, red-cheeked and breathless, running towards her. 'Listen, we've to go down the stores with our tickets. One of they sailors said we've to get our names set down on a list before we can get our food. He said it's not that good, but if we talk sweet to the steward, he'll maybe let us have some of what they keep for the captain's guests.'

Helen started, as though jolted from sleep. She looked at Betty's scabby chin and rabbit teeth, her stained armpits and stringy hair. With a wee thump of shame, she saw the two of them on the deck together: a pair of flea-bitten peasant girls plotting for rich folk's titbits.

Letting herself be dragged back to the rear of the ship, she ducked in through a low doorway and followed Betty along a narrow corridor and down two ladders into the very belly of the ship. It gurgled like intestines at this depth, creaking and rocking, lit here and there by lanterns which spilt unsteady stains of yellow light on the dank boards.

'Phew! It smells worse than a tinker's knob down here.' Betty wrinkled her nose and squinted down the passage. 'Look, down the end where those folks are waiting. That must be the steward. Here, you're the bonny one. Take these tickets and show him a bit of titty –' And she thrust three wooden tickets into Helen's hand and gave her a shove.

The steward was sitting in a pool of lamplight, unshaven and grunting. He licked a stubby forefinger and riffled through a ledger on a small table wedged between his fat knees. His wig perched on a barrel beside him and a few long grey hairs clung to his greasy scalp. His small eyes flicked across the faces in the queue.

A few minutes later Helen was standing in front of him, holding out the tickets. At Betty's urging, she'd loosened the front of her blouse and shaken her copper curls around her face.

'Name,' he grunted, dipping his quill.

'There are three of us,' she said, and spelt them out while he printed them laboriously on his ledger. A fly landed on his head and staggered over the shiny skin as he wrote.

'Two lassies and a lad, eh?' He looked up and his eyes narrowed. 'And is Master Douglas your sweetheart, Miss Helen?' His eyes were level with her crotch. For a split second Helen saw herself running headlong down the passageway, running and climbing into the sunlight, running and diving into clean, bright water.

'I haven't got a sweetheart.' She forced her lips into a smile and swayed her hips. 'I'm still looking for the right man.'

'And what kind of man would that be?' He wiped his mouth with the back of his hand.

'We-e-ell,' she pretended to consider, 'it'd have to be a generous kind of man, one who'd take care of me and my friends. Do you know anyone like that?'

Now he was grinning broadly up at her. She could smell raw onion on his breath, see tufts of hair bristling from his nostrils. 'Well, Miss Helen, I may know someone exactly fitting that description. Why don't you come back later this evening, so I can introduce you to him?'

'You don't have to radge him,' Betty whispered excitedly on the way back to the cabin. 'Just let him squeeze your arse, and suck on your paps a wee bit.'

Helen shuddered. 'I can't, Betty. Did you see his teeth? I couldn't bear to let him kiss me with that mouth of rotten pebbles.'

'It won't kill you.' Betty rounded on Helen. 'You owe us at

least that much for bringing you with us. I don't know what you're moaning on about anyway. It's only a wee cuddle.'

'But I've never done anything like that before –'

'Well, aren't you the lucky one, Helen Gloag? Well, maybe it's about time you learnt what it's like. Maybe it's about time you had to waggle your arse like the rest of us for a bit of something decent to eat!'

'I'm not whoring for anybody's vittals.'

'So I'm a whore now, am I? And what makes you think you're any better? Do you think you're the only lass as ever canoodled with John Bayne?'

'What do you mean?' Helen's forehead felt clammy.

'I mean I've seen him giving money to a lassie in Crieff – and he wasn't paying for conversation. What's the matter? Did you let him have it for nothing?'

But Helen didn't wait to hear any more. She was running down dark passages and up ladders, elbowing past people, not caring where she was going. She saw a door half-open to her left and rushed through it, slamming it behind her. And suddenly she was in a different part of the ship – quieter, cleaner – and she was standing, panting, facing three narrow doors with polished brass handles. As she stood there, one of the doors opened and a tall man stepped out.

She recognized him immediately. It was the husband of the elegant woman on the deck. 'I knew I'd heard something!' he said. Then, over his shoulder to his wife: 'It's just some lassie – lost her way by the looks of it. I thought you were the cabin boy with our tea,' he explained to Helen with a smile.

Then a thought struck him and he took a coin from his waistcoat. 'Could you go and hurry him up? My wife claims she's dying of thirst.' And he put the coin into her hand and closed the door in her face.

*

Betty found her, hours later: shivering, wedged again behind the hen-coops on the deck. A sea mist had risen and the timbers were dark and wet.

'They've pulled up the anchor,' said Betty, taking her hand. 'D'ye want to say goodbye to Scotland?'

2

Marrakech, 23 May 1769

Being ugly, I have always been interested in Beauty. Not out of envy, *vous comprenez*. I have never felt the luxury of mere envy – for what is envy but the fantasy of possessing what one envies? No, my brand of Ugliness is so far removed from your ordinary Comeliness that I cannot image the series of approximations that might take me from where I am to where Beauty stands.

It does interest me, however. Indeed you could say that Beauty has become my profession. For am I not Chief Custodian of the Harem of the Emperor of Morocco? A thousand beauteous lasses, a fleshy rainbow of hues from every corner of Africa, all gathered here for the delectation of His Majesty Sidi Mohammed XVII: God may be their Creator but I am their Curator.

Ah, but Beauty comes in strange guises in this land of camels and *couscous*. You'll find no plucked eyebrows or boned bodices here; no waxed kiss-curls or bobbing ringlets frame the faces of these concubines.

Au contraire, many of my charges have their heads shaved, for nothing else displays a fine skull and cheek scars so well. Others' native hair is a bush of such dense corkscrews that you would think the skills of a gardener were required to clip it to shape. As to eyebrows: your Moor claims a muckle thick caterpillar is required to lend definition to the eye. For the best effect, the brows should be joined in the middle, and lasses who have not been thus blessed by their God will paint in a dark bridge betwixt the two with *kohl*.

Yet all other vestiges of hair on a woman are abhorred with a loathing that borders on terror, which I trace to that apoplexy that assails the Moor at any hint of Masculinity in his mates. So a woman must remove even the gossamer down from her cheek, and those sweet furrings on forearm and finger.

It is this fear of the Masculine in his women that accounts for your Moor's partiality to portliness. Believe me, I am not referring to any ordinary plumpness here. No, Beauty in Barbary must ripple and judder. She must cascade like candle-grease; wobble like a *blanc-manger*; quiver like oysters in aspic. There should be such a yielding softness about her that makes the most flaccid of *homunculi* seem hard by comparison.

Yet she must not be so large as to seem smothering. For the intent, if I have understood it correctly, is to give the man back his mother in a form he can command. Thus the desire for the big woman is a kind of revenge on the ogress who overwhelmed the wee laddie. Hence it is your placid Pantagrella who is in demand in this land, who combines Bigness with a beguiling Biddability.

But my pen is running away with me. Reader, let me introduce you to the Author of these pages. In the Land of the Dwarves, I would be considered a fine specimen. My teeth are straight, my skin good and my eyes (though I say so myself) are a perfectly enchanting shade of grey. But set on this Earth to live among Giants as I am, my finer attributes are, literally, overlooked. And it's my legs that define me, being somewhat truncated and bowed out at the knee; and my brow, which balloons forth above my eyes. In the Land of Giants I am the runt pup escaped from the drowning sack.

In my darker hours I muse on the motives of our Good Shepherd, for hauling my sack, and others like it, from the river. Far from culling His misshapen ewes and two-headed lambs, He would seem to desire a world teeming with every manner of Deformity. And I wonder how this *penchant* for the Crooked might have impinged on His early career as Carpenter. How could he ever have discarded His squint posts and skewed dovetails? His favourite chairs would have rocked like coracles on their uneven legs, while heaped plates slithered inexorably from His slant tables.

But should you question His apparent scarcity of Skill, I wager that He would simply take you by the hand and conduct you around the humbler bothies of Bethlehem. And there direct your eyes to protruding rocks and sloping floors, bulging walls and crumbling rafters, and in each irregular niche, triumphantly apt, would be one of his cock-eyed creations.

So perhaps I have finally found my true niche: sitting cross-legged here on my cushion with my pen in my hand. The whole Harem is snoring, drugged by the heat, and sweat gathers in the creases of my elbows and causes my fingers to slip on the quill.

The Emperor's Chief Wife, Queen Batoom, is slumbering like a sow beside me. Her huge mounds of dark flesh glisten like heaped aubergines beneath her muslin robe. And I am reminded that the Moors have a dish made from aubergines, baked in olive oil and allspice, which they call *imam baylidi* – meaning 'apt to make a priest swoon'. Thus is my sleeping Queen, steeped in her own musk, basted by the oil of her sweat, sweetly cooking in the midday heat.

And I might be swooning beside her, nuzzling beneath those hills like a runtling rooting for truffles – except, except, except, I have a pen in my hand for the first time in four years, and black ink in this wee tin beside me. So I am inclined to keep my blunter instrument dry for once, and continue with my scribbling.

For I can imagine that you are wondering how it is that a frog like myself should be basking alongside the very epitome of Moorish Beauty. The answer is that the wondrous Batoom is the most discerning of women, by which I mean that she alone – of the heedless hordes that dwell in the Harem – has perceived the princely heart that pulsates in this squat body. And came by and by to discover, by dint of some determined and deft exploration, the princely pego, all intact, all a-quivering in these eunuch's *salwars*.

In short, I am long in that spurtle that stirs a girl's porridge, well endowed with that wealth that is wanting in a house filled with women. The Good Shepherd, who snubbed my nose and dished my face like a saucer, domed my forehead and shrunk my limbs to a *dachshund*'s dimensions, was not so cruel as to leave me with no compensation. Indeed, I am inclined to conclude that God never made a man Little but He made it up to him in something else.

And just as I have invaded Batoom's chamber, so I have somehow become lodged in the heart of this great woman, like a sand grain in the brown flesh of a Tay mussel, there to be enveloped in secretions until I am become transformed to something precious in her eyes. Thus does Love layer every aspect of the Beloved with pearly perception, and judges flaw and fine feature to be equal exemplars. So by Love is Beauty finally dethroned.

For my part, once I came to relish the aesthetic of a shaven scalp on a lass, the shift from Admiration to Love was but a simple step. I look at Batoom now and my mouth fairly waters –

But I digress. For there is need, too, to explain how an intact man like myself came to be taken for a eunuch. The answer is simple. For though I was christened Jeffrey by the father who sired me and Joey by the wet-nurse who fed me in her fish-flavoured pouch, the name I call myself is Microphilus, which means, in the Greek, 'little leaves' – for though my stem may be stout, my limbs are like those of a child.

And it is these little limbs which have hoodwinked the Emperor, and hooked the key to his Harem on to my belt. For he believes that my armaments are as infantile as my arms, and that I am as unmanned, in effect, as the giant eunuchs he employs to guard his lovelies. Indeed, so taken is he with the lowness of my stature that he has raised me to the rank of Chief Eunuch – for the sheer amusement of seeing me surrounded by his gollumphing geldings, a wee spuggie fluttering around their fat black ankles.

Batoom alone knows my secret. It was she, cunning queen, who coined for me the *sobriquet* Fijil, which is Moorish for radish – a wee pinkie of a name to circumjack all conjecture about the secret neep she holds so dear. Because if the Emperor were to discover he has been cuckolded by a Dwarf, then death would be the very mildest punishment he'd mete out. More likely would be some excruciation copied from his grandfather, the Emperor Ishmael.

They say that this ingenious Monarch devoted much time to devising elaborate machines of torture. The breast-vice was one of his favourites, and something he dubbed the 'spiked *jellabiah*'. He also applied his mind to expanding the repertoire of his executioners and schooled them so thoroughly that they could ascertain, from a single gesture of the Royal Thumb, exactly which method he wished them to use with each miscreant.

What they refer to as 'tossing' was the quickest, in which the unfortunate is lifted, much as your caber is hoisted up by your Highlander, and tossed in the air such that he lands on his head with a conclusive crack. Far slower was crucifixion, or boiling in oil, or dissolving in the lye his builders used to mix with their clay. So many were liquefied in this last manner as to give the Palace walls a curious mottled quality. Indeed, if walls can truly be said to have ears, they must have been rendered deaf by the wailing that went into their rendering.

But let me not dwell on such horrors. My sweet whale is surfacing. It is time to emulate Jonah.

3

Three weeks out of Greenock, the main passenger cabin stank like a pigsty. It had rained steadily ever since they set sail, making it impossible to spend time on deck, so they had to do everything in the near-darkness of the cabin. The pitching of the ship meant buckets were always tipping over; food was forever being dropped or slopped on the quaggy boards. After a spell of rough weather, the sour smell of vomit was added to the soup of stenches in the dark, swaying barn. Rats nibbled unseen in the rotting rubbish and there were cries of disgust almost daily as another litter of pink young was discovered in the middle of someone's bag of clothes.

Helen tried to be brave. She took her turn emptying the close-stools and shovelling up the slimy sweepings from the floor. She borrowed Betty's spare blanket and was grateful, and smiled at her gormless brother Dougie and made him blush. And tried to forget they were from the poor end of the village, where the work was seasonal at best, and measles took off all the weans, and gin was used to warm the empty bellies.

They'd been kinder than she deserved: waiting by the side of the track when they heard her running after them that shameful morning; listening solemnly to her lies about why she needed to come with them. They'd exchanged knowing looks, but had never asked any questions, simply handed her a bundle to carry and moved apart to make space for her to walk between them. Betty had even insisted on giving her her shoes.

'How come you're so kind to me?' Helen asked suddenly.

They were kneeling on the filthy floor, sharing a big bowl of pea soup.

Betty shrugged and shoved her hair behind her ears. 'It's nice having someone to blether with,' she said gruffly. 'And Dougie's no use – are you, man?' He humphed, dunking two ship's biscuits and cramming them into his loose mouth. 'See? I couldn't stand three months of that sort of chit-chat.'

'But there's the money too, for the stage-coach and ship. I'll pay you back, I swear, once we get to the Colonies.'

'I told you, it's not our money, it's the whole village's. Your father put his hand in his pocket same as everyone else – deeper than most, probably. So some of it's yours by rights anyway.'

Betty bailed green gruel eagerly into her mouth. 'The soup tastes different tonight,' she said. 'Someone must've added a dish of vinegar to the pot.' A green dribble snaked down her chin.

Helen's stomach churned with a mixture of hunger and nausea. How could they eat that swill? Nibbling the corner of a biscuit, she forced herself to swallow. It tasted of oat mould and barn dust.

'You feeling queasy again?' Betty leant towards her with a worried frown.

'Ay, a bit. I can't stomach this muck.'

'Well, you know what you can do about that.' Betty nodded towards the door leading to the rear of the ship, to the stores where the steward would be waiting.

Helen had visited him six times now – she counted them up: six foretastes of Hell. There, in a fug of sweaty cheese, she'd dodge and dimple, then let him press her up against a barrel of wet butter, where he'd slobber over her naked breasts until he jerked with some sort of release. Then he'd back away, fumbling for his keys, and unlock the cupboard where he'd put her reward: a dish of marmalade or apple sauce; once a whole honeycomb wrapped in a muslin cloth.

Helen made a face. 'He's been wanting more lately.'

'So? Give him more.' Betty shrugged, slurping soup.

'I can't bear to let him kiss me on the mouth, let alone –'

'So wank him then. You know, milk his thing, like whores do when they're on their monthlies. You can wash your hand after and he'll be awfully grateful.'

'Jesus God, Betty.'

Betty grinned and wiped her chin with the hem of her skirt. 'All right, dinna fash. Maybe you could try going all coy-like. Say you're not that kind of lass. That you're saving yourself for your true love.'

'He'll not fall for that. Last time I said it was only my monthlies that were stopping me.' He'd given her a whole bag of sugared figs that time. And she'd eaten half of them straight away, crouching in a dark corner and stuffing them guiltily into her mouth, swallowing so quickly she almost gagged. She'd wanted to fill herself with sweetness, choke on it, not give any of it away.

'So, tell him you're scared of getting pregnant.'

Helen dropped her biscuit into the bowl. Sweat prickled hotly on her scalp then went cold. The only things of Betty's she hadn't borrowed were her monthly rags. She counted the days in her mind. Betty'd been bleeding when they'd set off from the village. She remembered thinking then that she wouldn't be due until they were on the ship. But that was over two weeks ago now. Which meant she must be carrying John Bayne's bastard.

The sea was rough again that night and the hammocks swung wildly. Helen lay awake for a long time, listening to the sounds of the ship as it lurched through the towering waves:

the squealing timbers and slapping sails; the thud and rattle of every loose box or latch or barrel. And around her, the retching and coughing, the belching and scratching of a hundred bodies; the swearing of those crawling in the filth beneath the hammocks towards the wooden partition in the corner.

She unbuttoned her skirt and slipped her hand inside, knuckling it into the flesh where her bastard wean was growing, fisting into the pink maggot God had sent to remind her of who she was: a common slut like all the others. Hot tears burnt her eyes and ran into her ears as she lay on her back and sobbed silently in the darkness.

When she woke the next morning the cabin was almost deserted. Two oblongs of sunlight lay beneath the two trapdoors like white paper and she could hear talking and laughter above her head. She climbed the ladder and found that the sky was blue and the sea sparkling and everyone was sitting about on the deck in the first sunshine they'd seen since they'd set sail.

Blankets were draped everywhere and the women were scrubbing clothes and washing their hair in big tubs of seawater they'd winched up from over the side. The men sat in noisy groups, passing pipe tobacco. Helen picked her way through the scattered bodies to where Betty and some other lasses were combing one another's hair.

Sitting down, Helen untied her own matted curls and began dragging a comb viciously through them.

'Are you trying to make yourself bald?' Betty slapped Helen's hands away. 'Here, let me,' she said, kneeling up and starting to tease out the tangles. 'Oh, I wish I had hair this colour, instead of my mousy mane. So how's the sickness this morning?'

Something in her voice made Helen look up. Betty's brown eyes were full of concern. 'You're carrying, aren't you? We guessed as much that first day, when you said Meg had thrown you out. Then when you started being poorly I said to Dougie that's a sure sign.'

'I didn't realize until yesterday.' Helen felt a tear trickle down her cheek. 'I don't know what to do. I'll not be able to get work with a wean to look after. And no man'll ever marry me now.'

'Don't be so daft. Dougie'd marry you like a shot if you wanted. There's a dozen men on this ship'd be proud to have a lassie like you for a wife – baby or no. As for getting work, my sisters never had any bother. We just took it in turns to tend the weans,' Betty's eyes began to shine with excitement. 'God, I hope it's a wee laddie. Our house was always full of lasses.'

'You mean you'd help?' Helen wiped her nose on her shawl and stared at the other lass. It began to seem possible. She started to imagine a neat little house with lime-washed walls, and a bonny blond laddie toddling unsteadily in through the door. And Dougie bringing in the wood; and Betty tending the stove.

'I've always loved bairns,' Betty said quietly. 'But I don't think I can have one of my own. I was carrying twice last year, but I lost it both times. If you had a baby we could all share it.'

4

5 June 1769

S o we have had a purging! That is why I have neglected these pages for so long. I have been playing cat and mouse with the housekeepers, moving my cache of papers, much as your squirrel would his nuts, from this hiding-place to that in the wake of their furious brooms. For we have had such sweepings and scourings these last weeks; such shakings and scrubbings as would make your humble cockroach tremble in fear for his life.

Indeed, this very morning I saw a dozen such creatures, drowsy and dust-clogged, stamped on by the child of one of the Harem scullions. For what other being but a cockroach could succumb to this lowliest of children? Thus is power wielded constantly downwards, like a very waterfall of tyranny, from the Emperor at the apex, inexorably down through the hierarchy of wives and slaves, such that his smallest whim can result, *in extremis*, in a veritable Slaughter of the Innocents in the world of Insects.

So the Emperor eats an overripe quail's egg and conceives a slight itching in the armpit. The result is this turmoil, as his scratching sets us all a-jumping like fleas on a dog's back.

Normally we are alert to his moods, as a band of nose-quivering conies catch the scent of a fox on the prowl. But there has been such a heavy Heat in the air these past weeks, that has dulled all our senses and flattened us like flounders in a pool. So on Thursday, when he comes to select his diversions for the week, the women are drooping like limp cabbage leaves as they shuffle out to the courtyard to greet him. And they sag like lumps of dough as they position themselves before him, subsiding on thick feet in the heat.

His lip curls in disgust as he surveys them: silk stuck to their skin, swaying in torpid parody of seduction. So he looks them over, with his anger growing. And paces up and down, scratching vaguely at his armpit, until at last his agitation rouses them from their lethargy.

Then the fidgetings begin; the nudgings, the fiddlings with jewels. And they look sideways at each other and roll their eyes like frightened sheep. Then he's spinning on his heels and sweeping past them down the passage to their quarters. And they're following him, bleating and waddling like seals, fluttering their hands and calling for their children.

It is to no avail of course. For he's already hauling carpets from beneath *kief*-sodden slaves and scattering baskets of fruit to the ground, flinging heaps of clothing aside and calling on *Allah* to deliver him from his plague of idle sluts. I am translating freely, *vous comprenez*. His exact prayer was for a giant pig to consume their children and all their belongings and then to position its anus in such a way that, when it loosened its bowels, his whole Harem would be drowned in an ordure of its own making.

Perhaps I should explain that the humble pig is regarded by your Moor as the foulest of creatures, to such an extent that every rich household keeps at least one of these despised animals as a pet, allowing it free run of the garden, for the sole pleasure of heaping curses upon it. For I have noticed that we humans do like to gloat over that thing which we abhor the most; to pick at it and torture it with a demented intensity that one is almost tempted to call Love.

The result of the Emperor's frenzy was this manic cleansing

we have been forced to endure, coupled with a thorough survey of his *seraglio*, during which fully half of his unfortunate women were disposed of.

For the Emperor, though the richest man in his kingdom, yet has something of the frugal about him. Indeed, such frugality is the very *sine qua non* of wealth. For what is wealth but the failure to spend what one has? The accumulation of riches is a sort of accretion of the world to oneself, not unlike the waves of flesh that gather up and spill over the bones of the new women in the Harem. For every new acquisition is subjected to an obligatory fattening, much as your Christmas goose is stuffed full of corn, before she is considered fit for the Emperor's bed.

Growing rich is likewise a process of consumption, a vast repast which must be munched on and savoured and conjoined to the swelling body of matter which comprises the wealthy man.

And waste is anathema to this agglomeration. It is the spilt claret on the Laird's waistcoat – or, in the Emperor's case, the greasy scented tea tipped over his green slippers, tea being the beverage of the wealthy of this realm: a cup of sweet mint tea with a lump of *ambergris* melting in it. For though your Moor will smoke himself insensible on this leafy opium they call *kief*, yet to allow just a drop of alcohol to pass his lips is tantamount to the vilest debauchery.

Thus is the Emperor in his counting-houses like a hungry man at his table. The difference being that the hunger for riches is an appetite which can never be satisfied. For are there not always more riches in the world? I have also observed that a man whose vocation is Accumulation often looks on that which he has accumulated with a sort of repugnance. Once a thing has been purchased it loses much of its value, much as the food, once chewed and swallowed, becomes a loathsome wet *bolus*, contaminated with gall-juices of the foulest kind. Thus the very Act of Consumption degrades that which it consumes.

Your young virgin is the perfect example of the phenomenon I have in mind. While she refuses a man and is, so to say, still on display in the baker's shop window, he desires her with a very frenzy. But once she has been brought home and tasted, her charms seem to fade in his eyes. She is the gatepost that some dog has pissed on, albeit that the piss he can smell has issued from his very own pintle.

Such are the motives that engendered the Emperor's sudden urge for purging – these and a certain more personal purging that was brought about by the aforesaid quail's egg. So he orders his carpets and cushions and has them laid out beneath the great olive tree in the Harem garden.

Then he summons Malia, his Chief Midwife, to come squat down beside him with her record book. This she does with a surprising agility, for she's as wizened as last year's pippin and has presided over the gynaecological affairs of the Harem for nigh on fifty years.

Now, if you have ever wondered how it is that a man with a thousand wives can arrange to impregnate them all in a matter of a few years, then here is your answer. The canny crone Malia can calculate to the very day, if not the very hour, exactly which of the Emperor's heifers is worth humping if she is to be got with calf. And what is more, she keeps notes on the pedigree of his entire herd. For, strange though it might seem, it is deemed the highest honour to be able to boast that one's daughter is amongst the throng who flaunt their charms before the Emperor of a Thursday morning.

Thus the Harem gates are under regular siege as various minor chieftains present their offspring as offerings to His Majesty. Most are rejected without ceremony, as being too ugly or too scrawny for the Emperor's taste. But there are those few who gain entrance, regardless of their looks, because the Emperor wishes to do Business with their fathers. These Malia notes most particularly, for it would not do to insult an ally: by inadvertently beheading a treasured granddaughter, or boiling the feet of a beloved niece without due cause. Hence the dual importance of the Crone's book in the business the Emperor was minded to conduct.

So, sits he down and claps for tea, and instructs Malia to parade all the childless women before him. They come running at once, perhaps three hundred of them; all sizes and colours, all twittering mightily. Whereupon he has Malia divide them into two groups: those hundred or so whose bubbles have not yet been pricked, and the remainder who have been amply pricked but have failed to swell as a result. His eyes flicker idly over the first group, assessing their untried charms, while Malia points out the few it would be politic to retain.

Perhaps ten are selected by this process and the rest told to bundle up their belongings and report to the Treasury the next day – rather as you would return your unworn hats to the milliners if they failed to match your coats when you got them home. Such women have a high resale value, *vous comprenez*. They are unspoilt virgins, hand-picked from the thousands that are presented at these gates every year, fattened on royal *couscous* and green butter, schooled for the bed by the most diligent madams in the realm. What merchant would sneer at such a prize?

Next turns he to the second group: those two hundred sweet creatures who have been thoroughly furrowed by his Plough, but whose soil has not yet burgeoned forth with its requisite crop of Royal Seedlings. These are sifted likewise through the fine mesh of Lust and political Pragmatics. This second sieving yields but three, leaving the rest to be wrapped in their veils and loaded like sacks of corn, each on a minuscule donkey, to be driven, as a spent caravan of concupiscence, slowly out through the Palace gates.

My heart went with them, those sad young sows, abandoned to the pimps of this city, rendered cheap by the loss of their virginity. For though I have seen inside many a low brothel in my time, yet there is nothing in my memory to compare to the muddy hives where these cast-off queens will live out their lives, in cells no bigger than a closet, there to be stung and stung until they die.

Ay, truly, I would save them all, marry them all, if I could. For though I can contemplate a skewered brain or bisected testicle with insouciance, yet the sight of a woman scorned makes me fairly tremble with rage.

5

'Are you mad?' Betty tugged the slops buckets out of Helen's hands. 'That's how lassies lose babies. It pulls on your belly to lug those muckle things.'

Watching her stagger off towards the ladder, Helen sighed. What if she wanted to lose the baby? No, that was a sin. She pushed the thought to the back of her mind. Anyway, it was too late now. It was there now, stuck inside her like a limpet on a rock, glueing her to Betty for ever.

Everything had been decided that sunny morning on the deck of the ship. They'd live together, the three of them, and raise the bairn between them. 'I can pretend to folk we're married if you like.' Dougie's big mouth had twisted with eager embarrassment. 'If you can't fine another – I mean, so you don't have to –'

'Oh, it doesn't matter what folk think!' Betty had been brisk and brimming with smiles. 'I'll go out skivvying or something, when he's really wee. Then, when he's not needing to suck any more, I'll tend him so you can find a job. You're bonnier and you've more schooling than me, so you'll find something that'll pay better. Oh Helen, I can't wait to hold him in my arms!'

'What if it's a wee lassie?' For a while Helen had found herself smiling too, caught up in their excitement.

'So long's it calls me "auntie", I don't care what it is. As soon as we land, we'll get a wee room, maybe a wee outhouse –'

Helen's smile faded. Like a wet cloth slapped across her face, the word 'outhouse' had wiped away all the bonny scenes she'd been imagining. Of course, an outhouse would be the best she could hope for. All her schooling had been for nothing. She was a ruined wench in borrowed shoes. Betty and Dougie'd been raised in a sagging turf hovel. How could she expect anything better? And she cursed the tiny leech she was carrying, that was feeding on her future, that was going to swell and swell and show everyone what a wilful slut she'd been.

At least Betty didn't expect her to go down to the steward any more, that was something. And she still had a few of the sugared figs he'd given her last time, hidden away in her pocket. She sucked them secretly, one each night, tonguing off the sugar, feeling them soften in her mouth then burst open in a rush of gritty seeds. They were her reminder: that she'd been picked out from the others, that she was bonnier; that she might still have a chance to escape.

And when the figs were finished, and there was nothing but sticky fluff in the bottom of her pocket, there was still the coin the gentleman had given her that first day.

She'd finger it secretly sometimes, trace the outline of the King's head on its surface. Or catch its old copper smell on her fingers. Then she'd think of them – the pale-haired woman and her brocade-coated husband – sitting in their cosy cabin, somewhere above her head. She was a fish in a mucky pool; the coin was a bright bait on a line.

She'd started watching the couple. She'd found a place to hide, a totie washroom the cabin boys used for drying the few rich passengers' clothes. She'd lurk there waiting for their door to open, peeping out to see the woman rustling away down the corridor in her hooped skirts. She played a game with herself, trying to guess which frock she'd be wearing, which way she'd dress her fine pale hair. Often she'd tiptoe right up to the door and press her ear against the polished wood, straining to hear the woman's breathy, high voice, trying to imagine what she was doing.

She became desperate to see inside the little room, trying the door-handle when they were at supper in the captain's quarters. She wanted to feel the empty slither of the woman's silk stockings; look at the sky through her salt-spattered window.

One day, sneaking down the passage as usual, she found her hiding-place was already occupied. It was the smallest cabin boy, Davie, crouching by a tray on the floor, sobbing with his hands clamped over his mouth.

'What's the matter, Davie?' Her whisper made him start to his feet.

'Don't tell the cook, Miss,' he pleaded, wiping his nose on his sleeve. 'He'll whup me if he knows I've been blubbing. But I'm that tired of running up an' down they ladders all day, an' being cussed and whupped. And now I can't recall what Mistress Baird asked for, an' I just can't knock on her door again for I already knocked twice today for misremembering something.' And he started crying again, muffling his sobs in his sleeve.

Helen stooped and picked up the tray. 'I'll see to this,' she said firmly. 'You go off by yourself for a wee whiley.' And she'd turned and knocked on the cabin door before he could protest.

It was the woman who opened it. Close up she looked pointed and pinched, clutching a crocheted shawl round her narrow shoulders.

'Wee Davie's not feeling so good, so the cook asked me to serve you today. What was it you were wanting from the kitchen?'

Later, when Helen had made several trips to the kitchen, the woman said to call her Melissa. 'It means "honey",' she'd explained with a giggle. 'Robert says it suits me, because I'm so sweet. But I don't feel very sweet today.' And she'd pouted her thin lips and started complaining about the food on the ship. 'A lady simply can't digest the sort of fare they serve up to the captain. Our stomachs are too delicate. Be a dear and bring me a boiled egg, will you? There's not much they can do to spoil a boiled egg, is there?'

It was nearly midnight by the time Helen finally climbed down the ladder into the big cabin. A wispy old woman was changing a baby on the floor beneath one of the lamps, folding the claggy rag in on itself and putting it in a bowl. Everyone else seemed to be asleep. Helen crept beneath the creaking hammocks to where hers was still looped against the wall.

'Where've you been?' Betty hissed, leaning out of her hammock. 'I was that feared for you! I thought that fat steward must've locked you in his dungeon.'

Helen untied the knotted kerchief she was carrying. 'Here, taste these,' she whispered. 'They're called *raisins*. From France. Mistress Baird gave them to me. She's that fine lady with the rich folk upstairs. Her maid took sick the day before they got on the ship and they had to leave her in Greenock. So she says I'm to work for her instead.' Helen clambered up into her hammock and popped a pinch of the wrinkled fruits into her mouth.

She didn't tell Betty what else the woman had said. That if they suited each other, she could travel on to Boston with them. And she'd teach her to be a proper lady's maid, with her own room in the grand house they'd be building. Of course there wouldn't be anywhere for them to live to begin with. They'd have to stay in a hotel. But Helen wouldn't mind that, would she? It would only be for a few months. Helen hugged herself in the darkness, sucking sweet shreds of black fruit from her teeth.

*

32

Once she started working for Melissa, Helen hardly ever saw Betty and Dougie. Before they were properly awake, she was down in the kitchen heating a pitcher of drinking water for the Bairds to wash in. Then she'd collect their chamber-pot and find out what they wanted for their breakfast. Then it was to and fro with tea and porridge and eggs and dirty pots. And back to sweep their cabin and find out if any clothes needed tending. And so it went on all day – dirty pot, fresh water, trays of food, washing – until she took a jug of sweet port in to them last thing at night.

The steward had come looking for her on the second day, filling the low doorway of the kitchen, squinting in the light, with his belly hanging over his breeks. 'Why've you been hiding from me?' he growled, pursing big sulky lips.

'I've not been hiding.' Helen had pushed airily past him with a loaded tray. 'I've just been that busy.' She'd heard his voice fading as she threaded her way back to the Bairds' cabin, and a small flame of hope had licked at the base of her throat. A door had opened. She had a future. She wasn't tied to poor folk any more.

Working for Melissa meant she could eat any food they didn't want, as well as the treats they gave her whenever they took a new box from their locker. Often she put some aside for Betty and Dougie, but sometimes she couldn't help just gobbling it all down herself, growing rounder and glossy-haired on her diet of cheese and chicken skin, dried apple-rings and eggs.

The truth was, she was avoiding Betty. She didn't want to hear her jabbering on about what they'd do when they got to the Colonies. And she couldn't bear the endless blather about the baby. She didn't want to think about the baby. She hated the baby. She wanted to screw it up like a filthy rag and thrust it to the very back of her mind. Her future was with

Melissa Baird now: with a frilled apron and little tea-spoons, perhaps even a bed of her own with proper sheets and a copper warmer.

She began copying Melissa whenever she was alone in their cabin. Stooping over the remains of their meals, she'd practise sipping cold tea without slurping, and holding a knife and fork in either hand to cut a piece of leftover mutton. She spent hours trying to work an embroidered fan, letting it dangle then flicking it up and open in one movement the way Melissa did. All the time puzzling: what was it about Melissa that made her the kind of woman men took care of? The kind of woman someone like John Bayne might want for his wife?

There were her clothes, of course: all those bright colours and stiff layers. And her hair, set with papers and pinned up in curls around her face. She washed more often too, and smelt of rose-water as well as sweat. And she spoke differently, with the words sort of separate and finished, instead of chopped up and bunched together the way poor folk talked. All these things made Melissa seem beautiful, but when you looked at her properly she was rather a weasely sort of lass under all those frothy petticoats.

So how did she make all those fine men do what she wanted? Her husband, the captain, the ship's doctor, the parson – they all bowed and opened doors for her. Was she weak, was that it? Did the sun really make her feel faint? Helen watched Melissa's husband carrying her parasol when she strolled on the deck. Couldn't she carry it herself? She saw him striding proudly along, with his wife's wan arm tucked under his elbow.

Helen looked at her own strong arms, nutmegged with freckles; at her sturdy legs and the hard soles of her feet. I'm like a horse, she thought with disgust: bred to work, to ride. Was that what John Bayne thought of her? Sweet Helen Gloag:

good for a canter on a warm summer's night, and bonnier than most. But not to marry.

She squeezed her eyes shut at the thought of that night. She'd gone to him barefoot and stinking of sweat. And he'd done what any gentleman would have done, bedded her in his servants' quarters and left her there. Well, next time it would be different. In the Colonies *she* would be different. She'd go to Boston with Melissa as she'd promised. Then in a few years, she'd start tutoring gentlefolk's children and being introduced around. If all went well, she'd be married to a gentleman before she was twenty.

But first she had to get rid of the baby, cut the cord that bound her to Betty and Dougie. She resolved to start asking some of the older women: there must be someone on the ship who could help.

6

I have been writing this Treatise on Royal Paper. I stole it from beneath the nose of the royal *Alim*. It was a crime which gave me particular pleasure, for the *Alim*'s nose is no ordinary nose. No, his is the Sacred Nose of Morocco. His is the nose whose occupation it is to sniff out every whiff of sin in the Emperor's edicts. He is the Church's chief bloodhound (by Church, I mean that institution of washings and wailings within which these followers of Mohammed worship their God).

Sniff, sniff, goes the *Alim*, over this proposed new tax or that carefully revised law; sniff, sniff, riffling through his *Q'ran*'s ponderous pages; sniff, sniff, while the Emperor stands respectfully by, gritting the Royal Teeth and clenching the Royal Fists; sniff, sniff, then – snuff! – out it goes, with a single stroke of his rasping quill. For in Morocco it is priests who ratify the laws, not kings.

This is a source of exceeding frustration for the Emperor, who is one of Morocco's more modern-minded monarchs (which means that he uses his enemies' heads to adorn the city gates, as opposed to having their bodies woven into bridges, as his grandfather, the Emperor Ishmael, used to do).

One of the Emperor's most cherished ambitions is to expand his trading with Europe, an ambition which forces him to wade through a veritable treacle of religious resistance. This is because trading flouts one of his Church's most cherished Taboos, namely intimacy with members of the despised

Infidel. Indeed, to those that love money (and your Moor, it must be said, does love money) trading is more pleasurable than tupping. Thus to do business with an Unbeliever is far more sinful than merely beavering away betwixt his buttocks.

Now the Emperor could not be called a man of Conscience. Or rather, he finds it more comfortable to carry his Conscience outside his head, in the person of the royal *Alim*, preferring to find himself, as it were, beside himself. This convenient separation of the sin from the scruple is a trait I have observed in many True Believers, both here and in my homeland of Scotland. To such people, Conscience simply entails contriving one's vices in forms that circumvent the letter of one's religion's laws.

For the lucky folk of Morocco those laws amount to a mere handful, one being the removal of that piece of skin which protects the male Member from frostbite (which covering I suppose they have no need of in this sun-baked land, though I do wonder that their God should evince such an interest in so trivial a matter). Another is the requirement for Prayer, which your good Moor undertakes five times daily, prostrating himself in obedience to the wailing appeals of the red-hatted men who serve as bells in the belfries of their churches. Indeed, I have heard it said that once his sausage has been skinned and his prayers said, a Moor may rummage in life's frying pans in the sure knowledge that his Conscience will trouble him no further.

The Emperor is less fortunate than his subjects, however. Being sole ruler of this clammy kingdom, his Conscience is deemed to be the Conscience of the Nation, so much so that a flotilla of priestly skivvies is charged with the responsibility of keeping it free from stain. And their chief housekeeper is the aforesaid *Alim*, whose reward (apart from a personal Harem, crammed to bursting with the balloon-bosomed bunnies he favours) is to see the royal eyeballs bulge while he scrutinizes each line for the phrase that will consign the latest Royal Innovation to the Dusts of Oblivion.

It was under cover of one of these wrangles that I effected my sly plunder, flouncing off with a quire of clean paper under my arm. Of course, I could simply have asked the Emperor for paper directly, and he would no doubt have ordered reams of best vellum to be deposited in my quarters, along with a veritable Porcupine of quills. But my Treatise would not, I think, survive the scrutiny of his Royal Eyes. Indeed, the Emperor's largesse would have been larger with Curiosity than Generosity and he would have plagued me day and night with questions about my Enterprise. And, as I am vowed to be truthful in these writings, and as the Emperor will therefore be portraitured here in all his blemished brutality, I think it prudent to keep these scratchings a secret.

If I am discovered, I shall claim that I am designing embroidery *motifs* to be stitched on to a *jellabiah* for His Majesty. Since the Moors write a spiky topsy-turvy script, like a frayed woollen thread, they will never suspect the true import of my *curlicues élégantes*. And if the worst should come about, and the designs are despatched to the Royal Tailors, I shall have the pleasure of seeing the Emperor promenading before his subjects in a *jellabiah* emblazoned with damning descriptions of his own character. And if he is flanked by the *Alim*, as on most state occasions he is, I will be able to remark, to anyone who cares to hear me, that the Emperor has accomplished the impossible, by being both beside himself and outside himself at the same time.

7 June 1769

Today I bade farewell to the White Queen and helped her into her sedan with her three daughters. All hung around with green tassels was this conveyance, like a woodland bower, and the porters dressed in green pantaloons, rouched and puffed out like pumpkins. For there are no carriages in this country. Indeed, I have never seen a wheel on a vehicle at all, save on the tiny ceremonial barrow the Emperor drives when inspecting the ranks of his Black Guard, which more resembles a bucket than a *barouche*, rattling along like a tin cup tethered to his high-stepping horse.

Though her true name is Salamatu, I have dubbed her the White Queen to distinguish her from the Black Queen who is, *mais naturellement*, my glorious Batoom. For perhaps I have not yet explained that the Moor's god, Allah, though stringent in certain of his strictures, yet has the generosity to allow True Believers the luxury of four wives. (Indeed, it occurs to me now to suggest that this munificence might explain his insistence on that curious docking of the cock's stocking that I mentioned earlier. Being, as our own God is, Omniscient, he would have foreseen that a certain increased wear and tear might ensue from the satisfaction of four women's appetites.)

Thus the Emperor, though courted by a thousand concubines, yet has honoured a scant handful with the title of Wife. So we have our Black Queen and our White Queen, as I have said, plus two others of indeterminate hue but distinct ages, whom I have styled the Young Queen and the Old Queen respectively. And they have each their separate apartments and slaves and are in receipt of greater funds from the Emperor's coffers – which renders them, likewise, the recipients of a greater share in the prodigious funds of Enmity that are gathered up in this place. For I have observed that certain of the women maintain their own personal counting-houses in which they hoard, with fierce avidity, the bitter coin of Envy.

Thus there were many that were glad to see the back of

our White Queen; many who peeped in through the carved gates to her empty apartments, imagining their carpets and cushions arranged on her tiled floors. Indeed, there are now hundreds of stalls vacant in this rambling stable of ours, because the White Queen's departure was occasioned by yet further purgings. For the Emperor's scything did not end with that initial swathe of cast-off concubines. No indeed: that first swipe merely assuaged his more pressing of itches. Once old Malia's book was opened for his perusal, he became like your Tacksman's lady on the first day of spring, opening windows, brushing soot from the walls, tipping moulded oatmeal from the bottom of her sacks.

So two days later, to our dismay, it continues. Sitting down once again beneath the olive tree, he takes a tally of the women who have only delivered daughters and has them marshalled likewise before him together with their sweet shaven shrimplings – for all Moorish brats have their hair removed by way of a prophylactic against the plagues of parasites that thrive, like living paisley, in the warp and weft of these beautiful carpets.

Now here comes the White Queen flapping among them, gabbling wildly as usual in her elaborate hybrid of Irish and Arabic, making the others laugh and shake their heads – for these are your more senior women, rendered garrulous by their Motherhood as though their upper orifices had been opened by the same process that widened their wombs.

So the Emperor fixes her with his black eyes and she falls silent and kneels before him, and he takes her hands and kisses them and explains where he is sending her. And now the strangest thing happens. For I swear I can see a tear glinting on his cheek as he dismisses her and I am left wondering whether there is yet a morsel of soft clay in the flint of his heart that has been reached by this most unreachable of women. Indeed, it surprises me somewhat that she was not despatched moons ago. For it must be said that poor Salamatu is as mad as your proverbial March hare, having turned so suddenly when her son died two years back, poisoned, so they say, by a hand well greased by the coin of Envy.

So now the mad White Queen and the others have been despatched: off to Tafilalt, that green city of the East, which is peopled solely by Royal Offspring. For though hundreds of Royal Acorns drop to the ground every year, but one grows into that tree which becomes Emperor of Morocco. The rest are eventually clothed in garments of Royal Green and put out to pasture in the city of Tafilalt, where every man is a prince and every woman a princess, and they proliferate by the increments of Incest. Indeed, these transplanted seedlings become the very pasture itself, for in their green turbans and veils are they not all garbed in the colour of the grass? A very meadow of forsaken Filiation.

And tomorrow I am to be despatched likewise, though to different pastures. In company with the canny Crone and a bevy of eunuchs, we are off round the country on a mission of Replenishment, to herd up fresh horseflesh for our empty stables, a flux of fillies for the Emperor to ride.

Our route is already decided, as through an orchard of ripe fruit. First travel we east to the bazaars at the foot of the High Atlas Mountains, to pick our quota of the bronze Berber girls, each one tart as a wild apricot with her plaits to her knees. Next south to the markets of Sus where the sweet dark plums of Nuba are to be had – those few, I should say, which survive the bruising of their cruel transportation across the blazing deserts of this continent. Thence go we northwards, in a wide arc along the coast, scouring the Atlantic ports for corsairs' contraband. Here there are rich pickings indeed of the fair-skinned fruit that the Emperor particularly relishes.

For though most vessels that set sail from these shores return with catches of your usual finny variety, yet there are those that range further, after larger quarry, forsaking their nets and becoming Fishers of Men, in obedience, did they but know it, to Jesus' command to his followers in far Galilee.

Thus was I hooked, stunted fish that I am, and set out gasping and bug-eyed on the fisherman's slab, there to be prodded and ogled and finally set on a live turtle and carried before the Emperor like a mullet on a plate.

7

Helen had noticed the red shoes when she was tidying up the Bairds' cabin the very first day. Unworn and still in their paper, the soles were as blond as the day they were made. She picked them up and smelt the soft leather, ran her thumb along the rows of tiny stitches. When she was married, she'd have a pair of shoes like these.

The following day she scrubbed her feet carefully and tried on the shoes as soon as the cabin was empty. She'd expected them to be too small – they seemed so much daintier than the shoes she was used to. But they fitted like a second skin. She pointed her toe as though preparing for a polka, wondering what silk stockings would feel like smoothed up over her ankle-bones and knees.

The day after that it was a purple frock. Of all Melissa's dresses, this was the one Helen liked best. She eased it out of the locker and held it up against her body, lifting the whispering layers as though mounting the steps of a Boston mansion. Wedging a hand-mirror in the window-frame, she backed away as far as she could in the tiny cabin, trying to see how she'd look if she tried it on. Over the next few days she held all the dresses against herself like that: the white muslin with little flowers, the heavy blue velvet; the one with yellow stripes, the red and the two green ones. But she always came back to the purple.

It was such a grand colour, she thought: a colour to be noticed in; a colour fit for a queen. She examined every frill, every gather; turned it inside out to look at every seam;

danced with it in the cramped cabin. And one day, when she'd scrubbed herself thoroughly and washed her hair, and the Bairds were off playing cards in the captain's quarters, she decided to try it on.

The sea was flat that day and the sun hot. Helen bolted the cabin door, then threw the tiny window open. Slipping her own clothes off, she stood naked for a moment feeling the air cool on her damp curls. Then she lifted the purple frock and lowered it reverently over her head, worming her freckled arms through the rustling sleeves.

Her heart was thudding. The silk was cold, then warm on her skin. It was like purple water sluicing over her thighs. Craning sideways, she began doing up the long line of tiny hooks running from hip to armpit. At the waist the frock began to feel tight; then very tight. Was it this tight on Melissa? How did she bear it all day? Ten more hooks to go. She breathed in, praying her sweat wouldn't stain the armpits. Five more. She leant against the door and breathed in again. Yes!

Untying her hair, she shook it forwards over one shoulder. How bonny it looked, glinting like copper against the purple. Where was the mirror? She rummaged in a drawer: there. She held it out at arm's length and gazed at what she could see of her reflection. Gathering her hair up in one hand, she looked round for pins and a comb to secure it. How did Melissa get hers to stay up? She propped the mirror against the pillow and bent over it.

A corner of her mind was aware of folk shouting: some kind of rough game – perhaps a brawl – out on deck. Then suddenly someone was charging along the corridor, banging on the doors, bellowing, 'Pirates ahoy! All men and all weapons on deck!'

Helen spun round to the window. In the distance she could

see four longboats knifing cleanly through the water towards the ship, their lines of oars rising and falling like the ribs of four swimmers, breathing in and out, in and out. Behind her, someone was trying a key in the lock. It was Robert Baird, yelling, 'My pistols! They're inside. Let me in!' then battering at the door with his fists.

Helen stared at the closed door. How could she let him in? She was wearing Melissa's frock. In a frenzy, she began undoing the line of hooks. One, two, three. Her fingers were numb, soft as sausages. She turned back to the window. The boats were closer now. She could see the rowers bending and pulling on the oars. Four hooks; five, six, seven. She heard Robert start kicking the door and tried to wrench the frock off over her head. It wouldn't go over her shoulders so she tugged it back down and began fickling at the hooks again.

Eight, nine, ten. People in the main cabin were screaming beneath her feet. The kicking on the door became thick thuds as he began ramming it with his shoulder.

Eleven, twelve, thirteen. Now she noticed a new sound, above the banging on the door, the shouting and screaming on the ship: a rhythmic grunting, like her stepmother Meg when she was giving birth. It was the rowers. Whirling round to the open window, she could see them clearly now, bending and straightening, speeding towards the ship.

Their skin was black! Helen froze: was she imagining it? No, a few were paler, but most were dark as bladder-wrack. As they sped closer, she saw some of their backs were criss-crossed with red wounds, and clouds of flies hovered and settled again each time they hauled on the oars. She could see their faces creasing in pain as they rowed. Who'd whipped them like that? Her eyes flew to the bearded men standing over them, the whips coiled in their hands; their lances and long-bows; the pistols and knives at their waists. Why were they dressed like women, these other men, in those flapping white frocks and coloured sashes?

There was a sudden shout and the rowers lifted their oars from the water. The grunting stopped and the boats sliced silently through the water towards the ship. Behind her the door splintered and crashed open.

8

We have been travelling three weeks now, and I have lost count of the varieties of biting beastie which have battened on my poor freckled skin. This kingdom is so various, with its howling deserts and teetering mountains, its lush forests and meadows, its miles of roaring surf spiked with the bones of dead ships. And each place with its special collection of small Vermin to sting the earlobes or scuttle up the neb, deposit eggs in the hair or burrow between the toes. So that if I were to present myself tomorrow at the Edinburgh Zoological Society, there would be brawling in the halls as the whiskery Members vied to examine me.

The oases are the worst, where each suck of brackish water raises a cloud of midgies with the appetites of vampires. The new women are protected, for the most part, by their *haiks*, but we men are driven to lighting up brushwood fires whenever we stop, to dispel the smoke of insects with a smoke of our own.

Despite these torments, and the tireless toadying of the *sheikhs* and *khalifs* who have been our hosts, I am relishing this excursion away from the Palace. I had not realized how I'd been missing the sheer movement of the outside air: its dizzy green breezes, the sting of salt spray, even the puffing dust the animals kick up. The only wind in the Harem comes from the waggling of a thousand tongues, the waving of a thousand tasselled fans. And the vistas out here! My first day aloft my white stallion, I was like a veritable weathercock, spinning my head this way and that, trying to encompass the wild beauties of this land.

Since we embarked on our journey, we have spent three-quarters of our allocation and acquired nigh on fifty new lasses. The Crone and I have become quite the *connoisseurs*, huddling *sotto voce* over the merits of each proffered *pulcher*, then haggling with various flint-eyed kinsmen and procurers over her price.

What a strange process this is, to choose mistresses for another man: to judge the flavour of each woman by his tastes. There are certain basic requirements, of course, such as fecundity (which the Crone, by some alchemy, ascertains), plus a certain symmetry in the features, and the plumpness I have mentioned before.

Yet compared with these fleshly young virgins, with their dimpled wrists and doughy breasts, my big Batoom seems so sure and substantial. Where they giggle and cover their mouths, she throws her great chest out and roars. Where they call peevishly for some slave to tote their bags, she hoists hers up without a thought. And I challenge anyone to name a more stirring sight than the Black Queen, tall and magnificent, gliding gracefully along, barefoot, barrel-arsed, with her water jar on her head.

This is true Beauty to my mind: her gusty laugh and honest heart, her vast backside bending among her sorghums and millets (for she insists on growing her native food in her private garden, and cooking it herself in her own cauldron). Batoom, my cook and my gardener; my sea-lion, my she-bear; how I've missed her tart wisdom and sour porridge!

We are billeted in the *seraglio* of the Governor of Sallee – to the *chagrin* of his incumbent concubines, who had to vacate twenty-three of their dank chambers to accommodate us. For we are now an unwieldy company of four score, comprised of the hand-picked bonnies themselves (including the Governor's own pustular daughter, whom we could not, in all politeness, refuse), plus assorted slaves to groom and feed them, and a battalion of our heftiest eunuchs for their protection.

We are to remain here two more days, while the Crone completes some business of her own – involving, I would hazard, the secret disposal of the sacks of coins she has strapped beneath her garments, which cause her valiant mule's legs to buckle and have rendered her yet more bent and shift-eyed than usual.

She aims to thwart the Emperor's tax collectors by depositing some portion of her fortune with her numerous offspring who reside in this city. At least that is what I suspect, for this has become the avid preoccupation of each citizen since the Emperor reformed his Revenue, with some burying their treasures in the goat-shed and going about in rags to simulate poverty.

I have communicated my suspicions to the Crone by lurking nearby while she gingerly dismounts, and casually commenting on the strange clinking that accompanies all her movements. This knowledge will stand me in good stead, I hope, if she should ever discover the true nature of my relationship with Batoom. For, though we have established a wary *camaraderie* on this journey, I cannot imagine it would prove sufficiently strong to counter her absolute adherence to the Emperor.

Observing Malia in such close proximity these last weeks has taught me much about the *arifahs*, or wise women, of this kingdom. I have discovered, for instance, why they grow the nail on the smallest finger of the left hand into a two-inch talon. Men whisper that it is a claw to signify their kindred with the feared Hyenas, which are held to be witches in animal guise by reason of their sloping backs and ungainly gait: the very image of a human on all fours. Further proof is their *penchant* for gobbling goatherds' weans (fresh neonate flesh was ever your Hecate's habitual titbit).

Though I doubt the Crone's withered lips would ever smack on so distasteful a morsel, I can confirm that the uncanny claw serves the function of terminating pregnancy. I have witnessed this operation any number of times now, and it is conducted with surprising delicacy. Indeed, it is a procedure all potential concubines must endure *en route* to the Emperor's couch, for it would not do to introduce a cuckoo into the Royal Nest.

Wincing at the sight of the cruel talon, I did once venture that an examination of the hymen might serve as well, at which the old Witch cackled uproariously, declaring that we men are utter idiots in this regard. Chortling all the while, she then goes on to detail some of the subterfuges women concoct to convince some sap that he is shafting a virgin. To wit, I can now assert that a man would be better advised to check his mother-in-law's hen-house for a missing pullet than to examine his sheets for maiden's blood on his wedding night.

Ay, the Crone likes to flaunt her claw and pretend to supernatural powers (and holds the whole Harem in thrall to her abilities), but having observed the ceaseless flickering of her eyes, I am now of the opinion that what masquerades as uncanny Intuition is naught but canny Calculation. I cannot say what the bits and bobs might be that are totted up in this way, but I believe those eyes, shuttling back and forth like the beads on an abacus, are what account for her legendary skill – and the extraordinary fertility of the Crone in her youth.

I put this hypothesis to her only this morning, and a sly smile shifts a few cheek-folds in an upward direction. 'When you love your husband,' she says with a modest shrug, 'naturally, you notice things.' Whatever the things were that she noticed, our shrivelled Sibyl claims to have whelped thirty weans in as many years – and all of them sons.

Her notoriety began spreading, so she says, after her sixth confinement, until, by the tenth, her house was under veritable siege from heirless wives clamouring for her secret. At this point, her astute husband (a baker by trade) auctions off his oven and sets up a *kioshk* outside his gate to profit from his wife's more fleshly cooking abilities.

By her fifteenth confinement she is quite the Queen Termite, ballooning up to gigantic proportions on the *glacé* fruits she is brought by her *clientèle*. And a new son slipping out, smooth as soap, around the time of the *Eid* festival each year. And here she chuckles and slaps her knobby knees, because this precise timing was a miracle in its own right, for are not pregnant women excused the Ramadan fasting before the *Eid*?

The decades have diminished her dimensions since then, leaving a formless aggregation of empty wrinkles, like your crumpled night-shirt hanging on your chair. And her lips have quite puckered up over her toothless gums, which munch incessantly on the *qat* leaves she obtains from the Soudanese eunuchs. 'I just ate for thirty years!' cackles she, showing her green gums. 'While the other women were growling with hunger.'

9

The seagulls began feeding at first light. Helen lay with her eyes closed and wished she was still asleep. Every morning they jolted her awake with their foul squawking, dangling the image of poor Robert Baird's corpse in front of her mind. Every morning they made her relive, in a rush of horror, all that had happened in the last week: the pirates swinging up the side of the ship with their frocks flapping, then swooping down the corridors like white bats; the babies skewered on swords and shaken off, one by one, over the side; the nudie brown men squatting on deck, fickling through great heaps of clothes for money, flint-boxes, pocket-watches.

She shuddered. It had all been so cold, so organized: everyone herded up on to the main deck, then checked over like sheep at a fair, and the smallest weans and old folk hoiked out and tumbled over the side into the sea.

She remembered how she'd tunnelled to the back of the crowd, terrified of Melissa spotting her in the purple dress. As if it mattered any more. As if she still had a chance of going to Boston. She'd thought perhaps the rich folk would talk to the pirates, give them money or something. Then she'd heard a woman gibbering and had craned her neck to see what was happening.

It was Melissa, cringing in the centre of the main deck. She was surrounded by five white-frocked pirates, who were taking turns swiping at her with their swords. After a few moments Helen realized they were trying to slice off her clothes. Strips of sprigged muslin and lace fluttered down like feathers as, bit by bit, her white body was revealed, latticed with blood where they'd cut right through to the skin. When she crumpled to her knees, they started on her hair instead, laughing and flicking off her fine curls until she was tufty as a pullet.

Helen winced, picturing what they'd have done to her next if their fox-faced Chief hadn't emerged then from the captain's cabin and stopped them. He'd barked angrily at them in that strange language of theirs, nudging Melissa's body with the toe of his foot and pointing at her wounds in disgust. 'She's worthless now,' he seemed to be saying. And spat on the deck, unsheathed a long knife, and slit her throat.

There'd been a moment's shocked silence, then a terrible howl as Robert Baird had staggered across the deck, trailing a bleeding leg, and hurled himself at his wife's murderer. The Chief's response was instant. Neatly side-stepping the flailing man, he grabbed a handful of his hair, sliced off his scalp and ordered him to be tied to the mast. Then he gathered up a handful of sprigged muslin and carefully wiped his blade on it. Shrugging towards the rest of the passengers, he made it clear that this punishment was intended as a lesson to them all.

Robert Baird had lived for three days, tethered just outside the place where Helen and Betty had been locked up with six other young women – away from the rest of the passengers, in the small cabin the ship's cook and his mate had used. For three days they'd sat dumbly with their hands over their ears, trying to block out his fevered moans as the gulls stabbed and yanked at his flesh with their beaks.

Helen listened to the birds' webbed feet puttering on the wooden roof above her head. Weren't they finished with him yet? There must be some bits they couldn't get at: in his groin perhaps, or at the bottom of his boots. Tears squeezed out through her closed lids as she listened to the birds bickering; imagined them jabbing at his cage of stinky bones, making his dead body jump like a puppet against the brightening sky.

She shifted in the hammock and the silk dress rustled. Thank God they'd picked on Melissa to play with instead of her. If they'd spotted her first, they'd have thought she was one of the rich folk. If they'd seen the purple dress . . . She imagined them slashing at her, and her hair falling in coils like cedar-shavings. Thank God she'd found that brown shawl. Thank God she wasn't down below in the main cabin with the other prisoners.

They were being given food and water, she'd heard the pots being taken down. But something dreadful was happening in the black barn below deck, some sickness spreading in the oily darkness, so that every time the trapdoors were opened, and light spilt down into the thick stew of people, there were groans of anguish as more dead bodies were discovered in their midst.

How long was this going to last? If only she could sleep like the others: close her eyes and drift off somewhere, wake up when it was all over. She sighed, then stiffened suddenly, hearing the *shush-shush* of the pirates' pointy-toed slippers on the deck outside. But it was too early for the pirates to be up. Rolling out of her hammock, she peered out of the window at the grey dawn.

'Wake up,' she whispered, nudging Betty. 'I think we've arrived somewhere.'

They'd known, from the moment the ship was attacked, that they were going to be sold as slaves. Back home in Scotland there was a special collection at the kirk every month for the missionaries who paid to free Christians who'd been captured by pirates from Barbary.

'Maybe we'll be bought by a rich man with a grand house,' Helen whispered as the young women were chivvied out of their cabin and stood blinking in the bright sun.

'More likely a poor man with a whore-house.' Betty reached

for Helen's hand. 'Mind you keep ahold of me,' she warned. 'I don't want to lose you.'

Out on deck, Helen saw the other prisoners clambering up through the trapdoors from below, gaunt and grey-faced. She saw the steward being kicked towards a rope ladder, and big shy Dougie leaning on someone's shoulder like an old granda.

On the glittering sea a scatter of small craft was gathering around the ship, bobbing on the swell. Nearer the shore, where the waves crashed in a haze of white spray, a herd of tall brown men, with long tarred manes, waded through the water like horses, lifting people from the small boats on to their shoulders to carry them ashore.

A dry, crackling sound made Helen turn back to the deck. What was left of Robert Baird was being cut down and thrown overboard. She watched his sun-bleached clothes darken and fill as he was swallowed by the green water. Dear God, let that be an end to it, she prayed.

'Look at that grand city.' Betty was staring at the towering red walls perched on white cliffs overlooking the bay. 'And those great gates with the bonny carved heads all round the top –' Her voice faltered and Helen followed her gaze. The heads decorating this city's gates were not carved. She could see rusty smears on the stones beneath them; bare eye sockets staring out to sea. A dry sob shook her body. Here was her answer: there might never be an end to it.

In through the dreadful gates, and the streets seethed with men in long brown gowns. They peered greedily at the line of dazed Scots lasses, shackled together by ropes, stumbling along behind the pirate Chief. Hard fingers prodded Helen's breasts and arse as she passed; bearded mouths leered and spat at her. Heat thundered down from a white sun and boomed back, like an echo, from the red clay walls. She could feel her face burning, and her chest; her bare arms and the tops of her feet.

She scanned the crowds for a woman's face, hoping for a glimpse of pity for a lassie in trouble. But there were none to be seen, not a mother or a daughter; just men everywhere, brown-skinned and bearded: sucking smoke from water jars and snakes from grass baskets; lying face-down on wee rugs and muttering; squatting and blowing on tiny cups; and the endless whispering of their flat yellow slippers, shuffling through mule dung and smashed fruit: a whole city of men shambling along in their night-gowns in the middle of the morning.

Twice they had to edge past a monstrous yellow horse the size of a byre, with shaggy two-toed feet and a great lump of flesh on its back. And here and there, backed against the walls, were clusters of smaller figures, shrouded from head to toe in brown cloaks, jabbering and peering out through tiny slits.

She saw a black-skinned man singing for money, beating out a rhythm on his own leg, which was as huge and hard as a tree-stump. Jesus God, what was wrong with him? There must be some sickness here that turned folk – and beasts too – into monsters. Perhaps that was why so many had to cover themselves in those heavy cloaks in the heat.

They arrived at last outside a huge studded door in one of the clay walls that lined the shuffling streets. The pirate Chief rapped loudly and a wooden grille rattled open at eye-level. Moments later a series of bolts were drawn back and Helen found herself being tugged into a stuffy dark hallway, then shoved out again through another door into a sunny courtyard.

A mountainous Matron stood waiting for them, wiping her hands on an expanse of striped skirt. Her face shiny with sweat, she surged towards the pirate Chief, patting her baggy red lips with the kerchief she wore over her oily plait. He backed away slightly, and she veered towards Helen and the others with a hungry gleam in her eye. Waddling around them, she yanked open their blouses and mouths, and poked their bellies with an expert finger.

Two of the lasses revealed inches of bare gum and, snorting with disgust, the Matron stomped across the courtyard and disappeared behind one of several floor-length white curtains. When she emerged a few minutes later, she had a purse of coins in her hand, which she shook at the pirate Chief, jabbering accusingly at him until he clutched the purse to his chest, bowed hurriedly and left.

As soon as the door closed behind him, the curtains were flung back and a dozen plump wee lassies, about eight years old, scampered out into the sunlight. Helen looked around warily. Perhaps this was a school and they were to be teachers. Or pupils: perhaps they'd been brought here to learn that strange yelpy language. The place seemed clean enough, and a delicious meaty smell was wafting from the smoke-blackened kitchen. Saliva flooded her mouth.

The wee lasses fluttered around the newcomers, giggling and shyly touching their clothes. Their palms and the soles of their feet were a bright yellow colour and flashed like goldfinches' wings as they moved. Three bulky brown women emerged a moment later and stood in a stolid group. Helen stared at their hair. How thick it was, like sheep's wool, and short like the brown men's on the ship. And their lips: fat and swollen. Was that what the cloaks outside were hiding?

At a word from the Matron, one of the brown women began untying the ropes around their ankles while the other two carried brimming basins of water and clods of greyish soap to a shady corner of the courtyard. Betty nudged Helen: 'Looks like we're going to get a wash,' she whispered.

'Ay,' Helen hissed back. 'But I don't fancy stripping off in front of those muckle brown –'

A stinging slap across her cheek interrupted her. The two brown women grabbed her and made her stand with her arms aloft while they unhooked the purple dress and pulled it over her head. Then they led her over to the corner of the courtyard like a muddy horse and began scrubbing her from head to toe. Helen hung her head with the shame of it. No one had seen her naked since she was a wean. Squeezing her eyes shut, she tried to pretend she was six years old again, and they were her granny's nails scratching in her armpit, her granny's hands lathering between her legs.

But there was worse to come. When she was clean, she was taken into one of the curtained rooms where a smelly yellow sludge was seething gently over a charcoal brazier. There she was laid out on a reed mat and one brown woman held her down while the other slapped a burning pad of the yellow sludge on to Helen's pubic hair. She waited a few moments while Helen writhed with shock and pain, then suddenly ripped it off again, pulling a big patch of pubic hair out by the roots.

Helen stifled a scream. What were they doing to her? But it soon became clear: they were removing every scrap of hair from her body. It was agony: apart from the sting of the hair being plucked, there was something in the yellow mixture which burnt her, over and over, until the skin in her crotch and armpits, on her arms and legs, was red-raw and smooth as satin.

The sun was low by the time all the Scots lasses had been done. They stood naked and shivering in the centre of the courtyard, avoiding one another's eyes. How strange they all looked, Helen thought: white backs peppered with flea bites, limbs red as scrubbed carrots.

The Matron came out to inspect them, her flabby mouth stretching into a greedy grin as she ran her hand over their smooth flanks. She seemed especially pleased with the fairer lasses: two sisters with pale eyelashes and wispy blonde hair; and Helen with her heavy amber curls.

Clean clothes were brought out: baggy striped cotton breeks and loose white blouses down to the knee, coloured sashes and embroidered waistcoats. The Matron grunted approval as they began dressing themselves. Then one of the brown women pointed at Helen and hurried off to fetch something.

It was the purple silk dress: newly washed and ironed, it billowed and glimmered in the woman's arms. The Matron stroked it with pudgy fingers, peering at the tiny stitches along the seams. Then she looked over at Helen again, and a look of pure greed stole over her sweaty face.

That night they ate well and slept on mattresses for the first time in two months.

'Did you see Dougie?' whispered Betty when the lamp had been blown out. 'He looked awfully peelie-wallie.' Then, into the silence: 'Do you think we'll ever see him again?'

Helen didn't answer. No one answered. No one had said a word since they'd been stripped by the brown women. They felt raw and defenceless. Their legs felt smooth and cold; their groins stung. They'd no men and no money. They couldn't even speak the language so there was no point in escaping. Anyway, the city outside seemed even more scary than inside this house of hard women.

Helen put a hand on her belly, thinking of the tiny baby inside; and of silly-soft Dougie who'd offered to be the father. Then moved it lower, wincing, to the shameful baldness between her legs, wondering what kind of men these were that needed their women as bare as bairns.

10

I have become quite attached to the new eunuch, Lungile. I noticed him last week, when we stopped to water the animals, sitting away from the others against a termite hill. His head was hunched down between his shoulders like a vulture, but there was no concealing him, for his size is quite gargantuan. Even seated he is as tall as your average wench and it must have taken the hides of at least three goats to make his boat-sized yellow slippers.

He appeared to be in pain, so in my capacity as Chief Eunuch with a certain responsibility for the well-being of my charges, I went to speak with him.

'It's nothing,' hisses the giant, creasing his vast forehead in a wince of awesome dimensions. 'It will pass soon enough,' and grinds his great molars and bends over his melon knees.

'Shall I fetch Malia?' I persist, knowing that the Crone keeps a variety of powdered remedies in wee cloth packets hanging around her wattle neck.

'No, please –' and now his apish arms wrap around his tree-thighs as though trying to conceal something. 'It will pass, I tell you. It always does.' But there's a passion in his voice that tweaks my curiosity. And I ask whether there is anything I can do to ease his discomfort. Whereupon he laughs bitterly: 'There's nothing anyone can do for what ails me.'

Undeterred, I perch up beside him on a rock and begin a long blether on the merits of green butter, telling how the

Governor has promised us a vintage tasting when we arrive at the port of Sallee. I should explain here that your Moor, being forbidden the pleasures of wine, lays down butter instead, sealed in goatskin parcels and buried in the ground for up to twenty years until it acquires a level of rancidity your duncest Dunbar dairymaid could scarcely imagine.

'After four years, I'm just acquiring an appreciation of the stuff,' I remark, and am rewarded by an outsized sneer of disgust.

'In my village, you'd send a wife back to her father for serving muck like that – and get a refund of your cattle. Give me fresh curds any day, with honey and sesame paste. Or salt-cheese and sour-dough –' And while he's talking, I notice that his knitted brow has started to unravel and by the time he has progressed on to stewed wildfowl with *cayenne* (via some kind of leaf his mother used to fry in goat-fat), he is licking his bulbous lips with nostalgia.

This prompts my own reminiscences: on colcannon, skink and stovies; clootie dumplings and kale soup. And we continue in this vein for a while, comparing our native dishes, until he stops (in the middle of winding chitterlings on to a skewer) and claps me so heartily on the back that I am bowled over like a rolled-up hedge-pig.

'My dear brother, you have cured me! All this talk of food has quite distracted me from my – er – trouble –' Whereupon he casts a dubious eye downwards, to the folds of white cloth gathered between his thighs. And confesses that the winces I'd witnessed were the result of one of the women hoiking up her *haik* to inspect a tick-bite on her ankle.

It turns out that our poor giant is like those men who, having lost a leg to gunshot or gangrene, are driven insane by a phantom itching of the absent limb. Likewise is Lungile tormented by a Lust he cannot assuage. It seems his tender *goujons* had been hacked off but scant weeks earlier and the rest of his immense body is still a-roiling in confusion. So his Horse still rears up at the sight of our fresh fillies, but there are no Sacks of Seed (as it were) on his Cart. What's more, the wretched Cart's as raw as a burst gumboil, and stings like stoury whenever the Stallion stirs.

'I wake in agony every morning,' groans he. 'Before my eyes are even open, I'm doubled over with the pain of it. Then again, numberless times during the day. If he'd put me to work in the kitchens it wouldn't have been so bad. But in the Harem! When I've been so long away from my own wives. Brother, I do not know how I will survive. Oh no –' and he creases up once more, clutching at his ankles with mammoth brown hands. 'Quick, speak to me of food again.'

So I oblige and we proceed in this manner, alternating true conversation with inane extemporization on our native *cuisines*, until we are both hiccoughing with laughter. And when the time comes to remount, I realize I have found me a friend in this crestfallen Colossus, the first man in four years who has reached through my ribs to touch my heart.

Since then we have journeyed together, me aloft on my mild-mannered white stallion, he alongside on foot, trailing his rangy nag by the rein (for I need hardly remind you how sitting astride would inflame his poor wound). Proceeding in this manner, our two heads are on a level, which gives ample opportunity for strengthening our acquaintance.

It seems he was trussed up like a monstrous chicken after some tribal skirmish in his Nuban homeland, and sold off to a Berber merchant with a sullen dromedary to freight him across the desert to Marrakech. Polished up like best ebony, he was resold into the ranks of the Emperor's Black Guard. This battalion, or *Bokhary*, is the Emperor's personal army: ten thousand fierce tribesmen, dark as peat-bricks and sturdy as oaks. He keeps them, much as your Laird keeps his curs, to guard his house and savage his enemies. Ay, and breeds from them too, selecting several hundred on a whim, and mating them with the bulkiest slave-girls his procurers can find. The giant cubs that are born are then taken into the army in their turn, and raised so that riding and fighting are all they know.

So how, I can hear you ask, did this proud member of the *Bokhary* transform to this glum gelding a-plodding by my side? It happened one morning late in March, when the Emperor summoned the *Bokhary* in order to select the few he wished to breed from. 'He was surveying us from his horse, trotting between the rows with the Umbrella Bearers running behind to shade his head. Then he stopped suddenly – I can't remember why – and they ran straight into the back of his horse.'

I closed my eyes when he said this, and let my head fall forward into my mount's mane. The scene burnt itself on my mind: the toppling Royal Umbrellas with their spokes tangled; the Royal Stallion rearing and trampling the tumbling green turbans; the Royal Person sliding backwards, in a slither over his horse's tail.

'No one laughed. But it didn't make any difference. He remounted and ordered us to kneel. I fell to my knees as quickly as I could. But it wasn't fast enough. Or maybe I was too tall even when I was kneeling. Whatever the reason, it was enough for him to send for the *tabibs*.'

I saw Lungile's neck tighten. 'He watched the whole thing, you know,' he went on through clenched teeth. 'The cut itself, and after, when they smeared on that hot black stuff. He wanted me to beg for mercy, but I bit my tongue to stop myself screaming, and swallowed the blood, gulp after gulp of it, so he wouldn't know how bad the pain was.' He squared his shoulders for a moment, then slumped again. 'You know, Fijil, sometimes I wonder what would have happened if I'd howled on my belly like a whipped dog. Maybe then he wouldn't have gone on to do the others.'

This is the Emperor, dear Reader, who makes Harem hinnies swoon. If you met him, you'd judge him the noblest man alive. Yet all our fates are predicated on his pleasure.

11

Next morning, before the sun was high, the fat Matron opened for business. As Helen and the others were finishing their breakfast, she surged out of her private room in her layers of striped silk, and spattered scented water over the newly swept courtyard. Then she subsided in the shade of a tree and began painting her thuggish face until a thick black line joined her woolly eyebrows together, her button eyes were ringed with black and there was a neat circle of red on each cheek.

When she was ready, she nodded to the three brown women, who slapped the Scots lasses into silence and hustled them into one of the curtained rooms with the flock of little local lassies. Flies danced drowsily in the warm air above their heads as they crowded together in the dim space, straining their ears to discover what was happening in the sunny courtyard outside.

A pattern soon emerged: a knock at the outer door and a brief, low-voiced exchange, then the clatter of bolts being drawn back and shot home to admit someone through the dark entrance lobby. Next came tea. Helen could hear it being prepared: chunks clipped off the boulder of loaf-sugar; the clink of cups being set on the brass tray. When it was ready, the Matron would heave her great bulk through the curtain and squint down at them all crouching in the gloom. Raking her eyes over their upturned faces, she'd consider a moment before tugging someone to her feet to carry the tray out to her guest. Half an hour later the bolts would grate back again to allow the visitor to depart. Then the process would start all over again.

To begin with, only the local lassies were chosen, and they

fidgeted with nervousness each time one scrambled to her feet and disappeared out into the sunlight. After three had gone, Helen began to realize that none had come back. She stared at the remaining girls, but they seemed resigned rather than afraid. So she caught the eye of one of the brown women and pointed to the wee lassies, raising her eyebrows in a question and miming scrubbing the floor. Were they going to be housemaids?

The brown woman gave a bark of laughter and shrugged her big shoulders; then made a series of unmistakable rounded gestures with her two hands. They were to produce babies, the gestures said; as many as possible.

The Scots lasses stared at one another, shocked. 'But they're just bairns,' Helen whispered in Betty's ear. 'Better a wee wifie than a wee whore,' she whispered back. Still, there was something chilling about the image of a grown man's body rearing up over one of those plump little pigeons. What kind of man would want a bairn for a wife?

It wasn't until next morning that the Matron ordered the first of the Scots lasses out into the sunlight. She chose the two whose gappy gums had so angered her when they arrived. Terrified, the two lassies clung to Helen and the others. But the brown maids, obviously used to this kind of reaction, calmly clamped flat hands over their mouths and yanked them to their feet by the hair. A couple of vicious pinches later and they stepped meekly out through the curtain.

Helen craned her neck trying to glimpse the men they were going to, but the curtain dropped shut before she could see anything. Pulling on one of the brown women's blouse, she made the gesture she'd used before to mean 'babies'. The big woman sniggered and shook her head; then formed a circle with the thumb and forefinger of one hand, and thrust the forefinger of the other roughly in and out of it.

The following day two more Scots lasses were sold together, followed in less than an hour by Betty, then the two fair-haired sisters, one by one. By mid-morning Helen was the only Scots woman left.

She sat against the wall in the dim room, hugging her knees to her chest. She was on her own now. The thought pressed in on her lungs until her breath came in small gasps.

One of the wee lassies stroked her arm and passed her a dish of sweet-smelling red fruit. But Helen just stared straight ahead. There was a tiny hole near the bottom of the white curtain and her eyes seemed to be fixed on it. Betty had gone. Already she missed her blether and her buck-toothed grin; missed knowing she was there. She could see a leaf on the other side of the courtyard. Each time the curtain moved, she could see a different fraction of the bush outside. She tried to work out what kind of plant it was.

Soon some man would come and take her away. To a whore-house by the port, perhaps. Then what? She tried to block out the images that crowded her mind: of nappy beards and brown teeth, hot tongues and hot meat slabbed inside her –

There: a flash of pink. It was a rose bush.

She stiffened suddenly. The bolts were being dragged back again. She heard the Matron gabbling a welcome. Then she noticed that the brown women standing by the curtain had become quite nervous. She sat up straighter, scanning their faces. A moment later the curtain parted and the Matron appeared. She was flushed and a kerchief trembled in her dimpled hands as she patted trickles of sweat on her cheeks.

A flurry of hissed orders sent one of the brown maids hurrying from the room. She came back carrying the purple dress.

Fear clogged Helen's throat when she saw it and she wrapped her arms tighter around herself. Then a thought struck her:

why were they dressing her differently to the others? Hardly daring to hope, she pulled urgently at one of the brown women's arms and made the sign that meant 'babies'. The big woman nodded grudgingly and gave her a withering look. Her meaning was clear: who'd take this much trouble over a whore?

Five minutes later Helen stepped out from behind the curtain. The sun felt suddenly hot on the top of her head and beads of sweat sprang out on her upper lip. She looked down at herself: at the great swaying tent of purple silk round her hairless legs; the tight-boned bodice quivering with the thud of her heart. Shuffling clumsily forward in the stiff pointed slippers she'd been given, she stared across at the figures waiting beneath the tree, searching out the man who was to be her husband.

But there were no men there. Just an old woman and an ugly wee boy of about seven, dressed in a long white shirt and baggy breeks. She frowned, puzzled. Perhaps the boy's mother had died and his father wanted to let him choose a new mother for himself.

The boy scrambled to his feet and bowed in her direction, whisking off a small red hat. Then he was walking jauntily towards her, rocking strangely from side to side on his bandy wee legs. It was then that she realized that it was not a boy she was looking at, but a man. But a man like no other she'd ever seen, with his squashed face and swollen forehead and tiny, shrunken limbs.

He came and stood before her, his bulging head no higher than her thigh, and reached out a small, bony hand. Numb with horror, she looked down as he took hold of her hand and tilted his gargoyle face up towards it. His eyes were closed, his sandy-coloured eyelashes trembling, as he brushed his lips gently along the tips of her fingers.

Part II

12

Sallee, 2 July 1769

Alas, I am smitten! A kind of breathlessness palpitates my breast and rustles my papers in my lap. I might have suspected the *mal aire*, but these tremors have more of the *bon* about them. It is as though my senses had been peeled, like a bunch of wee grapes, and left quivering and wet as a pack of beagles' noses.

It came upon me all of a sudden at Madam Jasmine's today. We had gone there following a rumour that this was the source of some new white-skinned whores in Sallee's *salons des diversions*. The Crone and I were growing anxious, *vous comprenez*. For though we had gathered ripe morsels of many colours for the Emperor's delectation, we were still lacking one sweet pale Ingredient. And he would have deemed it a flat pudding indeed if our recipe had not been leavened by the yeast of fair skin (for nothing is better calculated to make his dough rise).

So we arrive, and *La Jasmine* ushers us in, quite suffocating us in a pall of welcoming frankincense, then straightway dousing us with orange-water, as though our garments had actually been conflagrated by the smoke. Then goes she immediately into a great blether about the young French Countess she has been saving for the Emperor, naming a preposterous price, then ordering her Amazons to reach the merchandise out from behind a curtain.

And suddenly there she is, swaying gauche as a harebell, all decked out in some ghastly purple dress that *La Jasmine* must have ordered from an addled seamstress in the Jewish *quartier*. So I watch her shuffle forward in those pointed red slippers all the women here wear, smoothing down the dreadful dress with her hands, and I feel my throat start to ache with a tenderness I vowed I would never feel again.

She didn't see me to begin with, or rather she was blinded: first by the sun, which made her squint like a dazzled newborn; then by her expectation of finding some tall bearded Moor waiting to greet her. I swear I must have loved her even then, for I leapt up and bowed as low as a primping Englisher, cavorting like a stupid lapdog to entertain her.

It was in vain, of course, my pathetic puppying. She had already recoiled by the time I'd gambolled across the yard. And when I tried to greet her in the polite Moorish manner, her face became so suffused with revulsion that I was compelled to close my eyes.

Meanwhile *Assayida* Jasmine is clogging the very air with her chin-wagging, apologizing for the narrowness of the Countess's waist, claiming such a shape is the latest French fashion, and so on and so forth, and on and on. But as soon as I touched the lassie's hand, I could tell this was no limp gentry paw. It was a working wench's hand I was holding, with strong fingers and broken nails, and an ingrained shadow of grime on the knuckles.

Then I heard her speak some few words, trying to communicate with one of the glowering madams at her side. Verily, I feared my heart would burst! For here were the long vowels and short consonants of my Homeland. I should have recognized that colouring immediately, for no Nation, I fancy, has ever produced that precise quality in the hair: a combination of red and gold strands that is wavy and thick without being coarse; with skin like buttermilk and a cinnamon of unfashionable freckles.

Peggy Doig had that exact same coloration, and now I come to think on it, perhaps it is this that has unshelled my wee crab of a heart. For wasn't poor Peggy my first sweetheart? And aren't we humans just creatures of Habit, such that what excites the Boy continues to excite the Man? Why else would we be so enamoured of a woman's breasts, when the purpose of our lusts should direct our attentions lower? We are but orphaned lambs sucking milk from a pig's bladder, fooled by a mere twist of dead ewe's wool tied around it.

So perhaps my fool's wool is this Scottish gold in the hair; though I must confess I never did get that suck I so craved. For pretty Peggy had an eight-month belly by the time I met her, and was so besotted with my brother James, who caused the swelling, that she scarcely noticed the concupiscent crab scuttling and sighing around her ankles.

She was blind, as this new lass is blind, to the gentle man that lives inside this gnome's skin. For what is a body except a clothing for the Spirit? And when we remove our clothes for the act of Love, do we not also hope to dissolve, for a few precious moments, this fleshly barrier which divides our Spirits one from another?

3 July 1769

The lassie is sleeping: I peeped into her chamber just now and found her snoring softly nearest the wall, hunched away from the others. She seems none the worse for her sojourn in the Crone's *chambre* this morning, though the thought of that cruel talon clawing at her precious pinkness was almost more than I could bear.

I begged the Crone to spare the lass, but she was adamant, pointing out the wench is with child. 'If you want the *bint* to come with us, I have to remove the other man's baby,' she says simply, and rattles her beady eyes curiously at me, no doubt wondering at my sudden concern. 'But I'll be careful, I promise. The pain's fleeting.' And pats me with her bony mitt, and shuffles off to fetch the poor wench.

In my anguish, I nearly cast aside my resolution to keep my Scottishness a secret. For I have conceived of a Scheme to masquerade as a Moor until she has grown accustomed to my appearance. Now is too soon. I am too shocking. Later, perhaps, when she has ceased to loathe the sight of me, I shall surprise her with our common Heritage and hope to kindle something akin to liking in her heart.

If appetite is any indication, the Crone was true to her word, and the lass's recovery has been swift: I saw her put away a fair few handfuls of the mutton at supper (though she rejected the pigeon, on account, I surmise, of its being steeped in the bilious green argon oil so beloved of these people). Already she is supping like a native, digging into the bowl with the rest of the wenches and balling up the *couscous* with her fingers, before flicking it to the back of the mouth.

Your Moor abhors to touch his lips with his hands, due to a curious conviction that an ague is got by ingestion, by a sort of smearing of invisible matter from hand to mouth. Hence his insistence on distinguishing most obsessively between the functions of his two hands, such that the left is reserved *pour les matières merdes* and the right for everything else (Allah, of course, has two right hands).

Thus, at dinner, you will find your Moor sitting sideways-on to the great platter they all share, wrestling right-handed with fish-bones and gizzard gristle, while his left dangles uselessly by his side. Indeed, it is possible to perceive a definite withering in the left arm of your elder Moor, from a lifetime of virtual disuse, and a kind of petrifaction of the fingers into a cup-shape from scooping up the water he uses to sluice his nethers.

Ay, they are a most cleanly race, washing as frequently and fervently as you might cross yourself in a normal day. Thus you can be sure that, however smirched be his soul, the Moor's arse will be clean when he meets his Maker.

I wonder where she got the wean. Some grizzled corsair, perhaps (Dear God, I pray not); a band of corsairs taking turns. No, calm my heart. Malia would have reported something, some scarring, if she'd been used in that way. A love child, then, by a lost sweetheart. How long will he occupy her heart? How long before she can look on me without revulsion?

What a queer enchantment Love is. On my way in to supper I found myself gawping at a common white *ibiscos* in the Governor's garden, marvelling at its luminescence in the blue twilight. I can be patient for ever, I think, while this Joy mints each minute with fresh perceiving.

13

The *tick-tock* of the mule's hooves on the track was hypnotic. Helen's head lolled forward and her eyes drooped inside the folds of white cotton. The cloak seemed to magnify the heat, sucking it in through the material and thickening it. Sweat dribbled from her armpits, between her breasts, behind her knees.

She'd given up looking at the passing countryside. It made her arms ache to hold the cloak open the way they'd ordered, so only her eyes showed: easier just to pull the sides across her face like curtains and be done with it. And it was comforting to be blind for a while; to be jolted along with no idea where she was going, hidden from the eyes that had been staring at her ever since she was captured.

Inside the *haik*, as they called it, she was almost helpless. If she wanted to see out, she needed both hands to hold the folds open the tiny amount the guards allowed. But then she couldn't *do* anything, because if she let go with either hand, the opening collapsed and she was blind again. Drinking, touching things, trying to talk to anyone, all took so much fickling with the material that she'd soon given up. But after a few hours of doing nothing, seeing nothing, her whole body had begun sagging with drowsiness, dulling her interest in everything outside, until she was aware only of what was inside her small, sweltering world: the damp blouse sticking to her back; the spasms of her empty womb; the rusty smell of her blood on the pad of muslin the old woman had given her.

'The baby's dead,' she whispered quietly, testing for the thud of anguish. But it was only relief that she felt. And the pain had been bearable, once she'd understood what the old hag was doing. 'Just get it out of me,' she'd muttered through clenched teeth as the gnarled hands had pressed her knees apart. One hot minute of agony and it was done. A moment later the cramps had begun. Now the baby was gone, perhaps it would all be over: the slobbering steward, the gorging seagulls, the stink of diarrhoea and death. They were then. *It* was then. This journey, this sleepy, hot pacing, was now.

The mule stumbled suddenly and she grabbed its mane. A gust of wind whipped up the free edges of her *haik* and flung them over her shoulder. She felt a brief draught of cool air on her throat, and caught sight of the mule train stretching ahead with its cargo of shrouded white figures; and the brown giants on their black stallions trotting lazily alongside. From horizon to horizon grew stands of cow parsley, high as apple trees, and great white hyacinths rearing twenty feet above thickets of sword-shaped leaves. Was everything monstrous in this land? Then one of the giants was reining his great horse around, and shouting at her to cover herself. The horse snorted, spraying flecks of foam in the bright air, as Helen pulled the flapping material back across her face. Then she was back in her white tent again, inhaling the hot odours of her own body.

An hour, maybe two, three hours later, the cavalcade stopped. She fumbled with the folds and looked out. They were in some kind of settlement: perhaps thirty animal-skin tents inside a fence of thistles. Straightening up from one of the low doorways was a stringy old man with a coil of dingy cloth around his head. He was followed by three stiff-legged dogs, who barked then cringed on their bellies as he kicked vaguely at them through his grubby white frock. Why were all the men dressed as women? Soon other folk began crawling out of the tents: naked weans with shaved heads and dusty bellies; a bleary grandma wiping her nose on her arm; younger women clutching rough woollen *haiks*.

Hearing the hollow clomp of big hoofs behind her, Helen turned to see the wee Dwarf-man who'd bought her cantering up on his huge white stallion. He slithered down from the saddle in front of the old man and bowed politely, waving towards the line of mules with a stumpy arm. The fear on the old man's face was replaced by a smile and he slowly bent his stiff body and lay face-down at his visitor's wee feet. The Dwarf-man must be some sort of laird, Helen thought, watching him bend kindly to help the old man to his feet. Was that why he had so many wives?

She'd guessed his name was 'Fijil', but she couldn't be sure, because when he'd said the word, and beat his barrel chest as though introducing himself, all the other lassies had started giggling. They giggled a lot when he was around, even when he seemed to be cursing at them. Was he going to do it to her too? Her neck tensed at the thought of his bandy wee legs straddling her; his bairn's hands scrabbling at her breasts.

Everyone began dismounting, so she dropped to the ground and found herself being ushered towards one of the tents. She crawled through the opening into a dark, smoky space with a small fire in the centre. In one corner knelt a young lass, naked to the waist, eating brownish lumps of what looked like porridge from a wide clay dish. There were four older women with her, also half-naked, smudged with soot and sour sweat. They shuffled sideways on their knees to make a space for Helen, then helped her off with her *haik* and handed her a bowl of water for her to wash in. When she'd finished, they patted the grass mat beside the younger lass and pointed at the heap of food.

Compared with the strong tastes of everything else Helen had been served, the brown gobbets seemed bland and sweet. She ate hungrily, smiling her thanks. The women grinned back and nodded for her to eat more, glancing approvingly towards the blank-faced lass beside her, who was munching steadily, reaching into the bowl over and over as though in a trance. She was very fat, with pudgy wee breasts resting on rolls of flesh the colour of uncooked sausages. Helen took another mouthful, wondering why they were the only two eating. The eagerness of the older women made her nervous.

She knelt back to show she'd had enough, but they pushed the bowl towards her, slapping their own juddering bellies. She shook her head, miming she was full, but they reached for her arm and forced it towards the food. She took another mouthful, beginning to feel sick. Had the Dwarf sold her to the old man? Was that why she was being given special food? She imagined coming out of the tent and finding the mule train gone, with just hoof-prints and dung piles to show where they'd stopped.

Sweat prickled on her forehead. Even though she'd no idea where they were heading, even though she hated the idea of being married to the Dwarf, there'd been something hopeful about the journey so far. Most of the other lassies seemed excited, happy about whatever lay ahead. There'd been lots of lewd eye-rolling and gusts of laughter among the ones who spoke the same language; plenty of good food wherever they'd stopped; finely stitched clothes to wear.

She looked at the fat women in their smoky tent: like crude Highlanders with their greasy plaits and stained skirts; the goat-stench of their mingin shelter; and the lumpy lass, munching like a milk-cow by her side. Strong fingers pushed her hand back into the heap of food and she took another mouthful; and another, imagining herself living here for ever; and another, forcing the stuff down her throat. There was a distant neigh – were the others leaving already? In a sudden panic, she began crawling towards the opening.

Behind her, the tent filled with shouting. Rough hands grabbed her ankles but she kicked herself free. As she scrambled out through the tent-flap, she saw a pair of red-slippered feet shuffling quickly through the dust towards her.

It was the old woman who'd made her lose the baby, flapping her hands to shoo her back inside. Beyond, she could see the brown giants driving the mules into a stockade. Helen ducked her head and backed slowly into the tent again. Old Malia followed her in, jabbering crossly and pointing at the *haik* the others were holding. Then Helen understood: she had forgotten her *haik* – that's why they'd tried to stop her. She laughed aloud, weak with relief. Then suddenly she was weeping instead.

Once she'd started, she couldn't stop. Her bairn was dead, Betty was gone, and she was surrounded by people she couldn't understand. A great wave of loneliness broke over her, leaving her sobbing and shuddering, rocking back and forth with her fists buried in her stomach. Malia knelt quietly beside her and, after a while, placed a clean kerchief on her knee.

Later, when she'd blown her nose and wiped her eyes, Helen looked up to find the older women deep in conversation. They stopped talking when they saw she'd recovered, and placed a bowl of hot water in front of her. Then they turned tactfully away while Malia helped her wash between her legs and supplied her with a fresh pad of muslin.

Afterwards some glossy brown fruits they called *balah* were handed round in a basket. Helen took one and bit into it cautiously. It was delicious: the sweetest thing she'd ever tasted. As she reached for another, she felt Malia watching her. The old woman smiled and placed the palm of one hand on Helen's belly. Then she lifted it off, very slowly. 'Eat well and grow plump,' the gesture said. 'Soon there will be another baby.'

The bleeding went on for five more days. In future, whenever she smelt menstrual blood, Helen would always remember that journey: the hot, stale air inside her *haik*, the many different places they'd stayed in, the different bowls she'd been given to wash with, all the strange dwellings she'd had to crouch in to clean herself.

She hadn't been allowed to remove her *haik* until she'd been hustled into some smelly tent or curtained room for the night. Apart from that one time it had blown away from her face, she hadn't taken a single breath of fresh air since the journey began. She'd become used to peering out through narrow openings; through tent-flaps, air-slits, door-grilles. The world outside had turned into something distant and dream-like: a series of peculiar fragments, framed by white cotton or mud bricks or black goat-skin: a woman yoked with a donkey to a plough; a man squatting in a church doorway razoring chicken throats; three giant geese with human legs trotting down a dry river bed. One day she saw a flock of goats climbing trees; the next, a herd of the gigantic humped horses kneeling to suck water from a green pond. There were fields of what looked like snow, lying glittering and unmelted in the sun; walls covered with blue hands; acres of jointed green turnips covered with thorns.

By the evening of the sixth day, Helen was able to shake her head when Malia offered her a pad of fresh muslin. The old woman wadded it back into her bag with a satisfied nod. Then she grasped Helen's upper arm and squeezed it to assess its plumpness. Clicking her tongue reproachfully, she gestured to a narrow slit in the wall of the room they were in, through which some half-naked brown lassies could be seen ferrying dishes of food into a long, flat-roofed clay house.

Helen sighed. She wasn't hungry. It was too hot and her teeth were still sticky from the *balah* she'd been given when they arrived. She knew everyone thought she was too skinny. But she didn't want to look like the other lasses, with their thick wrists and doughy necks. Some of them were so fat they couldn't even get up from the floor without help. And they all walked with the same slow, shuffling waddle, shushing along in their slippers with their rumps swaying and their thighs rubbing together. They seemed so soft and defenceless, big pillowy maggots: barely able to run, barely able to do anything but eat and comb their hair. It was as though they were submerged in their own flesh.

Helen had been singled out with three other lasses for special food. Two of them seemed to be ill: their conker-brown skin looked stretchy and dry and they hunched in their *haiks*, even indoors. The other was a rangy, black-haired lass with restless blue eyes and strange lines of dark blue dots along her nose and chin and down her long neck. Sometimes they ate separately from the others; more often than not they'd be given a plate of the brown *harrabel* pellets after their ordinary meal, or some dense honey cake to eat.

That night it seemed they were all to dine together. Shuffling in with the others in her pointy slippers, Helen shrugged off her *haik* and peered down the long, shadowy room for her usual eating companions. She spotted Naseem, the blue-spotted girl, beside a little oil-lamp at the far end, and made her way slowly towards her through the jabbering herd of lasses kneeling either side of the heaped dishes down the centre of the room.

'*Masal khair,*' she said, squeezing in beside her. Naseem

clapped her big hands, applauding Helen's attempt at the local language, then frowned, concentrating: 'Ghoot ee-ver-ning,' she said uncertainly, rasping the 'g' at the back of her throat. They smiled shyly at each other, then Helen grimaced at the mountains of food. Naseem pulled a face. *'Waja mi'deh,'* she said, clasping her stomach, then suddenly knelt up straighter and nodded towards the door.

The Dwarf was coming in, accompanied by the tallest of the brown guards. Dressed alike, in pure white frocks, they were chatting and laughing together: the one straining to look up, the other arching down like a stork towards its chick. A buzz of whispers followed them as they walked the length of the crowded room. What was happening? The men usually ate separately, with the laird of whatever village they were staying in.

Reaching the end of the room, the Dwarf turned and paused. For a moment he seemed worried, looking quickly round the room as though searching for something. His eyes met Helen's briefly, and she caught a flash of something – relief? triumph? – before they slid away again. Then he squared his shoulders and raised one of his wee bony paws. The lasses lapsed into a breathless, giggly silence as he began to speak.

What he had to say ignited his audience. They gasped and blushed; their eyes shone in the flickering lamplight. They began whispering excitedly, then chattering and calling urgently to one another across the brimming dishes. Some scooted along the carpet on their rumps for fevered discussions further down the room. The Dwarf grinned at the chaos and nudged the brown giant sitting cross-legged beside him.

Helen tugged Naseem's arm. 'What did he say?' she asked eagerly in English. But Naseem didn't seem to hear. She was sitting stiffly, with her hands clenched, staring into a half-eaten dish of meatballs. Helen shook her again, then turned impatiently to the lass on her other side, a noisy, big-breasted wench. 'What's going on?' she asked again, and was rewarded with a series of mimes, added to by some of the other lasses nearby: a big house with many, many rooms – they drew it in the air – beautiful clothes, more jewels than she'd ever seen. Soon. They would go to sleep. Then travel tomorrow. Then before sunset they would arrive at their final destination. There would be a man there: an important man. And sex. Babies. Soon. Tomorrow.

Their mood was infectious and Helen tried to say some of the words herself – 'man', 'sex', 'soon' – making them shout with laughter and clap their hands. They went on to test her with short sentences, correcting her accent and greeting her every attempt with gusty cheers. Then the big-breasted lass had an idea, and flapped her hands to silence the others.

'*Lahilah ill Allah, Mohammed nessul ul lah*,' she said solemnly and nodded to Helen to imitate her.

Helen hesitated. Their sudden silence made her nervous. She looked around at the others. They were all staring at her: all nodding, all smiling. What did the words mean? Why were they so important? She glanced at Naseem, but she seemed to have gone into some kind of trance. She felt the Dwarf's eyes on her and looked up. Were the words something to do with him? Did they mean she'd be promising something? She expected to see that triumphant expression again, but his face was in shadow. The big-breasted lass said the phrase once more, and the other lasses smiled: nodding, waiting, willing her to speak.

Seconds passed, and the phrase was repeated again. More women were falling silent now, smiling in that patient, encouraging way, waiting for her to say the words – until it became impossible to refuse and Helen shrugged and smiled and blurted them out as well as she could. Immediately the room was in uproar and they were all clapping and ululating, laughing and hugging one another.

Then suddenly there was another kind of uproar. The brown giant had sprung to his feet with a yell and was charging towards the door. Helen whirled round in time to see Naseem dashing out into the night.

Naseem was beaten for trying to escape: on the soles of the feet where the bruises wouldn't show. Helen could hear the blows, coming from a room at the far end of their sleeping quarters, and the grunts of the brown giant who beat her. But Naseem never even whimpered.

Later, when the other lasses were asleep, Helen heard their door being unbolted and saw the giant silhouetted for a moment in the moonlight with Naseem lying rigid in his arms. He carried her across the room, then knelt down and placed her gently on the mattress beside Helen. He was bare-chested and she could smell his sharp sweat, see the sheen of dampness on his back. So close, he seemed even more enormous, crouching over Naseem like a huge black cat, with his long, flat nose and slanting eyes, his filed teeth pointed and gleaming.

Helen held her breath. Why wasn't he leaving? Was he going to rape her? She could see the veins standing out in his thick neck, see him clench and unclench his huge hands. Naseem was glaring straight up at him, as though daring him to hurt her again. They stared at each other for a long time, then he pivoted on his toes and bounded out of the room.

'Why did you do it?' Helen whispered in English when he'd gone. Naseem sighed and sat up, wincing as her swollen feet touched the mattress. She pressed her hands to her heart then gestured towards the door. When it was clear Helen didn't understand, she crawled painfully over to a slit in the wall and beckoned. Helen knelt beside her and peered through it to see what she was pointing at.

A full moon was riding high in a clear sky, blueing the sandy ground and clay buildings outside. Two of the brown giants were patrolling, sweeping along like ghosts in their white gowns. Beyond the village was sparse wasteland: waving grass like silver mist in the moonlight, stunted trees with tiny leaves.

She could sense Naseem growing impatient at her side and looked again. Then she saw the mountains: towering peaks filling the far horizon, their upper slopes laden with snow. And behind them more mountains, higher still, like great waves capped with white foam, rearing up silently towards the moon.

She sat back on her heels and turned to Naseem. 'House?' she asked, using one of the words she'd learnt earlier. Naseem nodded with tears on her cheeks, and clasped her hands again to her heart. So that was why she'd tried to run away. She'd seen the mountains in the distance and she wanted to go home. She knew it was her last chance before they reached their destination.

Helen shivered suddenly and understood. This mysterious place they were going to, with all its comfort and wealth: once they were there, there would be no escape.

14

H er name is Helen! I discovered this at supper this evening. It means 'bright' in the Greek, if I'm not mistaken; which could scarcely have been apter, for her face glimmered like porcelain in the lamplight, her hair glinting like gairfish beside the seaweed tresses of the rest.

The lassies were all suffused with silliness, gurgling like fleshy fountains, after I had announced we would be arriving at Marrakech on the morrow. And they were teaching her some Moorish words, stubbing their fingers at one another, going 'Fatima', 'Maryam', 'Ayesha' and the like, naming each one, then squealing and throwing up their hands when she imitated them.

Thus they extracted her name (to the delight of my straining ears) then exchanged further fripperies, regarding fathers and houses, *et cetera*. And then something very odd happened. As if in answer to my prayer, the guileless wenches proceeded to extract, with ardour and smiles, that which might otherwise have been wrung out of her by Torture: namely, a declaration of the Mohammedan Faith. For I think I have already mentioned the disgust with which your Moor contemplates *Les Infidèles*, such that he will greet a scabrous slave with cordiality (as a fellow Mohammedan) but will whisk past a bejewelled Jewish merchant with his head distastefully averted.

Yet if that same Jewish merchant were to fling off his blue cap and utter a few crucial words of belief, a rolled prayer-mat would immediately be thrust under his arm, and he'd be spun round *tout de suite* until his beak faced due East, and urged to pray with his fellow Believers. Upon my soul, a man may embrace this promiscuous Faith as quickly as he may divorce his wife – nay, quicker, for the wife must be repudiated three times, whereas a man need only declare for Allah but once and they are joined.

Helen was ignorant of the import of her declaration, of course. But this Allah is not wont to quibble on such matters. Thus the lass has been spared the pang of denying her Christianity, and I may present her to the Emperor in the secure knowledge that she has been wedded to his God.

The irony of all this is that, though we have discovered her name, we shall now be forced to forget it. For each new convert must be rebaptized with a Mohammedan handle. There are but a scant few to choose from, *malheureusement*, which causes a deal of confusion, especially among the Emperor's slaves, who are named *en masse* according to their year of purchase, rather as your fine claret might be labelled with its date of vintage.

But now it's no longer moot, I'm left wondering whether Helen would have clung to her Faith. Faced four years ago with the self-same dilemma, I spoke my denial of our Good Lord without a second's hesitation, comfortable in the knowledge of His Almighty capacity for Empathy. Thus did I avoid a most uncomfortable grilling, tied to a spit and *rôtisseried* like a marinated grouse.

An act of cowardice, you say? Yet the Keys to the Kingdom of Heaven are brandished by just such a yellow-belly as I. For wasn't St Peter the most abject of all cowards, who, when mildly questioned by a Roman thug, divorced his Lord not once, but three times?

I have been likewise rewarded for my cowardice. For is not

the Harem a veritable *micro*-Heaven? And do I not carry the keys to this Heaven on my belt? So when we meet, St Peter and I, on some soft future cloud, he will wink and invite me in for a game of whist, to the vexation of those fools who suffered more for their Faith. For I feel sure our Good Shepherd does not take kindly to martyrs and looks on their sacrifice as a mockery of His gift of Life. Thus to choose Death is not evidence of a brave Faith but none other than overweening Obstinacy.

Our Young Queen, Douvia, is a precise case in point. Though but ten years old when she was captured off a Spanish ship, she refused to surrender up her Popish rosary beads. I can picture her now: braced back on her haunches and snarling like a kitten, with her tiny nostrils flared and her *mantilla* all askew. They had to break her fingers, one by one, to remove the ivory beads; then pluck every hair from her scalp, before she would consent to utter a grudging allegiance to Allah.

In case you are wondering, I am not in favour of Torture, though my position forces me to exercise some discipline in the Harem. For my first six months this was unnecessary, for the echoes of my predecessor's severity continued to ricochet down the corridors long after he was unaccountably skewered in the heart by a *shawerma kabab*. Since I took over, I have relied more on Disfigurement than Excruciation, having noted the torments women are prepared to endure for Beauty's sake. Thus I might singe a miscreant's fringe or shave her eyebrows; stain her breasts or her cheeks with green dye. Many's the time I've had them begging on their knees for a sound flogging, even offering to fetch the taws or the *chabouk* themselves, to avert the ignominy of a cochinealed neb.

And yet there are occasions when a drubbing is desirable, as with a foolish Berber lass this evening. I had foreseen that she might prove a handful, from the scratches on the cheeks of the brawny kinsmen who sold her. Indeed, Berber females are generally reputed to be fiery, like wild vixens in their remote mountain homes. Though Mohammedan, like their Lowland sisters, Berber wenches go unveiled, for there are few to see them leaping with their goats through the tumbled peaks. With their tattooed faces and powerful thighs, they are renowned for their passion in Love – which is why we purchased this unfortunate wench, reasoning that my Master would relish a wee dash of carnal *cayenne*.

Well, just as we are all congratulating ourselves on Helen's conversion, up this idiot lass jumps and skedaddles towards the door. The attempt was doomed, of course: Lungile caught her up in a trice and bundled her off to our room. And there, on my instructions, laid about the soles of her feet with a cat o' five, thus concentrating her heat most precisely in that portion of her anatomy that would flee.

Poor Lungile! He seemed quite dejected afterwards, sitting in the corner and clutching his great knees. He is unpractised at this, *vous comprenez*, and the shock of his unmanning has left him prey to fierce attacks of sweating, such as mature women experience when their wombs close, which soak through his *salwars* and drip down into his slippers so that they squelch and squeak as he walks.

So comes he in after administering the said drubbing, and slumps heavily on the divan, opening his giant's hands and staring moodily into those strange yellow palms the dark-skinned Negroes have.

'What kind of man is it,' sighs he, wringing out the sodden hem of his *kamise*, 'whose sole duty is the discipline of another man's wife?' and hangs his shaved head, and groans; for the answer, of course, is a eunuch, who is man no longer.

So now we have a hangdog eunuch to return to the Emperor, as well as the lame Berber besom I have mentioned

– plus a duo of limp Bagandan bonnies, whom we acquired for their legendary agility *d'amour* (embellished, so I am informed, by extraordinary crenellate *labia*, about which the Emperor had expressed a most fervent curiosity). But Malia says they are ailing, having aroused the curiosity of numerous minor chieftains *en route* to the merchant who sold them to us. She has tended them carefully, of course, and embarked them on the usual fattening *régime*, but they are still as flat and sad as two lugworms in a tin and have yet to regain their native gloss.

So I must confess to a slight nervousness about our reception at the palace tomorrow. For, though I have observed the Emperor's predilections for four years, I fear I may be as ignorant of the subtleties of his taste as I am of the precise measurements of the Royal Slippers. And herein lies the source of my anxiety, for few things try the temper as sorely as ill-fitting footwear, and should these pretty shoes chafe up a Royal Blister, I shall be the first to feel the kick of the Emperor's Wrath.

15

If Helen hadn't known they were arriving somewhere important, the change in the road they were following would have told her. Where there had been three or four narrow tracks, criss-crossing one another like a braid, now when she peered out through her *haik*, a wide brown road stretched ahead.

They began passing herds of goats and long-horn cattle tended by tall men with shaved heads and long plaits, stalls with reed awnings selling water and fruit. In front and behind her the other lasses started jabbering and calling to one another. Helen's arms ached with holding the tiny slit open. There were two more of those monstrous great yellow horses, heaped with rolled-up carpets; a young man riding in a sledge pulled by two black-skinned women, naked to the waist. Mules and dogs, barefoot bairns with shaven scalps. Why were some women covered and others shamefully displayed? What disease was it that made so many shave their heads?

Then there it was in the distance. Backed by snow-capped mountains and fringed by those strange trees that looked like ferns, was a red-walled city. Then Helen saw that there were actually two cities: one huge and sprawling, surrounded by clusters of brown tents and grazing herds, and a smaller, neater, walled city about half a mile to the east.

As they turned off towards the smaller city, she began to glimpse details. A sea of white tents to one side; green-tiled towers protruding above the thirty-foot walls; red-gowned figures trotting in formation on golden horses. Then they were there, and the gates were opening.

After that everything was a blur. The other lassies started barging forward and Helen's mule broke into a ragged canter, nearly unseating her. Grabbing a tuft of mane and clutching her *haik* around her, she careered blindly with the others for at least five furlongs until they all came to a chaotic milling standstill somewhere inside.

Dismounted and ushered through more gates, suddenly everyone was flinging off their *haiks*. At last she could see. There, a bonny fountain and patterned tiles on the walls; green roofs that sparkled in the sun; arches and covered walkways; carved wood, flowers – and women, everywhere she looked, in the brightest clothes she'd ever seen.

Perhaps that's why there were two cities; one for men and this smaller one for the women. This house was too big, surely, to be the one they were going to? Now they were being chivvied across a series of sunny courtyards, with fat lasses staring from every window and doorway. And overhead, washing lines: not sagging and dripping with grey and brown like in Scotland, but billowing up in great gauzy sails of turquoise, yellow, pink.

There was no time to take it all in. Helen was tripping over her slippers – why were they being hurried so fast? At last they arrived at a group of half-empty courtyards, where she was allocated a little white-walled room. Moments later a wee slave girl appeared with a bowl of water, soap and a chamber-pot; and came back again with a comb and mirror and a set of clean clothes.

She knelt respectfully in front of Helen, then tugged urgently on her arm. She must wash and change quickly, the gesture said. Someone, or something, was waiting for her.

*

The blouse was pale green silk, down to her knees, finer than anything she'd been given to wear on the journey. There were striped gold and green breeks to go with it and an embroidered waistcoat. Helen washed quickly and put them on, then dragged the comb through her hair.

Picking up a little pot of rouge, she looked around for the mirror. She'd never worn colour on her cheeks before and she wasn't sure how to apply it. There was *kohl* there, too – another mystery – and a little brush. But there was no time to try either: the Dwarf was outside, summoning them all into the courtyard.

A few minutes later they were in a bonny garden, shaded with bowers of honeysuckle and roses and great froths of purple flowers she'd never seen before. The Dwarf-man was trotting up and down trying to arrange the lassies in a line, but they kept giggling and clumping together. Then suddenly they were all on tiptoe and craning their necks in the same direction. Helen followed their gaze and saw a tall, white-gowned figure sauntering towards them, followed by a slave holding a wide green umbrella.

Was this the man they'd been brought all this way for? She hardly dared look. What if he was deformed or pockmarked? How would she endure it?

He was moving slowly down the line, greeting each of the lassies. Helen felt a trickle of sweat between her shoulder-blades. The girl beside her started whimpering quietly with excitement. The man's head was shaved, she could see that much, and his skin was the colour of Highland whisky. She could hear him talking; his voice was deep and even. Then he laughed, throwing his head back, and she glimpsed a black beard. As he came nearer, she could see he was about her father's age, with creases on his forehead and around his eyes.

Then he was talking to the lassie next to her, taking her by the hand. Jesus God, he wanted her to take off her waistcoat. You could see her big breasts clearly through the flimsy silk of her blouse. Wasn't she embarrassed? Helen stared at the lassie's face, but she was smiling and thrusting her chest forward, brazen as you like.

And now it was her turn. He was standing in front of her. She met his eyes briefly, then looked down. His feet were in green leather slippers; there was a dusting of pollen near the hem of his gown; she could smell mint and soap. Blood thudded in her ears, blocking all sound, as he touched her chin and tipped her face up towards him.

16

Dear God, what a day it has been! I am quite worn out from managing all these women: flopped on my divan like an old grey-muzzled sheepdog. The moment they glimpsed the palace in the distance, it was all we could do to prevent them heeling their mules into a gallop. The eunuchs managed to restrain them to a trot, by dint of some deft barging, but it was a most disorderly Caravan which broached the Palace gates, with them all squawking and flapping under their *haiks*, like fifty sacks of live chickens.

So we dismount them and take them to the Harem, and begin distributing them to their various rooms. Then word comes that the Emperor is anxious to view his new acquisitions. So we must gather them all together again, prising combs and *kohl* brushes from their flustered hands, and shepherd them out into the main garden where he is waiting.

Of course I am on tenterhooks as to how he will react to Helen, whom I have positioned at the end of the line (much as your good host serves up his finest *Cognac* at the end of the banquet). And when he sees her, his eyes narrow in an expression I have come to recognize in him, a look far stronger than Lust: of a *connoisseur* contemplating some rarity. And lifts her hand delicately to his lips, and coils a copper ringlet gloatingly around his finger. Then nods to the Crone to prepare her.

Then he bows to them all, with that flourish he copied from the Spanish Ambassador.

'You have read me well,' says he, turning towards me. And I feel an unaccustomed blush of pleasure chafe my cheeks, like a wee laddie praised by his father (for the Emperor is the most exacting of men and is normally quite stinting in his commendations). 'I had feared your northern tastes might have prevailed,' he continues, plucking the jewelled pin from his turban and giving it me. 'But you have learnt to appreciate women like a true Moor.'

He then sweeps off in one direction, while Helen is borne off in another to endure that succession of procedures that are deemed necessary to ready a woman for His Majesty's bed. Leaving me surrounded by gushing virgins, like a wee cork bobbing in the froth of a turning tide, while they prattle on about the Emperor: his charm and distinguished bearing, his fine eyes, noble mouth, and the like. Until suddenly I am utterly extinguished, and stand there staring at the gaudy bauble in my hand (an uncut emerald from some obsequious *sheikh*) and all I can think of are her green eyes looking up at him through trembling pale lashes.

Seven o'clock: she must be with him now. This damned palace is full of clocks, all ticking away, the only machines in this Godforsaken country. Tick-tock, stuttering out the minutes. Have his musicians performed yet, I wonder. Or was he too impatient to endure them? Sometimes he sends them all away, and his tasters too, and leaves his *tajines* and fruit bowls untouched.

I should have known he would choose her – what man would not? But so soon? I had thought perhaps the Berber first. Or that tall Hottentot from the Timbuktu trader.

Batoom came in just now, trailing muslin and jasmine flowers, with a flagon of illicit date wine. I pretended a distemper got on the journey and she stoops tenderly and kisses my brow, letting the muslin gape open, and offering to fetch Malia for me. I keep the flagon, but I want none of her, none of any of them.

How many hours will he keep her? I had not expected this excess of feeling – for have I not always lost what I have loved? Is that not the chief lesson of my stunted life? She is his: every curl, every eyelash. And I am his Pimp, with his emerald, my Pimp's wages, in my pocket.

17

M alia touched Helen's cheek briefly; then shuffled back out through the big double doors and locked them carefully behind her. Helen heard her murmuring something to the giants standing guard outside, then the *shush-shush* of her red slippers retreating down the long, dark corridor.

She sat still, not daring to move, just as the old woman had arranged her: leaning sideways against a mound of silk pillows. It was very quiet: only the fountain bubbling in the courtyard in front of her; the whirr and flick of soft moths around the oil lamps. She must be miles from the women's quarters, but Malia had rushed her so urgently through the shadowy cloisters that she'd lost all sense of direction.

He'd be here soon, the man who'd chosen her: the dark man whose hands smelt of mint. She strained her ears for footsteps, but all she could hear were muffled thuds, like loaded sacks being stacked in a distant granary. She was in a room like a small church, with white pillars and a high carved wooden ceiling. It was beautifully decorated, with patterned tiles over the floor and walls, and furnished with big embroid-ered benches and woven rugs which glowed in the lamplight.

A cricket started up suddenly by her ear and she leapt to her feet, stifling a scream. Trying to calm herself, she padded across the room and peered out. Bats were swooping down into the courtyard, their leathery wings rustling in the night air. There was a pair of double doors opposite: slightly ajar, with lamplight flickering inside. She tiptoed past the fountain and pushed them open.

This room was obviously a bedchamber: furnished in white, with floor-length muslin drapes around a divan heaped with cotton pillows. Was this where it would happen? An image burst into her mind: of the dark man's mouth grimaced in pleasure. Would she have to take her clothes off? A flush of shame brought the sweat out on her scalp and she stared round wildly for some means of escape.

She spotted a small door she hadn't noticed before and flung it open. Inside was some kind of washing room, lit by a small lamp; with ewers of water and white cloths hanging from wooden pegs. There was a wooden grille, high in the wall, and she ran over and tugged hopelessly at it. Then suddenly she glimpsed her face, reflected back from a mirror on the opposite wall. This time she couldn't stifle the scream.

What had they done to her? A thick black line across her forehead completely covered her eyebrows. Beneath it, her eyes looked enormous, outlined in black and slanting like a cat's. Her cheeks were stained with bright circles of rouge, and her lips had been reddened like a whore's. She'd known they were painting her – two brown slave-girls had spent nearly an hour preparing her – but she hadn't realized the effect would be so awful.

They'd left her hair loose. Helen stared at it, rippling around the garish face they'd given her and down over her embroidered waistcoat. She fingered the totie wee buttons on her blouse. Malia had undone them all, so the gauzy material hung open in a long 'V', drawing the eye down past the swell of her breasts, right down to her waist where it was cinched into a red silk sash. Was she supposed to be beautiful, this gaudy trollop with her paps half showing?

There was something shameless about the creature staring back at her. The colours they'd chosen for her clothes – shades of scarlet and gold – echoed her hair and the brassy stain on her hands, the rouge on her lips. There was fear in her eyes, but she looked brazen too. Helen gazed at this creation for a moment, then fumbled feverishly with the buttons and did them up. Grabbing a white cloth, she began scrubbing at her red mouth. Then a sound behind her made her spin round.

The dark man was standing in the middle of the white room. As she watched, he shrugged off his white cloak and let it slither to the floor, and dropped his coiled head-dress on top of it. Then he was walking towards her, smiling and holding out his arms. His head was completely bald and he had an upper tooth missing; and thick gold hoops through his neat brown ears. He was saying something in the local language, and laughing softly, taking the cloth from her stiff hands. Then he licked a corner of it and gently wiped her smeared mouth.

She could smell him now: garlic and incense and sweat; and the mint she'd noticed before. His tongue seemed pink, like a dog's, in his black beard. Her skin felt clammy where he'd wiped her. Standing back, he studied her with an amused smile, then reached out and began slowly to undo the little buttons.

Helen stared at the brown hand, spidering down the front of her blouse: at the black hairs on the long fingers, the white half-moons on the nails. She watched his forefinger slide inside the material and stroke slowly upwards over the underside of one breast. Feeling the tingle as it touched her nipple, she clawed suddenly at her chest to get it away from her.

He withdrew his hand at once, frowning with surprise, like someone who'd been bitten by a puppy he was petting. Then his lips were curling again, and his eyebrows arching in amusement. Giving Helen a mocking little bow, he gestured towards the water jars and said something curt. Kicking off his green slippers, he sat down on the white mattress and indicated that he wanted her to wash his feet.

Weak with relief, Helen filled a big copper basin and knelt

in front of him. Had she escaped? She picked up one foot and began to soap it. It arched like a horse in her hands as she lathered it: all hard bones and ridged muscles. She washed the long hairy toes, forcing herself to push her fingers between them, shuddering at his sighs of pleasure. After a while she felt his hands in her hair, lifting it in the lamplight and sifting it through his fingers. She soaped the toes of the other foot and he sighed again, lying back against the pillows and letting his knees fall apart.

She placed his feet on a cloth in her lap, drying them carefully, one after the other, trying not to touch the slick pelt of black hair on his ankles. He arched his feet again, breathing deeply, and pressed them rhythmically, like a cat, into the flesh of her thighs. Then he let go of her hair and eased up the hem of his long gown so that she could see the outline of his thing inside his baggy white breeks.

Trembling with horror, Helen ducked her head and picked up the green slippers, then thrust them quickly on to his feet. He laughed quietly and murmured something, placing his feet firmly on the floor on either side of her body and trapping her between his knees. She looked up at his face: there was a glint of menace in the laughing eyes, a streak of silver in the smooth black beard. He nodded meaningfully downwards and she followed his eyes to where he was loosening the drawstring on his breeks.

Helen looked at the twitching red thing that leapt out at her, raw as a chicken's gizzard and veined as a beggar-woman's leg. Was it diseased? John Bayne's hadn't been like that. She tried to pull away, but he tightened his knees. Waves of heat came from the dark cleft between his legs. He leant forwards and lifted her hair again with both hands, spreading it over his thighs like a shawl. She could see his lean hands on either side of her face; see his thing straining upwards like a death cap toadstool. Twining his fingers in her hair, he hauled her head slowly towards it.

It nudged her chin and she turned her face away, feeling its hot smear slide up across her cheek. He pulled harder on her hair, trying to steer her face towards it. Was she supposed to open her mouth? She lashed her head from side to side in a sudden frenzy.

He released her immediately, cursing under his breath, and she fell sideways on to the floor. Then, shaking his hands free of her long copper hairs, he stood up to retie his breeks.

Crouching at his feet, Helen began folding the damp cloths and piling them up. She picked up the basin but he moved suddenly and kicked it out of her arms, dousing her with scummy water and sending it clattering across the floor. The noise echoed around the room for a long moment. Black eye-paint ran down Helen's face and on to her wet blouse. Her hair dripped into the puddle around her knees.

She looked up warily. He was standing with his legs apart looking down at her. His face was full of contempt.

He clapped for the guards to take her away and they carried her out of the room, then dragged her back through the maze of dark corridors towards the women's quarters. Half-way there, they met Malia hurrying in the opposite direction with a tall, copper-skinned lass. The lass was wrapping a yellow sash around her waist as she walked, pulling a blouse taut over big-nippled breasts. Her eyes glittered with excitement, her skin shone with scented oil. She paused when she saw Helen's black-smeared face and wet clothes, then she laughed aloud and skipped triumphantly after Malia's scurrying form.

They were waiting for her when she came back, maybe fifty women. She could hear the buzz of chatter long before she was bundled in through the great gates. They flooded into the entrance hall, jostling to catch a glimpse of her, sniggering over her bedraggled clothes. Their faces loomed towards her from the darkness: a wall of jabbering mouths, filling her head with noise.

Clamping her hands over her ears, Helen pushed through them. They surged after her, shrieking with laughter, following her across one courtyard, then another. She started to run, kicking off her slippers, past row after row of open doorways. She glimpsed other women lounging inside: combing their hair by lamplight, changing their clothes, suckling weans. Soon her pursuers grew bored and dropped back, leaving her breathless and sobbing, trailed by a handful of curious, half-naked bairns.

She found a fountain in a dark corner and washed her face, then sat down wearily with her back against the wall. The bairns were bald too, each with a single long tuft of hair in a braid. They squatted in a silent semi-circle around her and stared with unblinking, black-ringed eyes. She stared back, shivering in her wet clothes, then lay down on the floor and closed her eyes. She heard them whispering; and their bare feet scuffing the cool tiles.

Feeling a gentle tug on her sleeve, she opened her eyes. One of the bairns was bending over her with a worried frown. He pulled again at her wet blouse, pointing down the corridor. 'Leave me alone,' Helen begged. But he kept yanking at her clothes until she gave up and stumbled to her feet.

Ten minutes later she was outside the room she'd been given when she'd arrived – what was it, five, six, seven hours ago? One of the bairns ran off to fetch a candle and they unbolted the door and pushed it open. There was her *haik*, like an old friend, on a hook by the door; her travelling clothes, washed and neatly folded, on a carved wooden trunk.

18

He has rejected her! Oh, most merciful God, my prayers are answered. It was Malia who told me, rushing in all of a lather, saying the Emperor has doused the lass in dirty water and sent her away.

'Why have you brought me such a stupid girl?' he rants at the quaking Crone, complaining that Helen seems wholly ignorant of the ways of pleasing a man, and is altogether too scrawny for his taste, and were it not for her magnificent hair he would have had her beheaded immediately.

I had heard the women's noise earlier, but like a dolorous dormouse I was burrowed too deep into my misery to twitch even a whisker of curiosity. Assuming it was some juvenile foolishness (the baiting of a snivelling slave-wench, or a frolic involving one of our more ludicrous eunuchs), I shut my eyes and lifted my flagon of wine to my lips, submerging away from the cacophony like a sodden orange in a dish of mulled ale.

Shortly after, in scurries Malia, and I must scramble about hiding evidence of my solitary debauch. But she is too flummoxed to notice, exclaiming, 'Ay me!' and 'What's to be done?', quite beside herself with alarm, so that I have to cork the bubbles of joy which well up in my chest at her news, and contain my wild smiles with a fierce scrunch of a frown.

'I should have schooled her,' laments the Crone. 'But he was too impatient! We should have stayed longer at the

Governor's and prepared them all –' And shuffles up and down, and gnaws on her grey plait, chuntering on about her precious Reputation.

'We'll have to get rid of her, of course,' she declares presently. Which throws me into an equivalent dither, for I had not foreseen that my Gain might so soon become my Loss. So I start up a wine-fuddled gibber of my own, to dissuade the fretful Hag, countering all her arguments with garble, yet somehow happening on a plausible solution: to wit, the invention of a sudden illness on Helen's part, to account for her shortcomings, which may keep her confined for a month or more. In the meantime we shall school her so diligently in the ways of Moorish Love, and cram her so full of Palace sweetmeats, that His Majesty will be enthralled when we present her again, and will expunge this smirch from the Crone's copybook.

This, I knew, would catch her. For the Hag's position in the Palace (and those clinking sacks which process so secretly to her coffers in Sallee) is predicated on her continuing Competence. Indeed, her entire *raison d'être* is to provide succour and sons for His Majesty. To this task she is so totally devoted that she is rumoured never to sleep and can be encountered at all hours prowling the tiled lanes of this sequestered city, cocking her old head and peering around with her shuttling eyes (much as your starling might search out beetles in a meadow) for scraps of information that might help in her quest.

So she agrees to the ruse and departs; and I am just subsiding with relief back on my cushions, when in comes Batoom, her night-gown billowing and her shaven head gleaming in the lamplight. She is anxious, she says, that my ague might have worsened. And draws closer and creases up her fine features with concern, for I am deeply flushed (so she informs me) and my eyes glitter madly as though in the throes of a high fever.

I am nonplussed for a moment, having forgotten my earlier excuses, and I burble on stupidly for a while, scanning my memory for some spark of recognition. Then I see she has fixed me with a penetrating stare and I find myself maundering off into silence.

'You have become hot for the new white girl, Fijil, haven't you?' she says quietly. 'That's why you sent me away earlier.'

Immediately I brace myself, expecting an outburst of injured fury (I think I may even have flung up my *k'sa* over my head). But she is silent. And when I dare to peep out, I see a strange, tender expression in her eye, coupled with a sweet sorrow that quite makes my chest ache. And I understand that her love for me is not of your ordinary, grasping kind, which would rather a lover maimed than untrue. No, Batoom's love is like herself: bountiful and disposed to generosity.

She has said as much to me before, many times, snorting her disdain at the jealous rages that shake the foundations of this place. Now she expresses surprise that I have never left my slippers outside the door of another woman before now, claiming she would not feel any injury so long as it made me happy.

After such Benediction, how my words tumble out! Like coins from a pickpocket's waistcoat, for I have not spoken of Helen except in these pages. So she listens, with that same look on her face – all solemn tenderness – until I conclude by explaining how the best course for keeping the lass in the Harem is to tutor her in pleasuring the Emperor. Whereupon she grins widely, and rolls back her magnificent shoulders, and offers her services as Governess.

I cannot tell what the expression on my face was, but it exploded her into a vast gust of laughter that set her breasts juddering and her earrings jangling. For I was deeply affected, as you can imagine. Indeed, I cannot think that I could ever summon such munificence myself. I say as much to Batoom, but she shrugs and laughs again, pointing out what I had failed to consider: that if Helen should leave, then Microphilus would feel compelled to follow. 'And I cannot bear the thought of life here without you, Fijil,' says she, fixing me again with that sad, loving look.

You will understand that I could not help but embrace her. Indeed, my heart was so bursting with affection as to create a general condition of constriction and overbrimming elsewhere (involving tears and other secretions), which she then eased with a particular balm of her own devising.

Afterwards, lying sated and serene in her arms, I quizzed her about her magnanimity in matters of Love. This she relates to the marriage practices in her native Mauritanie, which discourage rivalry between women. Thus a man may take any number of wives, provided he supplies each with a farm of which she is the sole mistress. This relieves the wives of their dependence on their husband. Indeed, the husband becomes dependent on the wives, for is it not their labour which puts the porridge in his bowl? And he visits each in turn (for they have each their own houses, too, albeit in a close configuration), taking sustenance and comfort in rotation, much as your itinerant might loiter outside a different kirk each Sabbath.

It is this emancipation of your Mauritanian wife (which puts me in mind of the washerwomen of Fife) which contrasts so strongly with our situation in Barbary. Here all women, save the ancient or indigent, are forbidden to range beyond the confines of their fortress homes, so have little to occupy their minds other than an Obsession with their men, and no provisions other than that which their husbands can supply.

'They are owl chicks squabbling over a dead mouse,' sneers Batoom, 'whereas we are out swooping for our own prey.'

Then she chuckles, and kisses my nose, saying that among her people the women are so occupied on their land that they may actually plague their husbands to get a new wife, so that they might ply their farms more convivially. 'And if he plays sex with one, the other is free to rest and tend her children in peace.'

Whereupon she leaves me to 'rest in peace' likewise. Except there seems to be no rest for me this night, despite my amorous exertions and the quantities of wine I have consumed. For though my heart skips to the tune 'He has not had her', my mind is tormented with the image of my bright lassie, fleeing through the dark corridors of this place, tearstained and soaking, pursued by a hundred shrieking banshees.

Thus I have resolved to visit her at sunrise and reveal my Scottish Pedigree, in the hope that kind words spoken in her native tongue might prove of some succour. This may be the ripe time I had foreseen, when she is so starved of the fruit of human companionship that even this wee crabbit apple might seem appetizing.

I have already done my *toilette*, scouring my little body with a *loofah* and scrubbing my teeth with the frayed root they use here, to try to banish the stench of date wine. And I have braided my hair into a frisky *queue de cheval* and donned fresh clothes under my compendious *k'sa*, such that I resemble a wee garlic clove in my hood and rustling white layers (though sweeter-scented, I trust).

19

Helen opened her eyes. Was someone whispering her name? She lay still, listening. It was very early: grey light seeped under her door and spread across the floor of the dark room.

'Miss Helen –' She could see the shadow of someone's feet outside. There was a quiet knock, then the soft thud of someone pushing their shoulder against the door. Swaddling herself in the *haik* she'd slept in, she crept across the room.

'Miss Helen –' The voice sounded gruff: too old, surely, to be one of the bairns who'd helped her last night? She drew back the grille and found herself looking down on a tiny figure in a white hooded cape. Smiling, she whispered the morning greeting – '*Sabahel khair*' – then gasped as the figure tilted its head up towards her. It was the Dwarf, grinning like a gargoyle under his hood.

'At last – you're awake!' he hissed urgently. 'Open the door –'

She backed away, her heart thudding. Was he going to punish her for last night? She thought of Naseem's bruised, swollen feet.

'Come on, lassie, don't be afraid. I'll not hurt you.'

Suddenly it dawned on her: she could understand what he was saying. The Barbary Dwarf was speaking the King's English. She edged back to the grille. 'What do you want?' she asked guardedly, trying to peer along the gloomy corridor outside. 'Where's that muckle brown man with the stick?'

'Dreaming of his wee bairns, I'll wager. He'll not be stirring for another hour at least. Please open the door.'

'Who learnt you to speak English?'

'My mother, of course – well, not my real mother. That one didn't keep me long enough to teach me anything save the folly of being born.' He was still whispering, craning his head up. 'It was Big Kath, in Pittenweem, who coached my first wee witterings –'

'Pittenweem?' Was it possible? She stared at his sandy hair and pale skin. 'Are you from Scotland?'

'Ay, Scots as the thistle, but not quite so prickly. And I should've stayed in the field where I was growing. But I uprooted myself in a righteous rage and jumped on a ship bound for *Le Hague*, to chase after my brother Jamie and make him come home. Och, I can't be whispering all the day! My throat's paining me already. Have pity, lassie –' And he gazed up at Helen with such a plaintive look on his face that she smiled and unbolted the door.

He bounded in and strutted around the little room: surprisingly dapper and elegant in his miniature white garments. Helen pulled the crumpled *haik* more tightly around her, remembering she'd nothing on underneath. She felt greasy and rumpled. Did she stink? Everyone here was so clean. Her scalp itched and her armpits were sticky. Was her face still covered with black smears?

'I'm sorry,' she said, shoving her heap of wet clothes into a dark corner with her toe. 'I didn't wash last night. I was that tired I never even folded my clothes –' Sweat tingled along her hairline at the thought of her meeting with the tall, hairy man. Did the Dwarf know? Of course he knew. Everyone knew. She realized she wanted to piss and noticed the chamberpot, and its contents, in full view at the end of the bed. 'Are you the only one here to speak English?' she asked, and sidled over to stand in front of it.

'Ay, but if you've a smattering of Latin, you'll delight our

Young Queen Douvia.' He was roaming the dim room, picking things up and putting them down again: a wooden comb, a flint-box, three candles in a palm-leaf basket. 'There were two French sisters who could speak it a bit, but they were despatched –'

'Despatched? What do you mean?'

'They were bonny right enough, but a wee bitty *languid*, if you understand me.' He picked up a chunk of soap and sniffed it. 'The Emperor prefers –'

'The Emperor? That baldy man with the tooth missing? Jesus God –' She clapped a hand over her mouth. She'd no idea he was that important. 'Is that like a king?'

'Ay, lass. The King of Morocco, though he's no crown to prove it, more a cushion of white cloth with a ruby impaled in it.'

A king: she'd been with a king. All the land she'd journeyed through, all the people, everything she'd seen was under his command. And she'd refused him. An image flashed into her mind: of a row of heads impaled on spikes above a city gate. When she spoke again, her voice was small and tight: 'What happened to them – they French lassies he didn't take to?'

'Taken off and sold somewhere – Sallee, Tangier, one of the ports. Mogador most likely. There's a new palace being built, with scads of carpenters and masons swarming all over. Tilers, plumbers –' He searched her face. 'Lots of men away from their wives.'

'I made him angry,' Helen whispered. Her legs felt weak and she sat down on the divan. For the first time the little man's grey eyes were level with hers.

'I know, lassie.' His voice was gentle. 'That's why I've come to see you. I've a wee plan.'

'To help me escape?' The words leapt out. For a heady

moment she was galloping away on his white stallion: to Boston, Perth, anywhere.

'Nay, lass,' he sighed. 'I'm afraid the safest place for a woman in this damnable land is where you are right now: in the Harem of the Emperor. As long as you're here, there's no man can touch you – save His Majesty, of course. And I can't think he'll bother you overmuch, with all they other buxom bonnies to play with. And even if he has you fifty nights in a row, isn't that better than fifty foul-mouthed roughnecks for fifty nights? At least the Emperor's clean – I mean, he'll not give you the pox. Malia sees to that.'

Helen flinched. A picture of Betty came into her mind suddenly, the look on her face as she was taken away. Clean, yes. She thought of the ship's steward: his swampy crotch and rotting gums. She thought of fifty stewards: with filthy breeks and claggy beards. At least the Emperor was a gentleman. He could have raped her; whupped her. At least he smelt nice. The Emperor! Sweet Jesus, she'd been caressed by an Emperor. 'But he sent me away,' she said in a small voice.

'Oh, don't worry about that,' waving a dismissive paw. 'I've told old Malia to say you were ailing. But you must be sure and please him when he asks for you again.' He stared meaningfully at her for a moment. 'It'll not be enough just to lie with him,' he warned. 'He'll be expecting certain *services*.'

She ducked her head in embarrassment and he turned abruptly away: 'I'm sorry. These're not things to be speaking of in front of a lady.'

'No! Don't go – please. It's just that I didn't know –' She hesitated and looked down, cheeks blazing with shame. 'I've only been with the one – I mean, it was only the once.' She could smell her fishy sweat through the tight folds of her *haik*.

'It's all right, lassie,' he said soothingly. And explained his plan to introduce her to a woman who'd instruct her in what he called 'the multifarious varieties of Moorish love'. 'If the Emperor's not besotted with you by the time you're gradu-ated, then my name's not –' and he laughed suddenly, and slapped his stubby thigh with his hand. 'Now, here's a con-undrum!' he exclaimed, highly amused. 'For I'm at a loss as to how I should style myself to you. My Mohammedan name is Mansur, but no one's ever tried lifting me by that handle – though I weigh scarcely four stone. And I daren't use my Christian name, even if I'd a mind, which I haven't, for it was my only gift from that callous mother of mine –'

'I thought you were called "Fijil",' said Helen shyly.

'By way of a *sobriquet*, ay. But don't tax me for its meaning, for I wouldn't embarrass you again for the world. And I don't like to suggest "Microphilus", for it's the name a totie wee Scots laddie gave himself for to feel bigger, and it's altogether too long to store in your memory, so that I would fear it would elbow out more important things.' He gave her a sly look.

'Microphilus? That's not so difficult,' she protested, then smiled at his triumphant grin.

'Which reminds me,' he added briskly. 'We must choose you a Mohammedan name *tout de suite*, for they are all here of that Faith, and consider Christians to be as animals, subjecting them to all the same torments and indignities –' He broke off: there was the sound of footsteps outside and he hurried to the door. 'Here are the slaves come to take off the chamber-pots. Quick, we must settle on a name for you.'

A dour brown parcel of a woman bustled into the room and knelt quickly in front of the Dwarf. He grinned broadly at her bowed head, gabbling a brief torrent of the local language before turning back to Helen. 'You're in luck!' he beamed. 'This old sourpuss is Reema. She's the tightest lip and the staunchest heart of any slave in the palace. And you'll be thankful for both afore long, for the Harem buzzes with mischief, which the slaves carry among their mistresses, like pollen from flower to flower.'

The woman shuffled around on her knees until she was facing Helen. She was bare-headed, with a woolly cap of grey curls, and a nose so crumpled from being broken as to be almost flat. 'Batoom must have sent her,' Microphilus explained. 'Reema was her slave, but it seems she's been gifted to you. Batoom's the woman I was telling you about, the one who's to be your Governess. What a blessed, sweet lady she is! This is kindness itself.'

Getting to her feet, the woman gave Helen a grudging nod and began gathering up the heap of wet clothing.

'I shall tell her your name is Aziza,' Microphilus decided. 'For there's no time to discuss the matter further.' And he spoke rapidly to the brown woman, who stared woodenly down at him until he'd finished. She then bent to pick up the chamber-pot and, cradling it in her arms, stood beside the open door, making it clear with every sinew in her solid, square body that it was time for him to leave.

From that moment, the dour slave took over: bringing hot water for Helen to wash with, and fresh clothes, then warm flat-bread and white cheese in a basket. Refreshed and in clean garments, Helen found she was ravenous. She knelt on the floor in the semi-darkness and began tearing great chunks off the loaf and dunking them greedily in a dish of delicious green oil.

While she ate, she looked around the room. It had two doors, she realized: the ordinary-sized one she'd been using was cut into a much bigger one which took up the whole of one wall. Now Reema unbolted the big door and slid it open against the outside wall.

Sunlight tipped in on to the tiled floor, making the oil sparkle and warming Helen's thighs through her fine muslin breeks. She could hear swallows chittering outside; a strange, flat-toed lizard darted in and began climbing the wall. Sitting back on her heels, Helen wiped her mouth on the back of her hand and sighed. At last: it really was over. She was safe, she was clean, she was fed. No one was going to punish her. And she didn't have to face the Emperor again for weeks. Anything might happen before then.

Outside her room, the courtyard was coming to life. Blue woodsmoke curled from the blackened doorways of the kitchens opposite, and two brown slave-girls began carrying great trays of food up the stone steps to a cloistered room above. Others plied stoically back and forth, naked to the waist, with huge red water jars on their heads. There must be a well somewhere near, Helen thought. No, lots of wells – she pieced together a mosaic of images in her mind – and lots of kitchens. The Harem was divided into separate courtyards, each with its own kitchen and slaves. Her own room was in a row of similar ones on three sides of the courtyard; outside was a shady cloister with narrow stairs up to first-floor verandas under sloping, green-tiled roofs.

She glanced round at Reema, who'd begun sweeping the floor. Her own slave! If only the folk back home in Muthill could see her now: in an Emperor's palace, with a bonny room and bonny clothes to wear. She'd have to ask Microphilus about the clothes; how many she was allowed; if she could choose them for herself. Perhaps Reema knew. Helen rummaged through her rag-bag of Moorish words for a few to patch into a question. But the slave seemed engrossed in her task, angling the dust together into a neat pile.

Then she did something very odd. Instead of whisking the dust out through the open doorway, she walked over to a floor-length white curtain and pulled it across the opening. In the familiar creamy twilight, Helen watched the stocky body crouch over the little heap. Sorting carefully through it, she picked out several of Helen's long hairs and wound them skilfully around her thumb and forefinger.

'*Afreet*,' she growled, lighting a candle and holding the little bundle of hairs over the flame. Helen nodded as the hairs hissed and shrivelled, filling the room with the stench of singed hoof. *Afreet*: she didn't need a translation. Among so many women, at least one must be a witch, collecting hair and bits of blood and fingernail for making spells.

Having disposed of the hairs, Reema went round the room placing a bit of cheese and a dribble of green oil in each corner. '*Ju'jinn*,' she explained, and Helen nodded again. In Muthill they'd have used oatmeal if they were moving to a new house – to make a friend of any ghost living there. And washed the floor with salt water to keep the devil away. As if reading her mind, the brown woman knelt by the tray Helen was eating from, picked up a handful of salt crystals and scattered them under the bed.

'*Shukran*,' Helen said quietly – 'Thank you' – and was rewarded by a grim smile.

Wiping her hands on her blouse, Reema went to pull the curtain open again. But Helen jumped up and stopped her: she could hear voices outside now, and she wasn't ready to face the other women. Not yet; not after the way they'd taunted her last night. Later, perhaps, when it was a bit quieter. If she put a kerchief over her hair, perhaps they wouldn't recognize her. Pulling the curtain open a crack, she peered out.

All the doors were open now and the courtyard was full of fat women of every shade of brown. Some stood in their doorways and bellowed for their slaves. Others were waddling from room to room with their breasts jiggling, trailing bright silk garments and scarves over their arms. Several had muddy-looking bandages around their bald heads or wrapped around their hands and feet. Did they have that swelling sickness too, or had they been beaten? And the bairns charging around everywhere, were they bald too, or had they been shaved like that? Some of the women were rubbing black ointment into their gums, snarling into brass hand-mirrors to see the effect. They seemed to blacken everything in this place – eyebrows, eyes, gums. Even the toddlers had their eyes done up like wee whores. And oil too – she saw a woman slathering it over her brown breasts – shining themselves like bits of furniture.

Helen searched for a face she recognized, and thought she spotted one or two younger lasses from the journey making their way up the stairs to the dining-room opposite, above the kitchens. Then another figure caught her eye, hobbling along like an old hag, bent over a stick with her black plait thudding against her knee.

'Naseem!' The figure straightened and looked around, then grinned broadly and shuffled painfully over to where Helen was beckoning through the curtain.

'*Keef halek* –'ow are you?' Once inside the room, Naseem scanned Helen's face with concern. 'I heard them chasing you,' she said in Moorish, putting her hand to her ear. 'But I couldn't help you –' gesturing helplessly at her bandaged feet. 'Stupid sows!' She waved a disgusted hand in the direction of the courtyard.

'Where's your room?' asked Helen in English, indicating her bed then pointing questioningly out through the curtain. By now she'd become adept at stitching English and Moorish words together with gestures and grimaces to make herself understood. It turned out that Naseem had been given a room in another courtyard, but she went to speak to one of Helen's neighbours and arranged to change rooms with her. 'She's happy – my room's bigger than hers.' Naseem drew a square in the air. 'She's moving straight away – you should see how much stuff she has!'

Helen peered out through the curtain again. A paunchy, buff-skinned woman was hurrying in and out of the next-door room, barking orders at a pallid monster of a man, with a massive belly and black patterns on his bald head. Yelling at him to 'Stand still!' and 'Hurry up!', she was dumping clothes in his arms and twining necklaces and scarves around his bull-neck. He fidgeted and pulled a face at her whenever she reappeared, sticking out his tongue and wrinkling his bulbous nose, then tossing his head and flouncing off down the cloister, with plumes of silk drifting back over his burly shoulders.

Two minutes later he was back for another load: two heaped baskets of embroidered slippers, three rolled-up mats and a bundle of striped silk cushions. So many bonny things! Helen clenched her fists with excitement, picturing her own plain white room crammed full of treasures. Where had she got them from? And who was that strange man? She thought only women were allowed in the Harem. If he was a slave, why was he being so rude to that woman? Perhaps he was really a kind of giant woman: his cheeks were so smooth, and weren't those titties quivering under his loose shirt? And he walked like a woman, with wee waddly footsteps and his great arse waggling.

She tugged on Naseem's arm and pointed through the curtain. 'Who's that?' she asked.

Naseem shook her head pityingly: 'A eunuch.' She grasped an imaginary scrotum and made a sawing gesture. 'He's been cut so he can't have children. The Harem's full of them. Look –'

Four more gigantic, smooth-faced men shuffled into the

courtyard and settled themselves down in the cloistered shade beside the kitchens. Clapping for tea, they took up the musical instruments they'd brought with them and began to play. The music was strange: a low rhythm plucked from a skinny kind of lute, and a high drone from a small set of bagpipes, plus the rattles of drum and tambourine. The instruments seemed so totie in the musicians' great paws: the lute like a wooden spoon, the bagpipes squealing like a tortured grey mouse.

The band was greeted with squeals of delight, and five or six women came hurrying out of their rooms waving long silk scarves. With lots of sniggering and eye-rolling, they began stripping off their blouses and loosening their breeks, tying the scarves around themselves – their foreheads, upper arms, hips – so the loose ends snaked down over their bodies. Helen gaped through the opening in her curtain. Were they going to dance like that, with their baldy dugs showing?

As she watched, they stretched their arms out sideways and began wriggling their shoulders and hips, making the loose tongues of bright silk lick over their skin. A part of Helen wanted to laugh: they looked so glubby, with all that soft flesh rolling, like offal fumbled off the butcher's block. Another part was shocked. Weren't they embarrassed? Every waggle of their fat shoulders, every jerk of their hips – as though they were doing it, in front of everyone.

One of the musicians picked some big red frilly flowers and pranced around pushing the stems down the backs of the dancers' breeks, between their buttocks. Screaming with laughter, they rounded on him and tore off his clothes, tying scarves around his enormous paunch and cheering when he began dancing too, jiggling his vast dimpled arse and twining the silk around his bobby stub of a penis.

Helen drew back from the curtain and turned to her friend. Naseem collapsed with laughter. 'Your face – you are so shocked! But you know this is a place of sex,' using the word Helen recognized only too well. 'It's all they think of here: the clothes, the paint, the dancing – it's all for sex, to make them good for sex, and good for carrying babies.'

'And those men?'

'Oh, their things are no use –' Naseem waggled a limp wrist. 'But they have tongues, don't they? And hands,' she mimed lewdly, then burst into laughter again at the look on Helen's face. 'And it's not only eunuchs who have hands, you know,' she grinned, trailing her fingers along Helen's bare arm.

Helen smiled uncertainly and turned back to the curtain. Outside the music had quickened and some of the women had formed pairs and were dancing face to face, matching their movements to one another, so close that their bellies were almost touching. The others were egging them on, clapping and cheering.

Then, without warning, the music faltered and stopped as, one by one, the four eunuchs noticed a tall, peat-brown woman in a plain white gown sauntering towards them across the courtyard. The women fell to their knees, and the eunuchs dropped their instruments and rushed towards her, warbling in welcome and crouching to kiss her bare feet. Waving them away, the big brown woman stood in the centre of the courtyard, spinning slowly on her toes and scanning the open doors.

Her eyes came to rest on Helen's closed curtain. 'Aziza!' she called, using the name Microphilus had chosen for her. 'Are you in there?' she said in accented English, adding some comment in Moorish that made everyone laugh.

Helen turned to find Reema's battered face at her shoulder. 'It's Queen Batoom,' she said, and her voice was warm with affection. 'Shall I pull back the curtain?'

★

Five minutes later Helen was strolling with Queen Batoom through the Harem. The sun was high by now and glinted off Batoom's heavy earrings, the only jewellery she wore other than a set of keys on a leather thong around her neck. She was at least a head taller than Helen, and twice as broad, surging across the courtyards like a ship in full sail: huge and unhurried, leaving a wake of prostrate and kneeling women behind her.

Was this the same Batoom Microphilus had been talking about? The one who was going to teach her how to please the Emperor? Why hadn't he said she was a queen? Helen tried to imagine the Emperor doing it with her. Did he like great fat baldy women? Those scars, like cats' whiskers, on her cheeks – did he think they were beautiful? And how could he kiss lips as thick and swollen as those?

Batoom caught her staring and grinned broadly, showing square white teeth in bright pink gums. 'You've never seen such a big brown lady before, have you?' she said in Moorish. 'Big – lady –' she went on slowly in English, seeing Helen's confusion, then threw out her vast bosom and slapped her enormous round arse. 'Fijil said there are no brown people in your country –' using the word Helen now understood to mean 'home'. 'So – how do you like our pretty prison?' she asked, flourishing a surprisingly dainty hand at their surroundings.

Helen looked around: it was the first time she'd seen the Harem properly in daylight. It was like a city preparing for a festival. Everywhere she looked, women were dressing or undressing, painting their faces, combing one another's hair. Most of the doors were open, revealing rooms like shops, full of clocks, mirrors and candelabras; divans piled high with bright cushions and draped with embroidered cloths. The contents even spilt out into the cloisters, with women slumped sideways on patterned carpets in the shade, suckling weans, sipping tea or painting dark patterns on their hands and feet.

'Along here is where the queens live.' Batoom steered Helen down a broad avenue shaded by arches of the brightest purple flowers she'd ever seen. 'There are four queens,' she explained, as they arrived at a huge deserted courtyard. '*Wahed, tnayn, tlateh, arba'a –*' 'One, two, three, four,' pointing at four huge ornate filigree gates, one in each wall of the great cloistered space.

Helen stared around. It was so quiet after the hubbub of the main Harem: no bairns running around; no jabber, no groups of fat women. And so grand; nearly as grand as the Emperor's quarters, with a fountain spilling over blue tiles in the centre. The two women began strolling through the empty cloisters.

'*Meen hadritha?*' – 'Who's that?' – Helen asked as they approached the first pair of gates. Inside was a lovely private courtyard, shaded with white rose-bowers and strewn with gold-embroidered carpets. A sallow, bony woman with a glorious froth of chestnut hair was pacing feverishly up and down, gabbling and scratching at her spidery arms. A group of agitated slaves hovered around her, proffering clothes, plates of fruit, jugs of water. And around her, on every wall, were painted blue hands, each with an eye staring out from the palm: accusing, unblinking.

'That's Queen Zara,' said Batoom in a low voice. 'She used to be so beautiful,' caressing her own glossy cheek and shaking her head sadly.

As they watched, the woman sagged suddenly, as though all the life had drained out of her. One of the slaves darted forward to wrap a *haik* around her knobby shoulders. But its weight seemed to exhaust her and she sank to her knees, beckoning weakly for a hand-mirror.

'What on earth's wrong with her?' Helen gasped. Queen Zara's nose and mouth were a mass of blisters and her skin was covered with brown blotches.

Batoom shrugged her great shoulders. 'Who knows? *Afreet*, maybe. Or poison.' She pinched her fingers and thumb together and brought them to her mouth as though eating *couscous*.

Helen frowned, confused: had the food made her like that? Then her brow cleared. 'Oh, you mean poison,' she said in English. Then: *'Khubz atel?'* – 'Bad bread?' – and Batoom nodded. 'Someone out there –' she spat, gesturing angrily down the avenue to the main Harem. 'They all want to be a queen.'

Now Helen understood. Somewhere in the Harem was a secret hoard of Queen Zara's long chestnut hair, or a screw-paper of poison crystals to mix with her salt.

They walked on. 'This is where Queen Douvia lives.' Helen peered through the next gate. Whilst Zara's courtyard was all cool white and gold elegance, Douvia's was ablaze with colour. Enormous clay pots stood around in great clusters, crammed with flowering plants, arched over with gaudy festoons of blossom.

The sound of laughter drew her eyes. A lassie of about thirteen was sitting cross-legged in the shade, with a chubby wean lying in her lap. She was tickling him with a bunch of coloured feathers, making him chortle and flail with his fists. Behind her, and on every wall, hung delicate brass cages full of little birds that filled the air with twitters and trills. Around her, scattered across the courtyard, was a slew of treasures: dolls in bonny clothes; a tinkling music-box on its side; glittering necklaces and bracelets; bowls of half-eaten food. Four strange creatures – like fat lizards in shells – trundled slowly through the clutter.

The young lassie was gorgeous, with dancing dark eyes in a small heart-shaped face; a tiara of red rosebuds nestled in her mass of blue-black curls. Unlike Queen Zara, she was as plump and restless as the fluttery songbirds in the cages around her. Douvia, Douvia – where had Helen heard that name before? Of course: this must be the 'Young Queen' the Dwarf had told her about; the one who spoke Latin. Helen hadn't realized quite how young she was.

'Is that her baby?' Helen asked, pointing and using another word she knew well. Batoom nodded, sighing, and there was a look in her eyes Helen couldn't decipher: something between pity and anger. The baby made a grab for one of the Young Queen's round breasts and a slave hurried out and whisked him away into an inner room. A surprised frown darkened Douvia's face for a second, then she picked up one of the dolls and began taking off its clothes.

'Do you have any bairns?' Helen asked as they made their way towards the third gate.

Batoom smiled. 'Three sons,' she said proudly, measuring three different heights between her belly and her chin with the flat of her hand. 'But they don't live with me any more.' She gestured vaguely into the distance and shrugged sadly. 'They're with the men now.' What did she mean? Helen realized she hadn't seen any laddies in the Harem, none older than about six anyway.

They reached the third gate and Helen looked in. 'That's where Queen Salamatu used to live,' explained Batoom. Within the gates there was no sign of life: just a pulsing haze of bees around the sprawling bowers. Dry leaves and brown petals littered the tiled courtyard and piled up in rustling heaps against the closed doors. It had been bonny, Helen could see: gold tiles glittered from the scummy green fountain and a red silk awning hung limply from one of the trees.

'Was she poisoned too?' Helen repeated the word Batoom had used earlier, but the big woman shook her head. 'No, the Emperor sent her away last month. To Tafilalt. Away –'

another vague gesture into the distance. 'So – here we are at last!' Extracting a key from up between her vast brown breasts, Batoom unlocked the fourth set of gates.

Helen stared around in surprise. It was even barer than Queen Salamatu's quarters, but spotless: no flowers or ornaments; just white walls and blue-patterned tiles, and a simple rush mat unrolled beneath a single tree in the corner. And so peaceful: only one totie slave ironing clothes in the shade, jumping up every so often to exchànge the flat-iron she was using for another heating on the kitchen fire.

Batoom scooped a cupful of water from a jar and drank thirstily. 'I only have one slave now.' She nodded towards the little lass. 'I like to do my own work. It keeps me strong,' and she drew back her loose sleeves to reveal arms as brawny as a man's. 'Work: good,' she repeated in English. 'Now, let's have some tea – you can help me collect the leaves.'

She led Helen through an archway to a square of land surrounded by a high wall. 'Over there, by the water-spout.' They waded through a forest of shaggy red seed-heads towards a plot of mint on the far side. 'I love this garden,' Batoom said, brushing seeds from her gown. Helen thought of the kailyard at home; the rich purple earth between her toes. Crouching beside the big dark woman, she buried her hands in the cool mint leaves.

'Fijil wanted me to meet you,' Batoom said, plucking the topmost shoots and gathering them into her blouse. 'Fijil: good,' she added simply. Helen looked up, surprised by the affection in the brown woman's voice. What had the ugly gnome done to make her so fond of him? They made their way back to the courtyard, where Batoom packed the leaves into a copper pot and began chipping lumps off a mound of loaf sugar.

'*Lazimni*,' Helen began – 'I need' – '*mu'allmeh*' – 'a teacher'.

She blushed and looked down. 'To help me with the Emperor.'

'Ah yes, the Emperor.' Batoom's slanting black eyes sparkled with amusement for a moment. 'The Emperor is a very hot man, very hot.' Helen frowned, not understanding, so the brown woman stood up and started thrusting her hips rapidly back and forth with a fixed expression on her face. She paused a moment, then started again, back and forth with gritted teeth, then paused again – then erupted into a gust of laughter.

'Oh dear!' she gasped, wiping the tears from her eyes. 'I shouldn't laugh. It's sad really. You see, the Emperor must do sex. He needs to.' She was serious suddenly, crumbling shards of sugar thoughtfully over the mint leaves. 'It calms him.' She made a soothing motion with her hand. 'Sometimes he needs to have two, three women in one night,' counting them out on her fingers, 'not speaking to any of them; just fucking, fucking, until he's exhausted.'

Helen watched the brown woman pour boiling water into the pot. She'd only understood a few words, but the gestures were clear. The Emperor didn't just do it and fall asleep like other men. He had to do it over and over, like a madman, like that bull in Muthill, who mated a whole herd in one afternoon. She thought of the glossy hair on the Emperor's toes; his raw purple thing butting at her chin. How many hours would it last? She felt her throat tighten with horror. 'I can't –' she burst out.

'Aziza, listen to me.' Batoom grabbed Helen by her two shoulders and shook her roughly, glaring angrily into her eyes. 'If you refuse the Emperor again, he will have you killed.' She let go and made a decisive scything gesture in the air. 'Killed. Dead. Do you understand?' Helen nodded dumbly. 'Next time is your only chance. You must make it good for him, really good.' Helen swallowed hard and nodded again.

'So, let us begin.'

20

14 July 1769

Today the heat has been like a hammer and we all nails, with our poor heads tilted sideways and our eyes asquint from its careless blows. We have been testy, all of us; spitting like cats. Even the cringing slave-lassies were shrewish, slopping samovars and banging down trays.

It is on such days that I long for my Homeland: for the crunch of hoar frost under my boots. Ay, even for the boots themselves, for I've not heard the clack of stout hobnails for four years, nor felt the kick of a braw toe-cap against a tussock. It is all slippers here, you see, night and day: shuffling along down at heel, as if there were no tomorrow; as if each destination were of like importance (by which I mean of no importance) and each appointment equally pressing (by which I mean not pressing in the least). It is impossible to move quickly in the things. To attempt anything faster than a brisk waddle is to risk tripping over the absurd tip-tilted toes, and cause all your garments to billow out like sails and catch on rose bushes and slap the wee faces of unwary weans.

Oh for a trudge along the front at St Andrews! With the salt wind nipping at my ears, and my neb running, and my eyes fair stinging with the cold of it! And Helen at home with treacle scones on the griddle and a dish of black tea a-stewing on the hearth.

These days all my reveries have the quality of a prayer about them. Dear Lord, let her be with me in Scotland, in a calico apron with a smudge of flour on her chin. Dear Lord, let her love me; spirit us out of this oppressive oven, where the only tea is greenish and the only wind hot and dry, searing straight from the desert in the east. And the only rain we'll see for three moons will be a rustling precipitation of locust husks.

She calls me 'Microphilus': how it thrills me to see her scowl of concentration as she sorts out the syllables! I fear I may have shocked her the other day with my talk of the Emperor's proclivities. I had assumed even a young country wench would have been more *au fait* with the ways of men. But it seems she is but lately a virgin, which leaves me yet more enamoured. There is something about her blushing *naïveté*, in combination with her braw peasant's bearing – like a princess in a fisherman's hovel, a Cinderella with scuffed ashy toes.

What a fool I am – as if she'd love me! And yet – when the Emperor tires of her, as he must do, who else is there to love in this place? I have more hope here than was ever possible in Scotland. Here, there is only me. And here I shall be, whenever she looks up. By and by, like a duckling new-hatched from the egg, she must follow me for there is none other.

Why does this please me? Why should a last-ditch left-over love please me more than Batoom's unstinting regard? For the Black Queen loves me, that is without doubt. Last night, while we were canoodling, she stopped my mouth as it was pleasuring her pouch, and raised me up the couch on to her breast like a smeary suckling, cradling me tenderly against her dark pillows. 'Poor Fijil,' she sighed softly. 'Why can't you be happy with this?'

Why indeed? Yet I am like a man possessed since I saw Helen . . .

*

I have just spent nigh on three hours with Lungile. I was poised, quill aloft, to pen yet more paeans to my duckling, when I hear the squelch of giant feet in wet slippers and see him lowering his great head to pass beneath the doorjamb into my chamber.

'May the flea gods be praised, you are here!' declares he, and concertinas his long body down beside me on the carpet. 'Where is your water?' reaching out with a long arm to the jar and gulping ladle after ladle. 'I'm like a sponge today,' he complains, 'dripping from every pore. Is it still hot? I can't tell any longer whether it's this damned fever or the weather making me leak like this.' And wipes a wringing sleeve across his forehead, enveloping me in a nidorous fug.

His pantaloons are sagging with moisture and he rolls them up like pancakes around his knees. 'I would go mad if I couldn't come here,' says he, leaning back against the divan. 'The other – er – men –' (How he stumbles over that word!) – 'Brother Flea, are they never silent? Do they stop their stupid chatter for a moment? Or their maidenish prancing? Perhaps in death –' And here he clenches his long fingers in the air, as around a eunuch's pulpy throat.

We have sat thus frequently of late, side by side in my quarters, continuing that intimacy begun on our journey. And have adopted the habit of sharing a *hookah* of an evening, a peculiar but convivial Moorish custom involving an elaborate pipe connected to a large urn of cool water. As with many pleasant pastimes in this land, only the men are permitted to partake and can be observed around the city, clustered in silent shoals in the outdoor hostelries, pursing their lips and puffing meditatively like dumb, flat-eyed fish.

This capacity for quiet is a crucial difference between the sexes. For I have observed that women fill up all the spaces between them with blether, as if prattle was millet which must be cast on the ground if the flock of friendship is to flourish. We men are quite different and silence is what we use to feed our fellowship, be it the silence of hard labour, or walking, or that concentrated quiet that accompanies a game of back-gammon or chess. But best of all is the silence of a shared plug of tobacco at the end of the day.

As far as I can discover, it is the same the world over, with the wifies garrulous indoors with the weans, and the men outside smoking dumbly in the darkness. In Nuba, so Lungile tells me, the lee of each house is actually forbidden to the women. And the prohibition is elevated to an obsession here in Barbary, such that women may not venture at all beyond their four walls to intrude their cacophony on the men's precious peace.

It follows that our eunuchs' verbal incontinence may stem directly from their unmanning. I suggest as much to Lungile, once we have lit the *hookah* and sucked companionably upon the mouthpiece for a while. And he nods lugubriously. 'But it's their vanity that's the worst,' he grumbles. 'The way they pluck their eyebrows and pout into mirrors. My nightmare is that I will come to resemble them myself. Once my manhood has finally leached out of me –' and he picks disconsolately at his sodden *jellabiah*, a very vision of dank despair.

I try to comfort him by explaining that our preening 'aunties', or *khalehs*, were de-uncled as mere adolescents, then presented straightway to His Majesty. Thus they have long forgotten the company of real men and women's ways are all that they know. But he is gloomy still. 'Do you know what they call me?' he asks, and a drip trembles at the end of his chin. 'Granny! Because of this old-woman's ague. As if I had never lain with my wives, or sired any of my beautiful sons. If they had known me then –' His jaw stiffens and the drip tumbles down his chest. 'I was a warrior, Fijil, with a thousand cattle and a Chief's head-dress to inherit.'

This is a recurrent theme with him: his noble status in his homeland compared to the ignominy of his current situation. 'At least when I was in the Black Guard I could imagine escape,' laments he, taking a deep toke on the pipe. 'But that's impossible now. Where would I go? I can't face my sons, my father, like this – with this wet woman's body. You know, Fijil, there are some days I think I would rather die than spend another minute in the company of those fat capons.' His chin is fair quivering now, and his voice hoarse with passion as he squeezes his eyes shut to stop the tears. But they seep out anyway and join the runnels of moisture already cascading down his face.

I pat him foolishly, trying to provide comfort, and look away while he slurps his sleeve across his face once again. Then we are silent for a while, me sucking, he blowing his wide nose, bubbles gurgling soothingly in the *hookah*. And I am just considering confessing my passion for Helen when he stutters out a confession of his own, whereupon I am left wondering whether there was some strange contagion in that desert air, that we should both have become so powerfully inflamed.

For it seems our great Gog has become enamoured of the Berber besom whose feet he heated so reluctantly last month. This passion has him in an utter turmoil, as you can imagine. For he has no notion of how to proceed, or whether – or even what with. So, though his rapier springs sharply from his scabbard whenever he thinks of her, he fears it may wilt when it is raised in true combat. And what a dull sort of duel would it be if no piercing could take place?

The dilemma has him clutching his big head. 'It would be better not to try,' he says glumly. 'But in my dreams, Fijil –' and now his eyes are glowing again. 'In my dreams I am as I was before. And my milk, thick as it has ever been.' Then he's scowling again and gritting his teeth. 'But it's worthless stuff, woman's stuff, without –'

For of course there is the vexed question of impregnation, which is crucial in the African mind. 'I am empty now, Fijil. A sham. That's how it feels. When it stood up before I used to feel proud, knowing what it was for: to go inside her and make children. I was a bull buffalo, an elephant, a storm-cloud at the end of a drought. But now,' sneering disgustedly downwards, 'it's an empty termite hill, a dead branch.' (Notice how his sense of proportion has remained intact despite his trauma.)

'Have you approached her?' I venture, and a hurricane sigh billows out my curtain like a sail.

'How can I? When I've no idea what I can offer – even if she'd accept me, which she shows no sign of doing. Especially after that night. But she looked at me with such fierce eyes afterwards! I tell you, Fijil, that look is burned on my heart.'

Then all of a sudden his demeanour alters. 'He's loving it, isn't he?' he hisses savagely. 'Have you noticed him in the garden? Sauntering among the women, then looking around and nodding in my direction. I swear that gives him more pleasure than all the women put together: to glance across at me like that, the strongest man in the *Bokhary*, his slave, his creature – no, worse: his women's slave.'

And I can see immediately where this is going, for is not Lust all caught up with Aggression in a man, such that the one excites the other? Why else do armies feel compelled to ravage their foes' females: even though they love their wives, even though they are exhausted and disgusted with war, even though they are gagging on the smell of spilled entrails? So Lungile is like a veritable pendulum on a fulcrum of frustration: swinging now to hatred of the Emperor, now to lust for the Emperor's wench, and back again, hate to lust, hate to lust, flexing his great hands and trembling with the passion of it.

'I will kill him, Fijil, I swear it. One day when he has forgotten all about me, and I am just Lungile the Harem auntie. When he is least expecting it. He must be punished for this thing he has done to me.'

21

'*Bi'tizer t'akhart* –' 'Sorry I'm so late.' Reema lowered the jug of steaming water from her woolly head and poured it into the basin on the floor of Helen's room. 'They're all wanting water this morning – the slaves are fighting at the wells. I had to go to Queen Batoom's quarters to get this.'

'*Shu sar?*' – 'What's happening?' – 'Why is everyone up so early?' Helen asked, pointing through the closed curtain. She felt she'd been awake all night; women had been rushing up and down with lighted candles, knocking on closed doors, arguing, screeching orders to their slaves.

'They're getting ready.' Reema sniffed and curled her lip. 'Today is *al khamis*' – 'Thursday' – 'when the Emperor comes to choose his women. Every week they are like this.' She jerked her head towards the noise in the courtyard outside. 'But not you, *Lalla*. Queen Batoom says you are to stay here.' Though she only recognized a few individual words consciously, Helen found she was gradually coming to understand the gist of what people were saying: this was the special day when the Emperor visited the Harem; but Helen was to stay hidden.

She washed quickly and pulled on her clothes: soft loose breeks and a long white blouse. '*Sa'dini!*' – 'Help me!' – wailed someone outside. Helen threw open the curtain. A lass of about sixteen was standing naked in the middle of the court-yard, sobbing and tugging at her hair. She'd been braiding it into tiny plaits, but something had gone wrong and strands of green silk were hopelessly tangled in her wet black curls. But no one was even looking at her. Right beside her two older women were snarling over a turquoise scarf. Another nude woman – bald as a plum – skeltered past with a basket under her arm, chased by a whale of a lass in ballooning blue breeks.

There was a waistcoat on the cloister floor outside her room. Helen picked it up and looked around for the owner. It was pink, embroidered with gold thread, with a lining of yellow silk: heavy, cool, slithery. She wanted to feel it against her skin. If it was hers – if she could get some yellow breeks, too, and a gold sash – where did all their bonny things come from? And the jewellery: they all had earrings; and necklaces, sometimes two or three at once; and bracelets, even round their ankles. Where did they get it all?

'What a mess!' Naseem snorted, stepping over a red blouse and a length of purple ribbon.

'Aren't you getting ready?' Helen dipped a finger into an imaginary rouge pot and put it to her cheek.

Naseem struck a mocking pose. 'And puff my chest like a pigeon and go dog-eyed for him? No. I'm going to hide in my room till it's all over.'

'What about Malia?'

'I'll say I'm dirty this week,' she said airily. 'You know –' She pointed at her crotch and mimed wringing out her rags. Helen looked doubtful. The old hag had known exactly when she had been bleeding. She doubted Naseem would be able to deceive her. Sure enough, when the others had waddled out into the garden a few hours later, a scowling Malia appeared to fetch Naseem.

Helen followed them at a distance, itchy with curiosity. She wanted to see what the other women were wearing: the jewelled armbands and nose-rings; the patterns some had painted on their hands and cheeks; the ways they draped their scarves and plaited their hair. And the Emperor – the word made her tingle. She wanted to see the Emperor again.

The women had gathered in some sort of tent, a huge white awning stretched between the trees. Malia was arranging them in rows, but they wouldn't stay where she put them. Helen hadn't realized there were so many – four, maybe even five hundred women: every shape, every shade of brown, from cheap whisky to murkiest peat-water, jostling and squealing, and a rainbow of silk scarves billowing. Naseem was in the front row, one hip cocked with impatience.

Set apart, to one side, were four smaller awnings, each one bright green and weighed down with gold tassels: the Queens' Tents. Batoom was kneeling beneath one, arranging gold cups on a low table. Beneath another, dressed in vivid pink, sat the Young Queen Douvia. She was pouting into a jewelled hand-mirror and rouging her plump wee lips; behind her sat a withered slave, fanning the sleeping baby in her lap. The two remaining green awnings were empty: holy niches without statues.

The women were nudging and pointing at the empty awnings, obviously all of a blether about the missing queens. Was Queen Zara going to die soon? The excitement was like spice in the air. When would the Emperor replace the retired fourth queen, Salamatu? Who would he choose? Maybe someone he selected today. Helen surveyed the restless rows of fat women.

A volley of gunfire and a sudden fanfare of trumpets brought silence to the garden. Then there he was: all in white, strolling down the sunny path with an apple in his hand. Helen crouched behind a bush just in time. She'd expected some kind of parade, but there was only Microphilus trotting along behind him with the great brown giant, Lungile, at his side.

The Emperor approached the queens' awnings first, greeting Batoom, and then Douvia, who jumped to her feet and curtseyed neatly, like a Perth lady. Taking his hand (how did she dare?), the little queen tugged him over to where her baby was sleeping. The slave proffered the baby and the Emperor stroked its cheek with the back of his hand. He's the father of that child, Helen thought. And of every other child in the Harem. One day – maybe this very day last year – he'd done it with Douvia and now she had a baby. She watched the hand caressing the baby's chin, remembered the black thatch of hair on his wrist; his bony toes and dog's tongue; his horse's legs. Had he trapped little Douvia between those legs too? How had she borne it?

But she seemed none the worse. Even from this distance, it was obvious she adored her tall husband, touching his sleeve, making him bend so she could whisper in his ear; making him laugh.

Easing her aching ankles, Helen shifted cautiously until she was kneeling in the stony dust of the garden. He'd left the queens now and was walking towards the other women. They bowed low, in a coloured wave, as he passed. Which would he choose? If only she could see his face. Malia was touching each of the lasses at the front, gabbling up at him like a stall-monger showing off her wares. But where was Naseem?

Helen scanned the first row, and the ranks behind, finally spotting her right at the back. She was the only one not looking at the Emperor. Helen chuckled to herself, following Naseem's eyes until they rested on the giant Lungile. He was looking back at her, his great chest rising and falling with some fierce emotion, his brow creased and shining with sweat. Was he still angry with her for trying to escape? His huge hands were twisting the material of his *jellabiah*. Then his gaze shifted to where the Emperor was talking to one of the women. Helen saw the giant's eyes narrow and his jaw tighten.

The Dwarf was pulling at his sleeve to get his attention, but the giant shrugged him off. Then the little gnome reached up and gently unbent the clenched fingers, one by one, from the white material. Helen watched the great brown face uncrease and the shoulders slump in a sigh as he bent over towards the Dwarf. What on earth was he so upset about?

But there was no time to wonder about that. The Emperor was taking one of the new lasses by the hand and making her turn round in front of him. Her arse was enormous, jutting like a bustle under her breeks. Helen could see the bay cheeks gleaming like a mare's rump through the thin muslin. He was caressing them, chuckling with admiration, and she raised her hands and began that shameless wiggly dance they did here, grinning over her shoulder at him with her wide mouth.

Dear God, so that was what he liked. And that tall damson-coloured one, with dugs as heavy as udders and a ring through her flared nostrils. He chose a paler lass next, short and sand-coloured with a fringe of short black plaits across her forehead. They all had big mouths, big white teeth, flat noses. And they were all fat: not just chubby like the two Robertson lasses in Muthill, but the kind of fat you never saw on a young lass in Scotland. Fat like Old Mother Crabtree at the manse: lumbering fat; jiggling fat. And brazen, showing off their bodies like that.

What had Batoom said? One after another until he's exhausted. She tried to imagine him with them, his gritted teeth and wild eyes. Tried to combine this image with the relaxed man in the garden; courteous, smiling, folding back his loose white sleeves. He was saying something and they were all laughing, all swaying and flirting their scarves around their faces; the ones at the back on tiptoe trying to see.

A moment later it was all over and he was walking back the way he had come, taking out the apple and biting into it. Helen held her breath as he passed. She could see him chewing, imagined the white flesh in his mouth; his wet saliva; the brown throat opening and closing; the black tufts poking over the top of his white gown.

He threw the apple away, half-eaten, and it rolled over towards where she was hiding. It rocked a little then lay still with dust stuck to its white flesh. A moment later there was a scuffle as four women raced over and tried to pick it up.

22

16 July 1769

Batoom has begun encouraging Helen to dance, teaching her those lewd undulations which the natives here substitute for *la gavotte*. It is part of some scheme she has conceived for banishing the lassie's coyness. 'The movements concentrate the blood in the loins,' she explains, which excites what she calls the 'macaque-mind'. This is an organ located near the base of the spine, which her people have named after a meretricious variety of monkey which scampers like a spider over the refuse heaps of their villages.

It is equivalent, she insists, to a second brain, which, when activated, has the effect of overriding the sensations of Shame and Vanity, which are the province of our Higher Minds and which impede the free flow of sexual pleasure. She demonstrated with me, gently scratching my sacrum, and I must confess that it engendered a most delicious sense of languor, along with a vague unravelling of the thought processes that I associate with my experiments with opium in Edinburgh.

So now I am in a fever to see whether a similar unravelling can be contrived from the lassie's first unsure gyrations. But I must wait until the morrow, for I have resolved to limit myself to just one visit each second day, hoping by this means to excite in her some kind of Expectation (if not actual Desire) to see me. Cruel experience has taught me that nothing wearies a woman so much as a surfeit of Attention. Such that the most unprepossessing of *beaux* can become well-nigh irresistible if a lass suspects he is indifferent to her charms: in much the same way as a common glove braiding can (by dint of the draper's judicious hoarding) gain such value that women will actually injure one another in their frenzy to purchase the last yard. Thus, by making myself scarce, I hope to revaluate myself in Helen's eyes (albeit that I am already about as scarce as a grown man can get, being literally the last yard of Microphilus, to the very inch).

The irony is that this ruse has had a greater effect on the Emperor (whom I did not wish to see) than on Helen (whom I did). For I have been avoiding him too, for fear he might order me to dispose of the lass. But this morning he sent word that he would avail himself of my scarceness and that I should attend him in the Treasury.

Abd el Kader, the *Alim*, was fidgeting in the anteroom when I arrived, tutting over some new consignment of clocks, totting up their value on his twiggy fingers and noting down their inscriptions in a leather-bound book. I do not know what he does with this information, but it both enrages and satisfies him in some profound way to record each new addition to the Emperor's cornucopian wealth.

The building is chock-a-block with valuables donated by importunate subjects. Three store-rooms, to my certain knowledge, are crammed with *accoutrements* for the appreciation of tea. Another six are home to a vast hotchpotch of equestrian equipment: to wit, saddles, buttoned and upholstered like divans; gem-studded bridles and spurs; saddle-cloths stitched as reverently as any chasuble (for your Moor holds his horse in far greater esteem than any wife).

The *Alim* stiffens like a gun-dog when he spies me, and his nostrils twitch with suspicion (for he has developed a loathing for me that is directly proportional to his Master's partiality to my company). I had a length of white *dulbend* cloth with me, and I unfolded it in front of him, begging him to teach me the art of winding it around my head into that grand *cochlea* the senior men wear. I was in mind to display my new emerald in a fashion which would amuse the Emperor, getting myself up like a whelk with an outsized *dulbend* and trailing *jellabiah*.

The *Alim* applied himself to the task with evangelical zest, holding forth ardently on the religious significance of each coil, and tucking the final end in place with a care verging almost on tenderness. For a moment I was in two minds about flaunting my priceless bauble, but the urge to twit his Piety was too great. So I toss it casually from hand to hand, as if to see it catch the light, and his eyes water with envy, and his twig-fingers quiver with the effort of not snatching it to his bosom.

'One-tenth, remember,' hisses he through his mean straggle of a beard, referring to the Mohammedan law which requires a tithe of all wealth to be surrendered to the Church for the relief of the poor. 'Certainly,' say I, 'but you must apply directly to the Emperor, for I am his slave and all that I own belongs ultimately to him.'

Just then His Majesty sweeps in with a flush of frustration on his cheeks. 'Fijil, speak to me!' cries he, stepping over the *Alim* who has prostrated himself like a heap of white washing. 'I am weary of advisors who refuse to advise, who stare at me with their jaws agape, and fiddle with their prayer-beads.' And goes on to detail his vexations with his new palace at Mogador: how there is no more money to pay the artisans, who are threatening to go home; how he can't simply behead them, for who then would come forward to replace them?; how even the slaves are unable to work, because the local peasants claim they have no food left to feed them. (I should explain here that the Emperor's slaves, like his army, are considered the nation's Guests, such that any Royal Excursion cuts a swathe through the countryside like a swarm of locusts, so much so that the leader of any real swarm of locusts is referred to by local people as 'the Sultan'.)

'And why is there no money?' he demands, flinging his *k'sa* tetchily back over his shoulder. 'Tell me, what is the use of establishing a Revenue if the collectors use my taxes to buy husbands for their daughters? I might as well go back to pillage and extortion like my father.' And sighs resoundingly, for he had cherished high hopes for his new Revenue, thinking that it would satisfy two needs at once; the first being his Avarice, which I have already mentioned; the second his quest for Refinement, which he fears may entail the perusal of Literature, and which certainly precludes the fund-raising habits of his bloody predecessor. Apart from frank thuggery, chief among these was arresting a wealthy *sheikh* on some pretext, then incarcerating him until his relatives have been prevailed on to pay his 'fine'.

The choice of victim was crucial, *naturellement*, since there must be many heirs who would rejoice at having an inconvenient patriarch conveniently removed. Indeed, the Emperor's dungeons are as full of these unransomed progenitors as his Treasury is of salt cellars and bedspreads. Yet where the selection is wisely made, the addition to the Royal Coffers is considerable (and in a far more serviceable currency than his daily deluge of clocks and counterpanes).

'Shall I roof the Palace with tea trays?' laments the Emperor, burying his hand in a crate of silver spoons. 'Pay the plumbers in embroidered umbrellas? When my father died they burnt sixty thousand silk cushions. Some were so decayed they disintegrated as they were carried to the pyre. Yet within five years the store-rooms were full again. Look at this: more clocks!' Sighing again, he caresses one with his fingers. 'Tell me, Fijil, is it like this in Scotland? Is your king burdened with beautiful rubbish?'

He is forever appealing to me in this vein, as though Scotland were some lofty citadel of Civilization and I its most erudite Exponent. So I describe our own Revenue as best I can, and proceed to outline our system of lending banks which hire out money by the day. 'Thus our king may profit from his hen,' I explain, 'plus all its eggs. Whereas you are only permitted to keep the hen.'

'A very civilized arrangement,' he comments wistfully. 'If I could lend out my taxes at a profit, like the Jews do –' Whereupon the *Alim* coughs reproachfully, for Mohammedan Law is most uncompromising on the question of Usury. 'Or employ Jews to operate a Royal Bank on my behalf –' Hope sparks in his eyes momentarily, then dies as the *Alim* clears his throat.

At this point three thousand clocks begin chiming the hour, and we are forced to clap our hands over our ears and retreat to the courtyard. By the time the noise has abated the Emperor has a new glint of determination in his eye. 'I shall levy a tax on the corsairs operating out of Sallee,' he announces triumphantly. 'I cannot understand why I have not done so before. For do they not reap a harvest like the peasants? There is altogether too much wealth in that region. Too many *kasbahs* and private armies. They make me uneasy. What do you think, Fijil? Fifty or sixty per cent? Of course it will make their ships far less profitable, and some will be forced off the water.'

I venture that this applies likewise to our true peasants; that his precious taxes have already resulted in less land being tilled. But he is in no mood for demurs, being ignited with a fierce surge of energy, envisioning how this tax on piracy would build him both a new palace and a new reputation in Europe: 'For it is demeaning to a modern monarch to be referred to as the Thief of Marrakech.

'It means a new Governor at Sallee, of course. Someone who is not in the pocket of the corsairs –' and so on, pacing restlessly among rows of unused carriages, planning how he will dislodge each perfidious Governor from his *baksheesh*-lined niche. 'I need my own people in place,' he declares to the air, 'to administer my taxes in a civilized fashion.'

Thus determined, he makes to depart, then checks himself and calls me to accompany him. 'I was forgetting the main purpose of our meeting,' says he, smiling (for all this scheming has quite transformed his temper). 'Tell me, Fijil, what ails the Queen Zara? She has not lain with me these last two months and her women claim she is too sick even to see me. They have called all our best *tabibs* to no avail and people are beginning to say that she has been cursed.'

I am so relieved that he is not quizzing me about Helen that I am speechless for a moment. 'Find out, Fijil,' he commands impatiently. 'And put an end to it. Let no one think they can harm the Emperor's wife with impunity.'

And goes on to remark (since I seem incapable of a coherent reply) that he has been informed that Queen Batoom has been teaching the new red-haired girl some manners. 'Let me know when the *bint* is presentable,' says he, 'and I shall gift her to my new Governor in Sallee.'

23

Helen closed her eyes and swayed to the music. She pretended she was standing in a warm sea, with an undertow sucking at her legs. The sash of her breeks was the water's surface, loosely looped around her hips. Waves lapped at her belly, making her body ripple like thick seaweed. She tried to forget the two women with her: Batoom, sitting cross-legged, rubbing scented oil on to her arms; and her skinny little slave-lass pattering on the drum with yellow palms, singing in a high nasal voice: the same melody over and over.

It was late morning and the heat boomed up from Batoom's bare courtyard. Even in the shade the air was gluey and warm. After three weeks of force-feeding, Helen's body felt swollen and heavy. Her breasts hung lower, lolling clammily as she moved, and sweat seeped from the new creases beneath her buttocks. It was easier to dance with her eyes shut: she didn't have to look at herself, at her joggling dugs and pink teats, uncovered for anyone to see. The women here didn't seem to care who watched them. Yesterday she saw one with a tame snake in her room: playing it out through her hands like a green rope, making it writhe under her arms, in her clothes, between her legs; her mouth slack with pleasure as it slithered through the crevices of her body. Helen wondered what that felt like: the head probing, the tongue flicking like eyelashes.

'*Formidable!*' Her eyes shot open as Microphilus's voice broke into her thoughts. 'You're moving like *une exotique vraie.*' How long had he been there? She snatched up a scarf to cover her breasts. 'My sweet Batoom has tutored you well,' he declared, skipping over to the great brown woman and pressing her hand to his lips. Batoom tugged affectionately on his little plait, pulling his head towards her so that she could whisper in his ear. Whatever she said made him burst out laughing, and he took her glossy face in his bairn's paws and planted a loud kiss on her forehead.

Perching himself on one of her cushiony thighs, he turned and grinned at Helen. 'Has she taught you yet about the fifteen kinds of kisses? No? Ay well, maybe your mouth's a mite too wee for such sophistries. The lassies hereabouts are mostly blessed with gobblers of greater girth.' He touched Batoom's lower lip with an admiring forefinger.

Helen stared at him in confusion. It was the first time she'd seen him with Batoom. Were they sweethearts? No, that was impossible: all the Harem men had been gelded. And his thing was like a laddie's anyway; Naseem had said so. That's why they called him Fijil. She had a brief image of his genitals: tiny, red and hairy, dangling inside his baggy breeks.

'The Emperor seems to have forgotten your encounter last week,' he remarked, smoothing a hand casually along Batoom's gleaming forearm. 'I saw him yestermorn and all he could talk about was how to squeeze more money from his straitened subjects. If 'twere possible to extract the stuff by compression, he'd set up a giant mangle tomorrow in the Palace forecourt.' He translated for Batoom, and they started gabbling in Moorish, heads together, like a mother with a toddler in her lap.

Helen pulled on her blouse and retied her sash around her waist. She'd never thought of her mouth as being especially small. But now he mentioned it, she supposed it was, compared with the others here. She looked at Batoom's thick lips, ridged and jutting as a bracket fungus. Nearly all the dark-skinned women had big mouths. And most of the paler lasses too: wide red lips and big, even teeth. And huge breasts, most of them, with proddy purple nipples. Not like her feeble wee rosy buds.

The slave went off to prepare tea and Helen wandered over to the water jar. She saw Batoom look up briefly, her glossy forehead wrinkled in a worried frown. What were they talking about now? If only she understood more of this stupid language. She picked up a brass ladle and lowered it into the water, stirring it slowly and inhaling the cool, mossy smell. She felt forlorn, embarrassed, like when her father and stepmother were together. Did they want to be alone? She hadn't realized they were so close.

More laughter made her look up. Microphilus was cradling Batoom's plump hand on his knee now, smoothing oil very gently into the crook of her arm. Helen stared at the big queen's billows of flesh; the long cats'-whisker scars on her plump cheeks; the nostrils wide as black caves. How had a creature like this become a queen? Then she thought of the seven women the Emperor had selected the other day: all fat as suckling pigs; all pug-nosed and big-mouthed as frogs. He must like his women like that.

So why had he chosen her first – out of all the new lassies? Out of curiosity, most likely. To see what she'd look like with her clothes off. Perhaps he'd never done it with a Scots lass before. But he'd sent her away without even looking. Maybe she disgusted him as much as he disgusted her. Her breath caught in her chest. At home, folk thought she was bonny. But here everything was different. Here the women blackened their gums and shaved their heads. They cut their cheeks and painted their faces like puppets. Here they were so fat they couldn't walk without panting. She'd never thought the Emperor might have found her disgusting. Was that why he'd sent her away?

'Despatched', wasn't that the word the Dwarf used? Off to the ports, to all those bearded men far away from their wives. Helen dropped the ladle back into the water, clattering it against the side of the jar. If these lumbering brown lassies were beautiful, the Emperor would be bound to think her ugly.

Microphilus seemed to be talking about the sick queen now: Helen recognized the name Zara. 'I saw her last week,' she said in a small voice, remembering the poor woman's whimper of pain as she stared at her reflection. 'All blotchy and knobbly, so she was, and half-crazy with scratching. What kind of sickness could cause such distress?'

Microphilus sighed. 'I can't tell, lassie. There are that many distempers in this torrid land, with its swampy crannies and fetid airs, never mind verminous insects,' he swatted at a red wasp diving at the oil jar, 'as bad as any plague in Pharaoh's Egypt. The *tabibs* have been summoned, of course, and have peeped and prodded at her as best they can through the wee apertures they're allowed. And they've prescribed various unguents and infusions. But her condition worsens by the day, so I'm told, and the Emperor's growing concerned. She's his favourite wife, you see.'

Batoom flared her great nostrils and loosed a torrent of angry Moorish. 'She says it's dangerous to be favoured in this place,' the Dwarf explained. 'There's ay somebody wishes you ill. She thinks the poor queen has been poisoned. But I'm not so sure. 'Twould have to be a crafty hand to circumvent her taster.'

'What d'ye mean?' Helen sat down shyly beside them.

'Poisoning's so common in this land that you can buy especially schooled slaves to sample your food afore it reaches your lips.'

Batoom nudged him off her lap and stood up with a grunt.

He flicked at her ankles with the hem of his cloak. 'Our Black Queen doesn't hold with tasters.' There was no doubting the admiration in his voice. 'She'd sooner cook her own vittals than have some poor wee lassie made sick for her sake.'

The big brown woman padded off towards the kitchen, rump swaying like a cow's udders. He watched her go, yawning and stretching out his stumpy legs on the grass mat. 'Anyway, if it is poison, why not finish off the job properly? Zara's been ailing nigh on half a year.'

'What if it's something else?' Helen asked, realizing suddenly that he could see her breasts and belly through the flimsy muslin of her blouse.

'Ah. You mean, what about the *afreets*? Not to mention the *ghouls* and *djinns*?' He chuckled. 'You've been listening to that old sourpuss, haven't you? Ay, well, you're not the only one asking that question. The Emperor himself set me off like a wee ferret only yesterday, to nose out the evil bunny who's to blame for this *maladie*.'

'But who'd want to do such a thing?' Helen shook two curtains of curls forward over her shoulders to cover herself.

Microphilus sighed again. 'Anyone who wants to be a queen – so that's everyone in the Harem for a start. But if I was to narrow the field, I'd think maybe someone without sons who's jealous of Zara's two strapping lads. Or someone *with* a son who she wants to see inherit the throne. It's not the eldest boy who succeeds, you see, but the one the Emperor names at the time of his death. And there's few things that recommend a boy better than his resemblance to a favourite mistress.' He seemed to be staring at her belly, at the henna stain on the palms of her blunt hands.

'So, what must a lassie do to be a queen?' Helen folded her arms over her breasts, not daring to look at him.

'No more and no less than you're doing,' he said quietly,

looking away. 'But when the time comes, make sure it's a wee laddie that you're carrying in your womb.'

'But not all the lassies with sons become queens.'

'That's because the Emperor's only allowed four wives. If all the vacancies are filled, you have to wait until one dies or is divorced by His Majesty. There's only the one vacancy now – because he divorced Salamatu barely four months past. But if Zara dies, there'll be only the two queens left: *La Batoom*, with her trio of sturdy young warriors, and wee Douvia, who pupped her first laddie just this spring.'

Tea arrived: fragrant, clinking on a brass tray. The music started again and Batoom reappeared and sashayed over towards them. Shrugging off her blouse, she tugged her breeks down to her hips and began to dance.

'*Regarde! La Reine de la Danse!*' Microphilus clapped his hands with delight. 'Is that not a braw sight? Akin to all the seven wonders of the world.'

Batoom smiled mischievously at him and raised her black eyebrows, shaking her extraordinary body until every part was in motion: a brood of tumbling brown seals. He smiled back. Helen followed his eyes: to the nipples, ridged as a man's thumb; the belly surging like treacle over her breeks. She felt pale and clumsy in comparison; pasty, heat-blotched.

'Do you think she's bonny?' She tried to sound casual.

'Ay, though "bonny" wouldn't be the first word on my lips. "Magnificent", maybe. Or "sublime".' Microphilus gazed at the big queen swaying in the centre of the courtyard.

'Even with her head shaved, and those plain clothes? And this place –' Helen gestured around the courtyard. 'Why does she not furnish it like the other queens, with bonny flowers and silk carpets?'

'Some folk say she's been hoarding her allowance from the Emperor. They think she dresses like this because her clothes trunks are full of jewellery and gold coins. For all I know they may be right. She's a whole suite of rooms I haven't even been into. She keeps them locked and the keys around her neck; says that way the slave doesn't have to bother cleaning them.' He chuckled admiringly again.

'She can't be bothered with all the *folderols* the others go in for. All she cares about is grubbing away on her wee parcel of land –' he raised a dainty cup and sucked in a mouthful of tea. 'And me, of course.' Grinning and smacking his lips.

Helen found herself staring at his little hands, still greasy with sweet oil. They were small as a child's, but veined and sinewy like a man's. The hair on the wrists glinted like gold over a dusting of tiny freckles. She remembered Naseem talking about the gelded men: 'They have hands, don't they? And tongues?' Needles of sweat stung her scalp and she scrambled to her feet and excused herself.

She stopped hurrying as soon as the gate closed behind her. She didn't want to draw attention to herself: no one hurried at this time of day. It was too hot. Panting sparrows crouched in the bushes with their beaks open. The women meandered slowly along the corridors, back to their rooms for the midday sleep, slurring their slippers, fanning damp faces with limp arms.

They still noticed her, of course, the other women. Even when their eyelids were drooping with the heat, they still managed to raise a curious eyebrow. Still managed to stare: at her hair, her pale arms, her belly. Always in that order: that new woman, that strange colouring, is she pregnant? Maybe a nod of greeting or a hissed comment, making Helen yearn for the concealing folds of her *haik*. Would she ever wear it again, ever step outside this stifling warren of fat women? Sweat rolled down between her breasts; her blouse was glued to her back.

'*Sabahel elkhairat*, Aziza!' A mocking voice was wishing her good day. It was the lass who'd replaced her the night the Emperor had sent her away. She was with a group of three others, ambling along like bay colts with big round rumps and nodding manes of tiny plaits.

Helen lifted her chin instinctively to return the greeting, shaking damp curls back from her sweaty face. The women were holding hands and blethering like sisters: happy, relaxed. Were they talking about her? Was she going to be stared at for the rest of her life?

She thought of Queen Salamatu's deserted courtyard: its stagnant fountain and froths of untended blossom. If she was a queen no one need ever see her; she could send people away, if she was a queen. In her mind she began sweeping up fallen petals and scrubbing scummy tiles; unrolling soft carpets across the floors.

By the time she got back to her room, curtains were drawn across every doorway. She heard snoring as she passed; quiet giggles and the murmur of invisible voices. On an impulse she stopped outside Naseem's room and called softly. There was the sound of scuffling and low laughter inside, then a strange woman's voice saying 'Go away!' in Moorish.

'Don't worry about her.' Naseem opened the curtain a crack. 'She's so rude.' She flashed a grin over her shoulder at someone inside the dim room. 'Come in, please.' She reached for Helen's hand and the curtain gaped wider. 'We were just playing.' She was naked, and her long plait was unravelled. Her lips seemed swollen and her strange, pale eyes shone. Behind her, another woman was lying on the mattress, a shameless sprawl of languid brown flesh.

'I'm sorry –' Helen backed away. Naseem shrugged her broad shoulders and pulled the curtain closed.

*

154

Back inside her own room it was stifling. Peeling off her clothes, Helen sat down on the edge of the divan. Her legs looked pale and lumpy. She dug her nails hard into her doughy thighs, staring at the red pattern of tiny half-moons she'd made. Two flies landed on her knee and began darting and butting at each other like tiny goats. A second later they were rolling over, buzzing and rasping their totie black bellies together. She flicked them off in disgust.

24

19 July 1769

My senses are swooning from the treat they have just received: of Helen dancing, with her blouse off and her pantaloons slung low on her hips. My eyes are replete from feasting on the pale hues of her nakedness, all the insides and undersides of Eden: the milky curves within a snail's shell; the silky depths of a leveret's ear; the gossamer veining on that shy anemone country wenches call 'windflower'.

Then she sat beside me. Oh happy nose, to be so filled with the smell of her! Enough to make me bless this damned weather if it can produce that tart waft of liquorice and mace; and that other scent which torments the monkey mind: of horseflesh and hay, and fresh fox-spray of a May morning.

It was the smell that really unhinged me, as though I was inhaling some essence of her, for what is a scent but a distillation of the skin's secrets, a steam rising from the deepest crannies of a body? She was talking to me, some nonsense about the queens. I suppose I answered, for the conversation continued for some minutes. But I was so overwhelmed by her proximity that it was some clattering clockwork creature that was blethering, while the real Microphilus was gulping down all the air in her vicinity, and ogling the coy folds of her belly, rolled up like rose-petals 'neath the silk of her *kamise*.

Earlier I did manage a passable brief dialogue with Batoom, on ways to subvert the Emperor's plans to send Helen to Sallee. 'I will deal with the Emperor,' declares the Black Queen with one of her grand shrugs. 'Now talk to her,' she orders, and takes herself off to the kitchen. She claimed afterwards that the sight was simply too droll for her to bear: the shy lass squirming to cover her bare paps, and the doting wee dobbin a-gabbling with his eyes fair popping from his skull.

Since then I have been maintaining a kind of abstinence, starving my famished eyes on alternate days, like a Papish penitent at Lententide. For she must not suspect that I love her; no, not now, while my form is abhorrent to her. Better let her think I'm attached to Batoom: a freakish puppet on a fabulous queen's strings. I must not, dare not, risk her scorn; for a woman's contempt is like milk on the turn. Once the curds have separated from the whey, nothing on this earth will amalgamate them back to creamy wholeness.

Meanwhile, I have been embarked on my activities as a Sleuth. The occupation proves the perfect distraction; otherwise I would be forever sniffing around Helen's quarters, like a terrier on heat, casting about for more whiffs of deliciousness.

I began by visiting the Queen Zara. Dear God, how she has changed in the weeks since I last saw her! She refused to admit me at first, fearing I had been sent by the Emperor to spy on her. The poor queen's mind is full of such fevered imaginings, like a very titmouse in a tree, darting and jittering, supposing and counter-supposing in the same breath, until I feel exhausted after just two minutes in her company.

She is thin as a crane-fly, all wrists and elbows, and fly-away-home hair like sheep's wool a-trailing from a hawthorn thicket. And her eyes glitter with a deranged intelligence, quite unlike the delicate queen I remember. For there was ever something calming about the *Lalla* Zara in the past, a poised stillness to her perfect features, like one of your more stately water-birds: a swan, perhaps, or a grebe, with her slender neck and small face looking mildly down, almost in surprise, at the swelling billows of her sumptuous body. I think perhaps this is why she so appealed to the Emperor: for the noble calm that so belies the wanton layers of soft flesh beneath her silks.

The flesh has quite disappeared now, and the calm. Today it was a gaunt carline who paced the cloisters of her rooms, with blood-caked nostrils and pink spittle at the corners of her mouth. She has a blue glass charm around her neck, in the shape of an eye, and it thuds against her painful breastbone, thud-a-thud-thud, up and down, as she moves. The emblem is thought to repel evil: she has had her slaves paint them all over her walls, in the palms of blue hands which are supposed to represent those of Mohammed's favourite wife. The effect is most unsettling, as though a disembodied audience has been bizarrely reconstituted and glares balefully down at the visitor.

So I sit myself down under this legion gaze, and begin asking information about her illness (when it started, if associated with any portents or foodstuffs, and the like). I can see she is trying to concentrate, but it is as though there is a hive of bees buzzing in her skull, so that I have to repeat my questions over and over while she agitates her bony head as though to shake them from her ears.

In the end it is her handful of five slaves who reply, while their mistress sits scratching at her scaly ankles, staring distractedly around and calling for water every few seconds, which she then pushes away after barely a sip. It seems the distemper began some four months past, with surges of black vomit which prostrated her for days at a time, and a scalp so hot and tender that she would allow no one to comb her hair, but demanded ewer after ewer of cold water to be dribbled continuously through her curls. Some days later the sickness would abate, only to recur the following week; abate and recur, abate and recur, accompanied each time by additional symptoms, *viz.*, strange splashes of brown pigment on the skin, inflamed eyes, black faeces, bloody gums.

'And she has visions, Master,' pipes up one minuscule *bint*. 'Yesterday I saw her crawling in the courtyard in the middle of the day. She was smiling, saying she was watching the baby mice. But I swear to Allah (who is merciful beyond our imaginations) there was nothing there but a few fallen jasmine flowers.'

I ask whether any have noticed signs of an intruder, and they look sideways at one another while one gets up and leads their ravaged mistress safely out of earshot. The rest then whisper details, with assorted wincings and shudderings, of some evil wee objects they have found in the queen's rooms: composed of birds' beaks, wasp-stings and the like; bats' ears and snakes' tongues. They are calling them '*afreets*', 'porcupines'. I have seen the like at home in Pittenweem (though with marine components, for we are fisher folk), and they appear the very embodiment of evil, with a power to affright that can only compound whatever curses they contain.

'Has the Lady Zara seen any of these things?' I inquire, and they shrug severally in a helpless manner, and eye one another again. 'Only the first,' admits one. 'After that we were so careful, searching every day.' And they all nod miserably, gripping the multifarious charms they all wear round their dark necks. 'Then last week, she found another. That's when her hair began falling out.'

I dismissed them to attend their mistress, while I sipped tea and pondered ways of uncovering the culprit (for I am loath to believe the porcupines came there of their own accord, however other-worldly they might appear). And, by and by, resolved to recruit a spy to be my eyes in my absence: *viz.*, the gnarled gardener who sweeps the litter around the queens' quarters. Indeed, the Methuselah selected himself, for I tripped over him twice before noticing him at all. Upon my soul, there never was a creature more suited to his calling, being the very image of a heap of garden refuse: in colour a mottled brownish and in texture rather angular and rustling, a veritable mullock of a man.

Requesting he examine an ailing rose in my garden, I hustle him away and order him to observe the activities in *Lalla* Zara's *ménage*, reporting anything untoward directly to me. With Invisibility on my side, I am hoping to ensnare our Witch (or whichever Familiar she has delegated to deliver her bristling deposits).

Next, I called on the *Lalla* Douvia, to discover (in as subtle a manner as I can manage) whether she has received any similar spiny harbingers. I found her among her flowers, peeping rosily out through the blossoms, a very picture of elfin majesty. Her courtyard is a cacophony of colour, her walls and arbours quite massed with gaudy blooms; and hanging among them like fruit, her jewelled cages of trilling finches.

'*Ave*, Fijil!' cries she, disentangling herself and presenting me with a yellow rosebud and a dimpled hand to kiss. '*Quis me visite?*'

I wonder if I have mentioned the lassie's *penchant* for conversing in Latin? It is a habit I find quite taxing, especially when interposed with her native Spanish, with the Moorish smattered throughout for good measure. I wish I had never let her know of my facility in the language (*hybris* was ever my undoing). We might have been better acquainted by now had our conversations been less conjugatory and declensive. It does please the Emperor, however, to hear her spout her subjunctives. She is his Madrid Madonna, a pint-sized packet of the European culture he so values.

Anyway, I embark on the painful process of explaining why I have come, making nouns and verbs agree as best I can, while her slaves set out tea beneath a bower of pink blossoms.

'I can hear her, you know,' interrupts the multilingual lass. 'At night, when it is quiet. Moaning as though her heart is breaking. It hurts me to hear her like this.' And knits her rosy brow in distress.

Without mentioning the *afreets'* porcupines, I ask whether she has noticed anything untoward in the four months since Queen Zara fell ill. 'Any strange ailments in yourself or your slaves, any strange person visiting or lurking by the gates.'

She frowns thoughtfully for a moment. 'There was that business with my slave Fatima, do you remember? Lots of the slaves were ill, all over the Harem. And she was one of the ones that died. But that must be more than a year ago now.' I remember only too well: a sudden virulent epidemic that had the *tabibs* all flummoxed, which stopped as suddenly as it started. 'But we've been well since then (praise be to Allah, the All-merciful).'

She claps for a basin and begins scrubbing mud from her hands with a *loofah*. (This *horticulture* is a real passion of hers, to coax and caress her plants, draping and tying them as tenderly as most women gird their own bodies. According to my Methuselah, she long ago dispensed with her gardener, and does all herself nowadays, save the disposal of her refuse, which he arranges for her.)

'I am puzzled, though,' she continues, rolling up her dusty *salwars* so the slaves can wash her scratched feet. 'Everyone says the *Lalla* Zara has been cursed. I mean, with all those hands painted on her walls, we all assumed –' Here her plump shoulders shudder briefly. 'But you are talking as though there is something else wrong with her, some disease –

'*Madre mia!*' Now her dark eyes widen in alarm. 'Are you saying we could all become like she is?'

Whereupon I hasten to assure her that no one else has

shown any similar symptoms, that as far as I know no one else is in danger, that it may be a curse or a spell, or poison, or even a form of madness brought on by the sun, that I simply do not know, but that the Emperor has charged me to investigate.

'Poor Fijil,' giggles she, seeming reassured by my blustering outburst. 'Has the Emperor been badgering you?' Then, growing serious again: 'Have you searched Salamatu's old quarters? They were always rivals. Could she have – oh, I don't know how this bad magic works. But no one's been in there for months. Maybe she left something.'

I reflect on this while sucking up more tea, and upon the *Lalla* Douvia herself, who, having dandled her baby briefly on her knee for me, is now itching to return to her garden. Even as she mouths multilingual pleasantries, she cannot resist plucking the dead blooms from a nodding fountain of nearby magenta and balancing her little bird-seed boxes into a tower.

It is strange, this patient obsession with her flowers and her finches: at odds with her habitual restlessness. Perhaps it feeds her somehow, to riffle her wee fingers through soft feathers and velvet petals, and let all her senses fill up with beauty and sweet music. Perhaps this is the secret of how she has healed herself. For though it is but three years since she was tortured into renouncing her God, she now seems a most carefree wench: dimpled and dishevelled in her leaf-stained silks.

Little remains of her injuries today (the corrective *khalehs* here know better than to make permanent mar of a maid's beauty): her curls are half-way down her back again, thicker and glossier than they have ever been. And you would never guess her bonny hands had been in splints for so long – except there is something in their movements, a kind of clumsiness when brushing the hair from her face, as if she'd forgotten the use of her fingers and must use the sides of her paws as a cat does to wash its whiskers. Indeed, there is something altogether feline about the Young Queen: her way of patting her garments when she settles down first on her carpet, as though arranging the stiff flounces of her Spanish petticoats; her pointy wee nose and plump cheeks, her mischievous wide eyes; and that slight sense that she will pounce any moment and steal the ribbon from your *queue de cheval*.

And canny, too, to suggest searching Salamatu's quarters. For though I cannot suspect the poor White Queen herself (she was far too deranged to engineer such subtle mischief), yet her vacant burrow might prove an ideal lair for our spider. So, I have searched out the keys and will hie tomorrow, at first light, to open her rooms.

20 July 1769

How quickly does Nature reassert herself! The White Queen has been gone but a scant few months and the Green Queen, Mother Nature, has quite taken over her quarters. Unkempt curtains of foliage, like green waterfalls, pour down the walls, and shoots and tendrils crawl across the tiles like the fingers of so many drowning Ophelias. Frogs lurk in her stagnant pools and there was one floating, belly-up and bristling with flies. I tug some old silk awning from a tree and it disintegrates in my hands. Even inside her rooms, my feet whisper through drifts of pale dust and fallen leaves which have somehow seeped in beneath the locked doors.

For a long while I forget my mission, and simply wander through the sad spaces, pondering on the dear daft departed queen. I remember her mad singing – some dizzy reels her Irish renegade of a father must have taught her – how she would clap her hands and skip some distorted version of the hornpipe, loud and wild and breathless, until her gates were plastered with children all jostling to catch a glimpse of the White Queen whirling in her silks like a dervish. And they'd copy her – what wean could resist? – until the Harem was full of wee spinning-tops, plaits a-blur and a-bobbing, all laughing, all shrieking obscene sailors' rhymes.

She was fond of me, I think. She would call me her Leprechaun and beg for stories like a wee lassie, as though there were spongy bogs outben the Palace walls, and peat-blocks a-steaming and whistling on the fire. Yet the Emperor loved her, for all her lunacy. They say she was very tender in bed.

By and by I recollect myself and set to searching all her rooms, not knowing exactly what I am looking for. A miniature butcher's table, with discarded carcasses heaped neatly alongside? A teeny *chiffonier* crammed with detestable fragments? There are some marks which might have been footprints; a clump of feathers, such as a sparrow-hawk might discard; plus the dried husks of two small rodents; some sewing-needles lodged between the tiles in one cloister. But nothing you would not expect in an abandoned apartment; nothing to prove or disprove that this is the factory for our porcupines.

So little remains of us when we are gone.

25

Helen leant towards the mirror and drew a careful line of the blue paste close to her eyelashes. It stung slightly and she opened her eyes wide to stop the tears overflowing and smudging the colour. Through the film of salt water, they seemed to be swimming in the mirror: blurred green fish rimmed with blue.

Was this any better than the black? Sighing, Helen stared at her bleary eyes, at the gluey blue flakes on the lashes, then down at her tray of smeary tins and spilt powders. Behind her, Reema moved quietly around the little white room; sweeping, folding clothes. Outside the slaves were topping up the jars, filling the air with the rumble of pouring water.

Did she look bonnier now than when she came? She tried a smile. Or just heavier, more stupid-looking? She was definitely chubbier around the face now, especially when she looked down. If she was lying next to the Emperor, leaning over him, she'd look like this, with these creases under her chin. And he'd be touching her with his black-spider hands, pulling her down to his dry beard and wet mouth. Her scalp tightened and she turned away.

'*Mniha –*,' 'Nice,' the older woman nodded grudgingly when she saw Helen's face. Then: '*Tfadali*' – 'Please,' kneeling with a bowl for her wash in.

A low table of food was waiting nearby: a plate of yellow beans steaming in mutton gravy, and a dish of that creamy mash they called *hummus*, with slabs of warm bread and some of those fat green fruits full of red pulp. Helen crawled over and began to eat, using bread to scoop the food into her mouth. It was delicious, as usual, the beans slippery on her tongue, and gravy dribbling down her chin.

At home Meg would be serving lunch now: scowling and red-cheeked with her hair uncombed, and the sour porridge popping in the pot. Helen tried to remember that knot of hunger she used to feel when it was cooking; the stinging spurt of saliva as it was dolloped into her dish. Here she was never hungry, just ate anyway, because food was always there, always wonderful; she could taste all those colours churning in her stomach. She thought of the slimy green soup on the ship. Was Betty eating now too? She'd have loved this: meat every day, as much food as you could eat; no turnips to dig or firewood to fetch. Perhaps she could ask Microphilus to send someone to look for her and bring her here: not for the Emperor, but as a slave maybe. She pondered the idea for a moment, imagining Betty here: borrowing her things, blethering on. She'd say something next time she saw the Dwarf.

A familiar sound made her stiffen: salt crystals skittering beneath the bed. Without turning she knew the expression on Reema's battered face: the narrowed eyes and pinched lips, as though she was flinging pebbles at a rat. Helen looked down at the bread in her hand, soaked with heavy brown gravy. Stuffing in one last mouthful, she dropped the rest into the remains of the beans and looked around for the bowl to wash her hands in.

Then she crawled back over to the mirror. She hadn't seen Microphilus since that time he'd watched her dancing. He'd stared at her so strangely afterwards. It might annoy him if she asked about Betty now. Later, maybe, if he seemed more friendly. Sometime when he wasn't with Batoom. The Chief Eunuch and the Chief Queen. He was probably with her right now. Or off searching the Harem, for smears of poison around the rim of a bottle; bits of hair in a kerchief; a secret wee pile of toenail parings. Helen shivered. Her blue-ringed eyes seemed horrible suddenly: evil and crude, like the ones on Queen Zara's walls.

When Reema had gone, Helen closed the long curtain and lay down on the bed. She could hear the women's voices; their slippers shushing along outside; see their wide shadows looming and distorted through the folds of material. She closed her eyes. Her stomach felt warm and full. Soon the clocks would begin chiming, and that weird shouting would start, from the towers that no one could see. And everyone would unroll their embroidered mats to say their prayers. She always tried to be out of sight when that happened. Though Naseem had showed her what to do, she felt embarrassed pretending to gabble all those foreign words, and patting her chest and her head like the others did, and the back of her neck, bowing to their Allah. And guilty, though Microphilus said Jesus would be bound to understand.

'Aziza –' Naseem was stroking her cheek with the back of her hand.

Helen sat up abruptly: had she fallen asleep again? This heat made her so drowsy. What time was it? She squinted at the triangle of white sunlight through the gap in the curtain.

'Ta'i la' – 'Come on.' Naseem smiled and pulled her arm. 'Wayn el bashakeer?' pointing to a thick folded cloth over her shoulder. 'It's so hot!' She lifted her heavy plait away from the back of her neck with one hand and fanned her face with the other. 'Ta'i la,' she insisted, making a splashing gesture then tugging Helen to her feet.

Helen hesitated. She hadn't braved the Bath House yet; everyone staring at her arse and teats. And all those rules to learn: which hand to use; which part to wash first. But Naseem was already gathering her things: her drying cloth and her comb, her jar of scented oil.

The Bath House was a great covered hall with coloured glass in the roof. It was dark and steamy, like an underground cavern with three deep blue-tiled pools, with steps leading down at each end, and a number of smaller steam booths heated to blistering-point by rows of bubbling cauldrons on clay braziers. The pools were full of naked women, lathering their hair, clambering in and out, submerging in a flurry of bubbles. Many were pregnant; many more were so fat it was impossible to tell whether they were or not. Helen had seen a herd of brown heifers once, fording the river at Muthill. They were like that: gollumphing and glossy, lowing and snorting with pleasure.

A crumpled old slave, with just a checked cloth knotted around her waist, hobbled over, exclaiming over Helen's pale skin.

'Don't worry.' Naseem squeezed her hand. 'They'll soon get tired of staring.'

The old woman led them into a side room, where she unrolled a straw mat and knelt beside it expectantly. '*Tjad-dalirtahi*,' she wheezed – 'For your comfort' – and motioned them to lie down.

Helen glanced uneasily down the long walkways surrounding the pools. A line of ancient slaves crouched over the prone bodies of perhaps thirty naked women, rocking backwards and forwards with their wrinkled dugs swinging, kneading flesh like oily brown dough or rubbing bits of grey stone on feet and knees.

Naseem shrugged off her clothes, then lay back and stretched out her strong legs. She was much plumper than before, but nowhere near as fat as the others. The tattooed design of blue dots on her face continued under her chin and down her neck, in lines like drops of water: over her chest and between her big breasts, across her round belly, all the way down until they disappeared into the hairless crease between her thighs. 'Like flies' footprints, yes?' She grinned up at Helen, walking the tips of her fingers downward along the blue tracks.

Helen blushed and began to undress, turning sideways to shield her body from the others. She wished she'd stayed in her room. She sat down and hugged her knees. Her hair was a hot blanket on her back; her nipples felt strange and tight. The new folds of her belly were sticky against the underside of her breasts. She glanced warily around: could anyone see between her legs?

Slick and streaming with water, the women in the pools hardly seemed human: more like otters with their blunt faces and bulging brown eyes. Or pond-frogs mounting each other in the springtime, gripping and sliding off, their fat thumbs in pale armpits, jerking in the slimy shallows.

After a while she noticed that one woman was watching her from the nearest pool, her small eyes on a level with her own. The woman's skin was purply-brown, like Perth slate, and there were six gold rings around her long neck. Smiling slowly at Helen, she began sluicing water over her high pointed breasts, pinching the teats until they bunched up like blackberries.

Why was she doing that? Helen ducked her head and shook her hair forward to hide her face. Peering through her curls, she saw the woman who'd been in Naseem's room the other day. She was wading towards the purple lass, splashing her and grabbing her hands, smacking them like a naughty wean's. Then suddenly they were wrestling in the water, squealing and tangling their dark legs.

Helen blushed and glanced around again. She couldn't get

used to all this touching. Didn't they mind people watching? She could feel the matting under her pillowy buttocks; soft warm air between her legs. Rolling on to her stomach, she buried her face in her arms. What did they do with each other?

By the time she looked up, the two women had left the pool and the old hag had begun massaging Naseem's big feet, cracking and pulling the long toes. 'My legs: like a man, yes?' Naseem bent her knee and clenched her thigh. 'Good for running,' she grinned.

A change in the quality of the sound in the pools made them both sit up. Everyone was staring at the entrance to the Bath House, where a white-veiled figure was walking, followed by two anxious-looking slaves. It was Queen Zara: even from this distance, Helen could see the pommels of her shoulders through her hooded *farrajiyah*, the sharp bones of her wrist as she flicked at the slaves to stop fussing. Though still blotched with brown, her skin seemed slightly smoother than before, and she walked steadily, with her head high, towards one of the steam booths.

When she reached the door, she paused and turned towards the staring women. Raking her eyes over their faces, she let the hood fall from her head so that they could all see her piebald scalp, and the few long dark wisps which were all that remained of her hair.

Microphilus was sitting outside Helen's room when she came back from the baths that afternoon. He jumped to his feet when he saw her.

'*Bonjour, mon amie!*' he cried, whisking off a red felt hat and twirling it by the tassel. 'I was wondering if you'd care to take a turn with me around the garden afore supper. There's a grove of cypresses on the far side where the shade's as cool as a loch and the air's sharp as a green needle.'

Helen put a hand up to her wet hair. 'Oh, don't worry about that,' he said. ''Tis curling up sweet as a mermaid's tresses, so that I will imagine myself truly underwater when we get there.' He picked up a turquoise parasol and handed it to her with a bow. 'To save your cheeks from the cursed freckle. Though 'tis a mystery why you ladies so abhor the pretty things.'

They set off, Helen walking slowly, the Dwarf rocking briskly from side to side on his bandy wee legs. Seated, she could almost forget his size, but walking beside him, she was acutely aware of his totie arms flapping like a puffin's wings; his little hooves kicking along in his yellow slippers. Looking down, she could see how his skull swelled above his eyes; how the tassel on his hat swung madly as he trotted along.

What was he saying? She kept thinking of Queen Zara, of what had happened to her froth of chestnut hair. Had she woken one morning and found it tangled on her pillow? She imagined the slaves combing it out, and wad after wad of it sizzling and melting on the kitchen fire.

'Would poison make a lassie's hair fall out?' she asked abruptly.

'So you've heard about our poor queen's latest tribulation. I've not consulted wi' the *tabibs* yet about the cause, but mixing poison's such a practised art in this land you can be sure there's some nasty haggie somewhere who's perfected the precise recipe that will provide any disfigurement you could require. It's the same all over this great Continent. Batoom says where she comes from half the men live in abject terror of their own wifies. She says it's because the men aren't allowed into the kitchen.'

Helen giggled. Was he serious? 'What do you mean?'

'She says the men can hear the clonk of the spurtle against the cauldron inside the cooking-house, and their wifies a-cackling together. But they can't see what's brewing so they imagine all kinds of evil being stirred into their vittles. The men always eat first, you see, and if there's just a wee pullet, the weans and wenches are lucky to get a few dregs of gravy to wet their porridge.'

'So the wife could poison the meat and her own food would be safe.'

'There you have it exactly! And wouldn't she feel tempted, too, if she's crouched slavering for hours over some savoury stew, only to see it gulped down an ungrateful gullet? Of course it's only the cruel husband who trembles when his supper is served. The man who respects his wife can tuck in with a *gusto*. It's your red-eyed ruffian full of millet beer, who wallops his weans just for sneezing – he's the one who fears his wifies are all witches.'

They reached the gate to the garden and he darted forward to hold it open for her. On the other side they were faced by a maze of paths radiating off through acres of formal garden and woodland. A group of women stood aside to let them pass, kneeling respectfully to Microphilus. Helen lifted her chin. She kept forgetting he was the Chief *Khaleh*. Feeling their eyes on her back, she followed him down a path shaded by arches of honeysuckle and roses, proud to be heard talking with him in a language they couldn't understand.

Now what was he saying? She bent over to listen. Something about Lungile, the giant brown man:

'– says he's taken a fancy to one of the new lassies.'

'You mean the guard on our journey, the one who skelped Naseem?'

'The very same. And a truer man you couldn't find if you searched all the nations of the world. Though he's not a man in the strictest sense of that word, if you know what I mean.' He nodded towards two sallow eunuchs lolling in the shade, one painting a design of curlicues on the shaved head of the other, dipping a wee brush into a dish of *henna*.

'That giant's been gelded like them? But he looks so different, not so fat.' She pictured him crouching over Naseem that night; the bunched muscles of his naked back; his narrow hips and sharp ankles.

'That's because the Harem eunuchs were mostly pollarded as wee laddies, whereas poor Lungile was lopped barely four moons past. Their sap's been dammed up for years in the bulky boles of their bodies, whereas his is still surging through his branches. He still dreams of his five wives in Nuba, for God's sake. While they're fluttering on about new ways of draping their vestments or cooking *glacé* fruit.'

Helen digested this for a moment. 'So which lassie is it he loves?'

'Nay, hen, he's sworn me to secrecy. I've already said too much – but my tongue's so happy to be tripping out its native syllables that it's fair galloping off by itself.' He smiled up at her. 'Walking with you like this, away from the others, I can almost believe we've been spirited back to Scotland.'

They strolled on in silence for a while. Then a familiar smell made Helen wrinkle her nose. 'Are there horses kept near here?' An image of her father came into her mind: his soot-smudged back bending; his hand splayed on a bay flank.

'Just over that wall. There's nigh on four acres of stabling, and as many grooms as there are women in the Harem. The horses are all stallions, of course, for your Moor wouldn't place his precious backside on anything less and keeps his mares for hauling sacks of wheat and beans to market.' He was plucking lavender flowers and crumbling them between his fingers. 'Now I come to think on it, I've not clapped eyes on a gelded nag since I set foot in this land. 'Tis as though the Moor feels his horse as an extension of his own body, so the very thought of the blacksmith's blade makes him clutch at his *couillions*.'

Helen smiled uncertainly. He was always doing this: turning some odd little fact into a parable. Like Jesus in the New Testament, though Jesus would never have spoken of such things . . .

'Castration's one of the worst punishments the Barbarian brain can devise. That's because your African measures his manhood by the number of bairns he can sire. So to slice off his sporran is to return him to his mother's lap in the eyes of his fellows. It's different for the real eunuchs, of course. They've never known life as a true man. Their cutting's more a calling than a culling and they've all been groomed for their vocation since they were weans.'

'Was Lungile punished then?'

'Ay. And it was the Emperor himself who ordered it – and watched it, too, though from a safe distance.' She could imagine it only too clearly: the Emperor's spider-hands resting calmly on his knees; his white gown and wolf's ankles. And the great brown giant thrashing wildly, restrained by a dozen men.

'What had he done?'

'Knelt too slowly, when the Emperor was inspecting the *Bokhary*. It takes a while to concertina a body that size.' His tone was light, but deliberate.

'You can't geld a man for something like that!'

'You can, lassie. If you're the Emperor, you can do whatever you like. He had one in ten of the *Bokhary* castrated that week – that's nigh on three hundred men. He was trying to tame the beast, by putting a ring through its neb, as it were – though there were many with the ring already in place, being from the blood-drinking tribes of the East. He pays them well, but he's never quite sure he can control them. And if you saw them, you'd see why he's so leery of them. They're the fiercest horde of hoodlums you could imagine.'

'That noise outside sometimes, is that them?' She thought there'd been some kind of uprising the first morning she'd heard them: the shouting and thundering hooves, the shock of gunfire and screaming horses.

'That's what they call "powder play" – though 'tis scarce a game for the poor horses, spurred at a twenty-foot wall to test their bravery, with foam flying from their mouths and muskets blaring in their ears.'

They were walking right beside the wall now; the heat shimmered on little thyme cushions between the paving stones. Helen tried to picture what lay on the other side: three thousand thick-necked stallions snorting in their stalls; and beyond them, acres of white tents like limpets on a beach; the angry glint of nose-rings inside.

Microphilus chuckled suddenly. 'Oh, our Emperor's a clever man, for all his cruelty. He sent a hundred of the poor geldings to work as grooms in the stables. And has them trot out the Royal Stallions each morning, in a sedate circle around the *Bokhary*'s encampment.' He tilted his jaunty head. 'Was that not a gesture of genius, lass? To make his entire army wince every morning? And he's decreed the time of this painful trotting to coincide precisely with the men's breakfast – which so dulls their hunger that he's been able to shave two hundred thousand sesterces a week off his bakery bills.'

Was he joking? She was never quite sure. Looking down, she saw his grey eyes were full of fun. She burst out laughing. 'I can't think a king'd concern himself with a few loaves of bread,' she protested. Then a thought struck her: 'Those men who were gelded, can they still – ?' She bit her lip. 'I mean, is it the same as with horses?' Blushing, she began unravelling the ribbon on the parasol's handle.

He chuckled again. 'Well, you're not the first to ask that question. And I've heard tell there are a few who can summon a wee something now and then.' Helen stumbled on the uneven stones of the path. Why had she said that? What must he think of her? 'But for the most part they're not interested. And the Emperor never even considers it a possibility. So, here we are.'

The path dived down into a shady little valley. Dark branches knitted together above their heads and dry needles whispered underfoot. Helen drew in a deep, sweet breath. Criss-crossed with spears of sunlight, the air smelt of peat and resin. Microphilus scampered ahead into a grassy clearing and threw himself down on his back with a sigh of contentment. Helen sat down against a nearby tree. She could hear swallows chittering, swerving through the hot sky high above, and some tiny little green birds darting among the topmost branches. Did he come here with Batoom? She found herself staring at his crotch, at the folds of his white *jellabiah*; his barrel chest, rising and falling as he breathed.

'I suppose you're wondering about me.' His eyes were shut, but he was smiling. He folded his stubby arms behind his head and stretched his legs.

'What d'you mean?' Her cheeks were blazing.

'Are you not curious about what kind of tricks this wee monkey can get up to?' Opening one eye and squinting up at her.

'I was just wondering how it was done –' His snort of laughter interrupted her. He drummed his heels with delight. 'Not that –' she stuttered hastily. 'I didn't mean how *that* was done.'

'I know.' Sitting up and wiping his eyes. 'I'm sorry, hen.'

'I was just wondering about the pain.' She remembered her father with the gelding iron; the horses' screams; the sudden smell of cooked horsemeat. Was that how they did the men?

'The knife's so sharp, they're off afore you can say "Allah". It's the hot pitch that makes them yowl. They pour it on after, to seal the wound.'

'How did you bear it?'

'Me? Och, I've not been cut.' He pulled up a stem of grass and chewed on it.

'No, of course not. I'd forgotten. Naseem told me about –' She bit her lip.

'Oh, Naseem told you, did she? And what exactly did she tell you?'

'That you were –' Was he angry? 'I mean, that you couldn't – because you didn't have – oh, it was only lassies' blether,' she trailed off. Why had she said anything? Now he'd hate her. She picked up a fir-cone and began snapping off its woody petals.

'So you've discovered why they call me Fijil.' The smile in his voice made her raise her head. 'Well, can I trust you to keep a secret? Nay, lass, don't just nod at me like a Wullie wagtail. If you breathe a word of what I'm about to tell you, I might as well sharpen up the gelding knife myself – and light the fire while I'm about it, to brew up the pitch. If I'm allowed to live, that is. Which I wouldn't be if my – er – *integrity* was revealed.'

'You mean you're just like any ordinary man?' The question was out before she could stop it.

'Not an *ordinary* man, no.' He spat the grass stem away and selected another. 'But I wouldn't want to embarrass you with the details.'

26

22 July 1769

Dear God, am I mad? I have told Helen my secret! We were walking cordially together in the garden, and some passing wenches knelt to me (it is their equivalent of the curtsey, which their bulk precludes). Vain fool that I am, it made me preen. Even now I blush to recall it: a gander waddling and honking with conceit, puff-chested and flaunting his petty power. And Helen so lovely, flushed and languid from the baths, with soft smudges of some blue around her eyes. She has acquired a new walk to accommodate her greater girth, a coy rotation of the arse that is utterly beguiling.

What was I thinking? That I could impress her? Intrigue her with my clandestine virility? When my head barely reaches to her crotch? Oh, numbskull Microphilus! You are not in control when that lassie is near.

This is Batoom's doing. Her regard for me is so partial that I forget the outlandishness of my appearance. But to Helen I am naught but a dwarf. And if I am intact, am I any less of a dwarf? Am I not the more deformed in her eyes if in this regard I am fully formed? Unmanned, I can be her pebble, her radish, the harmless small thing that keeps her amused. But with my turnip, I am metamorphosed to a monster.

And the power I have given her! What if she tells the Berber lass? (Lord knows she has little reason to like me.) One word to the Emperor and Microphilus will be no more. Turnip or radish, it will matter not in the sorry soup I will become.

My spy has reported back (though 'report' is altogether too precise a term for his crumbling ramble of an account). He waylaid me yestermorn, materializing suddenly from a thorn-hedge and half scaring me out of my skin. What a herbaceous hybrid he is, half man and half moss, such that anyone seeing us together must wonder why Fijil is talking to himself. Which supposition is not so far from the truth, for our mossy Methu-selah is so unpractised at speaking that his words emerge very ponderously, with long pauses while he reflects on his utterances as though amazed to find himself talking at all. Indeed, he has quite forgotten his name, it is so long since he was addressed by it.

He is a eunuch, of course, but quite unlike the other *khalehs*, for I cannot imagine his thicket of hair has seen a comb this past twenty years, and his beard is so matted with vegetation that I expect any moment to see a dunnock emerging from its nest there. It seems the gardeners are shunned by the younger *khalehs*, as being altogether too deciduous for their tastes, and so cluster together in rustling groups to exchange seedlings and cuttings, and fervent mutterings on the arts of pleaching, pollarding and the like.

'Another porcupine, Master,' hisses he, glancing cautiously around and passing me a tuberous bag. It seems he retrieved the spiny thing from Zara's cloister at sunrise, just where his mistress would step if she were going to her bathing room. 'It is a *ghoul*'s work,' nods he with a scattering of dead leaves, and explains that he has taken to sleeping across the gate to the queen's *appartements*, so nothing corporeal could have entered without waking him.

I took the thing back to my quarters and teased it apart, examining it most meticulously (with shudders a-scampering up and down my spine). It was just as the slaves had described: evil and cunning at the same time, with a plethora of unpleasant components all somehow bound together, like the indigestibles that bats and owls disgorge. I could not tell exactly how the things were joined, for my disentangling had destroyed much of their adherence. Some fine threads I noticed, as of gossamer or worm-silk, and a shiny residue such as snails deposit on the courtyard tiles.

I set the pieces out on my floor, grouped into various categories, *viz.*, parts of birds (beaks, feet, talons, feathers), insects (stings, pincers, horns, legs), animals (ears, eyes, toes, claws, tails, fur), and plants (thorns, roots, burrs, tendrils), plus miscellaneous entrails (including a wee heart, plus sundry shrivelled oddments I could not place but which smelled of fleshly origin).

I had set these occult oddments apart and was puzzling over their provenance, when it occurred to me suddenly that if said porcupine were anointed with poison, its spines would serve as perfect needles for its injection. Whereupon I scramble headlong to my basin to scour my hands, and thence to my lamp to examine them for wounds. It is during this fevered inspection that I recall that it is the slaves who have been touching these objects, not the queen. So whatever sharp mischief these prickles convey, it cannot be poison else the slaves would be their prime victims.

Yet if it is witchcraft, it is of a most precise and powerful type. For it seems the queen can be prostrated by these things without even touching them; nay, without even knowing they are there (for she has seen but one). Furthermore (if we are to trust our Methuselah), it appears the bristly bundles can appear from thin air. Farewell, then, to my fond fantasy of catching our miscreant red-handed, for no hands appear to be involved. Unless we have a flying witch . . .

I suppose I may yet hope to uncover some kind of workshop

in the Harem, chock-a-block with prickly paraphernalia. But the witch in question may not even dwell within these walls. There may be a market wench selling spells to the women. Perhaps – oh, enough of this. My mind is a *purée*. I am going to bed.

25 July 1769

What a night I have had, peopled with all manner of ghastlies, all strangely grizzled, all giggling and baring their needle teeth; and some wielding knives, and others drooling over spoons of brown liquid. I woke gasping and all of a lather, with a wet bed-sheet around my throat and my mouth full of feathers where I suppose I had been biting at the pillow.

Disentangling myself, I lit a lamp and sat trembling for a while, peering nervously at the bag where I had put the fragmented porcupine. I think I expected it to start moving, to knit itself together and come clattering across the tiles towards me. Ay, and it might have done, too, if I hadn't jumped up and dumped the lot on the kitchen embers.

It wasn't until they were burning, and the stench of singed horn and frizzled fur was in my nostrils, that I remembered the mystery fragments I'd set apart the previous day. (My only clues up in smoke!) And scratched hopelessly at the grate with a stick, and flicked out some burning oddments, and burnt my fingers, and showered my *kamise* with hot ash. Thus covered with recriminations, singed and shaking, and still spitting feathers, I fled my rooms and skedaddled to Batoom's quarters.

She was deep asleep, her dark chamber a very cave of velvet breath. And her gathered mounds softly heaving: a couch of comfort for my scrabbling soul. Trying not to wake her, I crept into the crook of her arm and there slept peacefully at last, in a blanket of musk with my nose in her oxter.

I have just been speaking with the Crone, who waylaid me and nudged me into a quiet corner.

'Have *Lalla* Zara's slaves mentioned the *afreets'* porcupines they've been finding?' she asks. 'They were burning something last week when she was at the baths, and I recognized the smell of lizard-tail.'

'Do you know how they got there?' I feel quite breathless for a moment, thinking the cunning Crone might have some knowledge that will lead me to our culprit. 'What else have you noticed?' But she will not be drawn.

'Zara is old now. Finished,' is all she will say. 'She has had her sons; there will be no more babies now. It is time for her to retire to Tafilalt and make way for a younger woman.'

And there you have it in a nutshell: the Crone's attitude to the women. While they are fresh and fecund, she prowls their lives like a very lioness. But once they have bucked and groaned and delivered their broods of boy-brats, she scrubs her knuckles clean of them. The intricacies of Zara's decline are as interesting to her as the crackling of a gorse pod once its seeds have burst forth. Far more pressing on her mind is the upsurge of what I can most nearly translate as 'fiendish frottage' among some of the women.

'Have you seen them, Fijil?' and now the beady eyes glint with real agitation. 'With each other! The Emperor's women! It is an outrage.'

She is referring to the intimacies the lassies indulge in together, as a substitute for conjugal canoodling. Indeed, I have heard it whispered that, once they have sampled it, many women come to prefer this softer love as being more satisfying (in both variety and duration) than the real thing. It is said that the participants become very enterprising, and that in the absence of the Star Performer, as it were, the Supporting Cast are inspired to disport most adequately (some would say superlatively) in the Act of Love.

The Crone fears that this flowering of love among the women will make them less respectful of the Emperor, which will result in a reduction in the quality of what she calls 'the Royal Cream' (which she believes can only achieve a proper thick consistency in the presence of a reverential mate).

'I'd have them all clipped,' she snarls, referring to an operation whereby the organ of pleasure in a woman is removed. The practice is prevalent in many parts of this Continent, among certain of the tribes which allow polygamy. Its purpose is to dilute the women's desire, which preserves for the poor husband some semblance of Authority. And I can just imagine the situation if it were not done, and a man was besieged nightly by his concupiscent concubines, or (worse still) rudely rejected because they preferred to do their porridging together.

Some two hundred of the Harem women have been 'clipped' in this way, including the ailing Queen Zara. The Crone claims it makes them more accomplished in love, because there is nothing to distract them from pleasuring the Emperor (and thereby extracting the Royal Cream). Indeed, she maintains that, in those places where the operation is commonplace, a husband refuses any wife who has not been 'clipped', believing such women are inevitable adulterers, being unable to restrain the vagaries of their lusts.

But I am not convinced, for what greater joy can a man have than to give pleasure to the woman he loves? If her pleasure is, as it were, curtailed, wouldn't his joy be likewise diminished? I venture as much to the Crone and she doubles up with mirth, rocking to and fro for a long while, wheezing and smacking her bony knees. 'Oh, Fijil!' she gasps eventually, wiping her eyes with the hem of her sleeve. 'You know nothing of true men! This "great joy" you speak of comes from the squirting of the man's milk. Nothing more, nothing less. Of course sometimes a man's milk comes faster if he thinks his wife is having pleasure – and a woman with a husband like this must make happy noises and move her hips to help the milk come. But other men prefer a quiet wife, who closes her eyes and keeps still while he is pumping. Or one who will not part her knees without a thrashing. It doesn't matter what the wife is feeling, as long as she makes his milk come.'

And, delighted by this evidence of my Ignorance, she treats me to a wide, green-gummed grin. But then her earlier pre-occupation recurs and she is soon scowling and snarling again.

Her wrath has focused on the new Berber lass, who has acquired a small following of lovelorn wenches. 'If it weren't for those blue eyes, I'd have despatched her long ago,' carps the Crone. 'The women are bewitched by her. I don't like it, Fijil. They are staying away from the garden on a Thursday.' And her hands begin, on their own volition, to knot up the material of her *kamise*. 'And the *bint* will not eat! She claims she is fat enough now. How would she know? As Allah is my judge (may His Name be praised), that one is dangerous.'

27

The heat increased over the following weeks, singeing the rose petals and crisping the columbine tendrils. At night the women hauled their mattresses out of their rooms and splayed snoring under the stars. By day they lolled in the shade, with their blouses off and their feet in basins of water.

Helen had never known anything like it. Her skin was clammy all the time; her clothes stuck to it like wet leaves. She took to lying on the floor of her room, her damp flesh flattened on the cool tiles, sweat trickling into her ears. Drifting in and out of sleep, she'd hear the swifts screaming high overhead; imagine blue air scything past their wings. She'd follow them in her mind, diving down into the courtyard, then whisking up and out again, over the baths and the laundry rooms, the towers she'd never seen, the army camp. Then where? What was it like beyond the palace walls?

She tried to remember the day she'd arrived. There'd been an open-air meat market, with carcasses hanging and scabby dogs nosing bloody dust; goats tripped down the tracks dropping pebbles of black shit. She'd seen a scatter of brown tents; rows of flat-roofed houses; in the distance the white tents of what she now knew was the *Bokhary*'s encampment. Beyond the Palace was a high wall with a shaggy beard of lean-to shacks. Within that was the city of Marrakech, narrow lanes full of flapping white-gowned men. Was it hot out there too? She felt like a pale grub in the middle of an ant's nest, cocooned in its wee cell, while the rest of the world scurried about its business.

How long had she been here? She tried to work it out. Malia had knocked on her door just last week with the pads of muslin – how did she know when to come? – and that was the second time since she'd arrived at the Harem. Nine weeks, then? Ten? Long enough for her thighs to thicken and her belly to plump up. When she knelt to eat these days, she could feel her heels sinking deep into her cushiony arse.

The old woman had seemed pleased with how she looked. 'At last, you are a proper woman!' she'd crowed, prodding a knobbly finger into the dimple on Helen's elbow. 'When Fijil said about the women in your country, how they pull in their waists, I couldn't believe it. You need a fat mama if you want a fat baby. The child needs room to grow. "Look at you," I said to him. "How tall would you be now if your mama hadn't laced herself so tightly?"'

Was that why he was a Dwarf? Helen had frowned. But the bairns of grand ladies weren't all like him. 'He's the only small man I've ever seen,' she'd said. 'And I think it was Allah (may His Name be praised) who made him that way, not his mama.' By now it seemed normal to speak the name of their god the way they did, with one of those little prayers they always used afterwards. It was part of learning their language.

Now she understood what they were saying, everything felt better. She could tell now if folk were gossiping about her or not, and knew to smile if someone shouted out 'pink-nose!' when she'd been too long in the sun. Now she was fat like the others, and knew how to behave, they didn't stare at her so much – except when she was walking with Batoom or Microphilus. But that just meant she was treated with more respect.

If it wasn't so hot, she might even start to enjoy this life: no buckets to lug or chickens to gut. Her nails were clean and pink now, like a new baby's, instead of split and wedged with kailyard mud. Her cheeks were chubby; her feet soft; her belly full of rich food. She had her own room and her own servant. Best of all, she had her own money for the first time in her life.

Microphilus gave it out on *al sabt*, the day after their Holy Day. And the market wenches came the same afternoon, to set out in the big courtyard by the Harem gates. Helen had never seen so many bonny things in one place: rings like heaps of cool gravel, she'd stir them with her fingers; bolts of silk and brocade, they'd be swooped around her shoulders with a flick of the wrist; tassels by the mile, scarves and ribbons; a field of carpets; cups, spoons, clocks, trays: all colours, all tinkling, ticking, glittering in the sun.

To begin with Helen hadn't bought anything: she couldn't haggle like the others and she had no idea what the different coins were worth. But once she got the knack, the market was the high point of her week. She loved weighing soft suede pouches of jewellery in her hand, then easing them slowly open. She wanted to touch it all, buy it all: the teeny crags in the little carved boxes; the slithery blouses and breeks. She wanted to own all the smells, take them back to her room: leather and beeswax; frankincense, sandalwood. And all the sweet things, taste them all: the sugared fruit and sticky pastries; honey cake and nut custard; trays heaped with sweetness and the market wenches waving the wasps away. She'd lick the sugar from her lips as she unwrapped her purchases in her room, crouching over them with the curtain drawn, as though she'd stolen them. But they were hers – the purple scarf, the bonny comb, the yellow pillow – and she was stroking them and deciding where to put them.

It reminded her of when she was wee, before her father remarried. He'd bring a surprise for her every time he went to the market – a sweet orange or a hair-ribbon, a bit of sewing silk – and make her guess which pocket it was hidden in. When the other bairns came along they seemed to get everything. She'd tried not to mind, but it hurt to see them burrowing through his greatcoat, even when the things they unearthed were treasures she'd long outgrown. Now at last she had treasures of her own.

Crammed full of sweetmeats, the women were always giddy after the market, as though honey was whisky. Last week they'd found a long branch in the garden and fixed a mirror to the end. Then, doubled over with giggles, they'd propped it against the massive outer wall, trying to spot a soldier, or a groom with his breeks down – even a sturdy slave-boy would have been enough. But the mirror had fallen off and smashed on the other side before they'd seen anything, leaving them squawking with frustration.

That was all they seemed to think about: doing it – they called it 'playing sex' – getting ready to do it, giggling about it afterwards. And who was playing sex with who; whispering and sniggering, listening outside doors or peeping through curtains. The bairns were even worse, scrambling under beds or hiding in the clothes-trunks of women they thought were lovers, then skedaddling out breathless to tell what they'd heard. Only last week Naseem had found a wee lad up to his armpits in her water jar.

Helen found herself pressing her ear against the wall too, trying to imagine what was happening in Naseem's room. Or she'd arrive early at Batoom's quarters, half-hoping to surprise her with Microphilus. She'd watch the lassies the Emperor chose when they came back from his rooms, all snooty and smug-like because they'd been playing sex with a proper man. Had he really hurt them or were they just pretending to walk like that, laughing and wincing as though their groins ached?

By now she understood that almost nothing of what she'd

thought about sex was true in this place. Lassies could do it with castrated men, with each other, with monsters. They'd probably use boy-bairns too, if they weren't taken away. A man could lie with a wife, a mistress or a slave, or all three at once if he had a mind to.

And all this food, all the mouths chewing, the tongues and fingers glistening with green oil; the clothes, soft and loose as night-dresses, and no chairs or tables, just mats and mattresses, so you had to lean or lie down; and it was so hot all the time, even at night, so you found yourself washing, maybe three times a day, and slipping on fresh silks, smoothing in more of the scented oil, which felt so good, and what else was there to do anyway if you'd no one to do it with?

Drowsing, flat and heavy on the floor, Helen tried to imagine Batoom and Microphilus together. Could he lift himself up on those wee arms? What had he meant about being different from ordinary men? At home once, she'd seen a little donkey put to her father's mare, to get a mule foal for the spring fair in Dunblane. Watching his little hooves scrabble at the mare's rump, she'd felt disgusted. His back legs jittered to keep a footing on the hill where they'd tethered him so he could reach; his huge pink thing stiffly waving about under its own weight as he jabbed blindly upwards.

Harem life revolved around two events: the weekly market, and the morning, four days later, when the women lined up for the Emperor in the garden. Those four days were days of preparation, when the women tried all their different scarves and paints, hair-styles and jewellery, growing more and more anxious as Thursday – *al khamis* – drew near, until, the night before, some lassies would be up until dawn crouched over a rush-light, plucking out stray hairs their slaves had missed. And afterwards, when the Emperor had chosen his women for the week, the rest would slump, clutching at their heads or their bellies, complaining they were dizzy, or sick, or exhausted, mythering on until market day, when the preparations would begin all over again.

'Why do they all love him so much?' Helen asked Batoom one morning. They'd settled themselves on a carpet in the shade and the big queen was sorting through a tangle of coloured threads.

'The Emperor? But he's every woman's dream!' Batoom clutched a skein of red silk to her chest and closed her eyes in mock ecstasy. 'Rich, powerful, handsome – what woman could resist?'

Helen made a face: 'But he's so hairy, and old –' she protested, then stopped, not knowing how to describe the strange lurch in her belly when she thought of his brown hand creeping like an earwig beneath her clothes. She'd seen a picture of the Devil once, with a black beard and the Emperor's beaked nose, and terrible dark shaggy legs with horse's hooves instead of feet.

'They like the way he looks.' Kneeling up, Batoom ran a comb through Helen's hair. 'See – you make a parting like this, then work backwards.' She took a lock of copper hair and braided it like fisherman's twine. 'They like his white teeth and smooth skin. Most men are covered with brown spots by his age. And his beard's still thick and black. And that nose – you must like his nose!' She was laughing now at the look on Helen's face. 'What about those magnificent eyebrows? Oh, the way they meet in the middle –' She wrapped a bit of the red thread around the end of the plait and bit it off.

Was he handsome? Helen tried to picture him through Batoom's eyes. Strong, yes, and lean. And clever – the look in his eyes told her that. And now she was used to seeing people with brown skin, he didn't seem that dark any more.

'There's the money too, of course.'

'What money?' Helen straightened her back.

'Didn't you know? Every woman he chooses is paid ten times what Fijil normally gives them. And if he's especially pleased, there's the chance of some real treasure. Once he gave me a gold saddle, and a bridle to match – and I don't even know how to ride!'

'Can I see them?' Helen started scrambling to her feet, but Batoom tugged her back by the hair.

'Do you want me to do this or not?'

'I'm sorry – what did you do with it?' Helen stared around the bare courtyard. Which of those locked rooms was the treasure in? She pictured it gleaming in a dark corner, beside a trunk full of jewels. This was like something from a fairy-story, with an enchanted king and unimaginable treasures. 'What else did he give you?'

'Oh, many, many things. But nothing else as foolish as that. Don't ask me for details. It's been years since he sent for me.' She finished three more braids, brown fingers flicking as fast as a lizard's tongue. Helen felt the tug on her scalp as Batoom started on another. Already she was feeling cooler. The big queen was right: these tiny plaits let the air through to the skin.

'You know, it's not just the gifts that drive them crazy,' Batoom said carefully. 'Have you heard them talking about the Emperor's cry?'

'I don't think so.'

'One thing you'll discover about the Emperor is his – his –' She screwed her broad face up, looking for the right word. 'It's a sort of coldness, except he's the fiercest man I ever played sex with. As Allah is my judge (may His Name be praised), no man ever tired me out like the Emperor. But always I had the feeling he is not really there. The body is excited, but the eyes just look at you.' She'd stopped plaiting and was just running the comb through Helen's hair. 'Always there was this cold thing, like another man looking out through the eyes, who is thinking: "So. Here we are, doing it again." Even with his big push of pleasure, he never cries out. It's more like a grunt, a little strangled thing, as though this other man does not want to let go of his milk.

'That's what makes the women mad for him. Because they know he's not always like this. The first time he played sex with Queen Zara, he cried out so loudly, people talked about it for weeks. It was the same with Queen Salamatu – you know, that pale-skin one who was sent to Tafilalt before you came here.'

Helen tried to understand what she was being told. Somehow, these two women had so excited the Emperor that he'd –

'He married them both, of course, soon after. And it was –'

'How is he with you?' Helen interrupted. Her brain was buzzing: could you really become a queen just by making a man cry out?

'Oh, there was never any true passion between us.' Batoom's fingers were busy again. 'He married me to end a war with my father. I excited him, yes, and he liked to wrestle me as though I was a man – because I was so strong, and tall like him, and could press his two shoulders on the ground.' She chuckled proudly. 'But I never made him cry out the way Zara and Salamatu did.'

'What about Queen Douvia?'

'No – though I expect she's tried. No, Fijil says the Emperor married Douvia because he'd been insulted by the King of Spain. Can you believe that?' Batoom's breasts heaved with merriment. 'Taking a bride out of revenge! He wanted a European wife, you see, and wrote to King Charles offering to marry his daughter. The letter he got back made him so angry that he sent word to the pirates to attack every Spanish ship until they found a girl with aristocratic blood.'

'When was that? She seems so young.'

'Poor little *bint*. I felt so sorry for her when she first arrived, clutching that disgusting old cloth doll of hers and her holy beads. And she was so brave – I don't think she's cried once since she arrived. Even the Emperor was impressed.'

Helen thought of the beautiful lass playing with her baby. 'Did he – I mean, how could he – ?'

'Play sex with her?' Batoom shrugged. 'He waited, of course, until Malia said it was safe. She's always careful with the younger ones, and he never insists. Not like some,' she added darkly, then flicked the last plait into place and knelt back to survey the result. 'So! How does it feel? If you are still hot, I will be happy to shave it all off for you. Then we will be like two eggs together, one brown and one white.'

28

Merde *alors!* It is so long since I have taken up my pen that termites have gnawed through the box in which I keep my Treatise and reduced the past eight weeks to dust.

It is my own fault, for forbidding my slave Maryam to tamper with my papers. It is only the vigilance of the house-keepers that prevents the entire Palace from passing by degrees through the stomachs of these creatures, which seem able to digest any substance, and have an uncanny knack of penetrating up through the floor exactly where you had forgotten your slippers. So that all that remains, when you discover them again, is an upper layer which comes away in your hand and a creeping orgy of consumption beneath. Thus it was with my papers – though it is no great loss, for the heat has sapped me of literary inclination these last weeks and propped us all against the walls like wet sacks. If it would only rain, how relieved we should all be! I am so weary of the brackish taint of this stale water; of the brownish dust that cakes my nostrils like snuff.

Poor Helen finds this climate very trying. She has not yet acquired that African trick of submission, which involves a certain slowing of all functions, as in hibernation. Thus she will fan herself continually, and agitate her garments; wipe her sweaty palms and mop her brow; or flop in a sodden torpor on the floor and consign herself to sleep, as if in hope that when she wakes it will miraculously be cool again.

Her fleshy cladding compounds her discomfort. For she is plumping up nicely, according to plan, as your cottage loaf rises on its tray above the range, and now has many more sweet creases to chafe with sweat, more dimples to waylay each salty trickle.

It is curious to observe the new women expanding. Some wax almost spherical, with all semblance of waist obliterated, like a sheep's tick when swollen with blood. Others balloon out like Batoom, with each part in perfect proportion, as a bunch of dessert grapes on the vine. Helen is of a third type again, where the choicest fruit is borne below the waist, in a great burgeoning of the buttocks. All her pertness is intact still: her sprightly smile and quirksome eyebrows; the stubborn jut of her wee squared chin. But her rump is become quite stupendous, curving out like the cheeks of a pumpkin from the stem of her back. And her belly is the plumpest pillow a man could ever wish to lay his head upon: sweet and round as a vanilla dumpling.

Her education, likewise, has proceeded apace and Batoom now informs me that there is nothing more the lass can be taught in the way of caresses. Her sole concern now is her pupil's reticence regarding the Emperor's person, which focuses most acutely on His Highness's hairiness. 'She speaks of him as some kind of *Shatan*,' laments Batoom, referring to the Mohammedan entity which is equivalent to our own Dark Angel, Lucifer. And the comparison is not wholly inapt, for there is something quite feral about the Emperor (that badger's beard, those lean shanks) which would cause any Necromancer to glance downwards for a glimpse of cloven hoof.

There are signs that Helen's worm of reluctance is on the turn, however, and may yet metamorphose into fluttering attraction. Just last Thursday I spied her crouched behind a *syringa*, bobbing her head from side to side like an apple on

All-hallows' Eve, for a glimpse of His Hirsuteness walking through the garden. And watched her afterwards, eyeing those he had chosen, marking their hair, their clothes, their paint. Soon she will be ready (*en garde*, my poor heart!); soon add her flushed cheek to the fevers of obsession which infect this sanatorium.

Meanwhile her cell is filling up with terrible trinkets: all kinds and all colours; all without any purpose that I can discern, save to fill all the baskets and carved boxes she has also been buying. Why is it that women so adore lace doilies and inlaid toothpicks? Is it, as Batoom claims, because their own lives are similarly petty and without purpose? When I stayed in Edinburgh there was a fashion among the idle for minuscule tea-spoons, differently decorated for each day of the week, almost too delicate for mortal fingers to hold; and teeny *tasses* to match, such that the upper lip must be contorted for each sip, with handles so wee the pinkie must be curled upwards, like a shepherdess's crook.

How I loathe this place sometimes, its fripperies and cloying oils, its petty concerns: the disposition of a kerchief, the merits of varieties of *henna*. There is a terrible *ennui* to these stifling days, when even Love loses its power to divert, as involving altogether too much glueing and unglueing of hot skin. Lately Batoom and I have been content just to lie beside one another, covered with a wet sheet, chuntering on like an old married couple.

22 September 1769

I have been trying to decipher what remains of my notes. The process is oddly diverting, with each fragmentary phrase conjuring some of its context and the mood in which it was written.

So we have here '. . . *tabibs all in a huddle, with their . . .*', which reminds me (how long ago this all seems!) of the week we expected the *Lalla* Zara to die. She had taken a sudden turn for the worse, with all her hair falling out from her spongy scalp and fresh sores on all her limbs, as though her very flesh was rotting away from the bones.

Each day she was conveyed to the examination chamber, a peculiar room abutting the main Palace, equipped with various screens and apertures (for however frail and wizened he be, however desiccated his vital juices, no intact man is permitted to enter the Harem). Now here come the *tabibs*, clustering around the cankerous hand the queen extrudes through the appropriate hole, cradling it in their bony claws and feeling for the blood inside her wrist. (This is how physicians here assess a person's health, by touching various points on the inner wrist and monitoring the minute changes they detect in the flow of vile or benevolent humours through the body. I have tried this with my own wrist and cannot imagine that they learn anything of value by this method, but it is at least harmless, which is more than can be said for the methods of our grand Scottish physicians.)

So here they all are, muttering and jutting their goaty beards, taking turns at the hand, while the unfortunate queen languishes on the other side of the screen, all hot bone and gristle and the air wheezing in her concave chest; and her slaves quite beside themselves with grief, keening and gnawing on their knuckles. And me a kind of Jack-in-the-Box, popping back and forth between the women's and the men's worlds, for here in the examination chamber we see the Mohammedan system at its most absurd, when it denies to its adherents the human contact they need.

The two princes, her sons, have been summoned too, and are squatting down behind the *tabibs*, bickering together over what this might presage. For while the queen is alive, each one's chance of becoming Emperor is at least significant. But if she were to die, they might as well begin wrapping their green *dulbends* around their heads and picking out their favourite slaves to accompany them into obscurity in Tafilalt.

Then, miraculously, she begins to improve. I use the word 'miraculously' because the *tabibs* are still bickering over an appropriate treatment regime when their patient falls suddenly into a profound slumber of some four days. Here is a taste of what I wrote at the time: '. . . *looked in on the Lalla Zara this morning and I swear her wounds are healing before my eyes, and a soft chestnut down is starting to appear on her bony scalp, like the silken lining of a beechnut mast. The slaves are . . .*' Well, you can just imagine how the slaves were: tiptoeing around as though afraid to break the spell, but beaming fit to burst.

Now we have: '. . . *hoping I can claim some responsibility . . .*'. Here is *Monsieur Microphilus le Révélateur* in self-congratulatory mood in the days after Queen Zara's recovery, wondering if his investigations have intimidated our witch into packing up her box of spells, so effecting the sudden reverse we had just witnessed.

Ah yes, '. . . *heaps of grass-seed . . .*' This refers to the rustling gardener, Methuselah, who has taken to lurking outside my quarters (hence the seedy deposits), hoping to waylay me so that he can deliver one of his interminable 'reports'. I am afraid I have become rather impatient with the man, for though he is always most agitated and earnest when he accosts me, yet his meandering accounts contain nothing but details of the condition of the plants in *La Zara*'s garden. Thus I spent an entire morning last week hearing about some unusual sprouting shoots on one of the jasmine bowers – when I could have been at the market with Helen.

Now, this is interesting: I am noticing how the writing

changes when I am describing my encounters with Helen, becoming thicker and blacker, as though I am pressing harder with my quill, with a plethora of small blots as the ink spatters wildly with the passion of my feelings. Thus, though '. . . *sunshine on . . .*' could refer to almost anything, the exuberant appearance of both up- and down-strokes reveals that this is a doting fragment of some tribute to the lassie.

I have been watching her at the market each week. It is difficult to describe the pleasure it gives me to see her wander among the merchandise, as reverent as any noviciate nun before an altar, touching each gaudy gewgaw as though it is a relic of the True Cross. It is money I have given her that she is spending, *vous comprenez* (though it comes from the Emperor, *naturellement*, and before that from some threadbare peasant in the Atlas foothills, who has amassed it, no doubt, as a *dowry* to rid himself of his ugliest daughter, so that he can then comfortably proceed to disposing of the bonnier ones). And it is to me that she comes, when her arms are full, eyes glowing with gratitude before skipping off to gloat over her treasures in her room.

'. . . *a more remote action, whereas obeahs . . .*' This is where I am describing the various kinds of spell they have here. As I recall, it was quite a sensible disquisition, which I will try now to replicate. I had categorized them into two groups, namely those which operate by remote versus proximal influence.

Thus you have your remote enchantments, such as the love charms women use, where the Beloved's name is written on a slip of paper or cloth (the scribes earn a fine income from the illiteracy of these lovelorn lovelies), which is then worn close to the body, or steeped and the water drunk, which somehow engenders love in the absent Beloved. There are remote malevolences too (*mais, bien sûr*), one being a red cloth packet tied to a chicken's ankle, which agitates as the bird scratches about and thereby excites ill-fortune to befall the hated person whose hair (or skin fragment or nail paring) is knotted up inside.

The proximal spells (which certain of the slaves term *obeahs*) can similarly be divided into two groups, *viz.*: the protective charms that people wear or keep beside them (such as the blue hands that surround the *Lalla* Zara, which, it must be said, proved powerless to arrest her distemper) and the vast array of objects and substances which intend harm to their recipients. The *afreets'* porcupines are in this latter group, along with all manner of virulences, such as powdered hyena brain, which causes a form of laughing madness when ingested (this is a magical effect, *vous comprenez*, as distinct to common poison, which a child can purchase at any spice stall in the city).

Setting this all out again, I can feel the self-same exhaustion that assailed me six weeks ago when I first considered this vast variety of possibilities. Who is to say, *par exemple*, whether it was a natural proclivity to insanity or some smidgen of hyena dust that scrambled Salamatu's sweet brains? Or whether our porcupines were (so to say) pointless, compared with the flock of hens pecking away somewhere with Zara's name strapped securely to their shanks? But no, I must take heart. Zara is recovering. It may yet prove that my work here is done.

Nevertheless, I have let it be generally known that rewards are on offer to any slave who can furnish evidence of infamy among the women. Which scheme I may be forced to abandon, due to the sheer volume of human fragments being deposited in my quarters (in the form of hair-tufts, blood-smears and the like), sufficient, I swear, to reconstitute an entire new woman (albeit somewhat of a scrofulous one).

I find I do not like the frame of mind this investigation engenders, where every dimpled hand might hold a phial of vile enemas, each comely *kamise* a very hotchpotch of horror. It is this bent of suspicion which bends the Crone Malia so low, grinding her *qat*-stained gums and scuttling her along like a cockroach near the wall. These days I feel my own eyes shuttling back and forth likewise, my own ears straining for whispers of mischief.

And I have found it, too, in every part of the Harem, though mostly it is petty stuff. But the most pettifogging wee pip of a slight can, in this hot-house, burgeon into a veritable vine of vituperation. So one poor wench has been pilloried for simply refusing to lend a pink scarf. I swear they have been breaking eggs in her slippers and pissing in her perfume pots, never mind the intimate fragments they have been stealing from her room. And there is an avid feud between two entire courtyards of lasses (involving plait-burning, fountain-fouling and worse) concerning usufruct of a mulberry tree.

'What else is there for them to do?' shrugs Batoom benignly yesterday, when I arrive spitting with indignation at her quarters. 'I'd be just the same if I couldn't work in my garden.' But she is dissembling, for she would never stoop so low as to stir spittle in another wench's *couscous*. And the proof is in her treatment of Helen, for has she not been like a mother to the lass? Ay, mother, teacher, sister, all rolled into one. Oh fool, fool, Microphilus, to lose your heart so carelessly, when it was in such safe and loving custody.

29

'*Tisbah 'ala khair*' – 'Goodnight.' Reema backed respect-fully from the room and pulled the curtain closed.

Helen stared at the swaying white folds: another day over. The rush-light was lit and her basin and cloth had been placed ready, but she was too hot and restless for bed. Though she had just washed and dried herself, her back was already damp with sweat and she could feel it running down from her armpits. She'd been lying down most of the day, in this cramped room with its thick air, and the three flat-toed lizards stalking dozy flies across the white walls.

The lizards were gone now, and the walls were dark. Standing up, Helen felt salt grit cut into her bare feet. There was a rustle of dry legs and a giant cockroach darted from beneath the divan and waved its black feelers at her; then another, from behind her clothes-trunk. Sometimes they seemed almost human, the way they watched her, waiting until she was alone. Was Queen Zara getting ready for bed now, washing her scaly, blotched face, pulling dead hair from her comb? Shuddering, Helen padded across to the curtain and pulled it open again.

Outside the sky was velvet and moonless, heavy with the scent of night flowers. On dark nights like this, everyone retired early. Gazing down the cloister, Helen spotted Malia's familiar bent form, shuffling around the bodies of two slumbering women, then pausing and listening outside a closed curtain where the faint glow of a rush-light shone through. She was prob-ably on her way back from delivering the Emperor's woman.

He'd been in such a tetchy mood in the garden that morning; the women were all blethering about it afterwards. How he'd hardly looked at them, and waved away the slaves who'd brought out the new babies for him to see. And that little slave-girl who'd tripped with one of the babies – Helen winced at the memory. He'd whirled round almost spitting with fury, towering over the cringing lassie. They said he'd had her beheaded, but that couldn't be true. He wouldn't have someone killed for something like that. The baby hadn't even been hurt.

Who was lying with him now? A picture filled her head: the Emperor with his eyes staring and his jaw clenched, arms braced above some soft-fleshed lass. She imagined that strangled groan, deep in his throat, as though a wolf was crushed in there. She pressed her thighs together. What would she have to do to make it howl?

She wished she could talk to Naseem, but she'd seen her linked in with some lass earlier and could hear their voices murmuring behind her closed curtain. If only Betty were here to blether with. She kept meaning to ask Microphilus about trying to find her. If only she was home again in the kailyard, with cold wet grass between her toes. Homesickness settled, like a dull ache in her belly. Without thinking where she might be going, Helen slid her feet into her slippers.

Ten minutes later she was outside Microphilus's quarters. She paused by the gate, hearing quick footsteps. What if he was with Batoom? She hadn't thought he might have company, too. While she hesitated, the gate squeaked open and a chubby slave-lass slipped out, scuttling away with a scarf pulled low over her face. Helen stared after her: how many lovers did the man have? A spark of something fierce propelled her through the gate and into the small courtyard.

She'd never visited his rooms before. She peeped into the kitchen: empty, with just a few embers pulsing in the darkness.

The door to his washroom was ajar and she could see a candle burning by a mirror hung at knee-height. Where was he? Something squelched beneath her heel as she crossed towards the main room.

There he was: inside, with his back to her. He seemed to be sorting through some papers, dusting them with his hands and blowing on them, then rolling them up and clambering on to the bed to shove them into a cloth bag on a hook on the wall.

Should she knock? An embarrassed sweat prickled on her upper lip. It was strange seeing him alone in his lair. Where had he got that canny clock with the gold horses on it? And those books? His things were so fine: the carved blond wooden chests; the silver tea salver and those matching wee cups; the heavy silk bedcover, striped with purple and red. She thought of her own heaped bonny baskets. Perhaps she should save up for some grand things, too.

Helen's eyes flickered around the room, searching for signs of Batoom. There: a filmy robe on a hook near the bed. And wasn't that her oil jar on the floor? So she did come here. The discovery made her feel foolish. Backing away from the door, her slipper skidded on the soft thing she'd squashed earlier and she stumbled loudly against the wall.

'For the love of Allah! Come in, will you,' he called testily in Moorish. 'I won't bite, you know, whatever you might have heard to the contrary. Now let me guess –' hopping down from the bed and padding across the room in his bare feet – 'is it a soiled kerchief you've brought me, or some poor wench's pulled tooth?'

'Helen!' There was no mistaking the pleasure in his voice when he saw her. Then, in English: 'What's the matter, hen? Are you ailing?'

'No, no – nothing like that.' What must he think of her? 'I couldn't sleep –' When had she said that before? Hot blood flooded her cheeks as she remembered: it was at John Bayne's house, when he'd caught her spying on him in the garden; before he'd taken her upstairs.

'*Mais, c'est vraiment bien, alors!*' Microphilus took her hand and bowed, as if her arrival was the most natural thing in the world. 'Now we can be night owls together. Sit yourself down, lass, and I'll pour you a nip of this rough date wine I've had smuggled in from the Jewish *quartier*.' He flourished a straw-covered flagon. 'And how about a plump green *teem* from my personal tree?' Prancing out into the dark courtyard, he returned with a fruit in each hand.

Helen knelt down and took a sip from the cup he'd given her. Immediately she felt a trickle of warmth spreading down her throat and into her belly. 'If I were a proper sort of host,' he was saying, 'I'd light up a wee morsel of that frankincense and waft the smoke around your head by way of a blessing. But I'm loath to do anything that might obscure my view of your bonny face.' He smiled across at her and tipped the flagon again. 'To you, my dear Helen,' toasting her, '*et bienvenue à la Maison Microphilus!*'

Laughing, she took another sip. She loved hearing him speak French, like a real gentleman. To begin with she'd felt ashamed when he used words she didn't understand. Now she was flattered he didn't talk to her like a peasant. She sipped again, relaxing back against the edge of the bed. Why had she never thought to visit him before?

'It's grand,' she said, waving her hand around the room. 'The way you've arranged all these things.' Then, spying a glint of green in a leather casket by the bed: 'What's this?'

'Oh, that – that's an Imperial Emerald from the Royal Turban,' he announced mockingly. 'Go on – pick it up. See how it feels to hold a king's ransom in your hand.'

It was cool to the touch; big as a starling's egg, but much

heavier. Holding it towards the lamp, she saw the flame reflected minutely, over and over, in its depths. A childish needle of greed tensed her body forward, towards him: 'How did you get it?'

'Just a wee token for pleasing His Majesty,' he said carelessly, and she was surprised to hear a note of bitterness in his voice. 'What you might call a nest-egg, for if I ever fly out of this chicken-coop.' He stared hard into her eyes for a moment and she dropped the emerald quickly back into the casket. Could he tell what she was thinking: that a treasure like this might be hers, if she played sex with the Emperor?

Her palms were wet. How many more emeralds were there in the palace? In her mind she was rummaging through her father's greatcoat again, bursting with excitement, trying to guess which pocket held the treasure. She tried to picture the Emperor's quarters: did he keep jewels right there, in his chamber?

To distract herself, she reached back into the casket and drew out a silver locket on a broken chain. 'And who gave you this?' she asked, putting a tease in her voice. The thing was a love-token, she was sure of it. Prising the two sides apart, she found two locks of hair: one copper curl, like her own; and, coiled within it like a shadow, a tiny crescent of fine black hair. 'Two lassies in the same locket! I fear you're maybe not the gentleman I took you for.'

''Twas that locket that brought me here in the first place,' he said quietly. 'It belonged to a lass named Peggy. That golden tendril's hers – it's the tip of a ringlet I snipped myself. And the wee dark wispie's off her bairn's new-born head. I was taking it to my brother Jamie. Peggy wanted him to have it – 'twas her way of telling him he was a father. The wean was dying, you see, and she hoped the sight of the wee laddie's elf-lock might bring his father back home.'

Helen looked down at the open locket and wondered about the red-haired woman and her ghost of a wean. 'I'm sorry –' She felt ashamed of her clumsy joke. 'Your brother, why did he flit?'

'Oh, he'd found himself some new rich friends who paid for his passage to Holland. And a rich mistress too, I've no doubt, for he always was a one for the lassies and they never could resist his bonny ways.'

Microphilus took the locket from her hand and snapped it shut, wrapping the chain round and round it as though trapping the memory inside. 'If she'd been my lassie, nothing would've taken me away from her,' he said savagely, folding it inside his closed fist. 'If that bairn had been my bairn –' Sighing, he laid the locket back in the casket.

'Was she very bonny?' Helen found herself envying this mysterious Peggy for inspiring such single-minded passion.

'No more than a thousand other lassies, I dare say. But she'd a sort of a way with her, a sweetness, that'd make a man do anything to make her smile.'

'But not your brother James.' It was a statement rather than a question. She wanted to remind herself that this Peggy had been rejected too. Dipping her hand into the casket again, Helen began sifting through the other objects there: a few coins she didn't recognize and a stone of some kind; and a flat mother-of-pearl button. She picked out the button and turned it over in her palm, admiring its rainbow sheen.

'Don't touch that!' He snatched the button out of her hand. The next moment he was contrite. 'I'm sorry, hen. I didn't mean to scare you. It's just that I've had that wee button ever since I was a bairn. It's from my mother's frock, the only fine one she ever had. My father sent it her: it was one my real mother didn't want.'

She remembered him saying something about this before:

how his real mother had sent him away to be raised by a wet-nurse, a fishwife somewhere in Fife.

'I'll wager folks in Pittenweem are still talking of that frock to this day.' He chuckled. 'How Big Kath downed a quart of whisky and danced all round the port in it, merry as a sow in butter, showing off her finery, until she tripped and fell off the pier. And would've drowned too, if the tide had been in!' He placed the button on his knee and stroked it absently with his forefinger. 'I found it in the mud by our door – afterwards, when she was sleeping it off. I never told her I had it – even when she trailed round the whole town asking for it, and they were laughing at her in her grand lady's frock, all covered with fish-scales.'

'Why were they laughing?'

'Oh, they were forever mocking my mother. She was simple, you see, so she couldn't answer back. And ugly, with a moustache like a man and muscles to match. And she always stank of haddock's innards, from cutting fish and forgetting to wash.' He smiled and shook his head. 'I reckon I did too, as a wean, for we shared the same cot. Anyway, I remember putting the button in my mouth to suck it clean, and tasting the perfume on it. Even after Kath had touched it with her feechy fingers and dropped it in the mud. And I thought: that's what my real mother tastes like. If she'd have suckled me instead of screaming for the servants to take me away, that would've been the scent in my wee nostrils.' He flicked the button in the air as though tossing a coin, and turned it over on his knee.

'Didn't it make you curious to see her?' Helen asked. Imagine: being raised by a dimwit fishwife and knowing your mother was a fine lady.

He shrugged. 'I was just angry my Kath had to wear her cast-offs. And didn't even know it – she thought the dress had been made specially for her. Even though it pinched in the oxters and wouldn't button around her waist.'

'I never knew my real mother either.' Helen sipped more wine. 'She died when I was born. Folk said she was too wee to be carrying. She was fifteen when she married my father, but she looked like a bairn still.' Why was she telling him this? She hadn't thought of her mother for years.

'Did he remarry?' He was stroking the button again, without looking at it, as though he'd been doing it all his life.

'Ay, after my gran died. I think that's why really, so he could get someone to look after me.' And she told him about Meg moving into the house, with her brown skirts and thick ankles. And the weans appearing, one after another, until the place filled up with noise, and chores to be done because she was always suckling one of them, or too pregnant to bend, and her father always seemed to have one wean or other on his knee.

'So you weren't awfully keen on your poor stepmother, then?' Microphilus was grinning at her. Helen realized she had clenched both her fists. She sat back with a little laugh and held out her cup for more wine.

'And what did she think of you?' he asked.

The question had never occurred to her. 'I never cared what she thought. I only wanted my father to myself again. I used to hide in the forge and watch him with the horses, or lie in the hay-loft – so's I didn't have to skivvy for her.'

'She sounds like a lonely lass, this wee Helen.' His voice was gentle.

She studied her knees. 'Not really. I liked to be on my own. And I'd friends at school – though no one close. They were so rough and silly, most of them. And they thought I was too clever for my own good, because I was quick at my lessons and tried to talk nice.' She thought of Betty suddenly, gruffly offering her shoes. Was this the right moment to ask about sending someone to look for her?

'I hated the bairns in Pittenweem.' The anger in his voice made Helen catch her breath. 'They used to march behind us with clothes-pins on their nebs. And they called her "The Ferry" on account of having had so many sailors inside her. But she didn't understand what men were about. She thought they were all going to marry her.' He drained his cup and slopped out more sweet brown wine. 'And I don't like to repeat what they called me. As the Lord's my witness, I'd have thrown myself in the sea if I hadn't had Big Kath to care for me.' He scowled into the lamp flame. 'Then later, when I grew older, I decided to get clever so's I could look out for myself. That's when I forced my father to send me to the Academy in St Andrews.'

Helen didn't know what to say. She'd been teased, yes, but not like that. And the thought of sharing a cot with that stinking wench made her shudder. If she'd been in Pittenweem, she'd have worn a clothes-pin on her neb too. Yet he clearly loved the wretched Kath. She looked at him with a mixture of distaste and respect: perhaps it was easier to love if you were ugly.

He flicked the button up again in the light. 'She found it in my pocket a few weeks later and wanted to sew it back on. But I liked it so much, she let me keep it. Do you believe things hold a bit of the soul of their owners?'

'I don't know,' she murmured lamely, shamed by the warmth in his voice. 'I left too quickly to bring anything with me.' What would she have brought anyway? She didn't have anything of her mother's and she wouldn't have wanted something of Meg's. The things her father had given her had all been broken or passed on to the bairns. As for John Bayne . . . She watched the Dwarf stroking the button. What must it

be like to be loved like that: for the sweetness in your soul –
even if you stank of rotting fish, even if you'd a face like a
teuchter?

'Would you like a wee something to remind you of Scotland?' he asked suddenly, reaching into the casket and bringing
out the stone she'd noticed earlier. 'It's from the beach outside
Big Kath's house. I used to carry it in my pocket and put my
thumb in this wee hollow.' He demonstrated for her. ' "Twas
such a snug fit, I used to fancy it'd been created by the
Almighty Himself, especially for me – as a comfort for a laddie
in need of a bit of comfort now and then. Here –' He placed
it in her hand. 'Like this. Try it for size.'

It was white as a new mushroom; smooth and warm against
her palm. She slid her thumb into the hollow and closed her
hand, surprised at how reassuring it felt to have it there: as
though something missing had been replaced. A wee bit of
Scotland. Tears stung her eyes suddenly.

'Sometimes I miss my home so much it makes my throat
ache,' she said, giving it back to him. 'Even Meg. Even the
bairns.'

'So, keep it.' He pressed it back into her palm. 'Please, it's
not really mine anyway. I mean, it's God's pebble, after all.
Maybe I've had it long enough.'

Helen folded her fingers around it again, amazed at how
empty her hand had felt with it gone. She smiled at him, sitting
beside her in the lamplight, with his soft mouth and clever
grey eyes. She could smell his sweat, like seaweed and damp
hay.

'Fijil? *Masal khair*, my dear Flea –' The doorway filled
suddenly with a flapping white *kamise* as Lungile ducked his
head into the room. Then emptied again as he retreated. 'Sorry
– I'm such a dimwit camel. The gate was open so I barged in.'

*

Helen was riding a little donkey, bareback, down the hill to her home, feeling its hard spine between her legs. She let her big buttocks roll from side to side as its tiny hooves picked their way down the steep ruts. It was raining, a warm rain that soaked through her clothes and snaked in purple rivulets down the hill. The donkey's flanks were slick with water. Feeling her thighs sliding as she tried to grip, she leaned forward to hold on around its neck. Its spine was jolting against her belly now, and its hooves were slipping in the mud. Tightening her arms and legs, she pressed herself harder against the donkey's back, praying it wouldn't fall, feeling a kind of tingling as it moved . . .

She woke up, face down on the bed, with a strange pulsing sensation in her crotch. Had she wet the bed? She sat up quickly, but the sheets were dry. The sound of sparrows twittering outside told her it was nearly dawn. Lying down again, she noticed something white glimmering on the trunk beside the bed. Of course: the pebble. She picked it up and smiled as her thumb slid naturally into the hollow. A wee bit of Scotland: her smile broadened.

Then she remembered the emerald. A king's ransom: she'd held it in her hand, watched it glitter in the lamplight. What treasures she could have bought with something like that!

30

24 September 1769

She has just departed. Oh, this was magic indeed, to have her here in my chamber for the first time, to see her touching my things. There is a crease where she leaned against my bedcover. She has taken my Pittenweem pebble: how it thrills me to think of it in her pocket, thudding happily against her broad thigh. Will she place it on the trunk beside her bed, to watch her slumbering, feet sweetly protruding from her thin sheet? My cup has the print of her blunt fingers on it. I have tasted the rim, the dregs her lips have touched.

25 September 1769

I have awoken filled with the magic still.

She has my pebble in her chamber. She sat beside me on my carpet and laughed and cried with me. Right here, on my carpet, she slopped some wine. Oh, joyous carpet, to feel the weight of her braw backside!

And she came to me: without prompting or urging. How I have longed for this moment. That she should come to me freely, without revulsion or loathing, think of me (me!) in the night when she cannot sleep. Never mind we were chaster than a nun's bed-sheet. There will be other nights.

Nay, Microphilus, do not hope for other nights. Today it is enough to be alive. Today you must bless today. Today there is nothing you cannot manage. For Love both sharpens and softens a man, lending him the keenest of skill combined with a preternatural sensitivity. So I have been the cleverest and kindest of men today, buzzing like a wee bee around my hive of queens, touching here an angry forehead, there an anxious wrist, scattering inspired words of praise and commiseration, leaving wreaths of smiles like garlands in my wake.

Enough of writing. I am too restless to sit any longer. I must talk of this or I will burst.

I found Lungile in the garden. He was sitting with his *kamise* off and his feet (they are too large for the basins the women use) steeping in one of the fish-ponds.

'I have been thinking of the different words in my native language for "heat",' he remarks glumly, unwinding a sweat-sodden cloth from his head and wringing it out. 'Dry heat, wet heat, the heavy heat before thunder, that fresh heat after a spring shower; hunting heat, worried heat, the heat of fear; anger heat; love heat –' Here he pauses and scowls at me.

'Why are you sniggering, Flea? Have you come to mock my affliction? Does it amuse you to see Lungile's knees, his elbows, even his ears dripping with old-women's sweat?'

Whereupon I try to conjure some contriteness and set about reconfiguring my face into some semblance of sympathy. But it is all in vain and the grin edges out again, elbowing my cheeks until they ache and I must speak.

'Brother Bison,' I burst out at last, 'your Flea has lost his heart!'

He stares at me a moment, while my words penetrate the steamy fug of his gloom, then a slow smile starts to spread over his features. 'So, the radish is in love! And what kind of heat would this be? Something fiery to be sure, but with a certain crisp bite.' And lifts me up in his ape's hands and dangles me in front of his face, laughing at the soppy grin that still stretches my cheeks. 'Is it Batoom, you sly pup? I always thought there was something between you.'

And now, strangely, I am suddenly coy, and can feel a blush oozing upwards from my neck until my face is a very furnace of embarrassment. 'It's the red-hair we found at Madam Jasmine's,' I mumble. 'The one they call Aziza. But her Christian name is Helen, which means "brightness". I loved her the moment I first saw her, but last night she came to my quarters and –'

'You kissed? Oh, Fijil, how I envy you! To touch the woman you love.'

'No, there were no kisses.'

'But you embraced –'

'No.'

His face is an acre of askance for a moment. Then he slaps the furrowed field of his forehead with a wide yellow palm. 'Of course. Forgive me, brother. I was forgetting the puniness of your – um – I mean the – I had forgotten your problem. So, what happened last night to make you beam like a little red sun?'

So I explain our encounter: how she arrived at my chamber ('She came to you? This is excellent,' comments my Bison sagely); how we spoke of our mothers ('This topic is very good; it is a lovers' topic'); how she stayed almost until dawn ('And seemed surprised that the hours had passed so quickly? Oh, Fijil. The wench is yours!'); until by the end we are both laughing and shaking each other by the hand.

And by and by, having repaired to my quarters and lit up the *hookah*, we compose ourselves for the pleasant task of comparing the charms of our two sweethearts, for we had naturally progressed to discussing his beloved Naseem, his passion for the Berber having deepened in the past months. So he embarks on a long speech about her silken hair ('Like water, Fijil, when she combs it in the morning. And when it is braided, there are these sweet wisps which escape at the nape'), which I counter with a hymn to Helen's heavy curls, which he then parries with observations on his Naseem's fine nose ('A noble nose, Fijil. Straight and strong, with tattoos marching along it like warriors into battle').

The conversation puts me in mind of the deranged dialogue we had when we first met, reminiscing on our native *cuisines* to distract Lungile from the agonies of his castration. I remind him of this and he laughs briefly, then subsides suddenly back against my divan like a punctured bladder.

'Why, what's the matter?' I ask, much concerned, for the change in his demeanour, from Lothario to Lazarus, is quite dramatic. 'Are you in pain? I had thought all your wounds were healed now.'

'Healed? Oh, yes. I am completely healed,' says he with a bitter laugh. 'There is nothing to trouble me now. Nothing at all to worry about. Nothing, nothing, nothing . . .' and trails off, hoarse with anguish.

And suddenly, with the heady perceptiveness that Love lends, I understand exactly what he is trying to tell me. 'How long has it been?' I ask, staring into the distance (for these are delicate subjects for men to discuss).

'More than two moons,' he moans morosely. 'It just hangs there like a goat's ear. Even when I – you know – *pull* it,' and he glares fiercely at me, as though daring me to laugh.

'Is that why you haven't spoken to her?'

He lolls his great head. 'It's the shame of it, Fijil. Worse even than these grannies' agues. It's different for you. You've never felt the surge of blood pumping into your skin-gourd, the pride as it rises before you, making your woman gasp and reach out. The tingling as it tightens your udders.'

Of course he is wrong here, on every count, but I dare not

tell him for fear of dunking him deeper in despair. Instead I remark blandly that there are some women who are not overly obsessed with the male member, who prefer the softer pleasures of the hand and the tongue.

Now I have tweaked his curiosity, for his head rises and turns slightly, and he arches a cathedral eyebrow at me. Surely he has noticed, I continue, how certain of the women seem enamoured of one another? No, he has not, I can tell, but he immediately starts putting one and one together in his mind and making a very pretty sum of it.

'You mean they pleasure each other?' The words emerge slowly, almost in wonderment. 'With no – using only –'

'Only hands? Yes indeed. And tongues, or so I've been informed. And teeth, for those who are inclined, and nails.' (I confess I am beginning to find this most diverting, watching his massive mask undergoing more transformations than any burlesque *Pierrot*.) 'It may be that some few use a vegetable substitute for penetration, a carrot or *concombre*, for example. But for the most part they are content to improvise with their own extremities.' Now he is actually gaping, his mouth opening and shutting as he frames one question after another, and rejects them all.

'How else did you think I hoped to seek fulfilment with Helen? Though I cannot tell yet whether she will be satisfied with the forms of caress I can offer.' (Oh, Microphilus, your wildest dreams have not yet taken you this far!) 'Your Naseem, on the other hand, is rather more –'

'Naseem?' He is gripping my arm with iron fingers. 'Naseem is more what? What do you know of Naseem?'

'Peace, Brother Bison! I was just going to explain that Naseem is more experienced than Helen. If Malia is to be believed, the wench has already practised with at least seven –'

'Seven? On my ancestors' graves, I had no idea. I have seen

her walking with other women, certainly, and envied their hands on her waist, their hips pressing together –' Now, of course, I am waiting for the import of what I am saying to sink in. 'But that means that she might –' he stutters out at last.

'Yes, my friend.'

'That I could –'

'Yes, my dear friend. That you could. But first, you must talk to her. For if there is one thing I have discovered in my dealings with women, it is that a tongue waggled in speech is far more seductive than any amount of slurping between the thighs.' Reader, I wish you could have seen the sheer size of the smile he gave me!

Now do you understand how my day has been? How perspicacious and astute I am? How I cannot, cannot go wrong? How even the rambling gardener has not the power to exasperate me today?

Buoyed up by my success with Lungile, I hied myself off to the Crone Malia's rooms. The Emperor has summoned me to appear before him next week and I am afeared he will quiz me on the progress of my investigations.

I have never visited her before (normally she simply appears when she is needed) and was curious to see how she had arranged her accommodation. I was expecting some dim cave of a chamber, with herbs hanging in pouches like bats from the rafters. Instead, when she finally opened the door (after much scuffling, for it was locked, strangely, in the middle of the afternoon) it was into a most sumptuous room that I was grudgingly ushered, hung all about with rich awnings, and the glint of gold on everything, the threads in her brocades, the rims of her cups, even the ladle and lid to her water jar – all quite at odds with the shambling shabbiness of her own appearance.

My surprise must have been obvious, for she waves a crabbed hand at her finery, asking, 'Does it surprise you that I like beautiful things? When I have dedicated my life to creating beauty for the Emperor?' Which shames me into a flustered apology, which she flicks impatiently away and begins setting out an exquisitely fashioned silver tea-set on her tray.

'I have been thinking about the *Lalla* Zara,' I begin, and see an expression of impatience pass over the Hag's face, for I never have been able to engage her interest in the Old Queen's *maladie*. So I explain that I have been trying to discover whether there have been any other mysterious ailments among the women in the last year, inquiring disingenuously whether she might have noted them down in one of her books (knowing full well that she has compiled a veritable encyclopaedia of information on the women).

'You are my only hope,' I declaim. 'For the *tabibs* have proved useless. Their memories are moth-eaten and their records patchier than a beggar's *burnus*.'

This flattery has her ferreting about in a twinkling and soon there are twelve tomes stacked in front of me detailing every sniffle and sneezle in the *seraglio* for the past year. The sight made me quail, for reading Moorish is a skill I have never mastered. But I need not have fretted, for she was in among them before I could ask, hauling them open and running her twiggy fingers up the pages (up, notice, as opposed to down, for the Moors read their writings from the back of the book, and the bottom of the page, and once there from the right to the left).

'Aha,' says she eventually. And then again: 'Aha,' flinging back her black sleeves and flicking faster and faster through the pages of the final tome. 'I knew there was something here, but I wanted to check the other books first.'

When she finally sits back on her heels and folds her arms triumphantly across her chest, I am on tenterhooks. 'This time last year,' she pronounces succinctly. 'Do you remember the slaves falling ill? And none of the *tabibs* knew what to do?' There is a distinct sneer in her voice when she mentions the *tabibs*, for she harbours a very warship of resentment against them. 'If they'd consulted me I could have told them that there was not one but three outbreaks of disease in the Harem at that time. The one that made all those slaves ill. And two more, far less serious, afflicting two other groups of the women.

'See for yourself!' crows the Crone, thrusting the tome under my nose. 'Ten women with itching skin, and scaly patches seeping with water. They complained their tongues were burning and they couldn't stop dribbling.' I find myself tensing forward, for here are definite resemblances to Queen Zara's illness. But these lassies had all recovered within a fortnight, whereas Zara was prostrated for months. Perhaps they had contracted it in a less serious form?

'And the other group?'

'Over here, on this page. Only six this time. They came to me because their bellies were throwing out their food and they thought they might be with child. But when I checked, their wombs were empty. They said they'd been dizzy too, and weak, with aching legs and belly-pains. I was worried because they were getting so thin, but they were back to normal again a few weeks later.' Lady Zara was weak and thin, too, but the other symptoms seemed too vague to be interesting.

'Did any mention finding porcupines in their rooms?'

'Not porcupines, no. But ten – no, eleven – thought someone might have put a hex on them. But they always think that – now look at this.' And she bends again over her book. 'Here.

220

And here.' I peer obligingly, but it is no use. Her curlicues are meaningless to me. 'The slaves who were ill,' she explains testily. 'Here are their names and here, beside them, I have listed all their symptoms.' Thrusting the tome into my hands, she watches as my eyes meander vaguely up the page.

'Shall I read them out to you?' she sighs at last, and I nod humbly.

'Bad, bad burning belly-pains and throwing out of all food. Running to the latrine all the time until only water comes out. The three who died only had these signs. By the time they stopped breathing they were like dried leaves: no tears, no spit, no wetness inside them at all. But the rest had many other signs. Here, look. Skin that itches and flakes, that leaves a mark when it is scratched. Cracked nails and broken hair. Some said their hair was falling out.'

Now I am leaning forward again. 'Were any bald, like *Lalla* Zara?'

'No, not nearly as bad as that. But they had all recovered within one moon. If it had lasted longer, who knows? Wait. I have nearly finished. Thin, they were all very thin, but this always happens when the belly is throwing out food. Thirsty: they kept a cup beside them, but could only manage a few sips at a time.' Again, just like the *Lalla* Zara in her *extremis*.

'Dark gums, dark stuff coming up from the belly. Four had red eyes and burning tongues. Two showed me brown smudges on their skin, like *henna* stains. But of course the *tabibs* were only interested in the grosser signs. As Allah is All-merciful, I cannot understand why the Emperor allows those fools near his women!'

'Do you know what was wrong with them then?' I ask, but she shrugs her bunion shoulders and begins stacking away her tomes.

'I will tell you what I think,' she concludes enigmatically

when she is done. 'I think we are seeing three colours here, but only one paintbrush.'

As always when I talk to the Crone, I have the feeling she is not telling all she knows.

31

'Can I use your blue *kohl*?' Without waiting for permission, Naseem padded over to Helen's tray and rummaged around. 'I've decided to be beautiful today!' She was naked, and her knee-length brown hair had been interlaced with lengths of blue silk ribbon.

'What's so important about today?' It was Thursday morning again, but Naseem normally sneered at the other women's frenzied preparations, and simply put on a fresh *kamise* and a splash of rose-water.

'Today I want the Emperor to choose me,' she announced.

'But why today?'

'Because I didn't want him before, silly!' Naseem was squatting beside the mirror now, licking the brush and dipping it in the pot of blue paste. 'It's Naseem who decides who she plays sex with. So now I want to play sex with the Emperor.' Her hair rippled down her back like dark water, puddling in gleaming coils around her bent ankles.

'But I thought you only liked –' Helen blushed. 'I mean, I didn't think you were interested in men.'

'Then you thought wrong, sweet Aziza. Naseem is "interested", as you put it, in anyone: man or woman. If I like someone and I am in the right mood, then I want to touch them. It needs those two things only: the liking and the mood.' She pursed her lips at her reflection in the mirror. 'And sometimes a little curiosity. Once I played sex with a very old man.'

Helen gaped: was there nothing she wouldn't do?

'He was a great musician who was teaching me to play the flute. I remember, he had these wonderful hands.'

'I'd have been sick.'

Naseem laughed. 'Then you'll be a frustrated old woman! What's wrong with the touch of an old man? If he is patient and skilled, and you are full of hunger.'

'You couldn't want a gristly old man.'

'Why not? If the hunger pushes me? Don't you find sometimes that a piece of dry bread is exactly what you want to eat – even if there's a big dish of sugared *teem* right beside it?'

'You're mad!' Now Helen was giggling. 'I'd have to eat every one of the *teem* first!' But the discussion intrigued her. She'd never thought of herself as being hungry like that: for a touch, any touch. An old man's, a woman's, an Emperor's. Hunger: what a good word for that restless, empty feeling she sometimes had.

'So, is the Emperor your crust of dry *khubz* or a juicy sugared *teem*?'

Naseem shrugged her tattooed shoulders. 'I am curious about him, that's all. How he will be when he is alone. The women say he's very fierce when he plays sex; very hot, very hard. And his body is strong and hairy as a lion's. It will be a change from the softness I've been used to. Anyway, it's time,' she added mysteriously.

A moment later: 'There!' she declared, turning round to display her painted face. 'How will he resist?'

She'd left her lips and cheeks unrouged, but painted first a blue, then a fine black line of *kohl* around her strange pale blue eyes. The effect was extraordinary: intense and glittering, surrounded by the arch of darker blue tattoos beneath each eyebrow which scrolled down around her cheeks and along her strong nose.

Naseem padded back to her own room and pulled on bright

blue breeks and an almost transparent white *kamise*. 'So he will see my flies' footprints,' she explained, smoothing the material over the tattoos circling her big breasts. 'More sexy than jewellery, don't you agree? Now, I think I should go. I want to make sure I am standing in the front row.'

Why was Malia scowling? From her hiding-place behind a rose bush, Helen watched the women shuffle into place. You'd think she'd have been pleased that Naseem had made an effort for once. But she seemed furious, was tugging at Naseem's flimsy sleeve to make her go to the back.

It did no good, though. By the time the Emperor was in sight, Naseem had somehow elbowed her way back to the front again. Then it was just as she'd predicted. Like a dog following a scent, he'd walked straight towards her. Malia had jabbered up at him, trying to interest him in one of the others, and he'd looked around vaguely once or twice to please her. But it was Naseem he wanted, that was clear, and he swept back out of the garden a few minutes later.

Emerging from her hiding-place, Helen stared after him. Soon Naseem would be able to tell her all about him.

A sound behind her made her turn. It was that poor giant, Lungile. Breathing heavily, with his white breeks stuck to his thighs, he seemed to be hurrying after the Emperor.

Helen lay on her back, straining her ears for the sound of Naseem's footsteps. Was she staying out all night? Why were the crickets so loud – as though knowing she was trying to listen? Her sheets felt hot and damp, creased from hours of restlessness. Perhaps she'd come back hours ago, and was fast asleep in her room.

Helen tiptoed outside and stared at Naseem's door, as closed as it had been when she'd first gone to bed, the only locked door in the row of white-curtained openings. The sight of it made her stomach lurch. This was the second night in a row that the Emperor had sent for Naseem.

'Listen out tonight – you'll be able to hear him from here!' she'd called back as she'd run off.

A layer of sweat broke out on Helen's forehead. The candle slipped greasily in her hand. Back in her own room, she lay down again on her side, watching the insects diving into the flame, then sizzling their wings and writhing on the floor. It wasn't fair: just when she was fat enough; just when she thought she might be ready to be presented to him again. Now it was too late.

She dropped her arm over the side of the bed and began squashing the singed insects with her finger. It was as though Naseem had cast a spell on him. No one was ever called back twice in one week. Helen looked at her fingertip, at the sticky smear of white and red, the black legs glued to it. She strained her ears. What if Naseem made him cry out this time? What if he made her his fourth queen?

But Naseem didn't even like him. She'd said so herself, only this morning. She'd been washing her hair at the Bath House, surrounded by some of the young lasses from the journey. 'Oh, the Emperor's too tight-hearted for me,' she'd announced airily, lathering the great tongue of wet hair and piling it on top of her head. 'He's exciting, yes, and clever. But he never opens so you can get to know him.'

Helen had stared at her friend: the Emperor had caressed those big breasts and lain between those strong legs. How confident she'd seemed, with her arms arched up like that to her hair. Like a queen already: brown and graceful, sparkling with diamonds of water.

'How is his heart tight?' someone had asked, and Naseem had looked around at her audience and laughed. 'I've heard people say that he's cold. But I think it's a kind of meanness. You know, if there are two halves of a peach, the Emperor will always take the bigger half. Even if the difference is tiny. Even if there are ten more peaches in the basket.' She bent her head forward so that she could scrub the base of her scalp with her nails.

'But what does he like? How did he touch you?' The lasses had splattered the air with questions until Naseem had held up a soapy hand. 'He can play a woman like a lute,' she'd said at last. 'But when the room's full of her music, he stops and smiles. Because he has won again. Because he has not made a single sound. Tight-hearted, you see?'

'It was fun, though,' she'd grinned. 'I enjoyed this battle with him. I especially enjoyed losing it. And he can laugh, this Emperor. But still, it's not as it should be with a lover, with both of you melting and taking pleasure together. With him it is a fight all the time, to see who will finish last.'

Helen had found she'd been holding her breath. She let it out slowly and began lathering her own hair. Then she stepped down into the bath and blotted out Naseem's voice with a roar of bubbles.

'You know, I'd hate to make an enemy of that man.' Naseem had still been talking when Helen had lifted her head from the water again. 'His hands are too clean.' There'd been a burst of laughter.

'I'm serious. You can't trust a man with nails as clean as that. He's vicious, I tell you!' They'd laughed again, splashing her with water. 'Remember when he had that poor slave-girl beheaded? What's to stop him hurting you?'

But later, when she and Helen had been alone, she'd leant over to whisper in her ear. 'I wasn't telling the whole truth when I said the Emperor was mean,' she'd murmured. They'd been sitting in Naseem's doorway, towelling their hair dry in the sunshine. 'Come inside – I want to show you something,' she'd said, pulling Helen inside and closing the curtain.

Opening her clothes-trunk, she'd burrowed a hand down inside, then placed a purple velvet pouch in Helen's lap. 'I didn't want the others to know, but this is what he gave me this morning. Isn't it beautiful? I can't imagine what it must have cost.'

Tipping out a sapphire necklace, Helen had spread it over her knees. Even she could tell how valuable it was. 'He must have liked you very much.' She'd forced warmth into her voice. 'The stones are exactly the same colour as your eyes. That's why he chose it for you, isn't it?' Her mouth was dry. 'Shall I help you put it on?'

She'd picked up the necklace and waited while Naseem gathered up her great shawl of dark hair so the clasp could be fastened around her slim neck. In the dim light of the curtained room, the sapphires glimmered like dragonfly wings.

'I had a ring once, with a stone in it like this.' Naseem had touched the jewels at her throat. Then, sadly: 'Undo it again, Aziza, will you?

'That's the trouble with this place,' she'd sighed. 'It's so comfortable, you forget you're in a prison.' Returning the necklace to its hiding-place, she'd pulled the curtain open again. 'That's where I should be,' she said, pointing at the misty mountains in the far distance, 'fighting my cheating cousins for my inheritance. Fastening my Chief's Gold around my neck. Not playing sex with a cruel man for trinkets. I can't even wear the silly thing in case someone gets jealous and stirs poison in my *couscous*.'

How could Naseem even think of leaving when she had the chance to be a queen? Helen rolled on to her back and stared at the dark ceiling. The sound of footsteps broke into her thoughts and she leapt up and peered through her curtain. But it was only Malia, scuttling across the courtyard like a brown rat. Did the woman never sleep? How could she wear that great dark cloak in this heat?

She let the curtain drop and wandered over to her water jar, stripping off her muslin night-gown and using a wet cloth to drip tepid water down her back. She imagined the Emperor looking at her. He was sitting right there on the bed, loosening the cord on his breeks. His legs were apart and he was beckoning to her, smiling that teasing smile. Now his hands were pulling up his *jellabiah*, pulling it right up and over his head.

Helen examined the picture in her mind. Would his chest be covered with hair too? And his back? She waited for her usual shudder of disgust – as if a spider had run across her lap. But all she felt was restless, heavy. Naked, she lay back down on the bed. What would it be like to have him pressed against her, to feel her breasts rubbing against all that hair? She breathed in, watching her breasts rise. This ache in her groin, was this the hunger Naseem had been talking about?

If only she'd felt like this when he'd first sent for her. She rolled over and buried her face in her pillows. They should have been her sapphires, not Naseem's. Except they'd have been emeralds, to match her eyes: a perfect string of emeralds, set in gold. What if he never sent for her again? Even though she was fatter now and knew what to do, what if he was still angry with her? What if she never got another chance?

Biting the sheet, Helen groaned aloud. Why did she never think before she did things? How could she have wasted that first opportunity? She thought of Queen Salamatu's empty quarters. If he married Naseem, she'd have all those rooms to herself, and as many jewels and clothes as she liked. If he married Naseem, he'd have four wives again and wouldn't be able to marry anyone else for years. Unless he sent one of the others away. Unless one of them died . . .

She thought of Zara's scaly skin and bare scalp: the Old Queen couldn't hang on much longer, surely? The thought calmed her slightly. Perhaps she'd get her chance after all.

32

Now here we have a sorry pickle! No sooner do I send Lungile off to plight his troth to the Berber besom, than she is selected by the Emperor for his bed.

The poor giant is quite beside himself with anguish, prowling the perimeter of the parched garden and scything at the plants with his hands. I have heard that bull elephants react similarly when thwarted, plucking up entire trees with their trunks and flinging them to the ground. Thus it is with our own Bull Bison. Indeed, the gardeners came to me yesterday in a delegation, begging me to prevent his perambulations (they dare not approach him themselves).

I tried to talk to him, hitching up my *kamise* and scrambling after him through the twiggy terrain. But he would not stop. 'Leave me alone,' growls he, splintering a *syringa*. 'I must cast this pain from my hands or they will smash your little body against the wall.'

So I let him go, though it saddened me to do so. For am I not the orchestrator of this turmoil? Ay, woodwind, strings, brass and percussion, what a sweet symphony of hope did I play for him.

Old Malia has been equally *distraite* by this sudden turn of events. Indeed, the Crone was so unhinged when the Emperor called for the lass a second night that she clenched her fists and impaled her own palm with her horrid claw, snapping the talon right off. 'The *bint*'s a witch,' growled she later, dabbing at the wound with a bloodied kerchief. 'She's cast spells over half of the women, and now she's started on the Emperor too.'

And I must admit that His Majesty seems almost preternaturally mellow at the moment. He sent for me this morning, quite the magnanimous Lord. 'Sit down, Fijil!' cries he, patting the carpet beside him. 'Why have you neglected me so long?'

Though the *muezzin* had already rent the air with the midmorning prayer call, he was still lolling in his crumpled *kamise*, with slaves scurrying like ants to carry off the remains of his breakfast. 'So, Fijil, tell me what you have been doing. For I have missed my little dog. Come, bark something sharp at me.'

Whereupon I find my mouth hanging open in a sloppy cur's smile, as always when he pets me like this, and I am all but rolling on my back for my stomach to be tickled. And I begin to regale him with tales of how the women have been trying to keep cool. Such as the pale Egyptian who bade the gardeners plant her in a shady corner and water her like a giant neep. Or the unfortunate who settled herself down for the midday sleep covered, like some great scaly lizard, with slices of cool red melon, and awoke squealing beneath a blanket of red ants.

'And the *Lalla* Zara?' queries the Emperor, when his mirth has abated. 'How are your investigations progressing?'

But his eyes wander off as soon as I begin elaborating on my investigations. And he interrupts me shortly with a weary 'Well, well, you must do your best,' as though I had just informed him that his tailor had been unable to acquire the silk brocade he had ordered for his waistcoat. By which I understand that the Old Queen has already been assigned to a back room of the Emperor's mind, with all the carriages and clocks he has no use for, where she will in time take on the character of an irritation, taking up space which he would prefer filled with other treasures.

Even if she were to recover her beauty, I think it unlikely he would ever return her to his bed. The disease has continued too long, such that she now has the taint of Death about her. And though she has refused to admit him to her presence, he must suspect the disfigurements she is hiding. Indeed, it seems likely that some malevolent wee cuckoo, with an eye on her nest, has twittered details of her transformation in the Emperor's ear and turned his squeamish heart against her.

'I have been enjoying the new Berber princess,' remarks His Majesty presently, probing his teeth with an ivory pick. 'An interesting woman,' he muses, and flicks a morsel of gristle to the floor. 'I gave her a necklace the first night and she thanked me nicely enough. But when I offered her a bracelet this morning, she refused it. The *bint* claims she isn't interested in jewellery. She'd prefer a horse – can you believe that? It seems her people allow their women to ride, provided they restrict themselves to the mares.' At which my cur's ears prick up with suspicion, for I have not forgotten the foolish dash the besom made for her freedom not three moons ago.

I recount the incident to the Emperor as a warning, but he just chuckles fondly over what he calls 'her hot spirit' and dismisses my anxiety with a flick of the Royal Wrist. 'That was before she met me,' scoffs he. 'What reason could she have to escape now?' Which silences me utterly, for I would hesitate to explain to any man why a woman might seek deliverance from his embraces.

Meanwhile, he is pondering the kind of mount he should pick out for her. 'A bay, perhaps, the colour of her hair? Or something white, like my own stallion? And a blue saddle, of course. You know, Fijil, she has the most amazing blue eyes –' And is impatient suddenly to embark on his selection, clapping for his dressers, who swoop in to preen him for the day. 'I wonder how much it would cost to have a white horse dyed blue?' he ruminates, as they wash and dry him, hopping around his extremities like sparrows, pecking at his fingernails and between his hairy toes.

Perhaps it was the pain of having a bristle plucked from a nostril, but his attention is suddenly diverted away from horseflesh. 'Did you send the scrawny red-hair to Sallee?' he asks suddenly. 'I should have received some kind of grovelling response from the Governor by now.' And fixes me with a suspicious eye.

This flummoxes me mightily, for I'd quite forgotten his instruction to have Helen disposed of. And I start extemporizing wildly on the mishaps which had befallen first the guards I had selected to escort her, then the replacement guards, then the mules, while he gazes at me with his arms folded and one eyebrow quizzically raised.

'You never intended to get rid of her, did you?' he says eventually, when my flare of excuses finally sputters and extinguishes itself. And frowns most severely, so that I am suddenly quaking with fear, for I have seen slaves garrotted for far less. At which point he relents and starts to laugh, throwing back his head and slapping his thigh. 'Oh, Fijil, Fijil! If you could see your face –' wiping his eyes, then leaning forward with curiosity. 'So tell me, what have you done with the *bint*?'

So now I must reignite myself and sputter on some more, about Helen's uncommon aptitude in Arabic, and her skill at dancing, while my poor mind is see-sawing with 'he mustn't send for her' alternating with 'he mustn't send her away'. How relieved I was when he swept off to the stables!

The encounter left me quite agitated, for I fear I may have piqued his interest in the 'scrawny red-hair', despite his new enthusiasm for riding. If I could only rewrite the script of this encounter into something less tantalizing.

What then? What then would Microphilus do? Upturn the logic of his entire life? Topsy-turvy the world so that a king must wait for crumbs from his slave's table? Nay, this will never be. I am the Emperor's taster: no more, no less. And though the taste was sweeter than I could have imagined, Helen shows no inclination to further our togetherness.

Thus I have waited in vain these past four nights with my flagon brimming for her to come again, patting anxious sweat from my oxters and retying my *queue de cheval*. Until midnight comes and I can bear it no longer. When I upend the wine straight into my gullet to numb the pain in my foolish heart.

29 September 1769

It is midday and Batoom has just discovered me: slumped forward from a kneeling position, where perhaps I had been praying, and snoring peacefully with my nose in a dish of sugared almonds. And lifts me up in her big arms, and bathes me like a wean, and tells me gently that Helen has just come to her asking when she can be paraded before the Emperor.

33

It was Batoom who'd suggested she wear white – 'So he will notice you, like a pale moth among all the gaudy butterflies' – and had plaited her wet hair, then brushed it out into a mass of golden tendrils. But when the time came, and they were all craning their necks towards the entrance, panic had surged through Helen's veins and she'd squirmed her way through the forest of slippery silk until she'd reached the very back.

'I don't believe it – you tried to hide?' Naseem clutched her hair in mock exasperation.

'I was so nervous, and the others were all glaring at me.'

'But he saw you anyway?'

'Well, he was looking for *you* really. But Malia told him you were ailing –' But by then he hadn't been listening. Helen hugged her triumph to herself. Because he'd caught a glimpse of her standing alone at the back: plump and copper-haired, dressed all in white. He'd made them all stand aside so he could get to her.

'And he wants you tonight? Oh, Aziza, I'm so excited for you!' Naseem grasped Helen's shoulders and kissed her on both cheeks. 'What are you going to wear? Let me help you get ready.' She flung Helen's trunk open and began pulling things out.

'Don't you mind?' Helen knelt down beside her. 'After last week, I mean.'

'Of course not! I've got my horse, haven't I? That was all I ever wanted from him. And I'll be glad to get some proper sleep for a change.'

Was she joking? Helen looked at her friend. Naseem was smiling, but her eyes were wild and bloodshot.

'You really are sick, aren't you? I thought you were lying this morning. So I'd have a chance with him.'

'I feel much better now, but this morning I couldn't keep anything down. And my mouth still tastes terrible, like rusty nails.' She pulled a face, then smiled again. But she didn't look well. Her skin was dull and dry, and there were brown smudges under her eyes. 'It's just tiredness, I expect. Come on, we've only got a few hours. Which of these are you going to choose?'

'I thought the green one.' Helen held a vivid *kamise* against herself.

'Oh no, Aziza.' Naseem was adamant. 'You need something much darker than that. Something to show off your skin. And your hair. A deep purple, maybe. Or – what's this?' She retrieved a pair of deep red *salwars* from the bottom of the trunk, and a matching *kamise*. 'I've never seen you in these.'

Helen looked at them doubtfully. She'd bought them without realizing how dark the silk was; like plum skin, shot through with a russet sheen. The colour reminded her of kirk vestments and spinsters' frocks. She was about to say as much when Batoom swept into the room and plumped herself down on the divan.

'Ah yes! This is perfect for you!' She pounced on the dark silk.

'I was just saying that I liked the green,' Helen protested weakly.

'No, no. Far too bright.' Batoom snorted her disdain. 'It will be night-time, remember. Your skin will look wonderfully pale against this, and the lamps will adore this coppery shine. It will be marvellous with your hair.'

'That's what I said!' Naseem was laughing. 'And no rouge, yes? She should be pale as a lily. Except on her lips. And her nipples, of course.'

'Of course.'

34

3 October 1769

She is going to him this evening. There, in black and white, it is written. I am not sure how I will endure the long hours until –

Until what? Until he rejects her again? And she is set on a mule bound for Sallee? Until she emerges from his quarters, flushed with love? No, Microphilus, there can be no happy end to this night for you.

I have spent the afternoon with Lungile in the stables, where he has been charged with the sole care of Naseem's mare.

This is the Emperor's latest prank. Having tired, I suppose, of taunting his pet giant with a cornucopia of unbeddable concubines, he has honed the humiliation more precisely by making him slave to a despised female nag. Never mind she is a creature of peerless beauty, having the black legs and face of an Abyssinian cat, fading to a shimmering silver on the body, with snowy plumes for mane and tail. Never mind she is as fleet as the wind, with a pedigree lost in the sands of time. She is still a mare, a lowly mare, and Lungile must groom and feed and water her. She is a mare, and he must shovel her shit – ay, and keep it separate too, in its own special bucket which must be emptied on its own shameful midden, well away from the manly mountain of the stallions' steaming sog-balls.

Worst of all, he must ride her: lope his long legs over (of course they reach almost to the ground) and trot her out to the paddocks where the other grooms are all gathered; feel the sting as his poor scar is stretched, but keep his face straight lest it be reported to the Emperor that the giant was seen to wince.

And there is yet more salt in this wound, for now he is back among whole men once more, billeted with the other grooms in long dormitories where all the talk is of outings to the city whore-houses. Ay, whole men and whole beasts likewise, for the dormitories are situated in the stable buildings, above the serried stalls of a thousand Royal Stallions.

But there has been little sleep for any since the mare arrived. So pent-up with lust are the stallions that the merest whiff of a nanny-goat in heat has their nostrils flaring and their sinews straining at their tethers. I wonder, then, if you can imagine the effect of a mature mare on this lecherous herd? Of course they have stabled her in the very last stall, with ten empty stalls as a bulwark. Still the air is rent by ardent whinnying and the crack of their saucer hooves against the splintering partitions. I swear they are biting chunks out of the doors with their teeth, and the carpenters have been working night and day to contain them.

I cannot describe how all this discomforts Lungile. Wherever he casts his eyes, they are confronted by male members in a state of engorgement. And these are no ponies, but stallions of eighteen hands or more. No wonder he speaks of suicide. Were it not for the date wine he has amassed in the mare's stall (no guard would dream of entering so contemptible a place), which drugs him insensible every evening, he would already have found a way to end his torment.

At least he can be private there, propped against the hay-bales with his wine. We have been side by side in the fragrant bed-straw all afternoon, passing the flagon to and fro, with the mare crunching on her hay and the dust dancing in a shaft of sunshine, the cacophony of crazed stallions like thunder in the distance.

'So, the giant and the dwarf are both cuckolded by the same man,' says he lugubriously after a long silence (they have all been long silences this long afternoon).

'If he likes Helen, you may have your Naseem back again.' This is me now, some half a flagon later. There are already two empty at my feet, rimmed with sozzled ants.

'No. It is finished. I can never approach her now.' He tips his head back and his brown throat engulfs another flagon. 'To be a mare's slave! I cannot even look at her now.' (I'm wondering whether the Emperor has caught an inkling of the giant's love for Naseem. Perhaps not in the front of his mind, but at the back, in its cunning recesses. What if, with the corner of his eye, he has seen the giant watching the Berber princess, glimpsed the depths of devotion in his eyes? How keen that would have made him to bed the *bint*.)

'I have been thinking.' Me again some hours later: maudlin, slumped sideways against my friend. 'I have been thinking I should marry Batoom.'

It is dark now. I do not know what to do with myself.

If she had not come to me that night, if she had not unbuckled the armour I wear around my heart, I would be better able to bear this.

All my thinking life there has been this wee red crab crouched within my chest. I know not how it came there, or when. Perhaps in my cradle, looking up in my innocence for the love that is every wean's due, and finding consternation, revulsion instead. Perhaps then was when my shell first began to form.

The other weans called me 'Mudskipper', for my wee arms and bulbous head, my scrabblings on the mud-flats with my mother. And they all so perfect – the least of them, the ugliest of them – all so graceful and long-limbed, compared with Mudskipper, whose blood-mother had tossed him back into the sea.

A mudskipper has no shell or claws; its entrails spurt on to the sand when it is stepped on. But all the while, deep inside, there was a wee Cancer in the making. Segment by segment, layer by layer, on went the armour around my heart. And so I have been ever since. Until the sight of a blunt thumb on a white pebble unshelled me.

35

The Emperor was sitting on the floor when Malia ushered Helen into his apartment. There was a tray of reddish fruit in front of him.

'The first *durra-ens* of the season,' he announced, waving Malia away. 'Come and taste – Aziza, isn't it? Who chose that name for you? It means "beloved", did you know? Here, sit beside me.' He peeled a swathe of downy red skin away from the fruit to reveal the yellow flesh underneath. 'See how easily it comes away? That means it's perfectly ripe.' He unsheathed a long silver dagger from his belt and sliced a crescent of the flesh. Impaling it delicately on the tip, he held it out towards Helen's mouth.

She flinched away, staring at the blade. 'Don't you trust me, Aziza?' His eyes were mocking. 'Are you afraid I will cut off your nose? But why would I want to do that when it's such a pretty nose, with all these small golden flecks?'

'I'm sorry, my Lord.' She bit into the fruit and sweet juice dribbled down her chin.

'Here, let me –' He leant forward and caught the dribble on his finger. 'You see, perfectly ripe,' he said, holding his finger to her lips.

Helen hesitated and he drew in his breath impatiently. 'I ordered Fijil to send you away,' he said. 'Did he tell you?' She shook her head and licked the juice off hurriedly. 'No, I thought not. You know, I could have had him executed for that. But when I saw you this morning, I was glad he'd disobeyed me. I hope you won't make me change my mind.' He finished the *durra-en* and held his sticky hands out expectantly.

Helen glanced around the room: where were the slaves? He must have sent them away when she'd arrived. Spying a basin of water nearby, she scrambled quickly to her feet to fetch it.

She knelt beside him with her head bowed while he washed. Was it the same basin he'd kicked over when she was here before? She squeezed her eyes shut to block out the memory. He mustn't send her away this time.

'Would you like to bathe properly, my Lord?' she asked cautiously. 'It is such a warm evening, perhaps it would cool you.'

'I see you've learnt some manners at last.' He smiled at her solemnity. 'Yes, Aziza, I would like to bathe. I would like everything. Let's see how well you've been taught.'

He led the way into an adjoining room, where wall-lamps reflected back from three separate mirrors and the tiled floor sloped into a neat gutter. Several pitchers of hot water were waiting ready, along with the usual giant cold-water jars. Kicking off his slippers, the Emperor strode into the centre of the room and held his arms out towards her.

Helen stared at him blankly for a moment, then understood: he was waiting for her to undress him. Kneeling, she took hold of the hem of his *jellabiah*. 'Be quick,' Batoom had warned her, when they'd practised this before. 'It's not dignified for the Emperor to have his head tangled in his clothing.' Pulling the *jellabiah* swiftly up over his head, Helen found herself staring at his naked chest.

The hair there was even thicker than she'd imagined. A sleek pelt of black, almost obscuring the skin, tapering down in a broad 'V' towards his waist. Additional tufts sprouted from his shoulders and upper arms and a strong, smoky scent seeped from thick wads in his armpits. Helen felt she couldn't breathe. Her head seemed a long way from her hands. She watched her fingers untying the knot in his *salwars* and letting them fall to his ankles. He stepped out of them and she knelt to whisk them away.

Dear God, he was naked. A smell of damp leather came from between his long toes. The bones of his ankles were bald as crows' eggs. Fetching the stool for him, she began busying herself with the water, mixing it to the right temperature as she'd been taught.

'So tell me, Aziza –' He was sitting down now, relaxed and elegant with his knees apart and his hands on his long, hairy thighs. 'How are Moorish men different from Christians?'

'In the body, Sir?' Why was he asking? Helen lathered soap in her hands and began working it into the hair on his chest. 'I think the men here are browner and of a more even colour,' she began carefully. Was he playing with her? Trying to trap her into insulting him? 'Where I come from, the men are white on their legs and bellies, where the skin never sees the sun, and red or brown on their arms and faces. And their hair can be of any colour: yellow, brown, red, black. Moorish men all seem to have black hair.'

'Go on.' He closed his eyes and leant his head back so she could reach his neck and beard. His eyelids were smooth; his lashes short and thickly curled. There was a feathering of fine dark hairs on his cheekbones and his scalp was smooth and recently shaved.

'The men here have much more hair than Christians. On the face and the body.'

'I thought as much.' He seemed pleased. 'And is it true that some of your men cannot even grow a beard?'

'Yes, my Lord. Men with fair hair often shave their chins because they don't have enough hair for a proper beard. Though I don't think a Christian would ever shave his head.'

She was soaping his head now, and behind his neat ears. 'And Moorish men are cleaner, I think, because of washing for prayers. Where I come from, even rich men only bathe properly once a week – before going to worship. But of course it's much colder there, so people don't like taking off their clothes.'

'How disgusting!' He leant forwards for her to wash his back. 'Common sparrows clean themselves more often than that. How do their wives stomach it? And is it true that the penises of Christian men stink, because they don't remove the covering of skin, and that they rot eventually because of the filth that gathers underneath it?'

Blushing, Helen moved around to wash his arms. 'Some have diseases there, my Lord. But I don't know the cause.' So that was why his thing was so raw-looking: he must have had the skin removed. He raised his arms automatically, one after the other, like a child, for her to lather his armpits. How bare his flanks seemed as she moved her hands down them, smooth brown sand-banks in the tide of black hair.

'I suppose that's why their penises are so small,' he remarked. 'The skin must prevent them from growing properly.' Standing up, he put his foot on the stool for her to reach his groin. When Helen bent to pick up the soap, her hands were trembling. Just do it, she ordered herself. He's been washed like this a thousand times. Reaching between his legs, she tried to remember what Batoom had said about his egg-sac: 'Be careful not to squeeze it, but be firm or you'll tickle.' She soaped the sac gently, feeling the two eggs jostling inside. She'd never been this close to a man before. Just like a ram, she thought, fascinated: a ram or a dog.

'That must be why Christians don't bother hiding their women,' he went on, shifting his feet slightly and raising one buttock, so she could get at his hole more easily.

'I'm sorry, my Lord?' Sweat trickled from her armpits: she

was washing the Emperor's hole! How like an animal he was, with all this hair. Even his buttocks were covered with it.

'If the skin's not removed, the penis can't expand properly. So the men can't get so excited.'

'I don't understand –'

'If the men can't become excited, the women are not in such danger from them. It's true, isn't it, that there are no walls around your houses? That a man can just look through the window at his friend's wives and daughters?'

Helen giggled suddenly, imagining folk gathered round the cottage window at home, trying to catch a glimpse of Meg in her night-gown.

'Have I said something amusing?' There was a note of anger in his voice.

'I'm sorry, my Lord,' she said hurriedly. 'Where I come from men only have one wife.' She began lathering the thatch of wiry hair around his red thing, cupping it gently in one hand. It thickened as she washed it, growing heavier and warmer. Did the skin really make Christians' things smaller?

'That's what I mean. They only need one wife because they are less virile.' Helen felt breathless. It was stiffening and rising out of her hands. Her lungs seemed to fill with fluttering moths. 'In Morocco the women must be kept hidden, otherwise the men cannot control themselves. See how you excite me?' It twitched, and she gasped and let it go.

Laughing, he sat down again, forcing her to kneel to soap his thighs. His thing was at eye level now: red, veined with purple, smeared with soap. Was he really going to put it inside her? Her heart thudded in her chest as she busied herself with his feet, massaging and pulling the toes as she'd been taught.

Standing up, she began mixing water in a pitcher to rinse him. 'Shall I –?' She wasn't sure how to deal with his soapy head: it seemed disrespectful to tip water over his face. His eyes mocked her for a moment, then he dropped his head forward between his knees. When she'd finished, he stood up for her to rinse the soap off the rest of him. Filling the pitcher again and again, she sluiced his body until he gleamed like a horse in the rain, black hair slick in the lamplight, water dripping from the tufts in his armpits and groin.

'When it's hot like this I let the air dry me,' he said, grabbing a large cloth from her arm and wrapping it around his waist. Then, smiling: 'I'm afraid you've wet your *kamise*.'

Helen looked down. The red silk was plastered to her breasts like damson skin. 'Now it's my turn, I think,' he said, reaching for her buttons. 'Let me remind myself how pale-skin women are different from our African ones.'

Taking her hand, he led her out of the washroom and sat her down on a carpet beside a lamp. 'First there is this wonderful hair.' He knelt beside her and lifted it towards the light. 'So fine, with so many different colours with in it. They say my grandmother had hair like this when she was young, but she'd seen so many horrors by the time my father was born that it turned pure white –

'And there's this pale skin, of course, which burns in the sun. If I remember rightly, it shows every mark.' He turned her arm over so its soft underside was towards him, then scratched it deliberately with his fingernail. Helen bit her lips to suppress a cry of pain, then watched the white line darken into an angry red weal. Didn't he care if he hurt her?

'And this pretty mouth, like a child's. So small, with its thin lips, so different from the mouths of our women. And so pink –' running a finger along her lips. 'Everything, so pink. Under the nails, inside the ears.' Helen shivered as he gathered her hair up so he could examine her ears.

'All this sweet pinkness,' he murmured, peeling away her wet *kamise* and dropping it on the floor. 'African women are more brownish here.' He caressed a nipple with one hand as though demonstrating something to a class of pupils, teasing it until it puckered. Then the other, making them tingle and ache. Helen tried to breathe normally, to stop her breasts rising and falling under his hand. A horse was galloping in her chest. Was he mocking her? A surge of shame brought blood flooding to her cheeks.

'Ah-h,' the Emperor sighed, and there was real pleasure in the sound. 'I'd forgotten about this, this sudden redness in the face. You cannot see this so clearly with our women. Salamatu used to colour like this too, when she was uncomfortable, or trying to lie to me.' He shook his head. 'She could never deceive me, my Salamatu. Her skin would always betray her.' He touched Helen's cheek, very gently, with his forefinger. 'I wonder if you will be the same.'

A moment later he was on his feet, clapping his hands. The room was suddenly full of people: slave-girls removing the washing things and setting out low tables of food; and the band of fat eunuchs who'd performed so often in the Harem. Turning her back, Helen grabbed her wet *kamise* and held it against her bare breasts.

'What are you doing?' He was laughing at her again, tugging the *kamise* firmly out of her hands. 'Do you think you're the first woman they've ever seen with me?'

'No, my Lord.' She felt herself blushing again. How stupid she was being. This was her one chance to please him: she mustn't let coyness get in the way. Taking a deep breath, she shook her hair back from her face: 'Would you like me to dance for you, Lord?' she asked demurely as the musicians began tuning their instruments.

'Thank you, Aziza. I can think of nothing I'd like better.' He bowed politely, but his eyes were full of amusement.

Feeling naked and exposed without her *kamise*, Helen found

the two red chiffon scarves Batoom had lent her for this purpose, and retreated into a dark corner to tie them around her upper arms. Then she loosened her breeks and tied them low on her hips in the usual way, not daring to look up in case she met someone's eyes. But when she turned round, no one was looking at her. There was no sign of the Emperor and the slaves had melted away, leaving a small banquet of trays and bowls. Only the musicians remained, talking to one another in low voices.

Ignoring her, they started to play. What had Batoom said? 'If you feel embarrassed, just keep your eyes shut. It will help you move to the music. Imagine you are in the sea.' Helen closed her eyes and started to dance, rotating her hips as she'd been taught, snaking her arms so the scarves slithered around her body. She was a mermaid with a tail of red silk, and water flowing softly over her skin.

The music changed and she opened her eyes. The Emperor was lounging on a divan, surveying her appraisingly. 'Come here,' he said, beckoning with a brown finger. 'Why are you hiding all this beauty in the shadows?' He'd put on a fresh white *jellabiah* and *salwars* and his beard was freshly combed. Helen walked towards him, aware of his eyes on her body. 'Good. Now, start again. Here in the light where I can see you.'

Feeling silly and clumsy, she began swaying again: nervously at first, then more confidently as her body began moulding itself to the rhythms she'd practised so often. She knew she should be smiling at him, teasing and inviting, as Batoom had taught her. But she couldn't bring herself to look at him, at those mocking black eyes, and found herself staring down at her own body instead. How huge she was now, and how pale. She watched the scarves lick her skin like dark tongues. Her belly juddered as she moved; her arse swayed heavily from side to side.

'I didn't know pale-skinned women could dance.' He sounded surprised. 'Salamatu never could get the knack, though she did try, poor dear.' He chuckled sadly. 'But why so shy, Aziza? What are you ashamed of?' The mocking tone was back, but when she looked up his eyes were gentle.

'I'm not used to your ways, my Lord. Where I come from a woman would never dance for a man dressed like this.' She made an awkward gesture towards her nudity. 'In Scotland men and women dance together, in a crowd. Never alone.'

'But you can't appreciate a woman's beauty properly if you are dancing with her. And if she excites you, what can you do if you are in a c owd? I don't understand your men.' He snorted his contempt. 'Don't they want to play sex with their women?'

Dismissing the musicians with a wave, he stood up. 'Come.' He took her hand and led her to a large mirror on the opposite wall. 'Look at yourself, Aziza. This is nothing to be shy about.'

He stood behind her and began untying her scarves. They slid silently to the floor and his hands moved to the sash on her silk breeks. Feeling the waistband loosen, Helen clutched at it with her hands, but he uncurled her fingers, one by one, until the breeks collapsed with a whisper around her ankles. She was naked: she could feel sweat drying behind her knees and beneath her buttocks. She hung her head in shame.

'See how lovely you are.' The Emperor lifted her chin with his hand, forcing her to look at her reflection. 'This pale throat, and these little round breasts.' She could see his dark face behind her in the mirror, the white stripe in his beard, the white teeth glinting in the lamplight. 'I prefer big breasts, but they don't have the firmness of these pretty round ones.' He cupped them in his palms. 'And this belly here –' grasping it like bread dough – 'with a navel so deep your finger disappears up to the second knuckle.'

Helen tried to breathe normally. 'In my country a woman is supposed to be much thinner than this, and to have a narrow waist.' Her voice sounded small and tight.

'But why? A man wants to feel softness when he presses himself against a woman.' She could feel his erect penis through his breeks. He was pressing it against her arse, moving his hips from side to side and bending his knees until it was nestled in the crack between the cheeks. 'A woman should envelop a man. Her flesh should yield to him, welcome him,' he murmured, pushing rhythmically up against her.

Was this really happening? Helen stared at herself in the mirror: at her fat pale thighs pressed together, almost concealing the shocking white triangle where her pubic hair used to be; her crack, bald as a bairn's. His dark fingers were splayed on her belly, pressing into the white flesh, pulling her back against him.

'And there must be nothing to impede him.' She felt his knees nudging the backs of her legs, forcing them apart; saw her thighs parting in the mirror, her knees bending; felt the sudden coldness of air between her legs. A sob of shame shook her body at the sight of herself: a mass of sagging helpless flesh in his hands.

He pressed harder on her belly, tilting her pelvis up towards the mirror: 'See, the pink is here too, in your secret parts.' Helen stared at her pleats of pink flesh and hot tears stung her eyes. He was hurting her, holding her like this. How had she turned into that fat creature in the mirror? How could she allow him to shame her like this?

Squirming violently out of his grasp, Helen wheeled round angrily to face him.

'So there is some fire left, after all.' He stepped back, raising his hands in mock surrender. 'I'm glad they haven't tamed you completely.'

Helen knocked tears from her eyes with the back of her hand. 'The men at home would never treat a woman like that,' she retorted, chest heaving.

'So, how do they treat their women, your wonderful, passionate men?' He was smiling again, that infuriating smile.

Forgetting her nudity, Helen squared her shoulders and raised her chin. 'In my country a man is polite to the woman he likes. If he wants to – to –' she hesitated, searching for an alternative to 'play sex' – 'to be with a woman, he goes to her house and invites her to walk with him. He would never order her to come to his room. Only street-women are treated like that.'

'And if she refuses?'

'Then he knows she doesn't want him.'

'And if she agrees?'

'Then he knows she wants to spend time with him. But even then, a man would never expect a woman to – to – play sex straight away. He'd wait until she was ready.'

'Until *she* was ready?' He laughed aloud.

'Otherwise he'd have to force her and she'd start to hate him.'

'Are you telling me that my women hate me?' He was smiling still, but there was a glint of something else there, something dangerous; a cat stalking.

'No, no, of course not,' she said hastily. 'They all adore you, but –'

'But?'

'But if a woman can't refuse a man, how can he be sure that she wants him?'

'Do you want to refuse me, Aziza? Is that what you're saying?' He spoke stiffly, coldly.

'No, my Lord.' She fell to her knees and kissed his feet. Oh no, what had she said? Was he going to send her away again?

The thought filled her with panic. She thought of Naseem's necklace, of Queen Salamatu's quiet, empty courtyard.

'So you do want to play sex with the Emperor, is that right?'

'Yes, my Lord.' She stayed bent over his feet, grateful for her curtain of hair.

'But how can I tell whether you're telling the truth?' He was taunting her now: she could imagine the curl of his lips as he looked down at her. Her mind raced: how could she mollify him? What had Batoom said? If your pouch is not wet, use saliva to make him think you desire him. Under cover of her hair, Helen brought two fingers to her mouth and silently dribbled saliva on to them. But when she reached back to smear it between her legs, she found she was slippery as egg-white already. The discovery brought a fresh blush of shame to her cheeks: what kind of woman had she become?

'Answer me!'

Stung by the anger in his voice, Helen scrambled to her feet. Her blush deepened. She couldn't look at him. Instead she slipped her fingers swiftly between her legs and held them out silently towards him. They glistened in the lamplight.

'So –' The word was a sigh, a moan almost, of satisfaction. He lifted her chin again, forcing her to look up at him. 'This is how a real man knows he is loved,' he said with a note of triumph in his voice.

Helen stared into his eyes. They were smiling again. There was a tiny brown mole high up on his cheek. Was he going to kiss her now, or slap her face? Either seemed equally possible. Her chest felt tight: she could feel stickiness where her thighs rubbed together.

'Come,' he said abruptly, leading her across the courtyard to the white-curtained room opposite.

★

Nothing Batoom had taught her had prepared Helen for the hour that followed. 'At the top, the man's penis is very delicate, so you must keep everything wet or you will hurt him,' the Black Queen had instructed. But she hadn't said the Emperor would treat her body like a pot of ink, dipping his fingers whenever he wanted more wetness. And then make her smell his hands, and lick them, and laugh when she wrinkled her nose and tried to turn her face away. Or that he'd dribble scented oil into the crease between her arse-cheeks, and make her kneel on all fours while he rubbed against her like a dog.

'Remember, he assumes you're a virgin,' Batoom had warned, and had taught her which muscles to clench to make her pouch tighter. But she hadn't said how that clenching would make her feel, when his fingers were inside her and his thumb outside, when he moved them quickly like that, sitting beside her and watching her face. She hadn't said how hard it would be to breathe; or told her what expression she should wear on her face. Or described the shameful sounds they made, these caresses, like a lamb suckling, or bare feet slurping through kailyard mud.

And where should she look while he was doing these things? At his face, with that gentle, mocking smile? At his thing, thick and gleaming, twitching in time with his movements? Should she be touching him too?

'Move your hips,' Batoom had said. 'So he thinks you're excited. But not too much or you'll make him angry.' Was this too much? Helen found she was pressing herself against his hand as he caressed her, as though she was still dancing; then against the mattress when he rolled her on to her belly.

'And never mount him like a horse.' But what if he sat on the divan and made her stand facing him? What if he forced her legs apart with his knees and grabbed her arse? And lay back on his pillows with his eyes closed, and pulled her forwards, until she was on top of his thing, sliding forwards along it, until just the red mushroom tip showed. And pushed her backwards along it again, until it re-emerged: the whole slimy length of it, with its knots of purple veins, as though it was growing from her own bald white crack. And urged her forwards again, burying his hard fingers into her arse, digging his clean nails into her skin.

She started moving by herself, watching it appear, red and glistening, in front of her; then disappear again beneath her, sliding slyly as a tongue against her secret parts. Her thighs were clamped either side of his body, two great triangles of marbled flesh, dimpling and puckering as she moved. She was glued to him with some shameful mix of sweat and slime. His brown belly was smeary with the stuff; its black hairs matted and shining. Where was it coming from, all this wetness? Were other women like this?

'Here is the pinkness again, spreading like sunset on the sea.' His voice startled her and she stopped moving. She looked at his face: the mocking smile was gone and had been replaced by a look she couldn't identify. 'On the neck, and over the breasts –' Helen looked down in astonishment at the red mottling on her skin.

'How fascinating it is, this pale skin,' he said. 'Like the roll-tail lizard's, which changes colour when its mood changes. Salamatu used to colour like this too, when she was excited.' His smile was full of sadness and affection. 'I could always tell how much she wanted me by this pinkness on her skin.'

It was a different man Helen was looking at now. His face seemed smoother, younger, as though some vague worry had gone. 'When she was near her release, it covered her neck too, and her shoulders at the back.'

Helen lowered her eyes. Was that what the pink blotches meant? She felt she was melting, like wax around a wick;

aching and itching at the same time. She wanted to move again, to ease her discomfort. Pressing down on him slightly, she felt his thing twitch in response. 'Does it feel good, Aziza?' he asked softly and Helen nodded, shaking her hair forward like a veil to hide her face. 'Do you want it inside you?'

She nodded again, tilting her hips instinctively to let him enter her, then pushing back against him with a sigh of relief. His own groan of pleasure sent a shock of sensation up her spine. She found she was moving again, but pressing down harder. The feelings were different with it inside her: vaguer and less intense. But he grabbed her arse again and began pushing against her too, making the feelings stronger and more urgent.

Forgetting where she was, Helen leant forward greedily inside her tent of copper hair. All her senses focused on the knot of pleasure in her crotch: worrying at it, trying to untie it. She pushed her pelvis down on him, harder and harder, digging her nails into his shoulders and sobbing with frustration. Then it happened, the feeling she was fighting for: the burst of pleasure as the knot gave, the sweet ripples as it unravelled at last. And she was aware suddenly of his dark body bucking beneath her, and her head filled with the roar of his voice.

Dawn was breaking when Malia arrived to walk Helen back to the Harem. The old witch was saying something about goats' milk, about how good it was with honey for young babies. But Helen wasn't listening. She was savouring the slight soreness between her legs, the slight tingling of her teats where his beard had rasped her.

'So, my Aziza,' he'd said with a smile. 'Shall I invite you, like a proper Christian, to go walking?' He took her hand and bowed over it. 'Would you do me the honour of meeting me this afternoon in my garden?'

'It will be my pleasure, my Lord,' she replied with a curtsey.

'And the night after?' He kissed her wrist and the soft skin inside her elbow. 'And the night after that,' pulling the red silk aside and nuzzling her shoulder. 'And the night after that,' fingering the buttons open again, 'until I have run out of places to kiss you?'

'And then what?' She smiled down at his bent head.

'And then – with your kind permission, of course – I shall begin again.'

36

8 October 1769

I saw Helen, but she didn't see me.

I was waiting in her courtyard. I do not know why. Perhaps I wanted to see for myself whether the rumours were true: that the *Lalla* Aziza (already this is how the women are addressing her) has grown yet more beautiful since she has been with the Emperor; that the Emperor's milk has brought a soft sheen to her skin; that she is plumper, rosier, brighter than ever before, and her face brims over with joy.

One glimpse told me that all the rumours are true.

I think I intended saying something, though I cannot imagine what that something might have been. 'Do you still have my pebble?' What would she want with it now?

Part III

37

'Tell me, Aziza,' said the Emperor lazily. 'How did you come here?'

He was lying on the divan in the ironed-out, deep-breathing, splayed minutes after love; his skin was gleaming, his chest hair matted with sweat. Helen was moulded along his flank, beneath his arm, drowsy as a sun-warmed cat, breathing his sharp liquorice smell.

'It seems so long ago,' she began. 'My ship was captured by pirates and taken into Sallee.' She was watching his chest rising and falling, the little brown teats barely visible in the pelt of black hair. She wanted to worm her nose in there and suckle like a kitten. 'I was travelling to the Colonies –'

'Alone?' The arm around her stiffened.

Helen's mind jolted awake, a hare with its ears up. Of course: a Mohammedan woman would never travel without a male relative. It would be like admitting she was a whore. She stretched and pressed against the Emperor, playing for time, while the hare raced around inside her skull. She dared not tell him the truth. Every part of her story – her sudden flight from Muthill, taking up with Betty and Dougie, sleeping in a hammock amidst a hundred strange men – all trumpeted she wasn't a virgin.

'My father –' she blurted. 'I was with my father. We had a little room – a – a room each,' she added, unsure whether it was permitted for a father to share with his daughter. 'Away from the other passengers.' Feeling a blush sting her cheeks, she began teasing out the damp tangles on his chest with her fingers.

'Your father.' His voice was mild. She closed her eyes as in prayer and moved her hand lower: she'd heard him speak in this tone before. It meant he was controlling himself; deciding whether to be angry. 'So. Who is this father of yours?'

'A laird, my Lord. Someone who owns land that other men farm. When my mother died, he sold his land and –' He was raising himself up on one elbow, rolling her away from him, back on to the pillow.

'And what happened to this father?' Still that dangerous, calm tone. The hare froze in the gun's sights. Had he guessed she'd been spoilt? Had she forgotten to tighten herself when they were playing sex just now? She tried to think. She'd been so hungry for him . . . What would he do if he found out?

'He was killed, my Lord. By the pirates. They –' The dead puppet of Robert Baird jumped into her mind: the tatters of shirt dangling from his empty rib-cage. 'He tried to protect me and they –' Could he feel her heart pounding? 'They sliced off his hair, then tied him to the mast for the gulls. They were going to kill me too, but their Chief stopped them and – and locked me up with the other *bints*.' She tried to breathe normally. Blood pounded at the base of her throat. He was disentangling his arm and sitting up.

'Why do you lie to me, Aziza?' He was smiling down at her, but his eyes were hard. 'Do you think I am blind that I won't notice this pink in your cheeks?'

Her hand flew to her blazing face, then down to wrench the damp bed-sheet up to cover her breasts. It was all over: he'd discover everything now.

'I'm sorry, my Lord. Forgive me.' How could he have changed so quickly? Ten minutes ago he was drinking her, moaning relief into her open mouth, like a traveller come home after years abroad. Now he was a stranger: face closed, lips tight.

'So. Now tell me the truth. This father –' That calm voice, like a threat. 'He was not some mighty laird, was he?'

'No, my Lord.' Why was he harping on about her father? Helen clutched the crumpled bed-sheet closer. The thuds of her heart shook her whole body.

'There was no land, was there?'

'No, my Lord. Just the house and the forge. He was a blacksmith.'

'Look at me, Aziza.'

Was he going to hit her? She tensed her shoulders and raised her eyes warily. He was still smiling, but it was a different smile now: tender, exasperated. 'Oh, my foolish Aziza. Do you think I care if your father was a poor man?'

He thought she'd been lying about her father! A great sob of relief doubled her over like a belly-punch. 'I was afraid it would turn you against me.'

'You see?' He caught a tear on his finger and brought it to his lips. 'You can never deceive me. Your pretty cheeks will always betray you. Poor Aziza, let this be a lesson.' Now he was sighing and laughing at the same time, tugging the sheet away, rolling her on top of him. 'There is no escape. Your body will always be faithful to me, even when your lips lie.'

Squeezing her eyes closed, Helen breathed a prayer of thanks. She'd been so close to confessing everything. She cursed her thoughtless tongue. What if she'd blurted out about why she'd left home? About John Bayne and the baby? All of a sudden she was exhausted. She felt like the hull of a fishing-boat after a long storm, beached at last above the high-tide mark.

But the exchange had left him exultant. He was teasing suddenly, full of affection. 'Come, let's wash and get dressed. I want to show you something.'

*

He took her to the Jewel Room. She'd heard the other women talking about it, but none, she thought, had ever seen inside. There was a shop in Perth the lassies talked of at home, where customers were served in a brocade parlour, one by one like guests, and jewels were brought out with the shortbread on trays. She'd dreamed of one day being bowed into that shop on the arm of a gentleman. But that was mean stuff compared to this.

Behind them, the guards locked the great doors. The room was silent, cushioned by pouches of kid leather and velvet that crowded the shelves like roosting owls; the silk-padded boxes and trunks herded against the walls, crammed with glistening intestines, a thousand, thousand kings' ransoms.

'Let me see. What would suit you best? Something amber, to match your curls. Or green, for your eyes. Or turquoise. Sometimes when the sun catches them, they look almost turquoise. But the turquoise has no depth, so perhaps –'

A plain purple carpet had been unrolled across the floor. Sunlight sliced in through the window bars and lay like white swords across it. Signalling Helen to kneel, the Emperor began tipping necklaces out on to the carpet in front of her: slowly, one after another, a rain of sparkling entrails. Soon the room was full of rainbow shards as the light shattered on the cut surfaces of the stones. Helen could feel them playing across her face as she gazed downward.

'So, Aziza likes jewels.' She started guiltily. Was it that obvious? Her urge to gather them all into her lap, the whole glorious, glittering heap; to dangle and trickle them through her fingers; sniff them, lick them; feel them cool and heavy on her skin?

But he seemed pleased. 'Aren't you going to try them on? Go on, choose something. Anything. There's a mirror over there.'

She reached out a tentative hand and began spreading the heap out on the carpet. The necklaces were warm where the sun had touched them, but cold as river pebbles underneath. Inlaid in gold or silver were rubies, sapphires, amethysts and a myriad other gems she couldn't name: yellows and purples; pinks and glowing russets. And emeralds, of course: cut and uncut, every shade, every size.

She knew immediately which one she wanted: a double row of big green stones in a heavy gold setting. But she tried on three or four others as well, pretending she couldn't decide. She wanted to stay there forever, dipping her hands in the cool jewels and trailing them across her skin like a princess in an enchanted tower.

It was better than sex: bending her head and pulling apart the heavy curtain of her hair; feeling the air on her white nape; his knowing fingers on the clasps; the long caress of rippled stones at her throat. At her neck, wrists and ankles, where her blue veins snaked close to the surface, she ached for the touch of cool stones. Desire – for them, for him – was rising out of her like smoke. He was breathing it in, turning her towards him. Outside, the clink of spurs as the guards fidgeted in the hallway. Inside, his minty tongue; the sweet pain as he spread her on the hard jewels.

Later, back in his quarters, after he'd washed again and gone off to do whatever he did during the day, and the slaves had finished fussing with the water and linens, Helen took out the necklace and laid it out on the new bed-sheet.

Her own emeralds. She touched each stone: bigger, every one, than the largest of Naseem's sapphires; altogether far heavier than Microphilus's puny pigeon egg. She lifted them and clasped them around her neck, then walked over to one of the great gold-framed mirrors in the washroom. Oh, yes.

The sweet weight of them, lifting her chin and twisting side-ways to make them catch the light.

Energy sizzled through her. She'd have to get some new clothes to wear with them. Batoom had said there was a special payment for every night with the Emperor. Well, there had been five in a row already. She'd have to find Microphilus and ask for what she was owed.

When was market day? She'd lost track of the rhythms of the Harem, had been living a separate existence ever since he'd first sent for her: awake by night, asleep by day. The Emperor's chamber, with its carved archways and snowy sheets, had become her whole world. She'd lain awake for hours beside him – too excited to sleep, too afraid of waking him to move – and had just gazed around the room: at the perfumed oil-lamps, turned down and glowing faintly in the darkness; the plumes of soot the slaves wiped off the walls every morning; the night-time fruit bowls, dewed with cool water; his white gowns and her silks tangled together on the floor; the shush of slippers as the tasters and guards shifted outside the carved doors.

There was a quiet knock on the chamber door: Malia, come to escort her back to her room. Helen scowled. Why did she always have to wait for that old hag, trail behind her through the ogling courtyards, as though she were a child who couldn't be trusted to find her own way? But she knew why. It was to make sure she was gone by the time the Emperor came back for his afternoon sleep. So he could send for a different woman if he wanted one.

Reaching up beneath her hair to unclasp the necklace, Helen hesitated. Why should she hide it in her pocket like a common thief? She shrugged her hair back from her shoulders. She'd give them something to look at. Let them all see how much he loved her.

*

'You know, you should be more careful.' Naseem was sitting in Helen's room, her long legs folded beneath her on the rug. 'They're all talking about the gifts the Emperor is showering upon the *Lalla* Aziza. Your one necklace has already grown into a whole chest of treasures in their minds. They are saying you are going to have a special guard to watch your room at night –

'No, don't laugh. It's serious. Haven't you noticed how they stare at you, some of them? With those slitty eyes, like daggers. It's bad enough that you are going to him every night.'

'Oh, they've always stared at me.' Helen was combing her hair. 'First it was because of my pale skin; then because of Fijil and Batoom. If I hadn't been wearing the necklace, they'd have been blethering about what I had hidden in the bottom of my clothes-trunk.'

Naseem shrugged. 'Is Reema being careful about your food? And what about your hair?' She picked up an amber strand and wound it around her forefinger. 'If I was a jealous sort of woman, think of the mischief I could do with this.'

Helen put her comb down. 'You're not, are you? Jealous, I mean. I assumed, after what you said – I mean, you seemed so –'

'Not me, you silly nanny-goat. I don't care if he never looks at me again. In fact I'd prefer it that way,' she added with a sideways smile. 'Then I could get on with my life in peace again.'

Helen stared at her friend. 'What have you been up to?' Naseem's cheeks were flushed and her eyes had that same reckless glitter she'd noticed the previous week. She seemed thinner, too, as though whatever secret she had was burning her up from the inside.

'Promise on your mother's grave that you won't breathe a word.' Naseem gripped her hand. 'You know that big eunuch, the one who beat me?'

'Lungile?'

'The Emperor has put him in charge of Naseem's horse.' She paused and squeezed Helen's hand harder. 'Well, Naseem has put him in charge of Naseem!'

Naseem and the giant? Helen felt disoriented; her world tilted slightly on its axis. Why would Naseem be interested in a eunuch?

'How long has this been going on?' she asked.

'Just a few days. But it's so *strong*, Aziza. I have never felt like this before; with a man or a woman. It's like he is inside my skin, in the vessels that take my blood around my body. When I look in his eyes I see my mother, my father. I see my people – myself as I used to be –' there were tears in the blue eyes – 'before I was locked up in this chicken-coop,' she hissed through her teeth.

'My spirit was dying, Aziza. My body was getting soft; my mind like a cushion. Every day: all the food we need, slaves to do our chores, nothing to think about except the market and the baths; how we look, what we eat; who is playing sex, who is quarrelling. Lungile reminds me there is another way to be a woman.'

'But where do you –?'

'In the garden. In the middle of the day, when everyone is asleep. He brings the mare from the stables for me to ride, and we find somewhere in the woods to be alone.'

'Fijil told me he was in love with someone.'

'He said it was because I was so quiet when he was beating me. He said any other woman would have burst his ears with her screaming. But he thought I wouldn't want him because he's been cut.'

Helen thought of his huge thing hanging, of the scar behind like a woman's crack. 'Don't you mind?'

'What? That he can't stick his tent-pole into me? That he

has no excuse to flop on top of me like a heap of goatskins? That he has to find other ways of giving me pleasure?' Naseem laughed.

'But he's so –' What? Huge. Brown. Sharp-toothed. Penniless. 'I mean, compared with the Emperor –'

'Compared with the Emperor, he's honest and generous. And he loves me, Aziza. Me. Not just my blue eyes and long hair. My *beauty* –' She almost spat the word, then shivered suddenly. 'Someone is walking on my grave,' she said, rubbing her arms.

Helen noticed how dull Naseem's skin was; she seemed pale, feverish. 'Are you feeling all right? You don't look well,' she said. 'Maybe you should ask Malia if there's something she can give you.'

'It's this place. It makes me restless. You know, there are mountains where he comes from, too. His people hunt up there and herd cattle in the valleys. I told him about my home, about the summer snow on the upper slopes; the black eagles; the *djinns* of the high caves.'

Helen had a sudden vision of the Ochil Hills and the Grampians of home, grazed with purple heather in the summer months, crackling brown with bracken in the autumn. The piping of the curlews; the clack of the stone-chats on the gorse. It was months since she'd thought of her home, months since she'd lifted her mind beyond the walls of the Harem. She didn't even know what the Palace itself looked like, wasn't even curious, hadn't bothered to try glimpsing along the corridor the Emperor walked down when he left her each morning.

Thinking of the outside world made Helen feed edgy, like being reminded of an important chore she'd forgotten. How long had she been here? Three months? Four? She'd lost count of the time. 'Look at these,' she said suddenly, to change the subject. 'I bought them yesterday at the market.' She took out a heap of new silks and flung them on her divan. 'They're from the Jewish trader. You know, the one with the little stall at the end. I could never afford her things before. But Fijil gave me so much money yesterday.' She was gabbling, scrambling back to safe ground. 'I thought I'd have to ask him for it, but he just knocked on my door and handed it over. He called me "*Lalla* Aziza".' She giggled. 'He was joking, of course.'

'It's not funny, Aziza. It's no joke to be loved by an Emperor.'

'But he doesn't love me.' She was fishing now. She wanted to hear Naseem say it again.

'Of course he loves you. They say he's not been like this with anyone since *Lalla* Zara arrived ten years ago. You are envied by every woman in the Harem.'

'Except you.' Helen smiled, then frowned as Naseem shivered again. 'I wish you'd go to Malia,' she said worriedly. 'I'll come with you if you like.'

'Don't worry about me. It's you who should take care. There is nothing wrong with me that won't be cured by a gallop in the mountains.'

After she'd gone, Helen went through the silks she'd bought again, spreading them across her bed. Each one she shook out hung in the air and floated down like gossamer. She'd bought seven different outfits, one for every day of the week. And matching slippers; softest leather, embroidered with gold thread. Next week, if he kept sending for her, she could buy more. And maybe a fine carpet, like Fijil's. Deep in the pit of her belly something shivered with hunger.

She thought of the purple carpet in the Jewel Room; the slimy stain they'd left there for the slaves to clean up; of his long fingers on her, in her. Dear God, the feeling was starting again. The itch and ache between her legs. If only he would send for her now. If only she could run to him now, through the cloisters and courtyards; push open the great double doors that led from his quarters to the rest of the Palace.

She imagined him sitting in a huge room beneath a lofty ceiling encrusted with gold leaf. There were ranks of benches in front of him, like in a grand kirk, though folk probably wouldn't dare sit before the Emperor. Carpets, then, instead of benches, with people bowing and kneeling before him. Acres and acres of them, bearing gold, frankincense and myrrh, the Magi multiplied a thousand times. She pictured herself there beside him on a matching throne: he in white, she in Royal Green bedecked with emeralds.

She riffled through the three green gowns she'd bought, choosing the one she'd wear. Then took out her emeralds and laid them on the whispering silk. She imagined the crowds gasping at the sight of her: the Empress with the translucent pale skin and hair of fire: Aziza, the Emperor's beloved.

Then she remembered that the queens in this country didn't rule alongside their king; they had to be content with the hidden grandeur of the Harem. But perhaps, when she knew him better, he'd take her outside the Harem into the main Palace. Late at night, maybe, when there were fewer people around. If she wore her *haik* –

Reema appeared with lunch. 'I used *Lalla* Batoom's kitchen, so there's no danger of poison,' she said shortly, eyeing Helen's purchases. 'And I've asked one of the eunuchs to fix a new lock to this door.'

She looked critically around the room. 'It would be safer if you combed your hair in here from now on. I'll wash it here too, instead of in the Bath House with the other women. Then I can be sure. And you should plait it and put it up if you're going to the baths. And never leave anything in the Emperor's rooms. You don't know which slaves can be trusted. I've known women pay slaves to collect hair and nail parings from the Emperor's quarters.'

38

16 *October* 1769

I t occurs to me that Jealousy is just as strong an emotion as
Love. Does it not take a hold of you, like Love, despite
your better judgement? And seek out situations that can serve
only to augment itself? And wallow in reflections that must
inflame it further?

Today, for instance, when the Emperor summons me, do I
wait for some seemly hour when I can be certain he has
performed his *ghusl* and is dressed? Or do I scuttle along *tout
de suite*, propelled by slavering Jealousy, and sidle into his
chamber, picking my way through the scattered debris of his
night's debauch with Helen, marking here a crumpled scarf,
there a damp cloth in a jewelled bowl? And the Emperor
himself, yawning and stretching, naked in the centre of the
room, smiling smug as I have ever seen him, lips bruised,
beard uncombed, with the scent of her still on his fingers.

And how do I know this last *morceau*? Because Dame Jealousy drove me forward, whining for the belly-kick, and bade
me take the Royal Hand and raise it to my cur's lips, and kiss
it, even though my very teeth were twitching with the desire
to bite, even though I must now perform the dratted *ghusl*
myself, for Emperors are rendered as unclean by the Act of
Love as dogs are, and we must all – all who attend him – hie
ourselves off to the washrooms straight after, as though we,
too, had been anointed by Love's unholy smears.

Ay, I could have closed my nostrils, it is true. Breathed out instead of in as I brought the hand towards me. And denied myself that exquisite *frisson* of pain that only Dame Jealousy can bestow, that ignites Anguish and Lust with the same spark, so that my jaw clenches and my member thickens in an instant at the faintest waft of her sweet slither. Thus does Jealousy create both the Punishment and Reward, a carrot and stick of contraries that keeps me cantering blinkered along the track of my Obsession.

So there I am in his chamber, zigzagging my eyes around the room, avid for each wee stab, noting here the mangled bed-sheet, there the dented pillow on the floor, and all the while attempting to carry on some kind of conversation with His Majesty. Thus he embarks on inquiries about Helen's origins, where she came from, where I found her and so on, clapping for water and wandering languorously into his washroom (while I note, with Jealousy's keen vision, the wondrous length of his stallion legs, the perfect straight proportion of thigh and shank).

'I discovered her in Sallee, my Lord,' say I, scampering breathlessly at his brown heels. 'She had been taken from a ship bound for the English Colonies in the Americas.'

So now I am in the washroom! With my senses fairly bristling for more needles with which to pierce myself. There! The wet soap; the oil jar with its lid askew. She bathed here this very morning; sluiced off his stickiness; first the left side, then the right; dreamily muttering her '*Allah akbars*'; smooth-ing plump arms and pale breasts until they gleam.

'And her travelling companions?' He is peering at his reflec-tion, waiting for my reply, and I realize he is checking whether he has been bedding a common whore.

I reassure him that she was purchased from one of the most reputable marriage brokers in Sallee. 'They are guaranteed virgins, every one,' I declaim. 'And of course Malia checks all the women herself.'

'You know, Fijil, she is far more passionate than she appears.'

'Yes, my Lord?' If I were truly a cur, my tongue would be lolling out shamelessly now. As Allah is my judge, I am as avid for this anguish as a dervish for his flails.

'When I saw her first she was like a tight bud. Now she opens like a flower whenever she is with me, like a rose which cannot resist the sun however hard it tries. She is still shy, Fijil, but the sun is so strong that it melts her shame and –'

'Yes, my Lord?' I am howling inside yet my ears are pricked, trembling, for more.

So now he seats himself while the bath water is poured, and leans back with his eyes closed, stretching out his long legs with a sigh. And I am staring at them again, at his baldy knees and *Shatan*'s calves and imagining him suspended above her, braced on his fine long arms, with his hard toes buried in the mattress.

'They tell me the *Lalla* Batoom has been teaching her.' The slaves hunker down with their bowls and begin lathering his feet.

'Yes, my Lord.'

'I thought as much. There are some tricks that I recognized. A way of squeezing when one is inside her.'

His pego is thickening before my eyes, yet I cannot look away. It has been inside her, milked by her slippery pink fist. Dear God, how shall I endure it?

Yet now I am writing it all down: living it again, but more slowly, lingering over each perfect detail, scratching the words, feeding my itch, dipping my quill over and over in a veritable frenzy, splashing and blotting the paper, dwelling on it, delving into it, like a dog rolling in a midden, until I am thoroughly steeped in its delicious stench.

This, in various versions, is the habitual pall which infects the entire Harem, to which until now I have been immune: this Incense of Jealousy, which wafts down into the hot courtyards, scrolling in through the nostrils of the women. And has them all staring mournfully into their mirrors, lamenting a lip too large, a belly too small, a less-than-nothing because he did not choose me.

He does not notice them, that is the cruel fact. Thursday after Thursday, for all their labours, they are invisible. Just as I am.

17 October 1769

Batoom interrupted me yesterday and freed me from my cycle of anguish, bearing down on me like an Archangel, scattering my quills and sweeping me off to her quarters. There she cradled me in her lap and dropped red grapes into my mouth, chortling down at me and teasing me for my glumness.

'But what did you expect?' she asks through her concertina of brown chins. 'She is pale, she is pretty, and she has been taught by the best mistress in the Harem. Of course he is besotted! And you are surprised that she feels the same? After I have worked so hard to this very end? Taunting her about the Royal Cry, tempting her with descriptions of my golden saddle.'

'What golden saddle?' I ask, whereupon she erupts and her lap rolls with mirth, which I take to mean that there is no golden saddle (nor ever could be, now I reflect on it, for what beast could be found to carry such a gurt-heavy thing?). So now I am chuckling too, at the youthful venality of the *bint*, then snivelling again for it's made nary a dent in my love for her.

'He said you had taught her well,' I sniff sepulchrally, wiping my nose on her sleeve. 'He mentioned that squeezing that you do.'

'Excellent! We had only vegetables to practise on, but I thought she showed promise.'

Which has me chuckling once again through my tears, and asking which variety of vegetables she means, whereupon she hies off to the kitchen and returns with some various examples (*viz.*, finger squash and carrots, and a kind of bitter small *concombre*) and proceeds to demonstrate until we are both aching with mirth, and I find I have somehow substituted my own turnip, and pressed my face between her big breasts, and am overcome by the familiar tart scent of aubergines. Then there she is all around me, mewing softly into my ear, squeezing like a lamb's gums round a shepherd's finger, until I am quite literally taken out of myself.

Re-reading this, I can see that it implies I was comforted by this. That when my ears were filled with the sounds of Batoom, and my mouth with the taste of her, that when I was in her and she was around me, and we were making that sumptuous *ratatouille* we have devised, that, for those precious minutes at least, I was free of Jealousy's miasma.

If I implied as much, then you have been misled.

18 October 1769

Is everyone in this damned world ecstatic but I? This morning I went to the stables, hurrying down aisle after aisle of lust-crazed horseflesh, to visit Lungile in his strawy box at the end.

I was hoping for a *reprise* of our sozzled commiseration last week, but discovered him whistling with a smile as wide as the Golden Mile. (Whistling, I ask you! A giant does not whistle. A wee flibbertigibbet of a bird whistles.)

'Good day, dearest Flea!' quoth he, taking out his brushes. 'A wonderful day for a ride, wouldn't you say?' And begins, most tenderly, to groom the bonny mare.

I'm afraid I responded rather snappishly, inquiring where he had hidden his flagon, then retiring rudely with it to a prickly bale. He was undeterred, however, and recommenced his idiotic whistling, buffing up the mare's flanks till they shone, then scrubbing and oiling her yellow hooves, while I glugged down throatful after throatful of Jewish Madeira and felt my mood darken by the second.

'Look, I've had a bridle especially made,' remarks the insensate Gog by and by. 'Naseem –' how he rolls the name around his vast mouth! – 'says the *Bokhary*'s bits are too severe. And the mare goes so much better now, don't you, Madam?' And strokes the animal on the neck and pulls her perky black ears, until I'm moved to remark tetchily on his altered attitude towards the beast. For it was barely a fortnight since he could scarce look at the nag, which he considered the very epitome of his humiliation. Now here he is petting it like a lapdog.

Whereupon he breaks off and squats down before me on his oak-bole haunches and gazes rapturously into my eyes. 'She loves me, Fijil,' he whispers, his face blithe as an infant's. 'You were right! Oh, my dear brother, I cannot thank you enough. If you hadn't told me about – I mean, if you hadn't encouraged me, I would never have dared –'

So now I must tamp down my seethe, and toast him and pat his knee and try to excavate up some pleasure in his joy. For it must be said that Love has quite transformed the man, so it is now Chief Lungile I see before me, who lately bestrode the mountains of his homeland, hunting ibex and slinging them across his shoulders. I swear he is taller by at least a hand, and gleams like a *pianoforte*, albeit these beaming ivories are sharpened.

So now he starts to regale me with details. How they wander the garden together, she on the mare, he ambling alongside on his yellow-palmed feet. How there are deep thickets where the gardeners never venture, all caparisoned with wild grapevines, where they study together through our somnolent *siestas* the many ways there are of pleasuring a woman.

'I feel so ashamed, Fijil,' declares he, looking the very opposite. 'If I had but asked my wives, instead of just assuming –' He hesitates for a long moment, his brow rutted as a Fife cart-track, then is off again, grinning like a slice of white melon. 'A woman's body is the most magical thing! Did you know, Flea, that they have their own small pleasure-pole? And when it is touched properly their burrow moves, like a throat swallowing, and sometimes a gush of milk appears, just like with a man. It is as though they are men really, only inside out, like your *salwars* when you have taken them off.'

'So now, you'll be galloping off with her into the mountains to live happily ever after.' I sound bitter, I know, but I can't help it. By now my store of magnanimity is exhausted. 'And I'll be left here alone with my broken heart.'

Now he stops his manic grinning and stands upright. And looks soberly at me so that my blood stops in my veins. For I see that this is exactly what he has planned.

39

'This evening you will stay in your room,' said Malia, escorting Helen back through the ogling, gabbling court-yards one morning. 'I will inform the Emperor.'

'But why?' Helen was taken aback. Was she being punished for something? She could sense the Harem's eyes following her like a wave, with a crest of silence and a long wake of speculative jabber.

'It will be your time for bleeding very soon. Had you forgotten? The Emperor must not see blood on his sheets. It is bad for the Royal Cream.'

Yes, she had forgotten. She'd forgotten everything except the nocturnal rhythm of her life: waking in the late afternoon, washing and preparing herself, then following Malia through the Harem to the Emperor's quarters. Then evenings with the Emperor: talking and eating with him; laughing, playing sex, washing and praying, then playing sex again – always playing sex. It was what she had been prepared for; all the afternoons with Batoom, all those strange exercises, they all made sense now. And all the dancing, the clothes, all the rich food: the Harem made sense. Playing sex was what she was made for. It was what she lived for now: once, twice, sometimes three times each night. Then gorging her eyes on him as he slept. It had been going on for nearly two weeks now; she really thought it would continue for ever.

'I thought we might have been successful this moon,' Malia sighed. 'But we were just a few hours too late. Your belly was already past its ripeness when you first lay with him. Never mind, child,' patting her with a withered talon. 'When you are ready again, I will tell him. And if he is still interested, I'm sure he will send for you.'

If he was still interested? Helen felt her ribs contract. Of course. If she wasn't available, he'd simply send for another woman. Helen glanced around: she was passing one of the many upper dining rooms. The air was thick with the scent of cinnamon and lamb, and women were pressing slowly up the stone steps with their weans for the midday meal. Every shade of brown and gold they were, plump and glossy: scarves rippling, shoulders gleaming, bellies bulging as they leant over the handrails to call to one another.

There was no question of him being faithful. He'd laugh in her face if she even suggested it. Even the poorest Mohamme- dan was permitted four wives. He was the Emperor. He could have any woman, any time he wanted. That was what the Harem was all about.

'Couldn't I just visit him? It is permitted, isn't it, as long as we don't –'

'Visit him? What for?' Malia stopped dead and turned to look at her. 'What is the point of visiting him if you cannot play sex in the proper fashion? Already you have been taking up too much of his time. Wasting the Royal Cream when there is no chance of a baby.'

He'd gone to the garden on Thursday, of course. He had joked about it, saying what a waste of time it was when she was all he wanted. She'd waited there for him, at the end of the front row in her new green silk, tingling with desire and triumph. The other women had backed away in glum silence as he strode towards her, ignoring Malia's urgent tugging on his sleeve. What a heady moment it was, when he'd pushed through them all to get at her, and had taken her hand and pressed it to his lips, and turned it over – there in front of them all – and had bitten the flesh where her thumb joined her palm. And had laughed when she'd gasped, and licked his forefinger and stroked it along her lower lip, and made her bite it, staring into her eyes as though there was no one else in the world.

How could he lock those feelings in a cupboard for a week? Just this morning, smoothing damp tendrils back from her forehead, he'd begun kissing her freckles, promising to love her one year for each one. Before fifty he'd reached her mouth and had stopped counting, and started teasing her lips with his tongue instead, while the slaves and tasters arrived with the breakfast, and silently withdrew, and the guards knocked and were ignored, and the *Alim* was kept waiting another hour.

Her place was in his chamber. Surely he'd send for her?

'I will come back later this evening with your rags,' said Malia, leaving her at the door of her room.

Helen unlocked the door with her new key and went inside. So. She was back in her little white box.

She looked around the room with disgust. It seemed cramped and tawdry compared with the Emperor's chambers. Why had she bought all these stupid cheap ornaments? Burnished brass and coloured clay; peasant stuff. She wanted to throw it all away and start again.

She imagined days stretching ahead in this hot little room. Evenings. Nights. What on earth used she to do with herself? Wash, pray, eat. Arrange her ornaments. Go and sit in Naseem's room. Experiment with face-paints. Wash, pray, eat. Change her clothes. Set out for a stroll to the fish-pond, but come back because it's too hot. Lie on the floor and doze. Wash, pray, eat. Sleep. Sit under the mulberry tree with Naseem. Come back inside because it's too hot. Lie on the floor. Drink tea. Wash, pray, eat. Sleep. Sleep.

Reema arrived with hot water and Helen began the systematic *ghusl* cleansing that had become second nature these last few weeks. Her body felt leaden, lethargic. Outside, clouds were closing in like a grey lid on the Harem cauldron, sealing in the heat.

She was back again, a Harem woman again. Waiting. What if he walked right past her next time? How they'd crow over her. *Lalla* Aziza, who thought she'd be the fourth queen. *Lalla* Aziza, who had better think again. What if the woman he went with tonight made him cry out too?

There was a knock on the door.

Malia! It had to be. Come to tell her the Emperor was insisting she come to him. Flinging on a loose gown, she threw the door open.

'*Bonjour*, Mademoiselle Aziza!'

Microphilus. Disappointment took the air from her lungs.

'*Comment allez-vous?*' he chirped, doffing his red fez and giving her one of his absurd extravagant bows.

She stood aside with a sigh and he pranced past her into the little room. 'I thought you'd like your money afore the market the morrow. I've been totting up the days and it makes a pretty penny. Enough for a whole camel-load of flimsies.' He took out a leather pouch and weighed it in his puppy-paw, wincing, pretending it was heavier than it was.

'Thank you.' Helen took the pouch and put it on her trunk. She'd been so looking forward to this moment. Now she just felt sick. It was all over; he'd had her and paid her and now she was back where she started. No better than a bar-hinny in Crieff.

'Is there something wrong, hen?' Microphilus was peering up at her, his bulgy forehead wrinkled with concern.

'Just tired, that's all.'

'Ay, well. Love can do that.' He was staring around the

room. Why didn't he just go? Couldn't he tell she wanted to be alone?

'Have you lost something?' she asked wearily.

'No, no –' He backed away abruptly. 'I'm sorry,' he murmured, and left, pulling the door quietly closed behind him.

Malia came back with the rags as she'd promised, after dark when everyone had retired to their rooms. 'Now rest,' she said gruffly, patting Helen's hand. 'And eat. Perhaps we can try again next moon.'

Big drops began falling on the tiles outside as she left. There was a peppery smell in the air. Helen could see lightning silhouetting the mountains in the distance. Rain. At last.

A moment after she left, Helen felt the familiar dragging cramps low down in her belly, like someone tugging at her womb from the inside. The rain was coming harder now, gusting in black curtains across the courtyard and hissing down the walls. She lay curled up on her side, cradling the pain. After a while she could feel a trickle of hot blood seeping into the wad of muslin. Soon there'd be that smell, of fish and old meat; the muslin would harden and darken. Brown. Rotten. Unclean.

Five, six, seven days till she could see him again. More if he didn't send for her. For ever if he didn't send for her. Thunder rumbled outside and rain blew in through the open doorway. Was he with someone now? She bit her knuckles: of course he was. That was why Malia had been so kind. She'd delivered another woman herself earlier that evening.

Helen tried to gauge the time, but the rain drowned out the usual evening sounds. She knew she should get up and close the door; light a lamp and get ready for bed. He could be undressing another woman at this very moment. A sob caught in Helen's chest and she squeezed her eyes shut. She' was just a woman, like all the rest, waiting for him to notice her again.

The pains ebbed for a while and she fell into a miserable doze, curled up fully dressed and unwashed with her *haik* pulled roughly around her. The night was damp and heavy; she felt as though she was underground. Crickets, cockroaches and spiders scuttled through the doorway to escape the rain. It had settled into a steady downpour now, pattering on the roof-tiles, rattling down the gutters. The air smelt of wet clay and black earth. After a while she heard the sound of Naseem's door being pulled gently closed and locked. A moment later there was a quiet knock on her own open door.

'Good, you're awake,' Naseem whispered. 'I wasn't sure you'd be here. But it's your bleeding time, isn't it? We're the same, so I guessed.' Helen fumbled for her flint-box and lit a rush-light. Even though it was the middle of the night, Naseem was wearing a heavy black *haik* over her clothes. Her hair glistened with raindrops and her feet were wet.

'I wanted to see you before I went to meet Lungile,' she said, coming in and sitting on Helen's divan. 'I wanted to make sure you were all right. It is hard when the one you love is with someone else.' She leant forward to peer at Helen's face. 'You've been crying! Oh, Aziza –'

'It's all over –' Helen was sobbing properly now.

'Don't be silly. You made him cry out, didn't you?'

Helen wiped her nose and nodded miserably in the darkness. 'But he's with someone else now. What if she –'

'She won't. She can't. It's something between you and him. Like between Lungile and me. It's not some simple thing that anyone can do. It's something you make together, something only you are that calls to something only he is. You can't find that with just anyone. It has taken him years to find you, Aziza. He's not going to forget you in a few days.'

'How do you know?' Miserable, sniffing.

'Everyone knows. That's why they call you *Lalla* Aziza. They saw him looking at you last Thursday. They know it's just a matter of time before he takes you for his wife.'

'Are you sure?' Helen sat up; she was beginning to feel better. 'I've been feeling like one of our rags. You know, like he's used me and thrown me away.'

'He loves you – as much as an Emperor can love anyone. You've managed to unlock that tight heart of his somehow. The others are just for play. They'll make him want you even more. Believe me. Come on now, smile and be happy for me. I'm going to meet my love. There –' reaching out and hugging her tight. 'That's how I like to think of you. Goodbye, sweet sister.'

'But it's still raining. Where are you –' There was something in Naseem's voice, a breathlessness, a catch. Too late, Helen made a grab for Naseem's *haik*. She was gone.

Hours, minutes later Helen was woken again. The rain had stopped. There were footsteps and loud voices outside; men's voices.

'Give me the keys!' one was saying. Then the sounds of them rattling something metal next door. Why were they trying to open Naseem's room?

Helen sprang out of bed and pulled the curtain open a chink. With no moon, it was hard to see what was going on. Three big guards were grouped around Naseem's door, two held smoking torches above their heads while the third bent over the lock, cursing, fumbling key after key with flat fingers. Dripping tallow hissed into the puddles.

Had Naseem been taken sick suddenly? Maybe Malia had sent the guards to fetch her some fresh clothes. No, that didn't make sense: the Harem was full of clothes. Perhaps she'd been discovered with Lungile in the stables, or wherever they'd gone. But why would they be trying to open her room? Maybe Lungile was locked in her room with her now and someone had reported them to the guards. But if he was a eunuch, why would anyone care? The women played sex with one another all the time and no one had made any trouble before.

Curtains all around the courtyard were beginning to be drawn back. Women were emerging like ghosts from their dark caves, slipping into their wet slippers and huddling together on the *verandahs*; whispering nervously, sidling nearer, holding their clothes up out of the puddles.

Suddenly a key turned and the door was pulled open. The guards rushed in, torches aloft. The women surged forward close behind them. Helen held her breath. But the room was empty; anyone could see that. The sheets were neatly folded; the chamber-pot unused at the foot of the divan.

The guards began opening Naseem's few boxes and trunks, tipping their contents on to the floor. There wasn't much there: a few sets of clothes; some slippers. They must be looking for the sapphires, Helen thought. Why else would they be searching her things? She remembered Naseem stuffing them down to the very bottom of the big trunk. She must have moved them. Unless she had them with her.

'Here's the slave.' Another guard appeared, dragging Naseem's little slave-girl. Wide-eyed and dishevelled with sleep, she cringed back against the wall when she saw the disordered room.

'Where's your mistress? We've had word she's run away with some jewels belonging to the Emperor.'

Run away? Helen grabbed a pillar for support. Around her the other women pressed forward, clucking and squawking in the darkness. She could feel them pushing against her like damp pillows; smell their humid scalps and sleep-sweat; their stale perfume; their garlic-and-honey-cake breath.

Naseem had run away with Lungile: suddenly Helen was absolutely certain this was what had happened. That was why she'd asked for the horse. She'd been planning it for weeks. At this moment they were galloping towards the mountains they loved; away from this fluttering hen-house; splashing through the puddles, leaping the streams, feeling the wind, the real wind, in their faces. Helen ached with envy for a moment. Leading their horses up through the foothills, with real rocks, real pebbles beneath their feet. And wild thorn-bushes tearing at their clothes, and no guard or gardener in sight.

There was a sudden scream. One of the guards was bending the slave-girl's arm up her back. 'Where is she?' impatiently, through gritted teeth. 'Come on, *bint*, you must know something.'

'As Allah is my Lord (the All-knowing, the All-forgiving), she never told me anything. I brought her supper, but she was sick in bed, so I took it away. Maybe she's out in the garden. Since she's been sick, she's started walking there at night. She says it soothes her.'

'The garden? In the rain? Who was she meeting?' The women shushed each other and pushed nearer, scenting scandal.

'No one! I don't know. She could meet anyone in the garden. How would I know?'

Helen backed quickly into her room and pulled the curtain across. She didn't want them questioning her.

There was a shout from outside the courtyard. A moment later another guard elbowed through the crowd and panted into the room. 'They've caught her!' he cried. 'And she has the necklace with her. You can leave this –' sneering at the snivelling slave-girl. 'The Emperor wants us all in the dungeons.'

40

19 October 1769

I have witnessed such horrors tonight, it has taken two hours to still the trembling of my hands. Even now they feel as boneless as a brace of plaice fillets and I can scarce summon the strength to wrap my limp fingers around the quill.

The blue-eyed Berber is dead – though her eyes are blue no longer, for they were gouged out by the Cutting Room thugs and thrown, with their entrails trailing like squid tentacles, into the basket on the torture-room floor, where they will swim for ever in my dreams.

The smell of her blood is still in my nostrils, though I have bathed my face a dozen times, scrubbed my feet, and kicked my stinking clothes out into the courtyard for Maryam to deal with. The Moorish Church has rules about blood, how clean it is, whether it be gushing from a live creature, or puddled in a dead one. I do not know when the Berber died. I do not know whether the blood on my clothes is clean or unclean. I pray unclean. I pray she was dead for her last tortured minutes. She was silent as the grave, for sure, but I fear not dead . . .

He said he was tired of the way she stared at him: defiant and unblinking while they sharpened their knives. If she would not close them, he would have them closed for her. Though, of course, they will never close now, will glare forever like St Lucia's on her golden plate, levered up from the caves of her skull.

I must compose myself. I have started my story in the middle, for that is where my own mind's eye keeps returning, tethered by the intensity of her last look.

It began in the wee small hours when two gurt Harem guards shook me awake, gibbering with fear and asking for my keys, saying the Berber had fled and the Emperor had despatched them to retrieve the jewels he gave her.

So I tumble out of bed and unlock my key-cupboard, reaching down the iron bunches and fumbling through them as long as I dare. By this means I hope to open a loop of empty time for the lovers to make good their escape. For I have no doubt that Lungile and his lass have fled into the moonless, trackless, wet night. And my mind begins racing likewise, debating how I can abet their absconding, and conclude I can serve them best by cantering *tout de suite* to His Majesty, to seek a means of damming the deluge of his fury.

So the eunuchs wade off with the keys – a large and complex bunch, I have made sure of that – while I don my clothes and make my way to the Emperor's quarters.

Have I said before that it was raining? Lancing down from a black mattress sky, stabbing at the tiles, overflowing the fountains and surging across the courtyards, so that my slippers squelch as I splash along the cloisters, and my *salwars* are all sogged around my ankles, weighted with leafy debris dislodged from the roofs.

So I arrive at the Emperor's door and dither, dripping, just outside, peeking around the jamb-cheek to discover what is happening. Inside he is pacing like a circus lion, snarling at the slaves who are attempting to dress him while they hold open his garments, like sails before a storm. Some glossy girlie he has been gulching is blubbing into the bed-sheet, all wet-nosed and smudge-mouthed.

'What do you mean you didn't see her?' rants the Emperor,

pausing to rinse his hands in a silver bowl. 'Were your eyes closed? Do I keep you to sleep on duty?'

He is addressing one of the guards who patrol the Harem walls of a night, a Goliath pillar now lately turned Atlas, grovelling on gourd knees 'neath the weight of Zeus's wrath and rolling his yellow eyes mutely.

Now comes a panting and a squelching behind me, which spins the Emperor round, spitting curses. Two sopping giants are skidding to a stop on the threshold, eyes teetering with terror (with me a little to one side, waiting for an opportune second to *segue* into the proceedings).

'What now? What new imbecility have you come to report?' Sometime around now, hail begins hammering on the roof like a mob at a stoning, lending a wild urgency – were one needed – to the atmosphere.

'We have caught her, my Lord!' blurts one (at which my heart lodges itself at the base of my throat, lamenting, 'Lungile is slain!').

'She is in the dungeon,' adds the other. 'What would you have done with her?'

'And the eunuch?' The Emperor is drying his hands. My throat feels full of mud.

'We have the mare, Your Majesty.' I can smell the soldiers' mutton-sweat, see the veins bulge on their rain-slicked necks.

'Did I ask about the mare?' His voice is cool and dangerous.

'The eunuch has escaped, Majesty.' So Lungile is safe! My heart bobs back down into my chest and air surges into my lungs. The soldiers tumble out an explanation, how he fought like a dervish, slaughtering ten men before galloping off towards the mountains. My grateful mind glories on him flailing at them in the rain, teeth flashing, clothes stuck to his skin. I ache to ask if he is injured.

'Ten men?' The Emperor's jaw clenches as he tots up the price, the cost of replacing them, the waste of their training. 'Inform their families that their sons have shamed them. And despatch a hundred more.'

'But the rain, Majesty.' Here is the first gargantuan again, rashly speaking when a sane man would rather swallow his tongue.

'Is there a problem?' The icy, soft voice; the ominous raised eyebrow.

'His tracks will be washed away –'

'Do you argue with the Emperor?'

'No, no –' But it is too late for the Emperor has already motioned to a handful of hovering henchmen, using a sign the brutes have been schooled to recognize, and the soldier's stuttering tongue is extruded and sliced off before he can gurgle a protest.

'So,' concludes His Majesty, pirouetting nimbly to avoid the bloody fountain that ensues, 'we will have no more arguments. I want him found. Rain or no rain. Do you understand? And take the *bint* to the Cutting Room.'

Now he espies me skulking in the doorway. 'Fijil, is that you? Come with me. I want you to see this.' And there is a glint in his black eyes that I have sometimes observed when he is looking over the women, an inner rubbing of the knuckles of Anticipation.

So his henchmen slop off down the damp corridors and he sweeps after, with me scurrying like a draggled puppy in his wake, while the whole palace thunders with rain, and water starts to seep through the window-frames and snake down the mossy steps to the dungeons.

I keep seeing her eyes. Blue and red *calamari*. I couldn't help her. She was so quiet –

And I did not speak –

This will not do. My silence will not help her now. I must return to the dungeons.

The Palace dungeons are quite palatial in their own right, having been lovingly created by the Emperor Ishmael himself, whose *penchant* for ingenious torments I think I have described earlier. Not the prisoners' cells, of course (which are as foul as any the world has to offer, and especially foul on this night as they begin filling up with flood-water seething with Palace effluent). No, I am referring to the torture rooms, of which there are many, each lavishly equipped and presided over by its own bespoke Practitioner.

Thus we have your Piercing Room, with its hinged caskets, lined with spikes like deadly mussel-shells; your Branding Room, with its great furnace and intricate irons; your Stretching Room, with its straps and pulleys; your Ducking Room and its jars of ordure; the Coal Room, which doubles as a Smoke Room – not to mention the Rat Room and the adjoining Rooms respectively of Snakes, Ants and Bees, plus the Acid Pits. And these are only the few I have seen myself. Plus the aforesaid Cutting Room, which is where the implacable Berber was awaiting us.

You can see I am digressing. I do not want to write this.

As Allah is my judge, the *bint* never whimpered: just rocked as they mangled her, silent as a mannequin in a seamstress's attic. My quill quivers as I describe this scene to you: the stubborn lass and the exasperated Lord; the grim thugs; the tilting torches on the walls, smoking and oozing tallow. And the prisoners below in their swarming cells, yammering as the foul flood-water laps ever upwards.

After her staring eyes have been plucked out, and red tears are gushing down her blind cheeks, I plead with the Emperor to allow me to leave the room, claiming a sudden faintness threatens to topple me to the floor. Whereupon he barks with laughter and chucks me under the chin, chiding what he calls my 'soft Scottishness' and observing that it is no wonder we can only manage the one wife since we have not the stomach for administering a proper discipline. And proceeds to hypothesize a like softness as afflicting the Scottish male's member, chortling and warming to his theme, while his thugs wait patiently with their hands swinging, and their blades shining in the torchlight.

'Very well,' he concedes eventually – and this concession pleases him somehow. 'Since you have not the mettle for men's work, you can wait outside. But do not scuttle back to your hole, for I want this lesson relayed to the women in full, that no one steals from the Emperor with impunity.' At which point his brow lowers and he returns to his bloody *tableau*.

I'm wondering now whether I could have stopped him. If I'd cajoled him at this point, staggered and swooned with extravagant squeamishness, and begged him to have mercy on his poor soft Scottisher. I wonder if he might have smiled and shrugged and spared the *bint*'s life.

Perhaps if she had cried out, to give him his pleasure, he might have relented. For howls of pain are sweetest music to the torturer's ear, which usher his climax as nothing else can. If she had opened her brave lips and released the screams that were writhing inside, perhaps he would have been similarly released, and sated enough for a poor Dwarf to lead –

But she did not and I did not, or perhaps could not, and slunk off and plunked myself down in my wet *k'sa*, listening to the rain jitter and gurgle all around and the prisoners moan with the chill of the rising water.

I could hear the sniffs and grunts of the cutters' men, the

rasp and clang as they sharpened their knives. Later one opened the door and shouted for a basket, and filled it, and passed it out again and shook it, sniggering, under my nose so I was forced to inhale the hectic smell of her blood.

Her hands were in there, like two crayfish in a creel; and her long feet, crossed tidily one over the other; her stubborn tongue, with the marks of her own teeth in it, and the white gristle of her windpipe, for he'd had his thugs cut out her voice, too, since she refused to sing for him. And her squid eyes, accusing, atop the lot. I cannot stop thinking about those eyes . . .

Now the Emperor emerges, suave as ever in his spotless white clothes, and laughs charmingly down at me and pulls me to my feet, and tells me to send the Crone Malia to his quarters. By which I understand that his man's work has given him a man's Appetite, and a wave of disgust wells up in my belly and threatens to spill out like a paisley waistcoat.

Yet, at the same time, that strange thing is happening which always occurs when I am faced with his insouciance. It is as though he is shaking me awake from a terrible doze, and all the rest has been a dream – the stench of blood, the charnel basket. There is his familiar face, smiling. His garments unsmirched and smelling of sandalwood. His gait graceful; his mien gracious.

This charming man would not harm a fly. Though I saw it with my own eyes. Though the basket is still in the room, its smell still in my nostrils.

We have a belief, I suppose, that only a monster can do *Shatan*'s work, and that his deeds must perforce be advertised upon his person. So we expect our murderers to sport a loose lip and slavering mouth; webbed fingers; the stump of a tail; a chameleon's contrariwise eyes.

By donning clean garments and a winning smile, a monster

may monster unmolested forever. And we will be dazzled by the white of his linens, and rub our eyes, and sigh with relief that the shadows have receded. And forget his dark deeds. And so become culpable too.

Later I came back to discover what they had done with the body. I had some notion of rescuing it from that place, and washing it, and wrapping it according to the gentle laws of Mohammed. I traced the Cutting Room guard to his cubbyhole and found him gloating oafishly over what he had seen.

She'd already been despatched, he told me, strapped to the mare and set loose for the hyenas to finish. Whereupon I open the gate and stare out at the hissing black rain. Some sallow dogs are snuffing at the wet sand and pawing at it.

I turn back and find the oaf still sniggering. 'What a waste,' says he, chafing at the long shape in his *salwars*.

It was then that my stomach truly rebelled, catching up with my mind, then overtaking it in a rush, so that I must skelter to the dungeon washroom and retch again and again into a bucket, while the cutters sneer and scrub the blood from beneath their fingernails.

How different everything seems today. Last night I laid my head down to sleep, the very epitome of tormented recrimination. This morning finds me counting my blessings: Lungile, the best friend I had in the world, is free; Helen, whom I love, is safe and whole in her quarters; Batoom, who loves me, is likewise safe and whole. But the Berber, whom I did not love any more than she loved me, is safe and whole no longer.

And I keep wondering what Helen would have thought had she witnessed the Emperor relishing the dismemberment of her friend. For whatever I say to the women, however red I embroider it, they will never truly know – not as I truly know – what their precious Lord is capable of. They are hens safely shut in the hen-house, while the farmer saws the throat of the rabbit in the far field.

41

Towards dawn, some of the women began to congregate in Naseem's room. Helen could see their candles glimmering along the cloister as they arrived, could hear their voices through the folds of her curtain.

They were going through Naseem's few things, holding them up, passing them around, putting them away. Helen sat stiffly on her divan, wishing they'd go back to their rooms. They were filling her head with their voices, like starlings flapping around their roost, stopping her from thinking.

They were speculating about what the Emperor had done to Naseem. The slaves were saying he'd called for four eunuchs to beat her; then ordered her to the torture rooms in the dungeon. They said he'd had her hands cut off for stealing and her feet for trying to run away.

Helen covered her ears and thought of the Emperor she knew. She pictured him sleeping beside her, his brown eyelids and thick lashes.

But each time she took her hands away, there was more. They said that he'd called for the breast-vice and the spiked *jellabiah*. That his fiercest hunting dogs had been forced to gnaw off her nipples. That she'd been skinned alive, peeled slowly along the lines of her blue tattoos. And taken out to the stables for the grooms to take it in turns, while the stallions were let loose on the mare.

And she remembered the woman who'd come skeltering into the flooded courtyard after the guards had gone, with her mouth smeared and her *kohl* running, sobbing that she'd been with the Emperor when word came of Naseem's escape. 'He was inside me, he was racing for his finish, but when they came in he just pushed me away.'

'Did you see her?' 'Was she alone?' 'Did you hear anything?' The women had pressed around her, greedy for details.

'No, no, nothing. He just got dressed and went off to the dungeons.' The woman began sobbing again. 'He was inside me! It was my only chance. He'll never send for me again now.'

In Helen's mind the starlings landed, but their cacophony continued as they squabbled and fidgeted for position. The Emperor counting her freckles; trickling jewels into her lap; wiping another woman's rouge from his lips; ordering Naseem's torture. Which was the man she loved?

And all the time her own bleeding continued. Each time she rinsed out her muslin, Helen thought of Naseem; how they'd always counted the days together. Each time she saw the blood running away, she saw Naseem's blood, and the Emperor watching; saw him plunging his meat into another woman; remembered the wee slave-girl he'd punished last month; Lungile's poor wound. What would he do to Naseem?

Perhaps there'd been a misunderstanding. And he'd lost his temper. And regretted it. Perhaps the slaves were lying. (Why would they lie?) Was the smeared rouge a lie? Were the castrated soldiers a lie? The starlings wouldn't settle.

The call to dawn prayers dispersed the women back to their rooms for an hour or two, but after breakfast they were back again; agitated, jabbering. Helen sent Reema for water to wash her hair and doused the sound with water.

Naseem couldn't be dead. Injured, maybe, or sent away. But not dead. They were just making things up, wild things, so they could gasp and squeal and hang on to each other, or waddle importantly up and down, poking their fat faces through one curtain after another, whispering, 'Have you heard?' and 'Isn't it terrible?' Pretending they cared when really it was just something to gabble on about.

Naseem had tried to run away and had been caught. That was all. And she'd been punished. Last time it was just a beating on the feet. This time she had the sapphires with her, so she'd be beaten harder as an example. He couldn't just let her get away with it. She was probably in a cell somewhere, recovering.

Around mid-morning, when the sun was sucking steam from the wet courtyards, the winged termites began swarming. Outside the washrooms, they massed at the entrances to their burrows like foam, lifting into the sky by the handful. Helen sat in her doorway and watched them go: up, up, rising with the steam; higher, catching the warm wind, circling dreamily, then off towards the mountains.

That evening the vigil continued: rush-lights flickering; low voices, quiet keening. And one voice moaning, 'No, no, no,' over and over.

'They're saying now that she was taken to the Cutting Room,' said Reema, handing Helen some dry rags. 'That's where they do the eunuchs.'

'Who's saying that?'

'The Emperor's slaves. I see them sometimes.' Reema took Helen's drenched muslins and dunked them in a basin. The water swirled red in the lamplight. Outside the rain began falling again, hesitantly, pit-pat. 'They're saying she died last night.'

So it was true. Helen felt sick. Her tongue filled her mouth.

There was a sudden rush of bare feet and a woman yanked her curtain open and spat at Helen, shouting, 'Bitch! Daughter of bitch! You've killed my Naseem.'

It was the woman Helen had surprised in Naseem's room. Her face was swollen with crying. 'She was happy before. Then the Emperor chose you and she couldn't bear it. I never saw her after that. She stopped looking for me and she was never in her room. Now she's dead and it's all because of you.'

'What are you talking about? Naseem never loved the Emperor –'

But the woman had gone. Helen stared dully at the swaying curtain.

Reema got up and pulled the door closed, then turned the new key in the lock.

42

It is *siesta*, but I cannot sleep. Each time I close my eyes, they are there, her squid eyes with their tentacles.

This morning, when I went to inform the women, I found Dame Gossip had been there before me and had done my work far better than I ever could. So they are all eye-rolling and breast-heaving, giving it 'Ay me!' and 'Isn't it dreadful?', flushed with unseemly pleasure.

Thus the Contagion spreads from the monstrous deed, in this relish that others gain from it, that polishes up the Horror and embellishes it and burnishes it into Spectacle. Thus are we all infected, all united in Iniquity, all pulling on our todgers like schoolboys behind the shed, while agreeing together how terrible a deed it was. Is the voice that abhors more innocent than that which applauds?

It is drizzling still, the clouds mounted up one upon another like bullocks in a barn, and enforcing a degree of propriety on the women by confining them more or less to their own courtyards.

I tried once to see Helen, but her door was locked. I thought she would send for me, to find out details of Naseem's fate, but perhaps she is too distraught to hear them. So I took myself off to the stables and sat for a while among the hay-bales. I was searching for some remnant of my friend, but the despised mare having been disposed of, the grooms had pillaged the small space, grabbing the little he owned, so there was naught

304

but a pair of his exorbitant slippers left to remind me of him – which I suppose they spurned because none had feet large enough to fit them.

I have been to the Palace mosque to pray for his safety. He has a horse, and weapons. And if he be not injured, and the rain but continue a few more days, he will be safe. Yet I miss him. There is no pleasure in my *hookah* without Lungile puffing beside me, and tweaking my plait, and displaying on the stage of his face the architecture of every human emotion.

23 October 1769

It has been raining for days now, the sky stooping over us like a wet grey hen, and we her chickadees dragging our drenched feathers through the mud. Thunder rumbles sometimes from her belly, but mostly it is just rain, sweeping the dust off the leaves and peppering them with fat droplets, so the garden is a boggy jungle, carpeted with sodden petals where giant snails and thick centipedes graze.

The Harem smells of moss and mould as our stocks of firewood burgeon forth with all variety of mushroom, and the rush mats take root and sprout green beards where they are rolled up in the corners of the courtyards. The slaves are forever sweeping up fallen leaves, which seem imbued with glue and adhere to the mosaics, and coalesce in slimy heaps which must be scraped up with shovels. Meanwhile, the twiggy brooms are themselves swelling with bud. Thus does the Green Queen reclaim her dominion.

And I am as glum as the weather, a muggy runt dragging aimlessly around: to Batoom's quarters, where I pace morosely back and forth until she orders me away; and so back to my own chamber for a solitary suck on my dumb *hookah*; then back to Batoom for some more hours, staring out at the dripping millet in her garden, at the slugs' long pilgrimage across her courtyard, idly wagering which will arrive first.

I knocked again on Helen's door, but she wouldn't speak to me. She must know I was in the dungeons. I thought she would be anxious to hear my account.

Reema says she is still on her monthlies, and more afflicted than usual. I have heard it said that some women are troubled with quite severe pains, as though a wound had opened inside. Others claim a certain emptying of the mind occurs during this time, as though their reason was draining away with the blood, leaving them aggrieved and prone to strange fancies.

I mentioned this theory to Batoom yestermorn, and she was most dismissive, demanding whether I have observed any regular falling off in her faculties – which I was obliged to deny. She maintains the very opposite to be the case, and that a woman's mind is actually keener when she is bleeding, being less clouded by what she refers to as 'pouch swelling', to wit the urge to mate. This swelling of the pouch, she avers, makes women slaves to the men they desire. Thus it is only when they are bleeding, and the said swelling subsides, that they achieve a sane appreciation of their situation.

She claims that in her country, women deserting their husbands do so overwhelmingly when they are on their monthlies, which she calls their 'clear days'. This is why men aim to impregnate their wives successively, so engendering fewer days of chafing reason; and why the wives lie about the return of their bleeding after childbirth, to gain some extension of their sanity before they are again burdened with fecundity. (It seems that in her land a man is forbidden to approach his wife for sexual favours until she has again taken out her rags.)

If Batoom is correct (and when, by my troth, is she not?), then Helen is at her sanest during her monthlies. And the women in her courtyard should be likewise afflicted with common sense, for do they not all bleed at the same time? As though the Crone Malia had contracted with Nature to sort them all into neat compartments and thereby simplify her myriad calculations.

Indeed, when I visited said courtyard to begin organizing the clearing of the Berber's room, the women billeted there were uncharacteristically indignant, bridling together at what they claimed was an intrusion into their mourning and muttering darkly about the excesses of the Emperor in tones I have never before heard in the Harem.

Why won't Helen see me? Perhaps it is too painful. She is mourning. I would not add to her distress.

43

When the rain finally swept back its curtains, day broke on an autumnal landscape. The mountains were on fire with orange and yellow, and steaming heaps of wet leaves were piled up in every courtyard. Mist diluted the sun and hung diamonds on the spider-webs that spanned every opening.

The vigil in Naseem's room ended and the guards came to clear her things and lock the door. The woman who'd attacked Helen lingered disconsolately outside for an hour or two, but then she too wandered back to her own courtyard.

Then somehow it was Wednesday again, time to begin preparing for the parade in the garden. Sitting in the doorway of her room, Helen watched those who were not bleeding getting ready. They were saying different things now. How the Emperor would have had to punish Naseem if she'd been stealing. How the proper penalty for such a crime was cutting off the hands. How the Emperor would have had no choice; the *Alim* would have insisted. Perhaps she'd bled to death, or died of a fever afterwards. Or been sent back to her father in disgrace. After all, there'd been no word of a burial.

By Thursday morning it was as though it had never happened. Helen's own courtyard was still rather subdued, but in the rest of the Harem it was like any other Thursday, with falls of silk draped over every surface, and water pouring, and *henna* heating, and slaves running, and children shoved aside.

When the time came for them to go to the garden, Helen stayed in her room, glad she didn't have to face him quite yet. Would he search for her? Or just let his eyes roam along the rows as if over a bowl of fruit. She thought of his confident hands peeling the *durra-en*, of the juice flowing down his fingers. A familiar pang went through her.

If he sent for her again, she'd ask him what had happened to Naseem. He'd explain, she knew he would. All that talk about torture was just gossip. He'd make her understand. He was no ordinary man reprimanding an errant wife. He was an Emperor, with an entire kingdom looking to him for guidance. He had to be strong; people expected it.

If he sent for her again.

The next day her bleeding stopped. Helen folded the dry rags and set them aside.

A moment later Malia appeared and began asking questions. 'So, the blood was thick, yes? Good, good. And strong pains? This is excellent. I have seen this before when the man's milk is coming every day. It strengthens the womb and feeds it.'

Helen stared at her. Why, the woman was positively beaming. 'Of course, you are fortunate in the Emperor. With most men, when they are giving milk every day, it becomes thin and weak and will not stay where it needs to be inside the woman. But the Royal Cream keeps its consistency however much is produced.'

'Has he sent for me again?' Helen hardly dared ask.

'No, no. He thinks you are still bleeding. But it is finished now, no? So – we will see. I will inform him you will be ready tomorrow – though this is not the best time. It would be better to wait a few more days, but he asked me to –'

'He asked you? What?' Helen sat bolt upright. 'What did he say about me?'

'He was just wondering when you would be available again, that is all. What did you think, child? That he would forget you?'

*

As soon as Malia had gone, Helen called for Reema. She'd neglected her appearance this last week; now there was work to do. A list formed in her mind: if she had her hair removed today, the redness would have faded by tomorrow evening. Which of her *kamises* were clean? She flung the lid of her trunk open and tossed its contents on to the bed. At the bottom she came upon two leather pouches: the green velvet one containing her emeralds; and a smaller one, of brown leather, with the money Microphilus had given her.

She stared at the two pouches. It seemed like months since she'd touched them; as though Naseem's death, and the rain, and her bleeding had filled far more than seven days of her life.

She tumbled the emeralds into her hand and felt their familiar cool weight. A sizzle of exhilaration began building in her chest. Soon there'd be more. A golden saddle and a silver carriage; a waistcoat of pearls. Soon she'd be with him again; his dark hardness inside all those deceitful white flowing robes.

'Aziza –' It was like a sigh.

He was walking towards her with his arms out, his face open and full of love. He seemed shorter than she remembered, and slimmer.

She dropped a deep curtsey, not daring to look at him. Her legs were weak; her hands cold.

Nothing had changed.

'When that old witch said you couldn't come to me, I felt like kicking her into the fountain. Come, let me look at you. I had begun to think I must have dreamed it all.'

He bent and raised her gently to her feet. That smell – how had she forgotten the smell of him? Frankincense, mint and sandalwood; liquorice and garlic. He'd bathed already, she could tell. She pictured his clean, lean body inside the loose white folds.

'Seven days – I thought they'd never end.' He was drawing her towards him. He was hard already, prodding at her through his breeks. An ache began inside her, so sharp and hot it made her wince.

'What's the matter?' His eyes were suddenly full of concern. 'Are you in pain?' She found she was staring at his mouth. Willing him to kiss her.

'No.' She shook her head. 'It's just –' How could she explain that she was tingling and flooding, like a mouth stinging with saliva? 'It's just that I've missed you, my Lord.' Her voice was a whisper. She pressed her thighs together, ashamed of the strength of her desire.

'I can't hear you.' He was whispering too now, pressing her closer.

Her breath was ragged; her mind focused just on the length of it pressing against her belly; she could see it in her mind, and his goat's scrotum, taut and drawn up to his body.

Soon. The slime was seeping out of her. Had the slaves gone yet? She glanced around; the door was closing.

He was saying something else. 'I want you –' Her knees were melting, her blood galloping along her veins. Why wasn't he kissing her? She watched his mouth form the words, but she wasn't listening. She was looking at his lips, the tiny scar at the corner of his mouth; at his tongue.

Now he was kissing her forehead, her nose, her cheeks, veering towards her mouth then away again, until her eyes closed and her lips were swollen, willing him to kiss her properly.

'Aziza, I want you to be my wife.'

44

26 October 1769

He has sent for Helen again. I have tried again to speak with her, to warn her what he is capable of, so she may guard her heart when they are next together. Ay, and her tongue too. For what if she questions him about that night? Lungile is not yet found and this rankles him beyond endurance. What if she should unwittingly enrage him?

She has instructed Reema to bar the door, and say she is too busy with her *toilette* to admit anyone. I showered the auld sourpuss with pleadings, but could not prevail, though her granite brow did lift an apologetic fraction. Which I take to mean that she approves my attempted intervention. It comforts me to know that such an Angel is watching over the lassie; an Angel, what's more, whose sanity does not wax and wane with the vagaries of the womb, for her womb loosed its grip on her mind many years since, and hatted her with grey wool, then deposited her back in Reason's house.

Not so Helen, now blinkered once more by Love, cantering blindly to the cliff's edge. Love's bridle is around her head, Love's bit in her mouth. She will not let me catch hold of the rein.

And what of my rein? How did Microphilus become so enamoured of such a heedless, wilful lass? Enough, I will rein myself in. She may flee from sanity, but I will not. It is time I put an end to this. I am putting this Diary of Obsession away.

45

The day of the wedding dawned bright and clear. After weeks of mist and rain, the air was fresh and cool, like springtime in Scotland. Helen pulled back her long curtain and breathed it all in: the blue air, the scuts of clouds, the scent of cold earth and new shoots. The other women were drowsing still, but the slaves were padding quietly up and down as usual, carrying water and firewood, baskets of fruit and cheese, steaming flat-bread.

Sighing, Helen turned and looked around her little room. Her last morning here. Tomorrow, when she awoke, it would be in the queen's part of the Harem, in Salamatu's old quarters. Tomorrow, when she awoke, she would be a queen.

Reema appeared with hot water and set it down in its usual place. Then, instead of bustling off as usual to prepare breakfast, she knelt in front of Helen and kissed her feet.

'I have made something for you,' she said stiffly, reaching into her pocket and pulling out a small object. 'Where I come from we call it *chifumuro*. It's something every mother gives her daughter on the day of her wedding.' She held Helen's eyes for a moment. 'It's for protection,' she added quietly. 'We wear them around our necks – or around our bellies if we need to be secret.'

Helen took the object and looked at it: a tiny blue silk pouch, no bigger than a thumbnail, beautifully sewn shut with golden thread.

'I know you will have your jewels today. But you can fix it to the inside of your gown. Look, I've found a little pin to tie it to,' Reema said.

Something old, something new, something borrowed – the Scottish wedding rhyme popped suddenly into her head. Something blue. Tears pricked Helen's eyes as she closed her hand over the little gift. 'You will be there when I get back, won't you? In the new place, I mean.' She felt nervous suddenly: it was not just a grand ball she was going to.

Cheeks creasing into a grim smile, Reema nodded and handed her a white kerchief. 'Come on now, dry your eyes. The women will be here soon to take you off to the Bath House. You don't want them saying that the *Lalla* Aziza was seen weeping on her wedding day.'

Led by Batoom, they arrived an hour later; a group of six senior women, laughing and ululating, carrying eggs and candles, and a white *haik* which they draped over Helen's shoulders. Accompanied by the band of fat musicians, they escorted her through the ululating courtyards to the Bath House, where they supervised her washing, then – taking turns – doused her seven times with clean water and prayed to Allah for her protection and fertility.

After they'd taken her back to her room, they sat around outside, telling the musicians what to play and presiding over a feast of food laid out in the upper dining room. Helen watched from the refuge of her room. Apart from Batoom, she'd barely spoken to these women. Yet here they were, organizing a wedding feast in her honour. Seeing their bossy, bold good humour, she felt a stab of regret that she was leaving.

But there was no time for reflection. The musicians struck up a new tune and everyone was ululating again. The *henna* painters had arrived, with three basins of steaming *henna*. Three eggs were cracked, one into each basin, and stirred into the *henna* mixture. Then the painters processed into Helen's room and pulled the curtains closed.

The painting took two hours. Helen had to lie perfectly still on the floor while the three women crouched over her naked body, dipping wee pointy brushes into a bowl of the steaming paste, tickling her, burning her, gently branding her with the wife's brand. She'd had it on her palms before, and on the soles of her feet, but never latticed over her entire body in the traditional curlicue pattern. Because her skin was so pale, they'd chosen a golden shade instead of the usual brown or black. When they rinsed it off and glazed her with jasmine oil, every inch of her skin – nose, breasts and fud, right down to her smallest toe – looked as though it was covered with a fine filigree of gold lace. Now Helen understood why Reema had been so meticulous removing her hair the previous day: the tiniest bristle would have spoilt the effect.

After the painters had gone, and Reema had left her to join the noisy feasting outside, Helen stood in front of her mirror and turned slowly. She'd been eating *harrabel* after every meal these last two weeks, to make herself even plumper than usual, and her skin stretched taut over her belly and buttocks. The big globes of flesh lolled and swayed slightly as she turned. She understood now that this was how a real woman should look: like a heap of satin pillows; soft and slow and dimpled.

Kneeling at her face-mirror, she applied *kohl* and rouge in the style that had become second nature now: green then black around her eyes; black in a broad line joining her brows; red on her lips and cheeks. Then she pulled off her protective headscarf and began unravelling the tiny plaits Reema had braided into her hair the previous evening.

When she'd finished, and was combing her hair out into a rippled copper shawl around her shoulders, there was a burst of ululation outside and Reema came in with her wedding clothes. There were heavy gold satin *salwars*, with tiny rubies embroidered on to the ankle-cuffs, and a filmy gold *kamise*.

Helen eased them on gingerly. She'd never worn anything so ornate. The satin slithered chilly over her lacewing skin; the *kamise* was light as thistledown against her breasts. Next came the waistcoat, stiff and heavy as a man's outdoor jacket with its encrustation of rubies; and matching tip-tilted slippers straight from the Royal Shoemaker.

Finally, the jewels. The Emperor had chosen them himself. 'Every fire-coloured stone the goldsmith could find,' he'd announced, scattering uncut gemstones on to a tray. 'A necklace made from these – all the colours of your hair. And bracelets to match; earrings, anklets. I want you to burn like a flame on our wedding day.'

Slowly, piece by piece, Helen put them on. She imagined the palace crowds gazing at her in admiration: the Emperor's beautiful new bride, chosen from a thousand women, pale-skinned and copper-haired, and clothed all in gold. The weight of the heavy jewels made her stand differently, with her head high and her wrists flexed. This is how a queen feels, she thought: proud and straight, weighted with treasure.

There was more commotion outside, and volleys of gunfire and drumbeats, coming closer. Helen peeped through the closed curtain. Led by seven guards firing muskets, a wave of ululating women broke into the courtyard and surged into every corner. In their midst, bobbing like a fat golden apple, was the wedding chair, borne on the shoulders of four burly, white-robed eunuchs. Microphilus strutted ahead of them with a golden *dulbend* on his head, accompanied by the biggest black slave-woman Helen had ever seen.

Turning, she found Reema's battered face looking at her with narrowed eyes. 'The big slave will lift you into the chair. Your feet must not touch the ground until you reach the Emperor's rooms. It is to protect you from bad dust. Do you have the *chifumuro*?' she asked, and Helen nodded, touching the wee lump pinned to the inside of her waistcoat. 'Good,' Reema said, pulling back the curtain. 'So, you are ready.'

The chair was more like a casket than a sedan. Seated inside, surrounded by cushions, Helen could only see out through a narrow golden grille at eye level on either side of her. It was like being inside her *haik* again: she could smell the eunuchs' sweat but she couldn't see them. The Harem lurched past the narrow gratings, two ululating ribbons of ogling faces interspersed with slices of rose bush, fountains, *teem* trees.

Suddenly the faces were gone and the women's noise started to recede as they left the Harem. She could hear the eunuchs' breathing now; their slippered feet slopping along the tiled cloisters of the main Palace. Dark wood carvings filled the little grilles; gold tiles, more fountains; bursts of sunlight and shadow as they passed through courtyard after courtyard; baldy-head slaves in ones and twos, their shoulders and heads only, staring; bearded men in white *dulbends*. She heard music approach, then fade away again; there was the clatter of cooking pots; the rich aroma of stewed mutton.

Now she could hear a different sound: people, a huge crowd of them, coughing and chattering, shouting to one another. Bolts were drawn back and the crowd began to cheer. A larger band of musicians started up, with trumpets and drums, and there was an explosion of gunfire. The images through the grilles lurched and darkened, then lightened, then darkened again before receding suddenly as Helen was carried out into a vast open space.

Where was she? She could see whole bodies now: men, thousands of them, restrained by lines of what she supposed were the *Bokhary*. The crowd was pressing forward, cheering and shouting, trying to peer in through the grilles at her.

Shrinking back against the cushions, Helen fumbled for her

chifumuro beneath her finery and wrapped her fingers around it. It was six months since she'd arrived in the Harem. She'd forgotten how frightening men could be in a crowd; how predatory; like hungry dogs with their white *dulbends* shrouded in brown winter cloaks; how crude and pock-marked, with their big noses and dirty teeth; their bristly ears and nostrils, their thick fingers.

Sweat prickled at her hairline and on her upper lip. She was back being chivvied through the streets of Sallee; pinched and prodded by strangers; drooled over; spat at. And she thought of Betty, for the first time in weeks. Betty was out there still, somewhere. Was she alive? Whoring, skivvying? Dying of some illness? Could any woman survive outside a Harem in this land?

The chair swayed to a halt at another gate and Helen realized they'd just passed through an immense courtyard. The grilles went dark, then brightened again, then they were crossing a second courtyard, even larger than the first. The crowd here seemed more unkempt and the noise was deafening: ten thousand, twenty thousand men, all heaving and pushing, and the guards braced back against them with their legs apart and their heels slipping in the red dust. What if they should give way? Helen imagined the multitude hurtling towards her, teeth reeking, cloaks flapping.

More gates. Microphilus had said she'd be taken right outside the Palace and along the outer walls before going into the Throne Room. 'It's traditional,' he'd explained with a tight smile. 'The bride has to be carried through the streets, from her father's house to the house of her husband. It's a sign to all the other men that she's been transferred to another man's keeping. Though in your case, of course, you'll just be returning to the Harem.'

Outside. She must be outside now, because suddenly there

were no walls in sight on one side. Just more men, poorer men, she could tell by the colour of their clothes. Duns and greys, peering and shoving, shouting and cheering. The guards were mounted now with their whips raised, reining in and spurring their horses to barge backwards, snorting and stamping, herding the crowd, trampling their slippers into the cold dust. She could see sunken cheeks and black teeth beneath grimy *haiks*; scars and bruises; the scabs of frostbite on nose and lip, like the wild Highlanders that stumped into Crieff with the first snows.

And out there, beyond them, the tree-studded plains; and beyond them in the distance, the mountains, Naseem's beloved mountains. Helen had to crouch to see the tops of them through the gratings: white peaks sparkling in the sunshine, crisp and clean as grace. And buzzards circling and dancing on the clean, cool air; the wisps of fresh cloud; scree glistening on the upper passes where the gentians grew.

Back at the Palace, she was taken in by a different route. This must be what visiting dignitaries saw when they had an audience with the Emperor: wide, lofty corridors studded with enormous jewelled wall-lamps; restive hawks tethered with delicate gold chains; soldiers hung with guns and swords; enormous cannons, clocks and mirrors in carved alcoves: all this unrolled like strips of coloured carpet through the grilles. Here must be where *sheikhs* and *khalifs* strolled and decisions were taken, where the Emperor ruled his kingdom. Where he actually ruled, over everything she'd seen outside; all those people; land as far as the eye could see; all the way to the sea. This Emperor, who could have any woman he wanted; who'd chosen her for his wife.

Any moment now. There was a fanfare and another volley of gunfire, followed by the sounds of shuffling and coughing.

Another crowd, Helen thought, fluffing her hair out over her shoulders: important men, rich men, especially invited for the Emperor's private wedding feast. She pulled out her kerchief and ferreted inside her *kamise* to pat sweat from her armpits. Black beards and jewelled *dulbends* bowed as she was carried past. Her palms were wet. What would they think when they saw her?

The chair turned and lurched one last time before finally being lowered to the ground. The chair door opened and the big slave lifted her out and on to the floor. They were in a small dark antechamber, lit by lamps. Helen could hear the restless crowd on the other side of the door. This was the moment.

But what was this? The big woman was stepping forward and covering all her glowing finery with a white *haik*. Before Helen could protest, the doors were flung open and the black woman was leading her into the great hall. Helen fumbled with the folds around her head to form the regulation opening.

There he was, waiting to greet her, clad in a golden kaftan covered by a gauzy white *jellabiah*. He had a sword in his hand, which he raised for her to walk beneath, as she had been told to do, to show her obedience and humility to her new husband. She tried to catch his eye, to say something, but the gunfire and cheering around them were deafening in the vaulted hall. Rows of turbaned men were reciting prayers, and someone was shouting names from the far side of the great room. The musicians began playing again, and a group of three men stepped forward with a steaming basin of *henna*.

Then another set of doors was opening and she was being ushered out through them, then in through another set of doors. They closed behind her and the sound was suddenly muffled. The slave lifted off her *haik* and Helen blinked in the light.

She was in a beautiful room with steps up to a small raised

platform, covered at one end with carpets and golden cushions. Apart from the stone-faced slave, the room was empty.

She didn't see the Emperor again until the evening. She could hear some kind of ceremony through the wall, with singing and chanting and an old man intoning some verses from the Q'ran. She thought perhaps he'd come to fetch her afterwards, but no. Then music began playing, and she could hear food being served. The black slave disappeared and returned with some trays for her; wonderful dishes, a feast for one, and sugared fruit wrapped in gold leaf.

Helen picked desultorily at the food, thinking that at any moment he would send for her. Tears burnt at the back of her eyes. Back at home she'd have been at the head of the table with her husband on one side and her father on the other. Everyone would have been staring at her, admiring her wedding frock. There'd have been daft speeches and slopped whisky; later, she'd have led the whole village in a dance . . .

In the great hall there was a burst of laughter, then angry voices. She thought she heard the Emperor, but with the music playing she couldn't be sure. There was a loud, screamed 'La!' – 'No!' – and someone calling on Allah's mercy. What on earth was happening?

The door opened and she stiffened with apprehension, but it was just one of the Harem eunuchs carrying an enormous mirror in an ornate golden frame. He held it up in front of her for a moment, for her to admire herself, then propped it against the wall opposite. Following close behind was another eunuch, with a cloak of velvet and silk over his arm, which he placed at her feet. He was followed by another, bearing a huge silver-framed clock; and another, who knelt to show her a silk-lined box full of inlaid tea-spoons. Wedding gifts! From the men outside, they must be.

Quite forgetting the disturbance in the great hall, Helen sat forward in excitement. Eunuchs were entering one after another, kneeling and piling beautiful objects around her. She saw herself reflected in the great mirror: a golden queen afloat on a sea of treasures. She hadn't expected that there would be wedding gifts; she had never seen things of such beauty.

She felt like laughing aloud. Still the eunuchs kept coming. After a while the room began to fill up and she couldn't see what was being added to the outer edges of the precious heaps. And it all belonged to the Emperor's special girl.

Hugging herself with delight, she felt the wee hard bulge of the *chifumuro* against her ribs.

'What happened in the hall after supper?' she asked the Emperor later. 'I heard some shouting, then everyone laughing.'

'Just some foolish slave-boy being taught a lesson.' He was caressing her cheek, easing her blouse open so that he could kiss her throat. 'I have never seen the *henna* done in this colour before. Like a golden spider's web.' She wondered what the boy had done. Spilt gravy, maybe, on one of the guests. 'Shall I be your fly tonight, Aziza? Will you catch me in your web, here –' loosening her sash – 'right down here where you are sticky?'

She closed her eyes and swayed against him. Inside her satin *salwars* she was all honey and oil. She didn't care about not being allowed at the feast. Being alone with him was what mattered, here in his chamber, where the Emperor took off his clothes and became a man. The man who loved her, who had married her and made her his wife.

Next morning she did not have to wait for the hag Malia to come to fetch her: the chair was waiting to carry her to her new quarters. Batoom and Microphilus were there when she arrived, each with a small tray of burning frankincense, which they wafted over her as she stepped in through the gates. And Reema, kneeling, smiling her reluctant stiff smile.

Helen walked into the centre of the courtyard and looked around. She had peered in through the gates many times, at the blowsy plants and scummy fountain, at tiles littered with bird droppings and fallen leaves. Now it was transformed: clean and bright, with the plants trimmed and the fountain sparkling in the sunshine.

Her own courtyard! And all those rooms: three, four, five at least, plus the washroom and kitchen. And the trees; her own shade. And no one staring and whispering about her all the time. Her own washroom; her own fountain; her own gate to lock.

'Welcome to your new home, *Lalla* Aziza.' Microphilus was smiling strangely at her. 'Is it everything you ever dreamed of?'

'Oh, yes! Was it you organized the cleaning?'

'Ay, me – and a small army of eunuchs. And auld sourpuss added a few finishing touches while you were at the wedding. Now I'm sure you won't want to be bothered with the likes of us while you're exploring, so we'll be gone.'

Helen wandered into the washroom and out again. So many rooms. There was even a little outhouse for brooms and spare water jars. An outhouse. She remembered Betty suddenly, and her sad small ambition: an outhouse; a borrowed bairn; a skivvy's job. Where was she now?

'I was wondering, *Lalla*, whether you'll be wanting more slaves?' Reema asked after a while.

Helen stared at her: of course, more slaves.

'A kitchen girl and a gardener,' Reema said. 'And maybe another girl to help me. The girls can stay in the rooms beside the kitchen with me. It seems a shame not to use them.'

'Yes.' Helen began walking towards the kitchen: her own kitchen, her own servants' quarters. John Bayne had shamed her in his servants' quarters. Now she was a queen with her own servants.

'Would you like me to ask around for you? You need people you can trust – especially now.'

She'd send someone to look for Betty tomorrow. And give her something far better than an outhouse to live in. She'd ask Microphilus about it first thing. It was the least she could do. Now she was a queen, she could do anything she liked.

After the lunchtime sleep, the eunuchs arrived, carrying trunks and baskets piled high with Helen's wedding gifts. She pulled open the door of one of the empty rooms and stood aside in an agitated daze while they brought them all in.

'So many, many pretty things!' Helen turned to see the little Queen Douvia skipping barefoot across the courtyard towards her. 'You should hear the women outside in the main Harem. They cannot believe it!

'*Ave!*' Douvia curtseyed comically, pulling out her baggy breeks as though they were petticoats. 'Aziza, isn't it? I have seen you in the garden with the Emperor.' She smiled and a dimple winked in her left cheek. 'Tell me, Aziza, why is it, do you think, that the men in this land dress like women and the women like men?'

Helen laughed and shook her head. 'Because of the heat? I don't know. It's the shoes I can't understand.'

'Yes! Slip slop, slip slop. Like a snail shuffling along. I have them on for a minute and I want to fling them across the room.' She kicked an imaginary slipper off a dust-covered foot. 'Over there by that pillar,' she barked suddenly, pointing an imperious finger at a burly eunuch lumbering towards her with an enormous plant in a clay urn.

'You see, I too have brought you a wedding gift. In my country we call this bush *ibiscos*. I chose the pale one with the red throat, because you are so pale. The flowers open freshly each morning to greet the sun, then die at the end of the day. But there are more each day. It is like the women in the Harem: whenever the Emperor sends a woman away, there is another fresh one waiting to replace her. It is a wonderful plant. And the sun-birds love them. So really, you see, it is two gifts at the same time. The flowers and the flying jewels who drink the honey from their throats.'

The eunuch set it down with a grunt, and Douvia immediately ran over to arrange the foliage. 'If you want, I could help you decorate. I know it looks bare now, but soon, you'll see, your home will be beautiful! Unless –' She hesitated. 'Maybe you are like Batoom. She doesn't like –'

'Oh, no! I love pretty things.'

'Good! I am so glad we are going to be neighbours. This place has been empty too long. And sad. *Lalla* Salamatu could never settle after her son died.' Douvia paused, frowning, then brightened again. 'But you will be happy here, I am sure. I was so excited when I heard you would be coming, someone young like me. Batoom and Zara, they are so – oh, I don't know. They have the ways of older women, always talking about their sons, what they will do when they leave here.'

Douvia danced around Helen's courtyard, darting into this and that corner. 'I am sorry to be so curious. But Salamatu was crazy for two years before she went to Tafilalt. So it's a long time since I have been here. Look!' The wee queen caressed a curling green stem. 'Here is a wonderful white jasmine, and you have all these bougainvillaea. They don't look like anything much now, but they will be marvellous when it gets hot again. Purple, red, pink. Are you going to get a gardener?'

'I think so – I hadn't really thought about it. Reema said she would find someone for me.'

'I do my garden myself,' Douvia said proudly. 'I will teach you if you like. And you must come and see my birds.' She smiled infectiously at Helen. 'I would have become crazy myself when I first came here if I hadn't had them to occupy me. I couldn't understand what anyone was saying and I thought they all hated me – even my slaves. For ages I was afraid they were going to poison me, until Malia found me a taster. Shall we have tea?' She clapped her dimpled hands as Reema emerged from the kitchen.

'I didn't go into the main Harem like you when I first came here, so it took me years to learn Arabic,' she continued, plucking a small rug from the growing heaps the eunuchs were delivering, and unrolling it beneath the jasmine bower. 'After he converted me, the Emperor married me straight away, so I was on my own nearly all the time. Except for the Emperor, of course.' She smiled fondly. 'And Fijil visited to make sure I was all right. He could speak Latin, so he helped me a lot in the beginning, especially after – I mean, to begin with I couldn't –' A look of confusion clouded her face briefly, before her dimpled smile burst through again.

Helen sat down, trying to remember what Microphilus had said about Douvia's conversion to Islam. Hadn't she been tortured into renouncing her Christianity? Had her nails ripped out, or her fingers broken, or something? Helen aimed a wincing glance at the plump little hands. They seemed a bit stiff, maybe, and covered with fresh scratches, but nothing like the twisted, deformed things Helen was expecting.

Perhaps Microphilus had been lying. The Emperor she knew would never break a ten-year-old's fingers. Punishing a grown woman was one thing; deliberately hurting a child was something else altogether. Anyway, if he had tortured her, she'd hate him, surely? But she seemed as obsessed with him as the rest of the Harem. It must have been someone else who dealt with the conversions.

'Would you like a little bird? I have mostly canaries, but there are some goldfinches too, and greenfinches, though their song is not as pretty. I pay one of the gardeners to get them from the *soukh* in Marrakech. They're my babies.'

'But I thought you had a real baby?'

'Yes, but the slaves won't let me near him. They're afraid I might hurt him by accident, and then they'll be blamed. He's a prince, you see. When he grows up he'll be the next Emperor. So no one trusts me to touch him. When you are settled, please come to visit and I will show you everything.'

46

Having vowed never again to set pen to paper, here I am scratching once more at my vellum. Batoom has sent me away in a fit of rage, claiming she cannot suffer my maudlin moping a second longer.

She is referring to my continuing obsession with Helen, whose own obsession with the Emperor was requited last week by a wedding of unprecedented expense (which the avaricious Emperor reaped back thrice-fold in tributes, and coffered a canny profit – even allowing for the traditional showering of coins on the crowds gathered outside the Palace).

So she is married. And Microphilus is forced into the role of doting Father, procuring her fineries and packing her, decked out like a crusted doll, into a box to be flaunted around the walls of the Palace. And here I am, as bereft as any father whose treasured daughter is gone from his household for ever.

'Three moons, Fijil!' thunders Batoom, bundling me up in the bed-sheet and tipping me off the divan. 'It's not that I mind you whimpering after the wench. It's the fact that you are so hangdog when you are with me! It has become an insult.'

The fit came on her suddenly this morning, like a ripe purple fig which swells on the tree until its satin skin can hold no more, and a seam splits, and a red gash gapes and spits out a great gob of gritty pips.

'If you were a young boy I could understand,' rants she, rifling in her clothes-trunk to extract my pressed *salwars*. 'I've known boys so enslaved by their monkeys that they lose all control of their higher minds. But you are not a boy.' How she glares down at me: nostrils flaring, breasts heaving with passion!

'If you were a man without a mistress,' she continues, unhooking an armful of my *haiks* from beside the door, 'with no way of discharging your milk. If your *durra-ens* were aching and your monkey's tail up and knotted around your throat. But you have *me –*' Her indignation grows as the heap of my belongings mounts up on the floor.

'Am I invisible, Fijil?' Now she stands before me, wide as a barn, feet planted, hands fisted on her hips. 'This body, which comforts and pleasures you each night – is it worth nothing at all to you?' And stoops and scoops and thrusts the heap into my arms.

I confess I am speechless, for this is the first time she has ever expressed herself in this way to me. Even last month, during the fasting of Ramadan, when the kitchens were all closed until nightfall, and the Harem bellies grumbled with unaccustomed hunger, and tempers frayed and snapped while all willed the sun to sink – even then Batoom kept her equanimity.

And will regain it again, I feel certain – perhaps even before sunset this evening. For she never was one to bear a grudge.

'I hoped when she married, you would come to your senses,' she continues. 'But now she is but a wall away, I can see it will be even worse. And you will be craning after her every movement, listening for her voice, counting the days the Emperor sends for her, checking the washing on the line in her courtyard. At least when she was tucked away with the other women there were some days when you did not talk about her, when I felt you were truly with me.'

And now a sneer wrinkles her magnificent broad nose. 'An

African man does not treat his women in this way. When he is with one wife, he is hers and hers alone. He does not do what your Scottish men do: play sex with one woman while thinking of another; keep one to tend the house and secret others to tumble.' I search for mollifying reassurances to muzzle her anger, but there is nothing I can say. Every word that she speaks is the truth.

'Well, Batoom refuses to be a Scottish wife. It is bad for her spirit to know her man is always yearning for another. Batoom is weary of this man, this piece of meat that has been chewed and spat out. Batoom deserves better.'

So I trail around the place, gathering up my comb and my razors, my best slippers and my comfortable old ones, chiding myself for my stupidity. When my *paniers* are all packed and my clothes piled to my chin, I sidle up to the glowering queen to take my leave, glancing hopefully up at her face for the twinkle that will show she has relented. Her face has softened, it is true, but not in tenderness. It is a mask of mourning that she turns towards me.

'What if she never tires of him? Have you thought about that?' she asks quietly. 'What if she is like Zara, and continues in her passion long after he has ceased to send for her? How long, Fijil, will you degrade yourself in this way? Yearning after someone who sees your little limbs and not the bigness of your spirit? Oh, you betray yourself, Fijil!' And sighs and subsides on to the divan with a stately ballooning of white garments.

'Go, Fijil,' says she, and her black eyes are suddenly bright with tears. 'Batoom will not love a man who values himself so cheaply. If you wish to return to Batoom's bed, come as a whole man who wants her for what she is, not as some half-man torn by unrequited longing. Until then – go. Batoom has had enough.'

And with these words ringing in my ears, and a flat-foot eunuch to carry my baskets, I trudge back to my own quarters.

Of course, I have always kept my own quarters. The Chief Eunuch cannot be seen to be ensconced with the Chief Queen. Though we must consult regularly, *naturellement*, on matters regarding the smooth running of the Harem. Ay, and meticulously too, mindful of our onerous duties, and often into the night, and beyond, and during *siestas*. So avid have we been, it proved practical to keep a duplicate set of my things at her *appartements*. And she had things of hers here, too, for those times when she visited me, though those times were fewer, for *La Batoom*'s stupendous progress through these cloisters is far more likely to cause notice than the busy scampering of the *mus minimus* about Harem business.

Thus, Batoom is unlikely to come directly to me when she relents. She will send her wee slave-lass on some pretext to call me back. Ah, there is the door now.

Just the wind knocking.

My *paniers* are at the foot of the bed. I have not unpacked them, for I am convinced she will call me back; if not tonight, then tomorrow when her anger has abated.

My ink pot was quite dry and encrusted when I took it out; I replaced the cork carelessly all those weeks ago. I had to send Maryam off to the scribe to beg more, and soak my quills for an hour to loose them of their craggy deposits. But it feels good to have the instruments of Reason at hand once more, and to scratch away like an ant-bear at a termite hill.

I see I was holding forth on the subject of Sanity three moons back, accusing Helen of Delusion, and concluding in a flurry of indignant blots. So much for those insights. According to Batoom, it is I who have been insane. Certainly I have cut myself adrift from this paper harbour, where wisdom is the quay and passion the boat, and ink the painter that tethers one to the other.

Why have I allowed myself to drift so long, with Dame Jealousy at the tiller, so far from Batoom, my safe island? Why sever the rope of Reason that has anchored me since boyhood?

Helen has capsized me. Since the Berber died, she seems to feel my very presence as an irritant. She is polite, sure, as the proprietor of a shoe-store is polite, with all the requisite 'Good morning's and 'I thank you's. But the warmth, the *craic*, is gone. And she will not, will not, look at me . . .

With my first love, Peggy Doig, there was always an intimacy, such that every detail of her *affaire* with my brother was mulled over in my company. Though we never embraced, I could think myself her true Lover, and he the Counterfeit, for did she not confide in me her true feelings, and dissemble with him? I thought it would be like that with Helen. But she has left nary a chink in the tight armour of her days. If I knock in the morning, she is preparing for sleep and wafts me drowsily away. In the afternoons, I am permitted a few minutes at most, while she dizzies around with her paints and perfumes with a fixed gaiety that enamels her discourse, and repels all my sober gambits. On the sane days of her monthlies she is less elusive, 'tis true, but insists on involving me in various practical plans which preclude any true intimacy. So she wishes a mirror hung – can I organize her a skilled eunuch? – and a series of small coat-hooks; her door needs planing as it has swelled in the rain; she wonders, can I arrange for fresh lime on her walls?

She has become quite the night owl, emerging at sunset with her eyes circled in some new green *kohl* she has discovered, to drift languorously after Malia along the cloisters, while the slaves kneel before her, murmuring her name. And in the mornings wandering back heavy-lidded, with her lips bruised and the Emperor's *haik* draped around sultry shoulders, looking around vaguely for her water and her breakfast, doing all like a sleepwalker until her curtains are drawn on the day.

Nothing can pierce the quilts of her satisfaction. Not the Berber's death – save, I suppose, for the first few days when we were all in a stunned stupor. The fasting of Ramadan was endured effortlessly, for was she not already a night creature? So while we are all chewing on our sleeves to assuage our hunger, she is just starting to stretch her elastic limbs on her divan, yawning and showing her little teeth, combing her hair and preparing herself for a long night of feasting.

And I am left with crumbs. But Dame Jealousy was never a finicky eater, and can batten as fat on scraps as she can on a banquet of lurid confession. Though I am not the only one feeding her. The entire Harem is hissing with resentment, for while the Emperor saves his Cream for the one strawberry, the other fruit wax peevish and sour. And the Crone has become quite demented to see the Emperor so engrossed with one woman. That Helen has failed to conceive further agitates the Hag and sets her to kneading her twiggy hands so rapidly that I fear they will smoulder and burst into flame.

At least the lass is not with child, I intone like a prayer. For I have developed an oddly comforting Superstition that the Body is truer than the Heart. As long as the Emperor's seed has not rooted in her womb, I may hope for a space in her heart.

21 January 1770

I keep expecting Batoom to relent. Even as I am snuffing my rush-light ready for sleep, I fancy I hear a quiet knock at my door and rush to open it, expecting her smidgin of a slave to say that I have forgotten something in the queen's quarters, which she desires me to retrieve.

But the knock does not come.

22 January 1770

Still no word from Batoom. I wonder how long she intends this to continue?

It is strange to be so much in occupation of my own space. Maryam is quite discomforted. She has become accustomed to using my kitchen as a Parliament of Scullions, where they gather for a Late Sitting of an evening. There was quite a procession of them knocking yesterday, which she turned away, one after another, with an apologetic shrug and a glance over her shoulder at me, until I felt compelled to apologize to the *bint* for inconveniencing her.

I shall visit Batoom tomorrow to seek some kind of *rapprochement*.

23 January 1770

It seems I am to get used to this solitary existence. Batoom welcomed me, it is true, and served tea. But when I stroked her glorious brown arm she disengaged herself decidedly, before my fingers could reach the soft fold of her elbow (this is a very sensitive part of the Black Queen, who has been known to moisten from this touch alone if performed delicately enough when she is in the right mood).

'Will you insult me, Fijil?' says she with a reproving look. 'You may be prepared to love a woman who thinks you are nothing, but Batoom will not endure it. No, don't start –' she interrupts me, for I have begun protesting my deep affection for her. 'I saw you pause at Aziza's gate as you came here. And you will do so again as you leave, will you not?' At which I sigh, but cannot deny.

When I come to leave, she stands in her gateway to watch me traverse the wide yard to Helen's quarters, and knock vainly, and find she is with *Lalla* Douvia, and trail shamefacedly away.

It seems the Young Queen Douvia will soon replace the Berber as Helen's *confidante*. These last few days they are for ever to be seen scurrying from one courtyard to another with tawdry baubles. I had hoped that Helen's association with Batoom might continue, now they are neighbours, and serve as a corrective to her petty venal concerns. But I suppose the two younger lassies have more in common, both hailing from Europe and finding themselves (in this, as in many other things) somewhat alienated from the rest of the Harem.

Certainly they share an obsession with the Emperor, for *La Douvia* regards him almost as a Deity, her bright eyes guileless with love, such that you would think she would martyr herself for his sake. Perhaps it is because she is so young, and has neither years, nor companions, nor God, to temper her attachment. Ay, she is a strange, sweet lass. When she first arrived in the Harem it seemed the more the Emperor tortured her, to drive out her God, the more avidly did she embrace him as her new object of worship. Like a puppy who knows his Master by the feel of his boot.

As though pain were love.

9 *February* 1770

I have been settling into my eunuch's existence and spending time in their company, something I haven't bothered with for nigh on three years. (My quarters are sited somewhat to one side of the eunuchs' chain of courtyards, but near to their main entrance so that I can mark their comings and goings without being drawn into the particulars of their society.)

There are some who play a fierce game of Backgammon, wagering their combs and *kohl* brushes (in flagrant disregard of Islam's prohibition of gambling), and flinging their counters on the board. I find I have quite a knack for the game, though it has been necessary to plunder the tawdrier of the market stalls to purchase a stock of gaudy kerchiefs and rouge pots to play with. When I tried to wager a brace of *qat* pouches, they refused me a seat on the carpet.

They have a kind of humour all their own, involving the giving and taking of offence, such that one will accuse his fellow of vulgar taste (for pairing, say, a yellow *kamise* with cerise *salwars*), whereupon the other will huff up like a vast turkey, calling his accuser a brazen bitch, or somesuch, flinging a tasselled scarf over his barn shoulders and sniffing in monumental *pique*. They can continue like this for an entire afternoon, flouncing hugely into and out of one another's chambers, squawking in theatric effrontery until called upon to perform some task.

Their duties are few, namely the patrolling of the Harem walls (which task they abhor, for it requires them to clean off their cosmetics and don the uniform – 'so *bland*' – of the Palace guards), and chaperoning the women to certain rooms within the Palace (when their sons visit from the Academy, *par exemple*, or when they need to be examined by one of the *tabibs*), plus sundry fetchings and carryings that the women require, for the Harem hinnies are so indolent their limbs are fairly devoid of strength, such that heaving a small pannier across a courtyard is beyond their capabilities.

A certain trio have decided to take charge of my appearance, for it is generally agreed that I am 'quite the most disgraceful harlot'. They object most particularly to my hair, which you may recall I wear long and unoiled in a wee braid down my back, and my side-whiskers ('so *vulgar*'). 'Why don't you let us shave you properly?' pleads one, poised to bound off for his razors. 'And his chest's a disgrace!' tuts another over my few pale curls. 'So *brutish* to see all *that* through the opening of your *kamise*.' 'Like a common peasant,' sneers the third. If they had their way I would be shaved bald as a plum, with a scarab tattooed on my cheek, and attired in an array of coloured scarves.

I still take tea with Batoom in the afternoons, and she will often invite me to join her for supper. But though I have lingered on occasion until bedtime, she has barred me from entering her chamber and crouches over me instead with her *kamise* gaping and her warm crevices all reeking with musk, and plants a kiss on my forehead with her marvellous wide mouth and shoos me off, tumescent and throbbing, into the chaste night.

So Microphilus is become a eunuch again.

47

Helen was squatting on the chamber-pot with a copper basin in her lap. Her forehead was clammy and a snake of cold sweat slithered between her breasts. She wiped her mouth and let her head hang forward, sighing. Would it stop now for a while?

She'd been sick for days now, for as much as an hour at a time: usually when she was in her quarters, but sometimes, as now, when she was with the Emperor.

'Aziza?' Oh no, she must have woken him up.

For an hour she'd been trying to keep quiet, as spasms doubled her over, throat burning, fingers gripping the basin, eyes staring at her distorted reflection, mouth gaping like a beached fish.

'Where are you?'

'In here. I won't be long.' Please, Allah, she prayed, who is so Merciful, don't let him come in and see me like this. Quickly she swilled her mouth out and spat quietly, then breathed out into her cupped hands and sniffed: he mustn't smell vomit on her breath. Getting shakily to her feet, she tipped the contents of the basin into the chamber-pot and laid a cloth over it to keep the stench in. Scrubbing her teeth with liquorice root, she stood up and peered at her reflection in the mirror.

'Aziza – you've been gone ages. Is anything wrong?'

Her eyes seemed huge and dark in her pale face; her freckles like mud splashes. Should she tell him yet? She watched herself smile, the small mouth tilting at the corners. No; a few more days and she'd be sure.

The Emperor's baby! Maybe now the old hag Malia would stop her incessant embarrassing questions: 'How thick was your blood?' 'Are your breasts sore today?' 'What is the slime like this morning?' 'And your smell, before you have washed? Is it of fish or meat?' As if she were some kind of animal, rather than the Emperor's favourite queen. Helen finger-combed the sweat-soaked curls off her face and opened the door.

'I'm sorry –' smiling and walking over to the divan. 'I didn't mean to wake you.'

'Are you ill? You're as pale as a ghost.' He sat up and looked into her face, his eyes full of concern. His eyes, the baby might have his eyes: black and fringed with thick lashes.

'Just a bit sick, that's all. Too much activity after supper, I expect.' She gave him a sideways look. 'My grandmother always used to say you should rest after a good meal. Lucky she's not here now. She'd give you a right talking to, Emperor or no, for exhausting her favourite grandchild.'

He raised his dark eyebrows. 'I'm beginning to understand why your men can only manage one wife at a time,' he said with a smile. His smile: it might have a smile like this.

'It's not a question of managing more than one at a time,' she retorted with a toss of her head. 'It's a question of loving more than one. Scottish men give their hearts –'

'Ah yes. I was forgetting your passionate Scottish men. How they love a woman so much, there is no desire left in them for any others.' This was a favourite theme of his, contrasting Moorish virility with that of Helen's compatriots. 'But this I am beginning to understand too. For have I not lost all desire for other women? Malia says they complain I never send for them. She says she has at least a dozen ripe for impregnation every day of the week if I would only avail myself of them.

'I'm sorry, my Lord.' Helen cast her eyes downwards in mock humility. 'I hope you don't think I have been wasting your time.' She could feel a smile hovering at the corner of her mouth. How pleased he'd be when he knew!

'What are you smiling at, Aziza?' He tipped her chin up towards him. 'Are you keeping something from me?' Tell-tale blood heated her cheeks as he searched her face.

'What is it? What is this secret?' Then suddenly he understood. 'It's happened, hasn't it? That's why you have been spending so much time in the washroom.'

'What are you talking about?' she asked, all innocence, but the joy was bubbling up in her chest. 'I have just eaten something that didn't agree with me, that's all.' His nose, it could have his nose too: strong and straight. And his long legs; his clever hands.

'Very well,' he whispered, gathering her gently into his arms. 'This is one secret I will allow for a while. But as soon as you know for sure, I want you to tell me.'

Back in her quarters, Helen called for hot water to be taken to the washroom. She remembered the other women talking about it. If you are sick, it is because the baby is lodged strongly within you.

The Emperor's baby! Dreamily, automatically, she performed the *ghusl* cleansing. Soon she would swell up like the other pregnant women in the Harem. Her breasts would fill with milk: already they seemed bigger. What if it was a boy? She could be the mother of the next Emperor of Morocco. A little dark boy: she could see him now, tottering across the courtyard towards her, his rosy face wreathed in smiles.

A jolt of nausea doubled her over and she vomited her breakfast up neatly into the white cloth she'd set aside to use as a towel. She folded it over with a little wince of disgust. Only a few weeks, they said, then the sickness would stop. It meant her lassie's body was turning itself into a mother's. She rinsed her mouth with soapy water and spat, reaching for another cloth to wipe her face.

'Ah, here you are.' Malia pushed open the washroom door with a gnarled hand and shuffled inside. Didn't the woman ever knock?

Sniffing, Malia peered round the wee room. 'So, how long has your stomach been sending up food?' she asked, wrinkling her knobbly nose and bobbing her head from side to side.

'About a week.' Helen wrapped the cloth hurriedly around her waist.

'There's a strange smell in here.' Malia's head was down now, like a hound on the trail of a cony, casting about for the source of the scent.

'Just this, I expect. I was sick just now.' Helen picked the sicky cloth up and dumped it in a basin.

'So –' Malia looked Helen up and down. 'Come out here into the light, child, where I can see you properly. You look pale. Your lips are dry.'

'I told you. I've just been sick.' Helen felt a surge of triumph well up in her chest. Wait until she found out!

'Well, it will pass soon enough, I expect,' said the old woman. 'Here. I've brought you these.' She shrugged off her leather bag and pulled out a package of white muslin. 'I will inform the Emperor this afternoon.'

Helen stared at the white bundle. Perhaps it was too soon for Malia to notice.

'You mustn't worry,' the old woman went on, packing things back into her bag. 'Sometimes it can take a little longer. Especially if there has been another time, and the seed has – er – been weeded out. It is unfortunate, I know. But much too soon to worry. Next moon, if we are not successful, I will give you some special herbs to drink.'

Helen watched the old woman leave, then smiled secretly

341

to herself. Silly old woman. Couldn't she tell? She didn't have to wait until next moon. She was carrying now.

When she was dressed, Helen wandered into the courtyard. Tea was already prepared and waiting for her in the sunny spot she'd taken to sitting in. Kneeling down, she sighed and looked around: her courtyard. The sun-birds were hovering around the *ibiscos* flowers, just as Douvia had said they would, darting forward and probing their long tongues deep inside the throats of the trumpet-shaped blooms. She rested her hands on her belly. 'I know you're in there,' she whispered, and closed her eyes to focus on the wee space she imagined within her. The sun was warm on her eyelids; her mind felt soft and red; she imagined the nourishing warmth seeping down inside her to the tiny being curled at her core.

Opening her eyes, she blinked and tried to focus on the courtyard. The warm red vanished and everything seemed greenish and dark as her eyes tried to adapt. She picked up the silver jug Batoom had given her and poured tea, green and fragrant, into a wee silver cup. She took a sip, feeling the thick, sweet liquid caressing her tongue, the steam filling her nostrils with sweetness. Then she put it down again. Too hot; too sweet. Suddenly she felt desperately thirsty; her mouth seemed to be burning.

Walking across to the water jar, she lifted the lid and caught a glimpse of her reflected face bending over the jar, the sun shining through her amber curls, her huge hand obliterating it, before the image was shattered as the ladle broke the surface.

She sipped, and the water was like balm on her hot tongue. She rolled it around her mouth and swallowed. Then sipped again, more blessed coolness into her hot mouth. How had she ever managed the hot tea? She leant back against the wall and swallowed again. Then she noticed something behind the water jar.

It looked like a half-fledged sparrow, all spiky and be-draggled. Was it dead? She knelt down to get a closer look. If it was still alive, perhaps Douvia would like it as a pet. She reached out her hand to touch it, then drew back sharply with a cry of pain. Her fingers were covered with tiny puncture marks.

Then she felt it: slight but unmistakable. The familiar drag-ging pain in her belly; the secret seep of blood between her legs.

'Have you ever seen anything like it?' Helen stood well back and pointed at the prickly thing. Shudders were chasing one another up her back. 'I thought at first it was a critter of some kind.' Bile coated her throat like green glue. She couldn't bring herself to look at it.

'With three beaks? I don't think so.' Douvia squatted down a safe distance from the water jar and peered gingerly at the thing. Helen's two new slaves pressed themselves up against the wall, clutching their neck-charms.

'Folk at home used to talk about this sort of thing.' Helen swallowed, trying not to retch. 'They said they're full of wee bad spirits, which crawl into your head when you're asleep.' She searched her *salwars* and pressed the reassuring shape of the *chifumuro* against her thigh.

Douvia stood up. 'I think you should burn it. Straight away. Before it can do any harm.' Shuddering, she turned towards Helen. 'Try not to worry. It's probably just some nasty joke – one of the women trying to frighten you. If you are a queen you must expect these things.' She spoke lightly, but the black eyes seemed troubled.

'Come on,' she said suddenly. 'We will get rid of it. Then you must come to my quarters for lunch. And when you come back, there will be no trace of it left, only a few grey ashes which we will toss to the wind.' She dimpled at Helen, flinging a plump arm out sideways and spinning on her tiptoes.

'Now, you –' pointing imperiously at the shrinking slaves. 'Take this thing into the kitchen and – I don't care how you do it,' she snapped impatiently as they began to protest. 'Just do it. Can't you see how it is upsetting your mistress?'

'Are you feeling any better?' Douvia asked later.

'Much better.' Helen sighed and leaned back against the warm tiles. 'Thank you.'

They were sitting in the afternoon sunshine, in the corner of Douvia's courtyard, surrounded by the scents of wet earth and new leaves. The birds were quiet for once, and still, as though calmed by the long purple shadows and soft honey light.

They'd spent the whole day together: chatting, laughing, drinking tea and nibbling the delicious titbits the slaves brought out. Douvia didn't seem to eat meals like ordinary people, but picked constantly throughout the day, like a bird, at this or that sweet or savoury morsel. How bonny she was, Helen thought, with her glossy curls and dusky rose-petal skin. But scruffy as a tinker. Her fingernails were always ragged – she wouldn't allow the slaves to touch her hands – and there were always fresh scratches on her hoyden ankles.

'It's so beautiful here.' Helen waved her hand around the pretty courtyard. 'I know fine about growing neeps and kale, but I wouldn't know where to start with flowers. Did your mother teach you?'

'What, and get her hands dirty? No. The only kneeling my mother ever did was at her pew in the cathedral in Madrid. And she always wore gloves in case she touched anything that might contaminate her. The only time she touched me was after my bath, and she always washed her hands afterwards.' Douvia laughed and rubbed a dusty ankle.

'She had four hundred pairs of gloves. Sometimes she'd get through four or five pairs in a day. I used to sneak into her dressing-room when she was out, and sort them into different piles. The little lace ones that buttoned at the wrist were my favourites. Of course they were much too big for me.' She laughed again. 'Then one day she caught me. I'd fallen asleep on her bed. With her gloves all round me – can you imagine? I must have been about four years old.'

Helen laughed. 'What did she do?'

'She had the maids wash all the gloves, and the bedcover, and change the sheets. And ordered them to keep her door locked so I couldn't get in again. Then she made me kneel outside the door all day praying to the Madonna for forgiveness. She said if you spent an hour praying in this world, you'd escape a year of suffering in Purgatory.'

She pressed her palms together and put on a pious expression. 'I imagined the angels counting up the prayers, and marking them down in a golden book. Then I started worrying whether all my prayers counted. I mean, if you just rush through the words, thinking of something else, that couldn't be worth as much as saying something with all your concentration, so I started trying to find ways of making myself concentrate.'

All this talk of praying was making Helen feel nervous again. She hadn't prayed to her God, to Jesus, for weeks now. Maybe the spiny thing was a sign that He was angry with her. Maybe that was why she couldn't conceive: she'd wanted her first baby dead and now she was being punished.

'So I started holding the crucifix tight in my hands when I was praying. Did you have rosary beads in Scotland? They're a sort of necklace to help you count out the prayers, with a crucifix attached. I began to stab the crucifix into the palm of my hand when I was praying, to stop my mind from wandering. See –'

She held out her left hand, cupped stiffly as if to hold water. There was a pale scar in the centre, a deep wound with several shallower spikes radiating from the centre like a star.

Helen winced, but Douvia laughed again. 'That's why I was upset when they tried to take my rosary away. I thought I'd go to Hell if I didn't have the beads to pray with.'

'Fijil told me they hurt you when you first arrived.'

'Yes.' Douvia shrugged. 'But only my hands. They were so stupid. They thought I'd renounce God if they hurt my hands. But I was so used to pain by then, it didn't affect me. I just closed my eyes and prayed to the Holy Martyrs until they gave up. And they didn't dare touch the rest of me in case the Emperor was angry with them for spoiling me. After he'd gone to so much trouble to get me in the first place.'

A look of satisfaction came over her face. 'So then he came to me himself and wrapped my hair around his hand and began ripping it out by the roots. I hadn't even seen him before then. But when I saw him – he was so handsome! After that, I just agreed to whatever he wanted.' She touched her curls and looked into the distance for a moment.

'He called me his brave little angel,' she said dreamily. 'And he washed me himself, and helped them put the bandages on. I thought afterwards, he would want to – you know, play sex with me. But Malia said I was too young. Interfering old hag –' She scowled for a moment, then her face cleared again. 'Brave little angel – that's what my father used to call me.'

'My father used to call me Nelly. I hated it. There was a toothless old whore in Crieff they called Nelly the Gobbler and it always made me think of her.'

'My Christian name was Maria Madonna. My father used to buy me blue dresses, and white ones, to remind him of the Virgin. He'd take me to the dressmaker in his own carriage, and tell her exactly what he wanted for me.'

'He sounds like a kind man.'

'He really loved me – and *she* never let him near her. He said I was his little wife. But he'd have hated to see me like this.' Douvia picked at her *salwar kamise*. 'He liked to see me strapped in really tight at the waist. He had all my corsets made specially and tightened them himself, a bit tighter each day, watching my face all the time to see how much it was hurting. He was always so gentle when he was hurting me. I must have had the smallest waist in the city.'

'I used to have a waist once.' Helen smiled ruefully down at her swelling belly. 'But they're not allowed here. Though if I go on being sick like this, I'll be in danger of getting my old figure back.'

'I thought you were feeling a bit better. You haven't been sick this afternoon, have you?'

Helen sighed. 'No. But I'm always better in the afternoons. That's why I thought – I mean – before I started bleeding, I thought I might be –' Her eyes filled with tears and she gulped into her kerchief.

'Pregnant? Oh, Aziza. I am sorry. But it's still so early. It was nearly a year before I had my little Sulaiman.' Her brow wrinkled sympathetically. 'I remember exactly how it felt. Every month, I was so disappointed. And terrified the Emperor would be angry with me, or stop sending for me. After Malia had made me wait so long. But it happened in the end. And it will for you too, believe me.'

Helen sat forward. 'It's that thing,' she said. 'I was so sure I was pregnant. Then as soon as I saw it, I started bleeding.' She shivered.

Douvia frowned. 'A sort of hex, you mean, to get rid of the baby?'

'What else could it be?' The more Helen thought about it the more convinced she felt.

'I'm not sure,' Douvia said doubtfully. 'I mean, it would have to be someone who knew you were pregnant, wouldn't it? But you weren't even certain yourself. Did you tell anyone? Apart from me, just now I mean.'

Helen tried to think. There was the Emperor, of course. But that was only a hint. Anyway, he'd never do anything to harm her. And the slaves. She hadn't said anything to them, but if they'd heard her retching, they might have suspected she was pregnant. But Reema had always insisted on getting rid of the vomit and washing her things personally. What about the vomit in the Emperor's quarters? His slaves dealt with that. Helen's stomach churned. She could feel the food swirling around inside, mixed with hot bile, pushing at her throat. The back of her neck felt cold and clammy.

'Malia came sniffing around just after I'd been sick this morning,' she said. 'She seemed to know I was going to start bleeding. But then she always does.'

'Yes, how does she do that? Interfering old hag. I hate her knowing what's going on inside my body.' Douvia wrinkled her nose. 'What about that sour old slave of yours? What's her name? Reema. I always wondered about her. Didn't she work for Batoom once?'

Helen shook her head. 'It couldn't be Reema. She spends all her time making sure nothing nasty happens to me. That's why Batoom sent her to me when I first arrived.'

'But why you? Out of all the other new women?'

'I think Microphi – I mean Fijil – asked her to. I think he was worried about me. You know we both come from Scotland, so I think he feels responsible for me.'

'What did she say when you showed her the – the – you know?'

'She wasn't there. Batoom came round when I was in the washroom and asked Reema to help her with something. You know she's only got the one slave now, and that big bit of garden she grows food in. So she sometimes asks Reema for help.'

'So either of them could have put the thing there while you were washing.'

'But why would they?'

'Or Malia. Or one of the slaves.' Douvia frowned, then jumped up suddenly. 'I think we should stop talking about this. It's making us suspect everyone. The thing's burnt now. Let's try to forget it. Come on. It's nearly dark. You must be exhausted. I'll escort you back to your quarters.'

48

15 February 1770

Mother of God, Helen has been cursed!

The sourpuss Reema was here just now, her face rouched with anguish, saying they have found one of those vile things in Helen's quarters. It seems she was with Batoom when it was discovered and by the time she came back it had been burnt. But she quizzed the other slaves and there is little doubt that it was the twin of the horrid harbingers that were discovered in *Lalla* Zara's rooms last year.

Is this what awaits Helen now? The agitated wasting that scraped away Zara's beauty and abandoned her on Death's threshold?

Our stout-hearted Reema blames herself. 'I laid fresh salt crystals beneath her divan every night,' stutters she through gritted jaw (for salt is used here, as in Scotland, to repel the Devil). 'But I should have done more – when we moved into the new rooms, I only laid offerings and washed the floors that first day with salt water. I should have thought of *Lalla* Salamatu's madness. I should have done it every day.' And so on, berating her good self and compressing the hem of her *kamise* into a crumpled ball.

'I am on my way to fetch blue paint,' concludes the stalwart. 'But I thought you should know. Lord Fijil, do you think –?'

And I nod dumbly, mind seething like a pot on the boil, popping with disordered images of the stricken Old Queen: her bloody gums and bony arms, her tufted skull and weeping sores; the sordid array of bowls and cloths that had always to be near at hand. Dear Helen, how can I protect you from this?

Thursday, in the garden, she seemed paler than usual, but I thought it a trick of the sickly light glimmering through her green awning. She was attired all in white, even to her slippers, and her hair braided with white silk: an alien mermaid in a green pond, and the women agog with conjecture over when she will be with child. Oh, greedy Jealousy, there was meat a-plenty for you that day. If suspects were needed for the origin of the porcupine, there were nigh on five hundred gathered in that garden last Thursday.

My worst suspicions are confirmed.

I have just come from Malia's lair, where she was crouched over a tombstone tome, squinting down at the spiderish entries. It seems Helen is indisposed with the same configuration of afflictions that Malia recognized from the early stages of *Lalla* Zara's prostration.

'Here, see?' croaks she with a triumphant gleam, prodding a frayed black cursive. 'Even the smell is the same.' Have I mentioned before the Hag's habit of sniffing her clients as she examines them, as though they were bushes and she a dog-fox, wrinkling her pendulous nose and closing her shuttling eyes to savour the fragrance more completely?

'So,' she concludes, subsiding back on her cracked heels. 'Our mischief-maker has found a new victim.'

At which my stomach contracts, opening a chill space beneath my ribs. And a sense of *déjà vu* seizes me, as a *tajine* ferments in a liverish belly, weighing afresh all the varieties of witchcraft and poison, all the possible culprits who might wish harm on the Emperor's new queen.

When I return to my own quarters, the *déjà vu* deepens.

351

For here is the gnarled Methuselah lying across my gate, a rustling memory of that time, not four moons past, when Zara danced the jig to Death's music. The mullock lurches to his feet when he spies me, and launches into the avid incoherence I recall so well, peering urgently from the hedges of his brows, and scattering a confetti of bark fragments.

I consider telling him of the new porcupine, but resist. I well remember how assiduous he was during *Lalla* Zara's illness: lurking in leafy ambush around every corner, and rustling along beside me like a heap of animated kindling, offering orts of observation until my patience was worn as thin as a beggarwoman's shawl. He guarded his mistress, 'tis true, like a mangy hill-dog outben the hut of the crofter. But he could not avert the evil that affected her.

I have just been to my washroom and he is still outside my gate. His presence torments me with images of Zara's ravaged mask. I will not see him. I have not the patience to decipher his ramblings.

27 February 1770

Helen grows worse by the day. The effects are subtle, but my eyes are sharpened by the keen edge of love. I see her weekly, as I have done from the beginning, delivering her allowance (as queen she has an augmented amount in addition to the special monies for each night spent with His Majesty). So I am able to mark a certain dullness to her skin, the limp greyness of a wilted flower. Her cheeks seem somewhat sunken, yet there is a puffiness about the eyes, and a redness there, and around the nostrils, as though she has been weeping (which she may well have been).

She was in the garden last Thursday, but I cannot imagine she will endure it again. Already the women are beginning to hop like gaudy vultures around the carcass. Soon they will have a chance at their Lord again.

Batoom invites me frequently to take supper in her quarters, though she is as obdurate as ever about her bed.

There is my door –

The Emperor has sent Helen away. I should be rejoicing, yet what a hollow victory this seems.

To do him justice, the fickle Lord seems full of perturbation. If it is possible for the powerful to love (when they can command, what need have they to love?), then I judge the Emperor loves his White Queen. But his love for his own Health supersedes her by far. Such that his furrowed concerns for the lass are harried by nipping queries about his own welfare. Thus 'What ails Aziza?' is o'ertaken, before an answer can be provided, by 'Is it the kind of thing a man can catch?' And though he has summoned the *tabibs*, his additional tasters and guards are in place long before the *tabibs* have arranged their stiff limbs on his carpet.

So now they are settled, a confederacy of tortoises, all nodding sagely and fingering their beards. I do not share his faith in these physicians, for they have never proved of any use with the women, being too jealous of their standing with the Emperor to hazard any true physic. When a prostrate woman recovers it is because the illness abated of its own accord, or from some remedy Malia has administered (for the women always consult her too).

'Should I send her away, to avert an epidemic?' asks the Emperor nervously. At which my spine bristles with alarm. But I need not have worried, for the *tabibs* are watching him like hawks to ascertain if he is seeking an excuse to rid himself of a troublesome queen. Having discerned his genuine reluctance, they look sideways at one another, then shake their jowled heads *en masse*, as though they have given the matter extensive thought, saying that as the ague appears to affect only the queens, and no eunuch or slave, it seems unlikely to spread wider.

The Emperor seems reassured, and proceeds to quiz them about the likely course of the disease. 'Will the same happen to her as happened to the *Lalla* Zara?' he asks with an ill-concealed shudder.

At which they comment vaguely, as only physicians can, that it would depend on this or that factor, and it being too early to tell, and the two women are of different physical types, and so on and so forth, until his anxiety effervesces into anger.

'Are you saying you don't know?' asks he in that dangerous, cool voice.

'We cannot be certain –' one begins.

'There are so many factors –' tries another.

'Of course we will do our best –' concludes a third.

'But your best did not help the *Lalla* Zara, did it?'

'The lady is well, Allah be praised,' protests one.

'The lady looks like a witch,' snaps the Emperor. 'And her mind is deranged. Is that the best you could do? Now, listen to me carefully. I love the *Lalla* Aziza. She is dearer to me than all of you put together. If you do not come up with a remedy before she has turned into a hag, I shall have you all fed to the pigs – is that clear? Now GO –'

At which they skedaddle, clutching their beards and their bags to their chests.

He does not dismiss me, so I remain. 'I have received word that the corsairs have captured an English doctor,' he says. 'I've sent my best horses and ordered he be conducted to the Palace at highest speed. Perhaps he will be able to help Aziza. When he arrives, you will translate his speech. You do speak English, don't you?'

'Yes, my Lord.'

'I miss her so much, Fijil. It is not the same with the other women. You would not understand, but when a man loves a woman, his body responds to her in ways it cannot with another. She is so shy, yet so passionate when roused. I loved watching those colours change on her skin, knowing how much she loves me.'

'Yes, my Lord.'

'When she was first sick we both thought it was because she was with child. I was so happy.'

'Yes, my Lord.'

'Fijil, I want you to spend time with the *Lalla* Aziza. Watch who comes and who goes.' Whereupon he places a long hand on my shoulder, and looks deep into my eyes. 'I love her, Fijil. I want her in my bed again. I want her to be mother to the next Emperor. Find out who is doing this to her.' And his black eyes brim, and his fine brow creases in an anguish so real that it almost obliterates the memory of the Berber's feet crossed neatly in a basket.

49

Helen opened her eyes and stared around her bedchamber. What time was it? Sparrows were stirring outside, but it was dark; too early for the dawn call to prayers.

Had she slept at all? The lamp behind the screen was burning strongly still, lighting the tableau of chamber-pots, bowls and cloths Reema laid ready each evening; close at hand in case Helen couldn't get to the washroom in time – though these days simply crouching over the pot made her legs tremble with exhaustion.

Bands of pain, the ragged remnants of hours of retching, were slung like hammocks across her belly. Was she hungry? Her stomach burnt and heaved incessantly, so that she could no longer tell whether the empty clenching was to beg for or expel food. Recently she'd given up eating altogether and just sipped water all day. She kept a jar nearby all the time now. There was the usual big jar at the end of the divan, which Reema refilled with fresh water at midday and last thing at night. But she'd had others, with ladles, placed around the courtyard too, wherever she might sit, so that she need never call for a drink. Thirst could grip her at any time, as fierce and sudden as a bout of retching, singeing her throat and flooding her mouth with thick saliva, making her lunge for the nearest gulp of sweet water.

Praise Allah, here was the call to prayer. Soon it would be light, and Reema would come to take the pots and basins away. And the rest of the stuff – the cloths, the soiled towels – all the feechy evidence of her restless night. There were lids on the pots, and cloths over the lids, but she was sure she could smell them. Or perhaps it was herself she could smell.

Maybe she should ask Reema to come in earlier, while it was still dark. Then she could clear everything away before the flies were awake. There was the first one now, crawling up the screen. And another circling, landing on the bed-sheet. It could smell her, she knew it could smell her.

It was the smell that was the worst. If she'd just been sick, maybe she could have visited the Emperor. But not when she smelt like this. She never wanted to see that look of disgust on his face again.

How many weeks ago was it? Three? Four? It was after her bleeding, so she hadn't seen him for seven days. And she'd been terrified of facing him: the last time she'd been with him she'd thought she was pregnant; she didn't know how he'd react to the disappointment. But he'd been understanding when she explained, asking after her health, full of tenderness.

'So, we will try again this moon,' he'd said, taking her in his arms and burying his face in her neck. A moment later, he stiffened and drew away.

'Have you come to me without washing, Aziza?' he asked, frowning. 'Surely an Emperor is worth this small courtesy?'

And she'd shrunk away from him. Of course she'd washed: had loofahed her whole body, scrubbed her tongue until it stung, her teeth until her gums bled. She'd hoped the smell was in her mind. Now she knew it was true. He was right to feel repelled; she was repelled herself. The smell seemed to seep from her pores; from her ears and underarms; between her breasts, behind her knees; no matter how much she doused herself with perfume.

Since that day she'd been haunted by the stench of her own body, a stinking shadow that followed her everywhere. The flies could see it, she was sure. She would watch them circling around her, tracing the outline of an invisible woman in the air; even when the slaves whisked them away, they'd zigzag wildly for a few moments, then return to their ghostly sketch.

On the orders of the Emperor, she'd been taken to the Examination Room last week to see the *tabibs*. She set out to walk there, but her knees buckled before she'd even crossed the Queen's Courtyard. So Malia sent for a stretcher and two eunuchs and she was carried through the Harem instead, in full view of all the women, who shuffled quietly after them, nudging and whispering. Their quietness had filled her with dread.

At the Examination Room, she was separated from the *tabibs* by a wooden screen so they couldn't see her, and the only parts they'd examined were her hand and her tongue, which she had to push through special holes.

After a long, muttered discussion, they'd pronounced that her symptoms were the result of her blood overheating. They proposed cutting her wrists and draining at least ten cupfuls of blood out of her. Helen winced, but lay back relieved on her pillows. Their diagnosis made perfect sense to her: she longed for someone to drain all the badness away. But Malia had refused to allow it. The blood was the river of the body, she declared. If a body was weak it needed more blood, not less. How many had they killed by this method, she asked, jutting her chin belligerently at the wooden screen.

'Why the Emperor insists on using those idiots is beyond me,' she'd muttered later, tipping the medicine they'd prescribed into Helen's chamber-pot. 'I am the one who knows the women. They think they can fiddle with their pulses and peer at their tongues and know everything. But I'm the one who sees them every day. I'm the one who knows what's happening in the Harem.'

But she hadn't offered Helen any alternative medicine; had

just shuffled off into the kitchen with Reema to inspect the cooking things. Why was she looking there? Everything Helen ate came from Batoom's kitchen now.

Bile rose in her throat at the thought of food, and she leant out of the divan and reached for the bowl. Then she saw it: on the floor just inside the gap between her curtains, crouching like a spiny crab silhouetted against the grey dawn light.

Her screams brought Reema running. She flung back the curtains and flicked the thing out into the courtyard as soon as she saw it. Then she systematically searched every inch of the room.

Helen hunched miserably on the divan, her teeth chattering, her arms cradling a bowl as attacks of retching convulsed her body and rasped her throat. When Reema was satisfied there were no more porcupines in the bedchamber, she helped Helen to wash, then half-carried her into the day-room, where she'd laid fresh sheets on one of the divans. 'Sleep, *Lalla*,' she said gruffly, touching Helen's cheek. 'I will clean your room, and put special protection there.'

When Helen woke up it was mid-morning. The sun shone in through the muslin curtains, warm and bright. Where was she? For a moment she couldn't remember, then the sound of brushes swishing and cloths being wrung out reminded her: the porcupine. They had put her in here so they could purify her room.

Clambering shakily to her feet, she called for hot water and began making her way to the washroom. She eased off her *kamise* and, standing as straight as she could, forced herself to look at her reflection in the big mirror. Tears scalded her eyes. She seemed to be getting thinner by the hour. Were those bones on her chest visible yesterday? And her breasts had never seemed this empty before, like punctured pig-bladders.

Where had all her bonny curves and dimples gone? Her skin was dull and flaking, her eyes dry and red-rimmed. Her scalp felt hot; her hair itchy and matted with sweat.

The mirror mocked her with a framed memory of how she'd looked on her wedding day: glossy and golden, brimming with health. As though beauty fed on love, and pined when love was withdrawn.

Reaching for the liquorice root, she scrubbed viciously at her teeth, then breathed into her cupped hand and sniffed: putrid again. And her feet, even though she'd just washed them. And under her arms, like the boggy land around the mill-pond in Muthill: slug-stink, frog-breath.

Sighing, Helen called for Reema. Perhaps if her hair was washed, she'd feel better. If Reema used cold water instead of hot on her tender scalp, and rubbed gently. Yes. And afterwards she'd ask her to take the mirror away.

The washing left Helen flat and chilled. She wrapped herself in her *haik* and lay down outside, propped on a heap of cushions in the spring sunshine. The slaves had moved into the washroom now, and were scrubbing it from floor to rafters with salt water, under Reema's critical eye.

The flies seem worse out here: wee ones above her head in a cloud, a fractured shadow-head hovering around her hot scalp. And bigger ones landing heavily on her *haik*, rubbing their rasping forelegs, probing at the cloth with their tubular mouths, trying to suck out the stench. She knew about flies. They liked dung and dead meat. Paddled in it and spat on it; lapped at it and laid their eggs in it. That was what she was becoming: dung and dead meat.

Helen dozed for a while, then jerked awake when Reema touched her arm. 'The *Lalla* Zara is here to see you, mistress. Shall I tell her you're not –?'

But it was too late. The older woman was already half-way across the courtyard, moving like a slow dancer with her heavy hips swaying.

'I'm sorry I have not been before, but as you can see –' gesturing at her face – 'I have not been in the mood for visiting recently.'

She settled on the carpet and shrugged off her veil. Helen tried not to stare. Short wisps of dark hair covered the other woman's skull; her face, neck, arms were spattered with brownish marks; her skin looked thin and tired, the skin of an old woman on the body of a younger one. Her old-woman's face and hands contrasted strangely with her undulating walk and voluptuous body.

'I wanted to comfort you. I was ill like you a while ago, you see. Perhaps you heard? Perhaps you even came to visit me? I don't remember much about that time. You are one of the new women, am I right? I don't remember the wedding. Was it recently? My slaves don't tell me anything.' Her voice was sweet and low, but she seemed confused, as though trying to focus in a fog.

Reema began clanking tea-things in the kitchen; soon there was a smell of peppermint and hot sugar. 'It has taken many months to recover, and I still get tired if I do too much, but my body has nearly returned to the way it was.' Zara smoothed brown-blotched hands down over her billows of flesh with a satisfied smile.

'The eyes you had painted,' said Helen, 'I wondered if they –'

Zara shrugged vaguely. 'I tried everything, but I don't know that anything helped. The porcupines kept coming, and then one day they stopped.'

'Porcupines?' Helen felt as though she was falling down a flight of stairs.

'I only saw one, but the slaves confessed to me afterwards that there'd been five. They'd hidden them from me; they were worried it would make me worse.'

'I've seen two.' Helen's voice was thin.

'Ah –' It was almost a satisfied sound. 'I thought as much. And you are being sick, and using the chamber-pot all the time? Of course you are; that is why you are so thin. And your hair is falling out? No? Well, perhaps you will escape this fate. And thirsty all the time?' She looked at the water jars. 'Yes, I can see you are thirsty. But never quenched, yes? And your head – it is painful to the touch. Tell me, do you see things too? My slaves said I was imagining mice and rats everywhere: scampering across the courtyard in the middle of the day, and on the wood-carving on the walls and ceilings. Wasn't that strange?' Zara laughed suddenly, and Helen glimpsed the gaps where her teeth were missing.

'When the Emperor refused to see me, I wanted to die. They told me afterwards that I nearly did die. But now I am recovering, as you can see. And soon he will send for me again.' She smiled brightly. 'That's why I came to see you. To prove that you can recover. Keep heart, sister. You will soon be yourself again.'

'Did you see her face?' It was midday and Helen was back in her bedchamber.

Reema straightened the sheets. 'She was sick for a very long time, Lady. It will take time to recover.'

'I don't believe she'll ever recover. She's mad to think he'll send for her again.' She felt hollow, stunned. The sight of Zara had shaken her even more deeply than the spiny thing.

'Zara is Zara. You are you. What happened to her will not necessarily happen to you.'

Helen looked at Reema's seamed face and felt a fierce lurch

362

of gratitude. What cruelty had she suffered to get a face like that? 'I never thanked you for coming to look after me,' she said shyly. 'I know you were happy with *Lalla* Batoom. I hope you don't mind being here. Especially as there's so much more work now –' She gestured weakly towards the screen in the corner.

'I don't mind hard work.' Reema's mouth was hard, but her eyes softened. 'And *Lalla* Batoom is wise enough to look after herself.'

'If anything happens to me –'

'Don't talk like that, Lady.'

'Please. If anything happens to me, you know where my jewels are. You could use them to buy your freedom. Or send the money home to your family.'

'Hush. Don't think about such things. What would I do with my freedom? My family were killed long ago. I never knew my home. This is how slavery works. This is my home now. My family is here: Batoom, Aziza, the little *bints* who share my room.'

'I just wanted –'

'I know, Lady. Rest now.'

After she'd gone, Helen slipped into a restless doze. The sheet felt too heavy, but she was chilly without it. And her skin itched all over in little spasms, as though the bed were infested by fleas. What if a witch captured a bedbug or flea that had bitten her? Could she make a spell out of that? Perhaps someone had found something in her old room in the Harem, in one of the cracks between the tiles: dust from her feet; a flake of dandruff. Reema might have missed something. A hair caught in a spider's web on the ceiling.

Once she woke to find Malia at the foot of her bed, peeling back the sheet and sniffing at her feet.

'I just came to leave these,' she murmured, placing a wad

of white muslin beside the water jar. 'You may need them, but I am not sure. You have lost so much flesh, your body may keep the blood inside this time.'

Then Reema was bending over her again. '*Lalla*, it is supper-time. I think you should try to get up for a while or you will not sleep tonight.'

The sun had moved round and was flooding the courtyard with golden light. Helen sat up gingerly. This was the time of day she felt best: late afternoon, when the sickness of the morning had retreated and she was light and empty.

She washed slowly and brushed her teeth, scraping the bitter grey fur from her tongue. Her nightmare morning seemed like a dream: the crouching porcupine; *Lalla* Zara's eerie cheerfulness.

She drew on a fresh *kamise*. It smelt of sun and wind. At least she didn't stink, and wouldn't for an hour or so if she was lucky. She slipped her *chifumuro* into the pocket. She'd once asked Reema what was in it. 'A herb, Lady, with protective properties. And dust from the Harem dining-rooms, where the women have gathered and left particles of their essence behind.' At least her hair hadn't started to fall out yet. Perhaps she had Reema to thank for that. The scent of fresh-baked flat-bread reached her and suddenly she was ravenous.

Stepping out into the evening sunshine, she saw Microphilus waiting for her on her carpet under the jasmine.

Her step faltered. Why hadn't Reema warned her he was here? She glanced around, but the kitchen was empty. Had she combed her hair? How would he react to the change in her? Now the mirror was gone, she had no idea how she looked. What did he want? Perhaps he'd come with her money. He seemed to be cradling something in his arms, something small and wriggling. Curiosity overcame her hesitation and she walked unsteadily towards him.

'*Bonjour, ma petite!*' he exclaimed, jumping to his feet. 'I heard you'd taken to your bed, so I've brought a wee playmate to while away the hours until you're back on your feet.' Beaming, he held a squirming black kitten up towards her.

It squeaked and waved its soft paws. 'It's a wee lassie, for I daren't allow a male animal in the Harem. The lewder women will have whisked it out your hands afore you can say "Kiss me quick". As Allah is my Lord, I swear it was waiting right outside my door this morning, mewing and scratching at the wood, crying, "Where's Helen?"'

Helen lifted the kitten from his hand and eased herself down beside him. It struggled out of her grasp, but instead of running away as she'd expected, padded carefully around her twice, then climbed into her lap and curled up with its nose tucked under its tail.

Microphilus chuckled. 'There now,' he said to the kitten. 'Are you satisfied? I said I'd take you to her and I'm a man of my word.'

'Where did it come from? Truly, I mean.'

The fact that it had simply curled up in her lap touched her deeply. Couldn't it smell her? Maybe it liked her smell. Maybe it knew that inside she was still the same lass.

'Are you calling me a liar? Truly, I did find it in my courtyard this morning. And I've heard tell black cats are good luck, so I brought it along to see if a few of its powers will rub off.' His eyes searched her face and she looked away, conscious of how haggard she must seem.

'The Emperor was asking after you in the garden this morning,' he said carefully. 'Malia told him you were still poorly and he near wrenched the head off the hawk he was petting. He hardly glanced at the other women, just waved to Malia to choose for him.'

'Did he really?' She stared suspiciously at him. Was this one of his jokes? But no, he seemed sincere. Her eyes filled with tears of relief. 'I can hardly remember what he looks like,' she said with a watery smile. 'It's as though I've been sick forever; like it was all a dream. I can't even wear my jewels. They make great red marks on my skin.'

'He summoned the *tabibs* again yesterday to put a flea in their ears. Not that I've ever thought they were much use. And he's sent for an English doctor captured from a ship out of Gibraltar –'

'An English doctor?' She sat forward.

'Ay, if the runners are not mistaken. The Emperor's ordered him to be brought directly to the Palace to tend you, so he'll be here in a week or three. Of course the women are all in a lather to see him too. By the time he arrives they'll all be prostrate with this ague and that, panting for the touch of his fine white hands through the holes in the healing-screen.'

An English doctor. Zara hadn't been treated by an English doctor. Maybe he'd know something the *tabibs* didn't know. If he treated her, maybe she really would recover.

Reema brought water for their hands, then began laying out the afternoon meal: a tray of flat-bread and soft cheese, *hummus* and fruit. She scowled at the kitten, which had woken up and was sniffing the air hungrily. 'I suppose it will keep the mice away,' she growled grudgingly.

'I don't think she approves,' said Helen with a smile.

'That's where you're wrong. I saw her face when you weren't looking. That scowl was just for show. Now, I've a little something else with me that you might like.' He reached into a cloth bag on the floor beside him. 'As a good Mohamme-dan wifie, you're not really allowed. But if the auld sourpuss will turn a blind eye, I think Allah will make an exception today. Think of it as a medicine to soothe your poor innards.'

And he took a small reed-covered flask out of the bag, along with a teeny cup, which he filled for her.

Helen took a sip and grinned at him. 'I like your medicine a might better than the stuff the *tabibs* gave me. Malia took one sniff and tipped it away.'

'Their aim is to fright the stomach into curing itself.'

The kitten wandered over and he began stroking it gently, letting it nibble his fingers. He scratched behind its ears and it purred loudly and toppled over sideways so he could rub its belly. Helen watched his hands, the little gold hairs on them, his blunt, clean fingers. Kind hands, casually caressing the kitten, knowing exactly how it needed to be touched. Generous hands: not expecting a response, not assuming a touch in return.

The sun was sinking lower and she shivered. Microphilus leapt up at once and fetched a soft woollen cloak which he lowered over her shoulders. Helen bent her head, so he could gather her hair up and out of the way.

'It's so tangled,' she apologized. 'My scalp's so tender, it nips to have it combed.'

'That's because it's not been done by an expert,' he said scornfully. 'Reema's a grand dam, but she's used to doing corn-rows and beadies, not ringlets from Perthshire. Where's your combs? If it wouldn't be too much of an imposition, I'd be happy to have a try.'

Helen smiled uncertainly. 'I wouldn't want to trouble you.' At least it was clean. And the flies weren't back yet. Suddenly she longed for her hair to be smooth and untangled again.

'Now, I'll start at the ends and work upwards. That's how I used to untaisel my mother's hair when she'd washed it. Not that she cared. If it hadn't been for me she'd have gone out with a head of rats' tails.'

He knelt behind her and started. 'Tell me if it hurts.' Helen nodded and closed her eyes. She could feel his warm hand on her neck, taking one knotted lock at a time, teasing it gently; careful not to tug on her poor inflamed scalp. Little shivers of pleasure rippled from her neck, down her arms and back. She remembered how little she was wearing. No *salwars*; just a thin *kamise* under the cloak.

Was this how he was with Batoom, she wondered. She remembered seeing him stroke the big queen's arm and kiss her mouth.

She could feel the warmth of his body the length of her back. Kneeling, he was the same size as she was. His liquorice breath was on her neck where the hair parted. She wanted to lean back, as though he was a tree, and feel the strength of his warm trunk against her.

He came round to the front and began combing the curls away from her face. Not looking at her face, to see how puffy and grey she was. Just focusing on her hair, one lock at a time, as if each were the most important thing in the world. She looked at his soft mouth, concentrating on the task; his small pink lips and clean breath; his even teeth. What would it be like to kiss him, she wondered.

She closed her eyes and let herself imagine it. She'd sway forward, with her lips apart. He'd put his hands on her shoulders. Their lips, their tongues, would touch very gently. Then what? What would it be like to play sex with someone who made you forget what you looked like?

He stopped combing and she opened her eyes. He had something strange in his hand: a fine brown silk scarf. No. She looked closer. Not a scarf. Hair, copper hair, trailing from his fingers.

50

I think Helen may be softening towards me at last, though it may be she can no longer summon the strength to repel me.

I have brought her a wee kittlin, to furnish a more frequent ruse to call on her, as the Emperor ordered. I planned to subvert her attempts to turn me away with some silly Pantomime, with myself in the role of Guardian to the feline Orphan, for women love all such nonsense, in which they can invest some doll, or lapdog, or any softish, roundish creature, with the personality of a child, and coo over it as a doting parent (while shunning the mewlings of their true offspring).

Whether it was her illness or the kittlin that prevailed, I know not, but she sat as mild as a milk-cow on the rug beside me, and even let me comb her hair.

Her hair was still damp, like pond-weed, and there was a faint smell of ponds about her too, a greenish smell, a slime smell, which told me – though I needed no telling – that my naiad was decomposing inside. Then, as I unravelled her taigles, I found great swathes of it coming away in my hands and hanging between my fingers as though I was carding copper wool.

Her eyes were closed and she was swaying slightly, then jerked awake and saw the hair, and was thrown into a storm of sobbing, telling me of the second porcupine she has seen, while I patted her knobby shoulder and told her of the English doctor the Emperor has sent for.

23 March 1770

I see her every day now. Sometimes for only a few minutes; other times for an afternoon or more.

My heart is full. I have heard women speak thus when their babies are new-born: 'My heart is full' they say, cradling some red-faced mewler. I did not know, until these days with Helen, what they meant: to be alert every moment, and brimming with tenderness. Ay, and anxiety, too, in equal measure. And elation; distress; wonder; such that the minutes expand and the hours contract; and you cannot sleep, nor want to.

I sit at her side when she is sleeping, poring over the map of her face. How parched she seems, her lips cracked as tree-bark, yellow tears caked in the corners of her eyes. And all the petty evidence of her waking agitations; beads of blood where she has gnawed at her hangnails, peeling back each little hook of dry skin. The grazes on her ankles where she scrubs herself raw with her *loofah*, eight times in one day according to Reema. She is a rag the washerwoman has yanked up from the suds and wrung out, and doused again, and wrung out and finally flung on the rocks to dry.

In sleep she seems at peace, but sinks so deeply that I am afraid she will never resurface, and must lick my hand and hold it under her nose to feel the soft breath entering and leaving, or place my questing ear on her flattened chest and listen for the knocking of the red fist inside her caged ribs. And I would stay there forever, and would judge my life to have been well spent, to feel that kick against my ear all my days.

Sometimes she starts awake with the vomit already in her throat. And all I can do is hold the bowl and the cloth, and empty the one and change the other, and mop her mouth, and murmur that it will pass soon, that she is a brave lass. And she nods dumbly, staring with round eyes, and I know she is not seeing me at all, that she has gone inside her body somewhere, where the bile is snaking back and forth, nudging now at her throat, now at her nether end, until she knows not whether to bend over the bowl or run to the washroom.

Once she was mistaken, and her anguish at soiling herself in my presence made me vow to come later in the day, when her snakes are cooler and more sluggish, and she is calmer. Then she sleeps, or we talk, or play with the kittlin, and I learn more about this lovely lassie from Muthill. How that first bairnie of hers was conceived, with the local Laird, and how he shamed her. How some kind wench took her on a ship from Greenock, and would have stayed to help mother the wean, and some gentle dolt, name of Dougie, who would have married her; and the fey Lady who offered her work, whose dress she was wearing when I first beheld her.

Whereupon I confess how I loathed the dress, which stings her to heated protest, which I counter, which she vehemently parries until sheer merriment declares a truce. Such simple pleasantries are like draughts of sweet water. Though there is gall too. To wit, how she yearns for the Emperor, how he is the most fascinating, most handsome, most exciting man she has ever met; how just a look from him makes her melt with desire; how he can be so ruthless with others, yet so loving with her; how he is really a boy at heart; how none but she sees him as he truly is.

27 March 1770

Today she was more listless than usual. Thursdays are always difficult, for she can hear the others getting ready, all their blither and blether, and the weans whingeing as their pates are shaved and they are attired in unaccustomed clean clothes.

It seems Douvia has been selected again, and skipped straight in to trill her good fortune, which Helen strove to applaud, summoning a gaunt smile and mouthing good wishes until I shooed the ebullient Young Queen back to her bowers. Afterwards there was nothing I could do to raise Helen's spirits.

I spent last night in Batoom's chamber. She had procured a flagon for me and the greater half was inside me before I felt its powerful effects. Yet this Jews' juice is less potent than your weakest whisky. How fickle the body is! In Scotland I could upend three quarts of claret and still play a fair hand of whist, whereas here barely half a pint has me rolling like a moggie in catmint.

I think I was urging her to drink with me, saying there was nothing like a drachm to warm the belly and soothe the mind, and she was pushing me away, saying she was quite warm enough, and needed no soothing. Whereupon I suppose I crumpled in a stupor, for the next thing I knew I was beside her in the divan, and dawn was pulling back her grey blanket. And I looked over at Batoom's peaceful face, at all the colours of her, her peaty neck and conker cheeks, the mushroom gills of her lips, the purple etchings of her cheek-scars. All so dear and familiar to me. And I knew in that instant that I could be happy with Batoom, and that all I had to do was wake her and kiss her and tell her I had put my madness behind me. And I could be content.

I lay there for a long time, just looking at her, feeling my fondness for her steal around my raw heart like a balm. Remembering our times together, our tusslings and burrowings, her big laugh and deep creases, her wise eyes resting on me and liking what she sees.

I slipped away before she could wake. I think if she had roused herself and found me there she would have relented. And we would have made love, but it would have been a lie.

And she would have known, the moment it was over. I don't want to see that knowledge in her eyes.

So I crept away with my *haik* wrapped around me and a mouth like the dunes of the Namib, and walked through the grey Harem to my chamber. The smells of spring were all around and the birds fair beating the air with their song. I found myself thinking of Pittenweem, of the ploughed land above the harbour, the thick earth heaving with fish innards, like the waves on a brown sea, and the gulls wheeling with the peewits, and the skylarks invisible above them all, clattering at Heaven's Gate and rousing the angels.

When I arrived home, there was the Methuselah athwart my gate. Who crackles in midst a confetti of gorse husks, and recites his Litany of botanical observations whilst I gulp water and douse it over myself and emerge, and it is Thursday morning, and we are back where I began with this day.

28 March 1770

William Lempriere, the English Doctor, has arrived at last. He is a clammy stick of a man, with a habit of cracking his knuckles when he is thinking. He has the narrowest lips I have ever seen, which he presses together a great deal, for it is obvious he is here under duress, despite the Emperor's effluvial hospitality. He is billeted in the city, with a merchant in the Jewish quarter, whither he escapes every night after dinner with a look of relief on his long face.

He is accompanied by a toity maid by the name of Julia Crisp. They claim to be married, but I suspect this is a charade concocted to preserve her Virtue. Indeed, had they not been travelling with a trader well connected in Sallee, I'll wager our prim Missie Crisp might have arrived here by quite different means.

I have been hovering by as Interpreter, and a most testing duty it has turned out. I burn to grab the Doctor by his collar and hustle him along to the Examination Room to see Helen. Instead I must stand calmly by as the Emperor strides around in his ceremonial *jellabiah*, ostentatiously fixing and unfixing his monocle (said item being, he thinks, the pinnacle of European fashion, such that he has all his *jellabiahs* especially made with an embroidered breast-pocket). He has ordered a feast of gargantuan proportions, which my translation duties prevent me from eating, and sets to boasting of his achievements at modernizing his 'Barbarian kingdom', satisfying himself hugely, while his guests wrestle one-handed with unfamiliar items of wildfowl bobbing in a bath of green oil.

And all the while Helen, the very reason for their presence, is dying not a hundred yards away. How is it that his memory is so short? A scant week ago he was the solicitous Lover, distraught with fear for his precious Aziza. Now he is the Enlightened Statesman, peacocking before his thin-lipped audience.

I swear he has conducted them through every room in the Palace, in a jumbled cavalcade consisting of six elephantine giants from the *Bokhary*, followed by the Bearers of the Royal Prayer-mat and Fly Swat (and lesser slaves responsible for the Royal Towels and Toothpicks, and all the other objects he might need), not to mention his expanded retinue of Royal Tasters. From the Palace, the Emperor diverts to the Stables, and would have had the *Bokhary* attired in battle-dress and staging mock skirmishes had not Mistress Crisp claimed a most severe headache brought on by the excitement.

At which he conducts them back indoors, where she is prevailed on to repose on a divan, which she agreed to with the *proviso* that her 'husband' should remain with her at all times. She is a most decided young woman, with clever blue eyes and a quantity of yellow hair which she has braided and wears wrapped around her head like a rope on a foredeck. In temperament she is that combination of honey and vinegar which puts me in mind of a Morningside governess.

The Emperor is quite taken with her, for she represents – more so even than Helen does – the very essence of that European refinement he would acquire. 'Find out, Fijil, whether they are really married,' hisses he with an acquisitive gleam.

'We met on the ship,' confesses *La Crisp*, all of a pother. 'I was travelling to join my *fiancé* in Gibraltar. Please, Sir, don't betray me. If the Emperor finds out –' But she has no need to finish her sentence, for we both understand how this tale would proceed.

And I must confess that a perfect cruel scheme formed in my mind at that moment, *viz.* to expose her to the Emperor and see her speedily installed in the Harem, as a decoy duck on a loch, where she would attract mischief away from Helen. The plan rose up and teetered on the brink of my mind for a long moment, tempting and tantalizing, before dropping back down into its nefarious recesses where it belonged.

Meanwhile, the slaves are all loitering nearby with their ears on stalks. Maryam says they are earning large sums for information about the English Doctor, which they transmit along servants' conduits, scaling walls and evading guards, to the very heart of the Harem. By this means the good Doctor's untried prowess has attained legendary status, so that when I return to my quarters, I must butt through a herd of distempered damsels, each claiming a mysterious ailment that the English Doctor alone can cure. In the end I was forced to summon a special guard to keep them at bay, otherwise they would have been knocking all night.

At least they have kept the Methuselah away, though I

suppose he may have been mistaken for vegetable matter and trampled underfoot. And I will discover him on the morrow, flat as a pressed bluebell in a Bible, with the marks of a thousand slippers along his spine.

I visited Malia this morning, begging her to devise some principle of *triage* with the women, for the Doctor will not be able to see them all. But she was in a sulk and refused to emerge. 'The truly sick ones will come to me eventually,' huffs she. 'The foreign Doctor is welcome to the others.' She is smarting at being excluded from the Emperor's palaver with the *tabibs*, but I do not have time to flatter her out.

At last the Emperor has released the Doctor to his doctoring. He will come to the Examination Room on the morrow. I prevailed on him to see Helen first, explaining she is a fellow countrywoman, but it seems *La Douvia* has staked out a prior claim, in a note of atrocious Latin, claiming symptoms that appear to mirror those of my darling.

Now this is strange. If it be true, we now have three queens afflicted.

51

Malia shuffled back out of Helen's washroom and knelt down with a grunt beside her beneath the jasmine. 'How long has it been that colour?' she asked, narrowing her eyes.

Helen sighed. 'A week, maybe two.' What did it matter? It was just coming out of her, that was all that mattered. Day after day, scalding her, as though she was rotting, dissolving from the inside, until she was a bag of burning empty skin.

'And when the food comes back. Is it dark or light in colour?'

'Dark – no, light.' Helen shook her head. 'I don't know. Dark in the morning, lighter in the afternoon.' Her tongue felt swollen and hot. 'Sometimes it's better in the evening. Other days it's nearly all the time, until there's nothing but water.' Until her ribs ached. Until her throat was raw.

'This is what I can't understand.' Malia stroked her long nose with a scarecrow finger. 'Why it stays like this: better some days; worse on others . . .' She trailed off, staring into the distance.

Reema came out with a samovar and cups. 'They are saying the English Doctor has arrived.'

'Where?' Helen struggled to kneel up. 'Is he staying at the Palace?'

Malia sniffed her disdain. 'He's lodging in the city.' She stirred her tea violently. 'The women have all discovered illnesses for him to cure. Even *Lalla* Douvia's begging to be seen, and she's as strong as a camel.'

'When can I see him?' The English Doctor here at last!

'Don't ask me.' Malia sucked tea through green gums. 'Tomorrow. Next week. As soon as the Emperor's finished welcoming them.'

'Them?'

'There's an English woman with the Doctor. Neat little thing: yellow hair, pink cheeks. Far too scrawny of course, in one of those dangerous tight gowns.'

Helen sank back against her cushions. A hole opened beneath her ribcage. It was as though she was dead already, eavesdropping on the future. Another White Queen. First Salamatu, then Aziza, now this new woman.

'He tried to buy her for the Harem, but she's promised to the Doctor.'

Helen reached for the water ladle, then let her hand fall back into her lap. Her bones felt so heavy, they made her skin ache. She could imagine it so clearly: the blushing newcomer and her attentive partner; the Emperor intrigued and charming. Determined. Of course he wanted her. What did they call them back home, those soft-heeled Southern ladies? English roses. He wanted her for his garden.

After Malia had gone, Helen lay for a long time with her eyes closed. Her throat clenched but she was too exhausted to sob.

It was over: she let the knowledge seep through her. She'd had it all, like a fairytale, everything she'd ever dreamed of. Her eyes burnt behind their closed lids, tears acrid as vinegar. How long had he been hers? Five moons, six? Flies were buzzing on the tea tray; she pictured them scampering around the rim of the cups, darting down, sucking up sugar dregs.

She could hear Reema tipping and swilling in the washroom; the slurp of wet rags, then the rhythmic long rasps of the broom, sweeping, sweeping for the third time that day. Though there were two other slaves now, Reema always did the sweeping herself, shaking every rug, moving every jar, then crouching and sorting, crouching and rising, pacing patiently back and forth across the courtyard to the kitchen fire.

Feeling a touch on her cheek, Helen opened her eyes. It was the kitten, reaching out a soft black paw. 'Pussy-baudrons, are you trying to scare me?' Blinking away the tears, she lifted the tiny body and shook a finger at it. It latched on to the tip with a set of needle claws and pretended to bite it. She could feel its heart pattering inside its basket of tiny ribs. How fierce and fragile it seemed, caught up in its wee world of pouncing and killing.

Sitting up, she held the kitten to her face and pressed her nose into the soft down on its belly. 'I'm finished, kittlin. Did you know? Ugly and withered as an old leaf.' It started to purr. 'Silly pusskin,' she whispered, 'don't you care what I look like?' Then: 'Shall I take you with me when he sends me away – to keep the rats out of whatever hovel I end up in?'

She scratched it behind the ear and it lifted its pointy chin, purring louder and butting at her hand with its head. 'So, you've had enough of that, have you?' She smiled as it tumbled over on to its back and stretched out with its eyes closed, waiting for her to stroke its belly. She rubbed it gently, in time with its purrs, cupping her whole hand around its tiny barrel of a body. 'You daft wee critter. I could kill you, gibbie, you know. Break all your bones like a handful of twigs.'

Microphilus had said the same thing yesterday when he'd visited. 'How does she know she's safe in my hand?' he'd wondered. 'It must be something she can smell – something that's different from the Harem urchins. They'd crack her like a wee nut if they picked her up.'

Since he'd brought the kitten he'd come every day. 'I don't mean to disturb you,' he'd say, bowing apologetically to

Helen, 'but the kittlin asked me to be sure and arrive early.' Or: 'She insisted I brought a ribbon for her to play with,' and he'd settle down companionably, as if he belonged there.

If Helen was feeling well enough, he'd sit beside her and tell her stories; about what was happening in the Harem; his adventures in Edinburgh and London. Sometimes she'd fall asleep while he was talking and wake to find him chatting to Reema or petting the kitten. Or just sitting quietly, watching her, like Gran used to when she was poorly; just sitting and watching. Often, when a sudden lurch of nausea yanked her to her knees, he'd grab the bowl and hold it himself.

'I'm sorry,' she'd whisper when the attack passed. 'It's bad enough the slaves seeing me like this.'

'Like what?' he'd say, holding the ladle for her to rinse out her mouth.

'Oh, I don't know. Stinking, puking, like a wean.'

'What's wrong with weans? I like weans.'

'But I'm not a wean. I'm a lass. And ashamed to think of a man seeing me –'

'Do you think you're the first lassie who's been sick in my presence? When I've a thousand in my charge?'

Gradually she began to believe him: that he'd seen this a hundred times before; that it was as normal and natural as sweeping out a stable; that he didn't find her disgusting; that he liked her as well now as he ever had.

Each time he visited, he combed her hair. It was something she looked forward to: the gentle tug of the comb, the coolness of the air on the back of her neck; the grey eyes that just focused on what he was doing. Not on her scabby skin or cracked lips, just her hair, one curl at a time: lift, untangle, smooth and drop; lift, untangle, smooth and drop; straightening her out like a sheet under the smoothing iron.

'Have you ever been to Tafilalt?' she'd asked him one

afternoon. 'You know, the place where the old queens are sent.'

No he hadn't been there, but he'd heard tell of the place. The summers were fiercer, he said, and the winters cooler. 'But a body from Scotland would laugh at what these soft folk consider cold.' There were some fine small cities, with all the amenities you would expect, and a fair few wild tribes, 'though not as untamed as your remoter Highlanders'.

What if she left the Harem altogether? The possibility raised its head. Left the Emperor and stopped being a queen. If she gave it all up, perhaps the curse would be lifted and she'd be well again.

Tafilalt. Though she knew it lay far inland, she pictured it as an island surrounded by glittering water. To begin with it was featureless, but each time it came into her mind, she would add some more details: a row of hills; a herd of goats; some tents and a *kaktus* stockade. A few fine small cities. In the calm troughs between her storms of sickness, the picture grew. Tafilalt: like a prayer. A place of rest; a place of clean air; a place of open spaces.

That night she fell asleep thinking of it; and woke again in the small hours with it still on her mind.

For once it wasn't nausea that woke her, but hunger. She pulled on her *haik* and wandered unsteadily to the kitchen, wary of disturbing the little slave-girls curled by the embers of the cooking fire. Cupping her lamp with her hand, she went over to the food shelves and lifted the fly-cloth.

There was plenty there: *teem* and grapes; goat's cheese and olives; cold *couscous* with almonds, and a couple of roast lamb-shanks crusted with herbs. Her stomach heaved and she let the cloth drop, then reached instead for the bread bag hanging on the wall out of reach of the ants.

Easing the bag open, she drew out a crisp new loaf, baked just that afternoon. She broke it open and buried her nose in the soft, crumbly centre, fresh and clean. Now she understood what Naseem had meant: 'Sometimes dry bread is exactly what you want.' Saliva flooded her mouth as she bit into it. It was firm and salty; simple and good. The kind of food you could trust.

The pitter of paws made her turn; the kitten had followed her in and was pouncing on the crumbs.

'Whisht! You'll wake the others.' It followed her outside, skittering after a cricket by the woodpile as she unrolled a grass mat and sat down under her favourite tree. Leaning back against the trunk, she took another bite. Such simple pleasure: fresh bread that stays with you and nourishes you. As she watched the kitten chasing white moths, more details began to form in her mind. Of Tafilalt: a simple house and simple food; a view of the hills. An honest tree to lean against.

Next day she was sick all morning, on jelly knees, bowed low over the bowl. Afterwards she crawled back between sweaty sheets and sank into an exhausted sleep.

She was jerked awake an hour later by Douvia shaking her arm. 'I'm sorry – Reema tried to stop me disturbing you –' Her voice was trembling. 'I know you're ill, but I didn't know who else to tell –'

'What's the matter?' Helen hauled herself up on her pillows. The sheets rasped over the knobs of her spine and her tongue tasted like sand. 'What's happened – are you sick?'

Douvia nodded; her face was the colour of dough. 'This is the third day now, but Malia thinks I'm just pretending because I want to see the English Doctor. But I'm not – Aziza, you know I never fuss. Then this morning –' She hesitated and suddenly Helen understood.

'You found one of those things, didn't you?'

Douvia nodded miserably. 'I thought I'd be safe. I mean, the Emperor hardly ever sends for me. I thought it was only you and Zara. But now –' she fluttered her pretty hands. 'It looks like it's going to be all the queens.'

'Did she keep it?' Microphilus asked gently. Reema had sent for him as soon as she'd seen the look on Douvia's face.

'I don't know. I expect she burnt it. That's what Reema did with mine. We just wanted rid of them –' Helen shuddered. 'I can't stand it!' she burst out. 'I keep thinking: it's killing us, one by one. All the queens. First Zara, then me, and now Douvia.'

'Now then, lassie. No one's died yet of this malady, and the *Lalla* Zara's improving by the day.'

'Better? Oh, ay,' Helen said bitterly. 'She's not puking out her guts any more. And her hair's growing back. But she's still as blichan as a beggar. Have you seen her? She talks all addled-like. She thinks the Emperor's going to send for her any day.'

'These things take their own time. And the Doctor's to see *La Douvia* this afternoon. And you on the morrow. And he seems a sensible sort, provided we can allow him a proper examination. But maybe his lassie can help with that. Mistress Crisp she calls herself, Julia Crisp. The Emperor's fair taken with her.'

'What did you say?' Helen wasn't listening. She was watching a logic unfold in her mind. First Zara, then me, and now Douvia. Every queen except Batoom. A feeling of dread, like cold water, trickled across her scalp. Why hadn't Batoom fallen ill?

'If Miss Crisp comes into the Harem – as she's permitted, of course – I was thinking the Doctor could direct her from the other side of the screen, and she could be his eyes, as it were.' He paused, noticing her face. 'What is it, hen? Shall I fetch the bowl? You're as white as the bed-sheet.'

He rushed off to fetch the bowl, and she hunched over it, cradling it on her knee. Of course, Batoom. Why had she never suspected her before? All those locked rooms. Three big sons to inherit the throne. Pretending she didn't care about the Emperor, when really she was scheming all the time. Helen clutched the bowl with cold fingers.

'Don't try to fight it, hen. Breathe deep and just let it come.'

Helen began to retch; deep, wrenching spasms that slammed her belly against her backbone. And Reema. Dear God, Reema was probably helping her. Her teeth began to chatter, her chin to judder uncontrollably.

'I didn't mean to upset you. The Emperor doesn't really care for the lass. It's you he loves. She's promised to the Doctor anyway. In a few weeks she'll be gone.'

'Gone?' She looked up. What was he talking about?

'So you see there's nothing to worry about. Just you wait and see. In three weeks, maybe less, things will be back as they were before.'

He fetched a ladle of water and she sipped it slowly, shivering. Her head felt huge and heavy, a lumpy boulder balanced unsteadily on her neck. Her skin was hot, but she couldn't stop jittering. He wrapped a thick *haik* around her and she sagged against him and let her eyes close. The red behind her eyelids began to darken. Then she was drifting in blessed darkness.

'I was telling her about Miss Julia and she fainted.'

'She's so weak now, poor lamb. Anything can set her off.'

Helen surfaced slowly, as though rising through grey waters. Two people were talking; she could see them congealing above the surface. Her head was resting on something warm.

'Do you think I should fetch Malia?' It was Microphilus, but his voice seemed to be coming from inside her own head. He seemed to be leaning over her. No, not leaning. Her head was in his lap; that was why his voice sounded so strange.

'I doubt there's anything she can do. But I think Reema should sleep with her tonight, just in case.' Batoom's voice. What was she doing here? Helen tried to lift her head, but a wave of dizziness made her fall back again.

A moment later she felt herself being lifted gently and set down on fresh sheets. Was this how it would be when she was dead? Voices drifting over her; covers pulled up. Batoom and Reema. They'd been so kind; she thought they liked her. All that concern about her food. All that sweeping and washing. When all the time they were just waiting for her to die.

She could hear the soft scuff of bare feet on the tiles; the echoey thud of the full water jar beside the bed. Microphilus was whispering urgently to Batoom in the doorway.

The top seemed to lift off Helen's skull for a moment, and a cold space opened in the middle of her mind. Of course, it was so obvious. If Batoom and Reema wanted her dead, then Microphilus would too. He'd always loved Batoom. They must be hoarding gold in one of her locked rooms and concocting spells in another.

'Leave her, Fijil. She needs to sleep.' Batoom's voice again, coaxing, soothing. 'There's nothing else you can do now.' Helen opened her eyes a chink to see Batoom's hand on his shoulder, drawing him gently away.

When she woke later it was dark, and thirst had welded her tongue to the roof of her mouth. Reema was lying beside her, asleep on the floor. Helen crawled quietly to the foot of the bed, reached the ladle from its hook on the wall and dipped it into the water jar. Hearing Reema grunt and stir in her sleep, she put the ladle down, grabbed her *haik* instead, and slipped outside into the courtyard.

It was a clear night, with a chilly wind and little clouds scudding across a fat moon. She walked shakily to the fountain bubbling from the wall and drank greedily from her hand. Standing upright, she could feel the water trickling down her hot throat and into her burning stomach, leaving a trail of cooler, calmer flesh.

She settled against her tree and wrapped the *haik* tighter, tucking it in around her bare toes. She looked up through the branches. The sky was a great arc of black, studded with winking stars. Was Allah out there somewhere? They said he had created a thousand thousand angels to watch over the world. Were any of them watching her now?

She thought of her first night in the Harem, running pell-mell through the cloisters with the bairns chasing after her. Lost and lonely and scared. At least then she'd had Naseem to talk to. And that other terrible time: on the ship, when they'd strung up Robert Baird; at Sallee, being spat at in the streets. Betty had been with her through all that. But now, when she was closer to death than she'd ever been, she was on her own.

Microphilus, Batoom, Reema wanted her dead. The people she loved – love had crept over her gradually, like the changing of the seasons – were plotting to get her out of the way. Her blood felt leaden. She had trusted them; even when the Emperor rejected her, they'd always been there. Except they hadn't been really; it was all a clever charade.

The wind made little rustling sounds all around her: in the tree, where the jasmine covered the roof, dry leaves dancing across the tiles. There was the sound of scratching over by the woodpile, the whisk of leathery wings above her head. She thought of the porcupines and felt her scalp tighten. Suddenly a small dark shape was charging towards her across the court-yard. Air solidified like stone in her lungs, then tumbled out in an avalanche of sobs as the kitten leapt into her lap.

She picked it up and pressed it to her wet cheek. 'At least you're with me, pussy-baudrons,' she whispered into its fur. After a while she got up and made her way back to her chamber. She fell asleep to the sound of the kitten lapping from the ladle.

52

I have just left Helen's chamber, where she has been swooning with pain over the Emperor's attachment to our toity English Governess.

These last weeks I dared hope – oh, what does it matter what I hoped? I was mistaken, there's the tall and the short of it. She is his, to her very entrails. Why, a mere mention of the corseted Madam Crisp and Helen blenched like a whelk and shrank back on to her pillows, fair gibbering with anguish.

We calmed her as best we could, but she flailed us away with bony arms as you would a bat in your hair. I explained that the maid was spoken for, but she was deaf to my protestations and just stared at us – Batoom and Reema were hovering beside me, as solicitous as you could wish – as though we were torturers from the Emperor's vile dungeons. And panted strangely, with her lips turning blue, finally toppling sideways into a swoon.

Microphilus, what more evidence do you need? She loves the Emperor with her very marrow. No matter he's as fickle as a buck rabbit; no matter he'd sooner brag and bluster to the Doctor than have him tend his dying wife; no matter he can put a lassie's eyes out with nary a shudder. She has gilded him; he is her Golden Man; and no other will do.

Peggy was the same, and tales of my brother's philandering made her sigh yet the more for him, as though his disdain of her person emblazoned him in her eyes. But never did she want me. Not before she knew him, nor after; never once did her eyes brighten when she saw me, nor rest on me, as Batoom's do: seeing me, and liking what she sees.

I have been weeping. It is a most strange experience. I suppose men are unpractised at it, so that when we cry the sobs must be wrenched out of us like vomit, or that puff of breath expelled by a punch in the belly. And we know not how to manage our voices; whether to wail like a woman, or moan in a more manly manner as with a corporeal pain.

I had not thought my nose would run so much and yield far more liquid than my eyes. Or that my whole face would become as hot and red as it has. Yet I do feel oddly refreshed, as though all this wetness had dissolved within it some confusion of pain, which, being gone, has left me more clearheaded than I have been for a long time.

I was holding my button when the tears came, debating with myself over its provenance. It was wrenched from a frock my true mother had thrown out as being too old or too unfashionable. I shall never know why she discarded it, for I never knew her; I only know that my father brought it as a gift to my foster-mother, who clasped it to her fishy breast as though it was the finest ballgown she'd ever seen, and wore it daily from that day forth, though it never fitted properly, which is how the button came to be torn off.

Anyway, I picked up the button when I was a wean, and have kept it in my pocket ever since. It was all I ever had of my true mother, you see: this one small, hard thing, torn off from something she had thrown away. Made of shell it is, with a soft rainbow sheen on the surface where it catches the light.

But when I held it in my hand just now (as I have done every day since I found it), I felt the strata of my mind shift and settle to a new understanding. All these years I have treasured it as a bequest from my true mother, who threw me away as lightly as she did the dress. Yet it is really a relic of my dear foster-mother, Kath, who loved me as fiercely as if I'd been her own, though they all laughed at her for it, calling her Mother of Mudskipper and worse.

I have had my true mother in my pocket all along, but I never saw it before, so caught up have I been with the false one who threw me away.

All those years I kept hoping that Madam Boswell would come riding up one day in her plumed coach, rattling grandly along the cobbles to fetch me. And the folk would all drop their nets and their mussel knives, and wonder why such a grand lady was coming to their village. And she'd step down from the carriage and bend over me, wafting her sweet scent in the fishy air, and would scoop me up and take me home to the grand house at Auchinleck. And I would have gone with her without a backward glance.

But she did not come, nor even sent word. Nor knew, less still cared, about the frock, or the button, or the laddie who held it so dear.

Now this button has unfastened my fool of a heart. I have true love in the palm of my hand. Batoom loves me with the deepest regard I have ever known. So I will love her in return.

Though my stature be that of a half-man, yet I will become whole in my heart. And offer her that heart, if she will accept it. And we will begin, like squirrels, to hoard up sesterces for our long winter in Tafilalt. Meanwhile I shall tend Helen as a brother would, and be content.

53

Next day Helen slept late into the morning, then drifted on the surface of consciousness until after midday. Sleep was the best place to be. Each time she emerged from that safe black burrow, she wanted to crawl back in again, away from the glare of awareness. Her stomach was empty, a limp, flat space; her head buzzed slightly; there was an ache behind her eyes.

She wondered vaguely whether she was dying. Perhaps dying was just discovering that you didn't want to think, move, or speak any more. If she was dying no one could hurt her: not the Emperor or Microphilus; not Reema or Batoom. She was journeying towards the Eternal Father who would cherish her for ever.

She lay like this for a long time, floating in a half-faint, waiting to die. Then a gnawing feeling in her stomach tossed her back roughly into the world of the living. She opened her eyes and looked around. The sun was high, judging from the light coming through the curtains. The water jar was gone and she could hear Reema swilling it out in the washroom.

A strange coughing sound caught her attention. It was the kitten vomiting in the doorway: hoarse, choking sounds, its legs stiff, its wee chin jutting. It vomited up a tiny dark puddle and stared at it; then backed away and began retching again.

Helen slipped her feet out of bed and reached for her gown. The kitten gazed at her with bulging eyes for a moment, then began retching again. She stood up and started to walk towards it. Her bones did not seem to be properly connected; the only thing holding her together was her skin.

Ever since that first day when the Emperor had chosen her, Batoom must have been watching and waiting. Making out that she was helping her; biding her time. And Reema too, seeming so concerned. Helen sank down on the floor and took the kitten in her arms. 'Now they're trying to kill you too.'

'Who's trying to kill who?'

Microphilus was there, opening the curtain. Reema was close behind with cloths and a bowl of steaming water. Their faces seemed full of concern. Lying faces: pretending to care while they watched her suffer. The kitten lay on its side, panting. Its lips were flecked with black foam.

'I hope you're satisfied now,' said Helen, her hand on the hot little body.

'What do you mean?' Microphilus sounded confused.

'She's dying – look. Why did you have to kill her too? The only thing I had left.'

'The kittlin? What's the matter with her?'

'Whose idea was it? Yours or Batoom's?' The pain behind her eyes had become a tight band around her head. 'Have you been enjoying yourselves? Laughing behind my back. It must have been such fun – watching me trying so hard with the Emperor, falling in love with him, knowing you could end it all whenever you wanted. Pretending to help me, when really you've been –'

'Helen, hen –' He made a move towards her, but she shrank back against the wall.

'Zara, Douvia, me. I suppose you got rid of Salamatu, too. The worst thing is, I trusted you. I thought you were all trying to protect me. I thought because you were Scottish that you'd be –' Exhausted tears dribbled down her cheeks.

'You can trust me –'

'Don't try that one again. Making out you're worried,

pretending you're looking for the culprit. When you know fine it's been Batoom all along –'

'Batoom?' A laugh burst from him like a sneeze.

'You said as much yourself.' How dare he laugh at her? 'Whose sons get to inherit if the other queens are dead? Who's been preparing my food in her kitchen? Who's the only queen who's not fallen ill?' The kitten crawled on its belly towards the water ladle and lapped at it greedily.

'Och, Helen, what weevil's been a-nibbling at your mind? Batoom would no more harm you than she'd sprout wings and fly to Peterhead.'

'Why doesn't she just finish it quickly? Do you enjoy watching us all linger, is that it?'

At least he'd stopped laughing now. 'How long has it been poorly?' He was staring at the kitten.

54

30 March 1770

I have just come from Helen's quarters, where I discovered her, a collapsed bag of bones on the floor, dripping tears over her sickly moggie. I fear the tentacles of this disease have gripped her mind now, for she was fairly pop-eyed with rage and anguish, raving on that Batoom has been trying to kill her, abetted by myself and the doughty sourpuss.

I think the moggie has deranged her. She is the miner trapped deep in the mine, who sees the canary-bird tip over from coal miasma and knows for certain sure that he will be next to succumb.

I tried to calm her, but she just hissed at me to 'leave her to die'. Reema is tending her as best she can, but the effrayed wench jitters like a startled faun whenever she is touched. The nightmares of her sleeping mind are stalking her waking hours, poor lass. I pray with all my heart that her reason returns soon, for if a remedy is not found, she will need the comfort of friends in the coming weeks.

Who, for the love of Allah, is doing this? The lass is right: Reason's finger points at Batoom. Yet I cannot suspect her. I know she does not love the Emperor. And in four years she has never spoken of any ambition for her gurt sons – save that they emerge from the brutalizing regime of Army and Church with some remnant of the humanity she imbued when they were weans.

Yet there is something snagged on the corner of my mind.

Why would anyone bewitch a mere moggie? To subvert its good luck? But folk here don't share that Scottish superstition. Perhaps this is naught but a cruel coincidence, and the pusskin chewed on a yew-berry or some nightshade or some other lurking poison I do not know of – a crunchy scorpion or earwig. A coincidence is a better fit for the facts. But the snaggle's there still. My coat-tails are caught.

31 March 1770

Now here is an interesting development. I have spent the morning with Dr Lempriere, who turns out a most perspicacious man; one whose oddnesses bespeak a most measured mind, that cares less about the niceties of Discourse than the determined application of his Science. These past days have been an utter endurance to him, the sitting and nodding, the pomp and pageantry, when he is itching to get to his patients.

I explained the situation to him, how he must examine the women as best he can through the small apertures for tongue and hand, but he does not believe me until he sees the screen for himself, and attempts to peer through the apertures – which he is prevented from doing *mais bien sûr*, for they are fitted with grilles which are not drawn back until the patient is *in situ*.

Whereupon he gives one of his high laughs, like a horse's whinny, and shakes his long head, snorting, 'How can I be expected?' and 'It is not reasonable' and the like, spluttering on, until I courteously remind him that his departure is predicated on his tending to the women. At which *La Crisp* places a governess hand on his arm and bids him do his best, for she grows hourly more nervous about the amorous ambitions of the Emperor.

So while we await *La Douvia*'s arrival, they commence to

interrogate me as to why the sexes are kept so strictly apart, which I explain by reference to the Moor's belief that a man's lusts are like dry kindling. 'And woman is the spark which ignites a passion he cannot control.' To illustrate the point, I relate the passing of a new law in Marrakech, whereby any man found carrying a mirror on his person during the hours of daylight may be stoned to death for the crime of *zina*, which is lust outwith the bounds of marriage.

'The women visit one another over the roofs,' I explained, 'as they are not allowed in the streets without their *haiks*, which are stifling in the summer. Thus they parade high above the men's heads, from flat roof to flat roof, along their own lofty lanes, with their heads bare and their silks blowing in the wind. And the men are forbidden to look up, for fear of being conflagrated at the sight.'

Now the Doctor is laughing, and the Governess too, for they have anticipated the end of my story. Which is that a group of enterprising youths have been discovered shuffling along with their heads dutifully averted, all the while feasting their eyes on small mirrors artfully angled in their hands.

As their jollity abates, rustling behind the screen announces the arrival of the *Lalla* Douvia in her Papish confessional. And by and by the upper grille rattles back and the queenly tongue is rudely extruded at her Priest, which he duly examines for taint of sin. And finds it too, for though dainty and pointed, the tongue is quite furred over and foul-smelling. Next she passes through her ragamuffin hand, thorn-torn as ever, which he duly fingers at the wrist to find the pulse.

Then: 'This is impossible!' huffs he, and drops the hand, which dangles briefly then disappears back through the screen. 'How can I work without seeing the patient?' And his knuckles pop like gorse pods on a midsummer day.

'Perhaps good Microphilus here could interrogate her for

you?' intercedes the emollient Governess. 'Now, Sir,' here she turns to me with a look that brooks no demurral, 'I am sure you would permit the Doctor to examine certain other portions of the Lady if he needs to? Provided, of course, that he does not view the whole of her person at one time?' Whereupon I nod and look at the Doctor, who shrugs testily and so it is agreed.

Thus we proceed, with me questioning the Lady through the lower aperture (which is at a good level for my mouth) and she replying through the upper one, illustrating her answers by inserting a scratched foot or inflamed ear, a bloodshot eye or puffy cheek, at alternative apertures as the Doctor requires.

'My first thought is that the Lady has been poisoned,' muses he when she has been taken back to her quarters. 'The black vomit and tremors are a certain sign. But there are additional symptoms which puzzle me. The pains in her limbs, for example, and the breathlessness she complains of, which would point to a rheumatic ague of some kind . . .' and trails off with a look of puzzlement on his equine face.

I explain that two more of the Emperor's wives are similarly stricken and, after a swift discourse on Mohammed's conjugal rulings (which they know, but cannot quite encompass, and shake their heads in agitated credence), the Doctor requests that Zara and Aziza be brought to the Examination Room.

Zara is already waiting in the outer chamber, having exerted her authority over a prior press of importunate *pulchers* whose cacophony belabours the doors beyond. So the Old Queen is admitted, and her tongue and hand protrude and are examined, along with sundry other portions, and questions posted in through the lower aperture like letters. With each answer, the Doctor's confidence grows until his knuckle-cracking ceases and his long fingers extend and flex in a veritable ecstasy of Enlightenment.

(Note that I have not mentioned the *Shatan*'s porcupine to him, for I do not want his mind stumbling into the maze I have been lost in, where all spells become possible and all culprits likewise. I am hoping that without these prickly signposts, the way may become clearer.)

Though he has not seen Helen (and I am wary of uprooting her while she is so deranged), the Doctor declares himself satisfied that all three queens are suffering from common *arsenicum* poisoning. His thin lips stretch in a broad grin, but words of congratulation refuse to jump from my mouth. For this is not the answer I am hoping for. *Arsenicum* was our very first suspect: having neither taste nor smell, the stuff is simplicity itself to administer and a favoured method of murder in every country where it is available. Every *tabib* in Morocco is familiar with the symptoms, so much so that the Emperor has a rota of *tabibs* standing by at all hours to watch for signs of such poisoning in his tasters.

My scepticism must have shown in my face, for the equine physician hastens to elaborate. 'The acute effects are well known,' he explains, pressing the tips of his fingers together, 'with the victim succumbing in a few hours and death following soon after. But when tiny doses are administered over a long period the effects are more like those we can observe in the Lady Zara.' It turns out he observed just such a case near his home in Shoreditch, where a small amount of the powder (which had been stored on a high shelf) fell into the family's flour sack and so became inadvertently incorporated into the bread. Over the following weeks the entire household became affected with the symptoms we have seen in our queens.

You can imagine how my mind begins racing at this, but there is no time to dwell on it now, for the babble of the women is bubbling like water in a pot, and threatens to boil over if I do not hie to the other side of the screen. It takes me nigh on an hour to organize them in some kind of priority, some to see the Doctor this morning, others on his return on the morrow. Some have brought cushions and plan to set up camp in the outer courtyard to ensure a good position in the forthcoming rampage. Thus are idle minds turned inward, and focus most avidly on their own concerns, and become thereby the more idle, the more inward-looking, in a tightening spiral of pettiness.

The Doctor sees perhaps ten more women, and amazes them mightily with some harmless concoction he has devised, involving common baking soda, which foams up as they drink and causes them to belch most spectacularly and expel, so he declares (winking at me), their bad spirits. Then we close up the apertures, as wee shutters over a shop, and leave the remainder chuntering aggrievances.

At last I extricate myself and canter back to my quarters to scribble all down, in the hope it will clarify in the writing, as butter does when heated and allowed to cool without churning.

The three queens are not bewitched, but poisoned. But slowly, so that their symptoms resemble a sickness. But not killed. Why not killed? Why, when Zara was hammering on Death's door, was not the fatal dose administered? It could not have been for fear of discovery, for no one – not the *tabibs* nor the Crone – suspected poison. The cunning placement of the porcupines made sure of that.

Oh, cunning, so cunning is our culprit . . .

And it could not be to prevent them from breeding (though the Doctor thought a protracted dose would prevent conception), for Zara had pupped her two princes and *La Douvia* her one long before they succumbed. Why, then, injure three queens but leave them alive? And how is it that no one else in their *appartements* was affected, though they all eat the same food and drink water from the same jars?

I will re-read my Treatise from last year. Perhaps there are some conjectures that might be of use to me now.

Nothing there of help in this enterprise. But enough about Batoom to fire up my resolve.

I will go to her now, while the Harem is slumbering in *siesta* and I may pass unmolested, and plead with her to visit my quarters tonight. I want to show her my button and all my Scottish things; explain to her how Microphilus is piecing his heart together at last, and offer her the torn and patched thing and beg her help with the healing.

She has agreed – though I thought I might never reach her, for my footsteps were dogged by the Methuselah, who it seems was but half trampled, sustaining but a bruised toe and wrenched shoulder in the *mêlée* outben my rooms the other morning. I said I was busy, but he was undeterred and limped after me for some four courtyards before I snuck down a side alley to elude him.

So, the deed is done. Batoom will come to me this evening and we will sup together. I have asked Maryam to make her *tajine* of new lamb with the fat garlic bulbs and dried apricots, and I will set out the fine flagon I was saving for my birthday. There is clean linen on the divan and the lamps are full of sweet oil.

There is not the ecstasy I felt thinking of Helen, the tender unpeeling of my senses at the sight of her, but perhaps that will come in time, when I am truly hers and she truly mine.

I have lain down, but cannot sleep. My mind is buzzing with images: all the tongues protruding through the aperture, red, purple, white, grey; and the hands, one after another, with bracelets jangling and rings buried in the flesh of fat fingers;

and the feet, all sizes, with toe-rings or *henna*, and wee Douvia's tinker foot, dusty and scarred from the garden, with its splash of fresh thorn marks on the sole; and the good Doctor bending over them all, like the men in Marrakech over their secret mirrors . . .

Now, here is a new thought. What if our poisoner (for I am convinced now that it is a poisoner we are looking for, with the porcupines just a distraction), what if our poisoner is climbing on the queens' roofs? What if – and now it is coming to me all of a rush – what if she discovers a hole in the ceiling of the queen's chamber and peers through it and notes the situation of the water jar (for we all sleep at night with a small jar of water beside the bed)? Or makes the hole herself, or several holes, until there is one precisely above the water jar? It would be a matter of moments to drop the poison through the hole. And none would be affected but the queen.

And any other creature that drinks from her jug. The kittlin! Now I am truly unsnagged, for did I not see it a-lapping at Helen's ladle?

Someone climbing aloft could bring the porcupines too, and drop them into the courtyard without setting a foot through the gate.

Oh, Microphilus, you are a man possessed! I will go straightway to fetch a ladder from the stores. If there are holes carefully sited on the queens' roofs, I will have my proof.

It seems I am mistaken. I cannot understand it.

I took a ladder as I said (and must bribe a Palace guard to fetch one, for ladders are not allowed in the Harem for fear the women would perch atop them all the day ogling the soldiers) and woke a burly eunuch from his *siesta* to carry it for me. And placed it against the wall in the queen's courtyard and clambered up on to *Lalla* Zara's roof. And there discovered, to my mounting excitement, the exact configuration of small holes I had predicted, each cunningly bunged with a tight-fitting cork such as is used to stop the bottles of argon oil. Whereupon I clamber across to Douvia's roof – it being surprisingly easy to move aloft in this way – and wave down at her, for the women are all beginning to wake now from their slumbers and she is out tending her finches in the garden.

But now, when I examine the roof of her chamber, I find there is no sign of any hole. At which point I regain a toe-hold on the top rung and, downcast, start to descend. And discover to my intense irritation that the gardener is grasping the sides of the ladder and will not allow me to alight until I have agreed to let him have his say.

I am too disgruntled to object, so he unrolls a bamboo mat he has been carrying for this purpose, and sits me down upon it and proceeds to tell me, with great urgency and at great length, about the *bougainvillaea* in *Lalla* Douvia's garden. They are not growing normally, he insists, because – here he strikes his chest for emphasis, ushering in a brief unseasonal autumn – because they have been *climbed upon*.

I thank him wearily and grunt to my feet, and he rolls up his mat and trundles off to wherever it is that he composts his wiry form in repose.

So, there we have it. *Lalla* Douvia's climbers have been climbed on. But there are no holes in her roof. Perhaps the poisoner is climbing down into her courtyard and creeping into her chamber?

Why do I keep thinking of her foot? Each time I close my eyes, there it is, poking out at me like a dusty giant's tongue, mocking me. The canny Governess remarked on the thorn marks, surprised that a queen should tend her own garden, but I explained that, along with her finches, *La Douvia's* blossoms are a cherished pastime. But why scratches on the sole of the foot as well as on the ankle? Perhaps she has been climbing on them herself. Her *bougainvillaeas* arch right on to the roof, so I suppose she must monkey up to clip them, for she long ago dismissed her gardener and has only the Methuselah to dispose of her clippings. So that is solved. Douvia has been climbing on her own climbers. Now sleep, Microphilus, your *siesta* is long overdue.

It is no good. My eyes close, but what they now see is the Young Queen clambering gaily among her flowers in the sunshine with a pruning knife in her hand.

What if it is not a pruning knife? What if it is a phial of *arsenicum*? And what if it be not sunshine, but moonlight that illuminates her ascent?

And what if, hearing the Doctor is coming, and fearing his inflated skills, she has taken the poison herself to put him off the scent? If she had the wits to decoy us with the porcupines, such subterfuge will be but a child's ploy. Ay, and added some strange additional symptoms, which she has concocted herself, to throw him off the scent. Oh clever queen, oh evil queen! Oh overweening clever Microphilus!

I must tell Helen straightway. She must not drink any more of that water.

55

Helen watched the shadows outside tilt and shorten, tilt and lengthen, as the sun passed overhead. The kitten lay on the floor, its breath laboured, its eyes flat and dull. The slaves brought her food and warm water to wash with, but she ignored them and they didn't press her; her limbs felt like water; she could barely stumble to the chamber-pot.

There was a slight commotion at her gate. Her ears heard Microphilus calling to Reema to unbolt it and she closed her eyes, bracing herself to face him again. But he was talking urgently to Reema, questioning her about the water jars. How often did she refill them, where did the water come from? And the small one in the *Lalla* Aziza's bedchamber, when did she fill that?

Helen sighed. What new ruse had he dreamed up to deceive her? She heard his feet scuffing up the stairs, his slippers kicked off against the wall. He bounded into the room without knocking. 'I know I'm the last thing you want to see, but I need to show you something.'

He was peering up at the wooden ceiling. 'Is this jar always here?' She nodded mutely. 'And do you always use this ladle to drink from?' Another nod. Why was he so interested in her water all of a sudden?

He moved the jar and hauled her biggest clothes-chest over in its place.

'What are you doing?'

Ignoring her, he scrambled up on to the chest and reached up towards the ceiling. 'Damn these wee leggies. I wish I'd brought that ladder. You'll have to do it, hen, if you've the strength. Or I can call Reema in if you've no –'

'What?'

'Stand on the chest and reach up to the ceiling.'

'What are you talking about?'

'Go on. If I'm right, you'll feel a wee eye-hole right above your water jar. That's how she did it. Climbed on to the roof like a wee monkey and bored a hole in just the right place. I expect she had to do a few before she got it just right. Then all she had to do was push a hollow reed through and drop the poison into your drinking water. That's why you're always worst in the mornings – that's when it's fresh in your stomach. Then by the afternoon you're feeling a bit better. I never suspected the water, because the jars are all filled direct from the fountain and Reema won't let anyone else in your chamber –'

Helen sat up, trying to absorb what he was saying. He'd discovered that Batoom had been poisoning her drinking water. 'How did you find out?'

'I clambered up myself on to Zara's roof, and there it was: all the evidence laid out nice as ninepence.'

'I mean, how did you find out it was Batoom?'

'Nay, hen. It would never have been Batoom. It's wee Douvia who's the evil monkey in this jungle.'

Helen shook her head; she felt muddy and confused. 'But she's sick herself – and what about the porcupine she found? I saw how scared she was when she saw it. She couldn't have been pretending.'

'Och, she's canny, that one. I think she was afraid the English Doctor would work out what was going on, so she thought she'd better swig a wee bittie of the same poison herself to put him off the scent. Come on, lassie, this is the last piece of the jigsaw. But my arms aren't long enough to set it in place.'

He put out his hand and Helen slid out of bed and climbed gingerly on to the chest. A shower of little grey specks swam before her eyes and she felt herself sway slightly. She put her hand against the wall to steady herself, then straightened and began to raise one arm until she was touching the ceiling. Not daring to look up, she began to rub her fingers over the oiled wooden boards.

'You're looking for a kind of plug, like a bung on a whisky barrel. Something you can push out and replace again without anyone noticing.'

Suddenly she felt something: a rough-hewn wee circle, like a knot in the wood. She pushed it gently and felt it move. She imagined Douvia crouching on the roof above her in the middle of the night, silently removing the wee bung and staring down through the hole at her. Douvia, creeping like a cat across the rooftops.

'I've found it,' she said quietly.

Douvia. Suddenly all the strength seemed to drain out of her. 'The kittlin – she was drinking my water last night. That must be why she's so poorly.'

Douvia was the poisoner. Not Batoom; not Reema. Helen stumbled down off the trunk and sank to the floor. Not Microphilus.

'I thought you were helping her.' She looked at him. 'Batoom, I mean. And Reema. I thought you were all in it together. Plotting, playing with me.'

'I know, hen.' He knelt down beside her and took hold of one of her hands.

'That's why I was so angry. I thought you'd – I mean, after you'd been so kind. I thought you were – oh, I don't know –' Huge sobs rose in her chest like iron bubbles; she felt her face crumpling. 'Then when the kittlin was sick too, it was like I had no one left in the world.'

She was crying properly now, big violent sobs that jerked her body forward until she was leaning against him and he was cradling her against his chest, with her arms around him, and her nose running and her mouth a wailing square.

'There now,' he was murmuring into her hair. 'Let it all out.' She could feel his broad back under her fingers, his cage of ribs. 'It's over now. You can rest now. No one's going to hurt you any more.' He hadn't betrayed her after all.

She wanted to hold on to him for ever, his safe chest, the kind curve of his neck. The man who'd seen her puke and shit and rage and weep. Had seen her through it all. And had liked what he'd seen.

Gradually her sobs quietened and she felt her body relax. Slowly unclenching her fingers, she was aware of his neck against her lips, the soft skin there, the wisps of fine hair escaped from his *queue de cheval*. She breathed in and found her lungs full of the smell of him: his smoky grass smell, his smell of sunshine and puppies. Without thinking what she was doing, she pressed her lips against his neck and slowly opened her whole mouth, tasting and smelling him, burying her nose in his hair.

Somewhere, a long way away, she heard him groan and felt him open his hands against her back, laying his small palms very gently against her shoulders. Not to pull her towards him, not to push her away: just to hold her where she wanted to be.

Closing her mouth, she moved her lips upwards, to the wee dent beneath his earlobe. Like a wean rooting, she moved her mouth along the line of his jaw to the hollow at the base of his throat, the ridges either side, the salty taste there, his blood pushing against her tongue.

'What are you doing?' His voice was very soft, his hands on either side of her head, pulling her up so he could look at her.

'I'm sorry –' She backed away. He didn't want her.

'Nay, hen – never say "sorry".'

'I didn't think.' Her eyes were filling again. She'd forgotten she'd grown so ugly: all bone and gristle, with her hair falling out. And the smell – dear God, what was she thinking of? 'I'd forgotten I was so – I mean, I haven't washed since breakfast. I probably –'

'Whisht, hen. It's not that. As if I'd care about a thing like that.' He was brushing the hair back from her face, his eyes dark and stern. 'It's just I don't want you to open your eyes tomorrow morning and find yourself wishing you'd never put me on your plate.' He pulled a kerchief from his pocket and dabbed beneath her eyes. 'I'm something of an acquired taste. And it can take a good while to acquire it. I want to be sure you've the stomach for it.'

She only half heard what he was saying. She was looking at the damp patch on his shoulder where her tears had wet his *kamise*; at the creases where she'd crushed herself against him. The front of her body felt cold and raw, as though the skin had been peeled away and his body was the dressing that had been laid over her wounds.

The tears were coming again. 'I don't know what to say.' She wanted to press against him again, hide her rawness like a limpet on a rock. '

'You don't have to say anything.'

'It was hurting so much, but when you were holding me it felt better. Oh, I don't know, like being wounded then being tended –' smiling uncertainly. 'But now it's paining again.' She willed him to understand. 'Here,' picking his hand up and placing it palm-down between her breasts. 'And here,' moving it lower, to the soft place below her navel. 'Raw, like. As though I've lost something.'

She glanced at his face. He was staring at his hand on her

belly. 'Like when you gave me that pebble, do you remember? And I fitted my thumb into it. And after, when I gave it back my hand felt so empty, and you said I should keep it.'

She felt the hand on her belly press down harder. And it was as if he'd pushed a lever on a machine, that hinged them both slowly forward and open against each other.

56

1 April 1770

Dawn is breaking and Batoom is dead.

I have written it, but I can scarce believe it.

She came to my quarters but I wasn't here. While I was making love to Helen – God, forgive me, but I could not resist –

While I was with Helen, Batoom was waiting here. And when I did not arrive, she drank poison. While I was easing Helen's pale thighs apart, Batoom was pressing my poisoned flagon to her lips. While I was relishing Helen's little mews of pleasure, Batoom was clutching my coverlet with rigoured fingers.

In the small hours, with Helen slumbering beside me, I remembered my tryst with the Black Queen, and skeltered barefoot through the Harem to my quarters. She had used her key and the rush-light was glimmering in my chamber.

I hesitated outside, wondering what I would say to her. That love for Helen fizzed like *Champagne* in my veins? That her scent was on my cheek, on my thighs, in my hair? That I was sorry? Two, maybe three minutes I waited. It was so quiet: my breath ragged from running; the coals sighing and settling in the kitchen grate; the *teem* tree whispering in the corner of the courtyard.

I pulled back the curtain and crept inside, trying to breathe softly so as not to wake her. She was curled away from me, her back humped up like a barn, the coverlet corkscrewed around her. It was as if she had become knotted into the bedclothes, like a clothes-pin in a storm, when the shirt tugs and twists trying to escape, and instead becomes wound ever more tightly.

Tiptoeing nearer, I saw her legs were mangled with the bed-sheet as I'd never seen them before. Oh Batoom, my softest pillow, how peaceful you always were in sleep. Not flailed about like this.

That was how I knew something was wrong. How long the moment seemed, the impressions piling up like clouds on a mountain: the clenched body, the sour stench, the dark puddle. And stepped forward to shake her stiff shoulder, and saw her roll back towards me, like the rock at Golgotha, cold as a boulder, knees up, fingers clawed into the coverlet, face a rictus of pain.

Blessed Batoom, I tried my best to smooth your face. Ungrit your teeth, plump the bonny cushions of your cheeks.

I ran to Malia, hoping there might be a flicker of life there that she could coax into a flame, and jerked her from her lustrous cave, and pulled her, plait askew and *haik* trailing, through the dark cloisters. It was she who discovered you were poisoned, who held the candle to your face and wiped your chin, picked up the spilt cup and set it aright on the tray. Put the cork back into the flagon and searched in vain for the phial.

Why did you use my wine to dilute the fatal drops? Were you hoping for a drowsier descent?

We laid you out, the Crone and I, raking coals and heating water by candlelight. Not speaking, just doing our work: unbending your strong arms and straightening your legs. You were warm still, behind the knees where the skin is purple. My tears are blotting the paper . . .

When I didn't come, did you search for me? Did you hear

us across the courtyard? Helen's yelp when her time came, and my groan; her sobs afterwards. Oh Batoom, I never thought it would hurt you so much.

My buffalo, my hippo, lying still now on your back on my divan. But not sweetly snoring, not rising up and down like a swell on the sea. Not rolling over, walrus in your foam of bed-sheets, snuffling softly and reaching for me with your fins. Never rolling again, save in your winding cloth, sad grub in your last cocoon, brown arms pinioned, breasts flattened for ever.

When I slipped from Helen's bed, and pulled on my *kamise*, and bent to kiss her sleeping cheek, I heard my button drop and roll unseen on the floor. And smiled in the darkness and left it lying there, thinking the Lady of Auchinleck has come for her Mudskipper at last; the Frog has been kissed and metamorphosed to a Prince. And forgot my pledge to you.

That first moment when I felt her mouth on my neck, and stopped her, and begged her to think what she was doing: if I had thought of you then, come to you then, while it was still afternoon. Stepped across the courtyard and knocked on your gate.

I cannot write more.

The Harem is awake now. The eunuchs are all at their toilet, with all their oils and razors, their foot-smoothers and nose-tweezers. I have slept an hour or two, crooked like a lamb 'neath Batoom's cold arm, praying to the Good Shepherd for forgiveness.

I have been thinking of all the nights I slept thus, dedicated in the brown chapel of her arms: her peat and frankincense; her red tabernacle. Talking, always in the midst of love, and laughing, with her telling tales of her homeland, how the men are this way, and the women that, planting the seeds of her wisdom.

She spoke to me once about death, about how her people believe their souls pass into the bodies of birds, and courtyard trees, burrowing deep into the heart, there to watch over the lives of their descendants. And visit punishment on those who displease them, and wealth and happiness on those they approve. 'So you will never be rid of me, Fijil.'

Is this my punishment? To discover you contorted in my chamber, with smears of my own poisoned wine on your chin? Is this revenge for the hurt I have caused you?

No. This I will not believe. I cannot think your whole life was a lie. Your kindness to Helen – all for show? Your patient tolerance of my madness with her; your wise counsel as the days stretched to months . . . Such a woman does not thirst for revenge, nor quench that thirst wantonly in a lover's chamber.

Think, Microphilus. You are blinded by Guilt. The Batoom you knew would never end her life in this way: spiteful, shameless, flaunting her pain. No, the Black Queen would go stately into her dark night: in lamplight, with a gentle sleeping draught in her own quarters. And bid farewell to her friends, lest they blame themselves, and do all generous and kindly as she was in her life.

She would not choose this howling end, I am sure of it.

And where is the phial? If she poisoned the wine, the phial would be there on the tray. Yet we could find no sign of it. And what reason would she have to hide it?

Another hand, then, brought the phial. But another hand could not have known that Batoom would be there. Which means – what other interpretation can there be? – that this end was meant for me.

57

Helen rolled over, and the last few shreds of sleep sloughed off one by one. Yawning hugely, she stretched out her limbs like a long cat in the sun. She felt ironed out and at peace. She'd been poisoned but now she was safe.

The sickness was going already. She could feel it draining out of her body. Her veins were flowing with clean blood. She could feel it pulsing in her ears and her wrists, flushing out all the badness: fresh and red, sluicing down through her belly, to the sweet ache between her legs, the red bud of memory.

Microphilus: how he'd surprised her. The thought made her laugh aloud. No wonder Batoom loved him so much. She'd expected some fumbling shyness, but he approached her body with the same confident skill as he combed her hair: careful not to hurt, or tire, or bruise her poor bones, but managing to tease pleasure from all the knots in her body.

'Is this all right, hen?' he'd smiled, padding her with pillows; or 'Let's try it this way,' arranging her like a crabbit granny. When he went to lift her *kamise*, she tried to stop him, ashamed of her ladder of ribs. So he'd caressed her arms instead, tracing the blue lines from wrist to elbow, until she relaxed back and saw his eyes on her, and read in them how beautiful she was. And pulled her *kamise* up with her own hands, and felt him climb the ladder with his lips, rung by rung, all the way to her little flat breasts, and cup them gently as birds, nesting them in the palm of each hand.

Her belly growled with hunger. Lying on her back, she began imagining all the things she could have for breakfast:

warm bread dipped in green oil; roasted capsicums with the skin blistering off; yellow curd cheese and partridge eggs; *teem* and *balah*, a huge plateful, with goat's cream and honey.

So careful he'd been, uncovering her piece by piece, then covering her again, with his mouth, his hands, his chest; piece by piece, fitting his body on to hers, until she couldn't tell where he began and she ended.

The scent of new-baked bread and woodsmoke came drifting through the curtain. Getting up, she padded unsteadily across the room and down into the bright courtyard. The tiles were warm on the soles of her feet and yellow roses nodded a cascade of waxy petals as she brushed past.

'Reema!' she called, looking round. 'Where are you? I'm starving!'

Feeling a little giddy, she put her hand on the wall for support and made her way to the kitchen. 'Is there anything ready? I've been lying in bed thinking what I'd like,' she went on. 'As Allah is my Lord, I could eat a horse.' She peered inside. Where was everyone? At the stores, perhaps. Or the laundry.

She was squinting up at the sun trying to calculate the time, when the gate squeaked open and Reema walked in.

'Oh, there you are – good. I'm so hungry!' Her smile froze when she saw Reema's face.

The older woman seemed to be in some kind of a trance; her mouth was set, her eyes blank, her scarred cheeks stiff as stone. 'Breakfast, yes,' she murmured, moving towards the kitchen. 'The bread's made.' She looked vaguely around. 'And water. The water's hot if you –' She made a limp flapping movement with her hand. 'Wash. If you want to wash.'

'What's wrong?' Helen asked.

'They've already washed the body,' Reema went on in a strange, matter-of-fact voice. 'So that's done.'

'What body?' Helen's belly seemed to collapse in on itself. Was someone dead?

'I would have liked to do it myself. But it's done now.' Reema lifted the cloth covering some loaves of flat-bread and a billow of trapped steam rose into the air. 'There's fish if you want some. If you sit down, I'll bring it out to you. I made one for her too, you know.'

'Made what? Reema –' Helen gripped the other woman's arm. 'Please tell me what's happened.'

'A *chifumuro*. She laughed when I gave it to her. But she wore it to please me. I said I wouldn't sleep otherwise. So she hung it around her neck with her keys.'

Helen leant back against the wall. Batoom wore her keys around her neck.

'There's fresh fruit in the bowl over there.' Another limp, flapping movement, as though the hand was moving of its own accord. 'They'll be bringing her back soon. I must prepare the room. There'll be salt in the kitchen, of course. And there should be myrtle –' That vague look again, as though she'd forgotten something. 'I would have liked to wash the body,' she repeated. 'Still, it's done now.'

Reema stared around the kitchen. 'The water's hot,' she said again, then turned and hurried back out into the Queen's Courtyard. On trembling legs, Helen followed her. Had Batoom been poisoned too? Was that what had happened? But she hadn't even been sick.

Reema crossed the courtyard and pushed Batoom's gate open. Helen started to follow, then hesitated, noticing Douvia's gate was open too.

Douvia was kneeling beneath one of her glorious rose bowers. She'd unhooked her golden bird-cages from the walls and was surrounded by bright, darting sound. Microphilus was standing in front of her, holding something in his hand.

Edging closer, Helen saw that it was the flagon he used to keep his wine in.

'It was meant for me, wasn't it?' His voice was low and angry.

'How should I know?' Douvia shrugged. 'What is it?' She started fiddling with the door of one of the cages. The finch inside chirruped in alarm and fluttered against the bars.

'For a while I thought she'd killed herself. Then I realized she'd never do something like that. In my room, where anyone could find her.' His chest heaved as he fought to control his voice. Helen saw that his eyes were red.

'What are you talking about?' Douvia tugged impatiently at the tiny door. 'You're frightening my poor chickies half to death.' A small breeze shook the branches around them; red petals thudded softly down.

'It was because you saw me on the roof yesterday, wasn't it? You knew I'd discovered how it was done.'

The door came open and Douvia put her hand inside the cage. 'There now, my sweetkin. Don't be scared. It's just a silly old eunuch.'

'So you tried to kill me before I worked out it was you.'

The bird's wing-feathers bent and protruded through the bars of the cage as it tried to evade her grasping fingers. 'There now, don't listen to him. He's had a shock and doesn't know what he's saying.'

'You came to my quarters last night, didn't you? And dropped poison in my wine. Deadly poison. Strong enough to kill a man in minutes. But it wasn't me who drank it.'

Douvia's fingers closed around the fluttering bird and pinioned its wings to its side. Helen could see its feet kicking downward, its wee head jerking in a frantic attempt to escape. 'Out you come, *mi querido*. Time for your medicine.' She brought the finch out of the cage and held it to her chest.

'She didn't even have time to call for help.' Microphilus's voice broke and tears began to run down his face. He swiped at them with the edge of his sleeve. 'The gardener kept trying to tell me, but I didn't take any notice of him. He kept talking about your damned flower vines, how they were bent and broken, always in the same place. That's how you climbed on to the roofs, wasn't it?'

'Why on earth would I want to climb on to the roofs?' Douvia moved her thumb and forefinger until they were either side of the bird's head. Holding it secure, she reached for a tiny spoon.

'To drop your poison into Aziza's water jug. And the *Lalla Zara's*. I've found the holes you made.'

Helen heard footsteps behind her and looked round. It was Reema, still as a statue, with a basket over her arm.

'This little chickadee needs medicine. His feathers are falling out and he's stopped singing,' Douvia said. Spooning up some brownish liquid, she nudged the bird's beak with the spoon.

'It was you who dropped those spiny porcupines into their quarters to make them think they'd been cursed.'

Douvia tilted the bird's head back and placed a finger either side of its beak, squeezing gently. 'Come on, open up for Mama. It will make you feel so much better.'

'Why go to all the trouble of poisoning them every day? Why didn't you just kill them and be done with it?'

'Come on, sweetkin, open wide.' Her teeth were gritted now, her fingers squeezing tighter. 'If they were dead he'd just go and marry some more,' she said calmly, looking down at the bird in her hand. It had stopped struggling. 'But if they're just ugly, then he has to love me. You know, those thorns really hurt. Sometimes they went right through the soles of my feet. I'd think of the nails holding Jesus to the Holy Cross, how he offered up the pain to His Father.'

Slowly she opened her fingers. 'He used to call me his brave angel, you know.' The bird was dead; eyes milky, head lolling sideways. Shrugging, she tipped it back into the bottom of the golden cage. 'Sometimes things die when you don't mean to hurt them,' she said, holding out her hands and looking around for a servant to bring her a bowl of water.

There was a long, shocked silence, then a sudden howl of fury as Reema hurled herself across the courtyard. She grabbed the flagon from Microphilus and forced it to Douvia's lips, kneeing her in the belly and yanking her head backwards with her free hand. The little queen struggled and tried to move her head, flailing and scratching with her hands, but the old slave was too strong for her.

A lurch of reddish liquid spilt from the neck of the flagon, splashing on to Douvia's clenched lips, down her chin, up her small nose. She breathed it in and began to splutter, eyes rolling mutely from side to side. Her face turned scarlet and her chest heaved as she struggled to breathe, to cough, to cry for help without opening her mouth. Reema's knuckles shone pale through her dark skin as she ground the neck of the flagon into Douvia's mouth, mashing soft lips against hard teeth as another heave of deadly liquid splashed out, spraying into the desperate eyes and filling the flared nostrils until at last Douvia stopped struggling and opened her mouth.

58

2 April 1770

I have brought my writing things to Batoom's quarters. She is the felled hunter and I the poor hound who will not leave her side, who whines and paws at her dead hand, nudging her cheek with his muzzle to make her head roll and wake her and bid her back on the trail.

Malia and Reema have arranged for the women to visit the body and they have been crowding in silently all afternoon. I see some have left food bowls, with lids against the flies, which I lift to discover all variety of grain, got from Allah knows where. And pestles, too, and mortars. How is it they all know about her sour-mashes? How is it she came to be loved so well?

It is night now and the guards have sent the women away. I did not know I had so many tears inside me. It seems now I have learnt to weep, there will be no stopping me. My shoulders ache and my nose is swollen with blowing and wiping. I keep thinking: it was my death that she drank. If she had not sipped from my flagon, it would have waited there patiently until I had tipped it myself. In death, as in life, all she did was for my well-being.

I have sent for ice to cushion her through the night. We will bury her in the morning. Batoom, your face is empty now. You inhabit this body no more. Have you chosen your soul's resting-place? Night's white owl or day's black eagle? Or the great argon tree in the middle of the garden, where the storks nest, haloed with bees? Or in your own *syringa* at the edge of your kailyard, with cooling mint at your feet and a skirt of rustling red millet? Perhaps you have gone further: south to the Mauritanian plains; to your own birds and trees, your own noble people. Free at last.

She often spoke of her homeland. Not as the slaves do, those that are brought here as adults, in tones of hopeless longing; but with easy familiarity, as one who has but stepped abroad for a week or so and plans to return on the morrow. I think she received word from her relatives, though I did not press her for details, and sent word too via some route she and Reema devised, passing clandestine despatches to trusted couriers, with coins to seal the secret. And I know these exchanges pleased her, and that Home was scored even deeper in her heart than it is in mine.

Malia says she will inform the Emperor in the morning. 'This is women's business,' she growled. 'There is no reason he should know more than he needs.' Thus is the Husband excluded from the Wife's world, as she is from his; and ever has been, and ever will be: in Morocco and Scotland, Nuba and France, and every place I have ever heard tell of. He fears and reveres her competences, as she does his, and they war continually, trucing only briefly 'neath the covers – and not even there, often, for the bed can be the bloodiest battleground of all. Batoom, I should have done sweet battle with you till the end of my days.

More tears. I have had to rifle her trunk for fresh kerchiefs. And burrow down through her wind-fresh white gowns, which yet hold the slight scent of her. And no gaudy silk, and no secret jewel pouches.

I do not know what they have done with *La Douvia*'s body. There were difficulties finding slaves to wash it, due to the

421

taint of witchcraft. Ay, and madness, too. I will not forget that calm little voice confessing atrocities, that pretty shrug as if murder were an unavoidable necessity.

It seems she had been practising the poisoner's art for the past two years, in the little locked room she used to store her treasures, experimenting with different substances and doses, on animals and humans alike, maiming and disposing of several unfortunates in the process – and causing the mysterious epidemics which so puzzled the canny Crone.

Now the poisoner is poisoned. The wasp will sting no more.

Helen was just here to take me off to her chamber. It seems a lifetime ago that I was in her arms, as though it happened to a different man.

That man has quit my body and leans against the wall watching me. He can stand there all night if he wishes. He is ignoble and faithless and I want nothing to do with him.

59

Helen closed Batoom's gate quietly behind her. She felt confused and lonely. Microphilus had hardly glanced up when she invited him to stay with her. It was too soon, she told herself. He needed time to mourn Batoom. They both did. In a week or so, perhaps he'd come back to her.

She could hear a quiet buzz of voices, and see light flickering, beyond the Queen's Courtyard; and the tall silhouettes of the guards posted to keep the mourners at bay. She looked around at the four golden gates. Yesterday all four queens had been alive. Now there were only two left.

She passed Douvia's gate. Light spilt from the chamber where she'd been laid, but Helen knew there'd be no one keeping vigil by her body. Her slaves had refused to sleep anywhere near. Before the corpse had even been washed, they'd started mixing blue paint and scrawling hands and eyes over the walls, wherever they could reach, slopping it in their haste, so big spots of it lay on the ground and runnels snaked down from the crude eyes like tears.

Helen pushed open her own gate and climbed wearily to her chamber. Lowering herself on to the divan, she found herself staring up at the wooden ceiling, searching for the wee hole Douvia had made. So clever: one queen after another, drop by drop, watching them grow uglier and uglier until the Emperor rejected them. Helen shivered and unfolded a blanket around her shoulders. How did such a bonnie wee lass come to have so much wickedness inside her? Planning it all. Gathering frogs' eyes and birds' beaks, beetle horns and bee-stings, secretly, day after day. Killing and cutting and binding, hoarding them all away in that horrid little store-room.

'Shall I light the lamp, Lady?' Reema stood in the doorway, a smouldering twig cupped in her hand.

'Thank you.' Helen sat up, screwing her eyes as the flame shivered and swelled. Then, peering at the older woman's face: 'If you want to go back to –' She hesitated, not wanting to mention Batoom's name. 'With Fijil. For the rest of the night. You don't have to stay with me.'

'This is my work,' Reema said shortly, and drew a fistful of salt crystals from her pocket. 'These things need to be done.' She paced the room carefully, trickling salt through her fingers like gravel. 'They're awake tonight,' she said grimly. 'And hungry. They've tasted blood and they want more.'

Helen watched her perform the reassuring ritual. 'I didn't know Batoom was waiting in his room,' she said quietly.

'No, Lady.' Reema wiped her hands on her *kamise*.

'I didn't ask him to stay. He was explaining how Douvia poisoned my water. We forgot the time . . .' She trailed off.

Reema sighed and picked up the big water jar. 'She wouldn't have blamed you.'

Microphilus came to her in the small hours. Helen woke up to find him sitting beside the bed in the darkness, cross-legged on the floor with his back to her, as he'd done so many times when she was ill.

She touched his shoulder. 'Are you cold?'

He shook his head, but she could feel him shivering in his thin *kamise*. 'Come on.' She folded back the blanket. 'Let me warm you.' She tugged gently on his plait and he turned slowly and clambered in beside her.

His body was icy, and she tried to warm him, wrapping her thin arms around him and pulling the blanket up over his head like a *haik*. She wished she was softer, bigger, deeper, to cushion the jagged shudders that convulsed him. His teeth were chattering against her knobby chest; his feet icy between her bony thighs.

Gradually his shivering stopped and he lay still in her arms, breathing so softly she thought he'd fallen asleep. His hair smelt of myrrh and *qat* smoke. She could feel his belly against hers, warm now, and solid; the slight rocking movements as he breathed in and out. She could feel her breasts tingling, remembering his mouth on them. She touched her lips very gently to his domed forehead. Sighing deeply, he moved drowsily against her, worming nearer. His breath was warm on her neck, his heart thudding against her ribs. No, *her* heart thudding. Was he really asleep? She moved her hands slowly down his broad back, the long mounds of muscle either side of his spine. Not thinking whether he was awake or asleep, just wanting to trace the shape of him through his clothes. He sighed again and she could feel his thing growing against her belly; tilting and turning, trapped by the folds of his *salwar*. Smiling in the darkness, Helen reached for the hem of his *kamise* and began easing it up, slipping her hands underneath and feeling the warm shock of her forearms against his bare skin.

Then she was kissing him again, tasting tears on his lips. They were face to face on the pillow, breathing each other's breath, barely moving. Her skin was singing. She could feel a pulse in her groin; an answering pulse where he was pressed against her belly.

'Is this all right?' she whispered against his mouth, and felt him smile and nod his head.

She smiled back, fitting her curve on to his, running the tip of her tongue between his lips, until they softened and opened for her, and they entered one another, wet as oysters, smile to smile.

They kissed for a long time, tracing and tasting one another with their mouths. It seemed right to be like this – slow and tender and respectful – even though she was red and aching, and itched to squirm up and on to him. At last they pulled away and lay staring at each other in the darkness. She could hear an owl screeching somewhere out in the orchard; further away, a dog barked then yelped as it was kicked into silence.

'I was going to ask her to marry me,' he said quietly. 'Last night. That's why she was in my room.'

Helen felt her throat close. Air curdled in her chest.

'She'd loved me for so long, I felt I owed it her. Of course, it wouldn't have been like a proper marriage until she moved to Tafilalt. But I wanted to promise her.'

'So why did you stay with me?' Her voice was tight. She began pulling her arm out from under him.

'Oh, Helen,' he sighed wearily. 'Don't go cold on me now. You know fine why I stayed with you.' He rolled on to his back and stared up at the ceiling. 'I keep thinking: if I'd only gone to say I wouldn't be coming. When I went to the washroom – after we finished the first time, d'you remember? I could have nipped over and told her not to go to my room. All I'd to do was walk across the courtyard. But I was so caught up with loving you, it never crossed my mind.'

'I'm sorry.' Helen laid a hand on his heart, pictured it clenching and unclenching.

'I keep thinking of her waiting by herself in my room, wondering where I'd got to. Then drinking that stuff –' His voice caught. 'I keep wondering what she'd have been thinking. When it started happening – she'd have known straight away the wine was poisoned. What if she thought that I'd done it?'

'But why would you?' Helen felt his chest heave under her hand.

'That's just what she'd have been wondering. All the time she was dying, thinking, "Why does Fijil want me dead?" Her last thought, Helen. "Why isn't he here? Why does he want me dead?"'

'You don't know that. You weren't there –'

'No. I wasn't there.' His voice was thick. 'That's the beginning and the end of it. Whichever way I look at it. If I'd have been there, she'd be alive now. But I wasn't there.'

She felt his chest heave with trapped sobs for a while, then quieten again. 'D'you want to be held again?' she asked shyly.

He sighed deeply, but made no move towards her. 'Oh, I don't know, hen. When we're kissing, my mind empties of everything. But I'm not sure that mindless is how I should be right now.'

Swallowing a little needle of pain, Helen nodded. They lay like that for a long time, side by side, staring up into the darkness. She tried to remember what had comforted her when she'd been too frightened and sick to speak.

'I could bathe you,' she suggested after a while. The words 'like a proper wife' were on her lips, but she didn't say them. 'It will help you sleep. I'll put some water on to heat.'

She lit a rush-light and laid out cloths. The night was warm and quiet as she enacted the familiar sacrament, reverently as a priest at the altar: uncovering and unfolding; chasuble, alb; blessing and pouring; bread, cup.

He lay passive, turning on his side when she asked him to, letting her move his arms and legs. It was the first time she'd looked at him properly, and was able to fit him together in her mind: the public parts she saw every day; the secret parts she'd only felt with her hands. He was very white; very broad; very smooth. Not like a tree at all, she thought. More like a –

Like a what?

She looked down at him. His eyes were shut, his limbs

relaxed, his chest rising and falling. His thing lolled to one side in his dark bush; there was a small triangle of sandy curls between his nipples. He was like a man.

60

3 April 1770

Thursday crept up on me early this morning and tapped me on the shoulder and bade me gallop to my chamber for fresh garments and hustle out to the garden to greet the Emperor.

I have been living in that place Papists call Limbo, suspended somewhere twixt Heaven and Hell, where none are saved and none damned, and all is Innocence and naught requires Forgiveness. My love is dead. My love lives. My heart is taut as a lute-wire. Now I must push feet into slippers, and slap slippers on to solid ground, and make them move forward and carry me back to normality.

So here is the Emperor eyeing four empty green awnings. Had I envisioned this scene, I might have prepared him. But I did not, and cared not, and so here we have it. *Naturellement* he was informed of the deaths – Malia told him herself – but it is not until he sees the row of bare niches that he realizes he has lost all his queens.

Of course the women are all jiggling and jostling as usual to catch his eye. Indeed, their excitement would be quite palpable, had you but a thumb and forefinger that could pinch the plump air. Not since he was a princeling has there been such a chance for advancement.

But he is oblivious, transfixed by this stark evidence of his Shame. For to lose one wife might be considered a misfortune; to lose four bespeaks a man who cannot husband his females.

In this sequestered kingdom, a man's ability to manage his women is as much a measure of Manhood as the size of his herds. For all here know that women are stupid, wilful creatures who must be corralled in their houses, with men their custodians and responsible for their actions, just as the cowherd is whipped – and not the heifers – if his herd tramples a field of peas.

Thus the Emperor is more incensed than bereft by his losses. 'First Zara, then Aziza with their beauty destroyed,' seethes he with beetling brow as he sweeps from the garden. 'Now Douvia and Batoom poisoned. I will be the laughing-stock of Africa!'

And so Anger vies with Vanity in his breast (Sadness having been o'ertaken at the first hurdle), and each triumphs in turn. First Vanity, which has him summarily despatching the good Doctor and his Governess post haste to Sallee, to be bundled off back to Gibraltar on the first ship before the news of the queens' deaths can reach them. He forbade me to bid them farewell lest I let slip some hint of his Ignominy, which would leak thence into Europe, on a tide of derision, until the Thief of Marrakech had been rechristened the King without Queens.

With Vanity assuaged, next Anger pulls his strings and he summons us all to his quarters – myself and Malia, the guards, the *tabibs* – and strides up and down before us, and tosses back his sleeves, demanding tea and *kief* and *balah* in succession, and sending them all away. While we wait, stiff wee pawns on his chessboard, as he moves us impatiently about to discover how his queens have been toppled.

And all the while this is happening I feel like an audience at a puppet show, where the action is petty and mean and occurs at a great distance. I keep thinking of the Black Queen buried in her yellow coffin outben the Palace walls. How her rich colours must be dulling now, all the browns and purples I loved; her glossy chestnuts and aubergines, all clouding and shrinking down as the life dissolves within them.

The Emperor rants on for an hour, but cannot penetrate us. The *tabibs* conjecture; the guards quail; and Malia and I outdo one another in eloquent ignorance. Together we are a very vision of respectful evasion. And though Anger is not appeased, Weariness finally insists we are dismissed. I am fearful, though, that Anger will not sleep easy. We have not heard the end of the affair.

Now to kinder matters: I want to describe how we have been with each other, Helen and I. How we first undressed each other like shy bairns, she my rag doll, I her Bruin. How, finding her so coy, hiding her wee flat dugs and the jutted shelves of her hips, I must coax them out with soft words and smoorikins, stroking beauty into them, until she has forgotten her shame and is spidering her skinny arms around me. So now I set to peeling her fruit, and tasting her, her fish flavours, and sweet monkey noises begin gibbering in her throat.

I bless Batoom for stripping me of my old shames, of my wee legs and pup's paws, all the brawn I have accumulated through the years to haul this bole about, my gnarled knees and axe-man's shoulders. Batoom loved them and so they are lovable, and can love Helen better than any Emperor.

I have hungered so long for this banquet; now she is here on my table I hardly know where to start. She was laughing at me this morning, for I had become transfixed somewhere at the base of her back, nuzzling the downy hollows either side of her tailbone, licking there to test the flavour and strumming the stacked cups of her spine, and ferreting lower with my small finger, nosing into her cony's burrow. 'Have you forgotten me?' she asks in mock petulance, and butts me off and rolls herself over and pulls me on to her. Allah be praised, she is so wet for me! So I must pause again, and go winkling with my fingers, and marvel how her fat frills are arranged, cunning as a sea-otter's lair, to sleek me into her.

Now she grows impatient again, but loving-like, squirming her bony pelvis crying, 'Fijil, please, no more fiddling!', tugging up my hand and kissing me, salty as eel-juice, and her cheeks hot and her breath coming in wee gusts, and all her jockey's bones circling me, spurring me, until I relent and go cantering where she wants me to go.

4 April 1770

Today we opened Batoom's locked rooms, using the keys she always kept around her neck. I do not know what we expected to find: bales of unwanted silks, perhaps, and jewel-chests; cabinets with all her wedding gifts; despatchments from her homeland, of gourds and head-dresses, and Allah knows what-all; or coins at the very least, slumped in leather purses, for she had her allowance from the Emperor each week, which I handed to her myself, and nothing to spend it on save her tweeny and her scythe and the gauzy white sails she attired herself in.

But when we unlocked the doors and pushed them open, every room we entered was empty. Helen and Reema were with me, and a brace of burly eunuchs I had summoned to sort and carry the stuff. Our footsteps echoed as we toured the vacant chambers, all freshly swept with nary a house-ant to be seen, the tiles pristine as we cluster across them.

She had always said they were empty, when I teased her for her keys, but I never thought she was telling the truth. As we toured them, and heard their shuffling echoes, it was as though each were shrugging as if to say, 'We are as you see us; nothing more, nothing less – and no good searching.' By and by I find myself smiling with them, thinking of the *Alim* waiting in the Royal Counting-house, rubbing his knob-knuckled hands in anticipation, with his quill aloft to inventory for the Emperor. (I have had occasion in the past to marvel at the Emperor's unwonted generosity to his favourites, while he tends to be so niggardly with the rest of his affairs. The explanation is here before you: the goods are but lent to their recipients, and return forthwith to the master's coffers as soon as their lessees have fallen from favour.)

Now Helen is laughing and twirling around on the bare tiles, and Reema smiling as best she can with her granite cheeks. So I send the eunuchs trotting off to the *Alim* and we set down on a grass mat under a *teem* tree (for there never were any carpets) and bless the Black Queen for having the last laugh.

Then I see that the sourpuss is glancing around as though she has some intelligence to impart, and is giving us the shrewd eye and the cocked brow. And by and by, when our tea has arrived and the tweeny has popped back into her box, she leans forward and whispers what has become of Batoom's wealth.

I have explained, have I not, how Batoom first came here? Given by her father in a pact for peace with the Emperor, who must wrestle her to the ground in full sight of her countrymen – as is the custom with her people – before he may carry her off on his stallion. Though ever Chief Empress in the Harem, it seems she never forgot she was a Prisoner-of-war. And was in receipt of frequent messages from her homeland, first from her father, and then when he died, from her younger brother who eventually inherited the feathers of his Chiefdom.

'Do you remember that time she was so unhappy?' demands the sourpuss, and my mind goes to a space of weeks some years back, when she took to working her kailyard day and night, swinging her hoe and hacking into the red soil, even though the clods were broken, stabbing it by moonlight with tears on her cheeks. 'That was when we received word about her father. She would have escaped then, risked her life to go home and wear his Chief's Headdress – except she loved you, Fijil.'

So she stayed here, and sent back what she could: coins, bracelets, buckles, all smuggled out by Reema and galloped southward to be traded for muskets on the Gold Coast. 'They are preparing an attack!' hisses sourpuss, and glee twitches up one corner of her mouth. 'They are tired of Morocco's marauding *sheikhs*.'

Now I am wondering whether there was, indeed, a golden saddle once, somehow spirited away with all the rest.

5 *April* 1770

The *Alim* was just here, with a hood over his head (for of course he is not permitted to see the women) and an escort of eunuchs. They are all frolicking and laughing behind their hands, inventing peculiar obstacles for him to avoid – 'Oh, not there, your Worship, for that is where the women dry their *salwars*' – making him bend at the waist and shuffle beneath an imaginary line of dripping nether-garments, or, 'Sideways here, your Holiness, for Zenaida is having her arse painted', and so on and so forth until he has gathered a whole procession of women, all giggling and falling into one another, while his discomfiture grows and his gnarled old twig nudges up inside the tent of his garments at the thought of the erotic visions he is missing.

He has insisted on inspecting Batoom's quarters for himself, for he cannot bring himself to credit the eunuchs' reports. I close the gates and wave the women away, and he divests himself of his hood and stands blinking in the middle of her largest room, all flushed and askew, scowling around at the empty space. Which he walks around, much as we did the previous day; glowering and scratching his ruffled head; perambulating irritably from room to room with his chin jutting, then returning to where I am waiting with his hood.

'The Emperor will hear of this,' mutters he as I enshroud him again. Which the Emperor duly does, and reacts as one might expect, with more wrath and more summonses, whereupon we all shuffle forth once more with our evasive faces, to be interrogated and shifted about. He sends us away, but keeps Malia. It will take four more lassies to assuage his itches tonight.

28 April 1770

Helen's flesh is returning. She complains she is ravenous all the time, blaming our loving exertions, and has been ordering all varieties of food, at all times of the day and night, such that Reema has taken to preparing a covered tray before she retires, heaped up with *hummus* and butter-cakes, *balah* and honey. So Helen pads across the courtyard at midnight, with the moths diving at her lamp, and returns with her mouth full and sweet grease on her chin.

My throat aches to see her thus: greedy, sucking her fingers, cross-legged in the lamplight. And me eating, drinking the sight of her, seeing her bones start to sink back under their quilts of pale flesh; cheeks first, next chest, the hard ruts of her ribs softened by ripples of snow. And her green eyes smiling at me, liking what they see.

61

Helen sat under her jasmine and sipped sweet mint tea, but she felt cross and restless. The thought kept coming back to her: Batoom had sent all her wealth away. She had so much, but it meant nothing to her. Somewhere far away men were preparing to fight with weapons bought with Batoom's jewels, the gold saddle she'd talked about melted down and exchanged for pistols and powder.

No wonder she'd no interest in scarves and slippers. What did she call the Harem? 'Our pretty prison.' All those hours she worked in the garden, her mind must have been journeying up and over the great wall, out along the tracks to her distant home where her brothers were waiting.

The thought of all that space out there made Helen feel dizzy. The slaves talked about oceans of sand, deeper than a man could dig, and no water for weeks. There were rivers full of man-eating lizards; forests full of baboon-people; trees so huge you could plant a garden in the clefts of their branches. Out there somewhere was Tafilalt.

Tafilalt: she could go there with Microphilus. Retire there, maybe even have children; a little courtyard; a fountain; a few nice clean rooms. It would be like home.

Helen thought about Muthill; remembered how she used to run down the tracks by the forge for the sheer joy of it. Easing out her legs, she looked at her feet: soft, silky, pampered. At her thighs: fubsy and dimpled. How had she ever walked all the way to Crieff? Naseem had been proud of her strong legs. But Naseem had planned to escape. Batoom had laughed and shown off her muscled arms. Batoom was hatching rebellion. The Harem was just another slave ship to them. Their horizon was far beyond its walls.

Helen thought of the bonny eighteen-year-old running down the lane to Muthill all those months ago; how she'd leapt across the puddles with her head bare and her skirt rising and the sun on her arms. How long was it since she'd run anywhere? Or walked, even? Since she'd been ill she hadn't ventured beyond the Queen's Courtyard.

She stood up. She wanted to face the world again.

'Here, Lady?' Reema brought in the big mirror and propped it against the wall. 'There are marks where the nails were.'

'Yes, good. That's perfect.' Helen stood back while Reema hammered in new nails and carefully lowered the big mirror on to them. 'It was the first gift they brought in on my wedding day,' she said, touching the gilt edging. 'I'd forgotten how pretty it was.'

'And this other one, Lady?' Reema was lifting a second mirror. It was one of three that used to hang in the washroom, but Helen had ordered it to be brought through into her chamber. Reema looked sideways at her mistress. 'A little lower, perhaps?'

Helen grinned. 'Quite a lot lower, I think.'

Reema made a mark with her thumbnail and picked up the hammer. When she'd finished, Helen moved in front of the big mirror. She was half afraid: it was the first time she'd seen herself properly since she'd ordered all her mirrors removed. She'd been relying on a wee hand-mirror for months: just to paint on her *kohl* and rouge, and check her chin for spots. Now she stared at her reflection.

The face looking back seemed older than she remembered. The girlish plumpness had gone from the cheeks and her freckles had faded. She seemed more serious: her eyes dark; her mouth grave and small. She was dressed simply, in a white *kamise*, with her hair hanging in a single plait over her shoulder. Her illness, her terror, her recovery had given her face a gravity it had never had before. The girl was gone. She looked like a woman.

'It's good to see you well again, *Lalla*,' Reema said quietly as she left the room.

Helen kept staring at herself. She couldn't believe it. She was bonny again. No: more than bonny. Beautiful. Allah the Merciful had given back her looks. Slowly she loosened the ribbon on her plait and shook the curls out around her face like copper ribbons. Slipping the *kamise* from her shoulder, she surveyed her body. She was thin, still, but no more than when she first arrived. The terrible flat bone of her chest was covered again with smooth flesh; her pommel shoulders were rounded once more; her breasts plump and taut. And her skin – thanks be to Allah – showed none of the cruel brown blotches that so disfigured poor Zara.

She opened up her trunk of silks. There were things in there she'd forgotten she even owned; things she'd bought in the first flush of the Emperor's money. For weeks now she'd worn nothing but simple white cotton. Half-way down she found her wedding clothes, wrapped carefully in clean muslin. Where were her jewels? She burrowed through her things, heaving out a rainbow swathe of silk and flinging it on the floor. At last: here were her jewel-boxes, jigsawed at the very bottom. And the keys? She flew to the loose tile in the corner of the chamber and prised it up from the floor.

Fitting each tiny key into its lock, she turned the small oiled parts, feeling them clicking back. She opened them all, then sat back on her heels and stared at the brimming boxes. How could she have forgotten them? Her pearl bracelet and her favourite emerald necklace; all her earrings and the jewelled combs for her hair. And here, in the most ornate box of all, her wedding jewels, glowing like live coals in their nest of gold satin.

Time stopped as she sat there among her treasures, picking them up one by one and examining them like old friends. This one, with its tricky clasp: she remembered the Emperor laughing as she tried to fasten it, then lifting her fall of hair and biting her shoulder. She thought of the Jewel Room, how he'd cascaded treasure on to her lap; the pain as he pushed her back on top of them, nudging her legs apart with his knees. She could feel herself blushing. How long ago it all seemed.

She picked up her wedding necklace and stood in front of the mirror, remembering the golden bride with her filigree face and shining satin. In a sudden flurry of excitement and decision, she unwrapped her wedding clothes and began putting them on.

First the cool satin *salwars* and filmy blouse; then the heavy waistcoat. Finally the jewels. And that strange regal stance: head up, shoulders back. There: she was an Empress again. The sun slanted into the room, glinting on her hair, on the golden embroidery, the scarlet gems. She could feel that wee flame of triumph catch and burn at the base of her throat. She was herself again, she was bonny again, she was the most beautiful and best-loved Empress in the Harem.

She backed into the room and began swaying her hips the way Batoom had taught her all those months ago, feeling the weight of her finery moving against her skin. Then suddenly noticed the reflection of herself in the other mirror: her half-reflection, truncated at the waist.

She stopped dancing and stared at the two mirrors: one high and one low on the wall. One for the Empress; one for the Dwarf. Moving to one side, she imagined Microphilus standing beside her, pictured his reflection in the empty mirror. Pictured them walking together, the Empress and the Dwarf, his little feet kicking, his balloon head rocking from side to side; his hand reaching for hers like a bairn's.

A jolt went through her. Three moons ago she was playing sex with an Emperor. Now she was the sweetheart of a dwarf.

There was a quiet cough behind her and Helen whirled around to find Reema stooping over the sea of silk. 'I'm sorry for the mess,' she said. She felt guilty, as though she was back in Melissa's cabin all those months ago, wearing clothes that didn't belong to her.

'Can you iron this, please, Reema?' She bent and picked up some garment at random.

'Yes, *Lalla*.' Reema looked at her.

'It is Thursday tomorrow, isn't it?'

'Yes, *Lalla*.'

'I think it's time I went to the garden again.'

'I can't stay hidden away for ever.'

'I know.' Microphilus put down the piece of bread he was holding and looked at her over the low tray. They were sitting in her courtyard, eating their evening meal.

'Zara went last week,' Helen said.

'I know. I was there, remember? It was me who told you about it.'

'And he asked after me.'

'Ay.' And they'd laughed about it together afterwards: the Emperor waving an angry hand at the three empty awnings, asking was he a Christian that he had only one wife?

'I have to face him sometime.'

Microphilus sighed. 'You don't have to explain, hen. We knew it would have to happen.'

'So you don't mind?'

440

'Does the fox mind when its leg's being crunched in the trap?' He smiled, but his eyes were dark.

Helen balled *couscous* in her fingers and stirred it to and fro in the gravy. She couldn't look at him. She was afraid he'd ask why she wanted to see the Emperor. And she didn't know the answer. Because she wanted to see if he still loved her? Because she longed to be the talk of the Harem again? Because she was ashamed of loving a dwarf?

'I'm so scrawny still, I don't expect he'll send for me.'

'Don't make it worse by lying,' he said sharply. 'You're as bonny as ever and well you know it. He'll know it, too, the moment he sets eyes on you.' A slave brought water and he washed his hands. 'Oh, don't worry. I'll not throw a jealous fit if that's what you're thinking. I know you've to go to him if he wants you. I know you've to perform as best you can, so he's not suspicious.'

He took her wet hand and dried it. 'This is my favourite hand in all the world,' he said, turning it over and tracing the blueish veins in her wrist with his finger. 'It was the first bit of you that I touched. Do you remember? At Madam Jasmine's? You were in that dreadful purple dress and I bowed and kissed your hand. Your nails were broken and smelt of *smeen* and mutton. I remember thinking: this is a good working hand. She was trying to make out you were some kind of French countess, but when I held your hand I knew better.'

'What do you mean, you knew better?' Helen pulled her hand away.

'I mean a countess doesn't have callused thumbs and scars on her knuckles.'

Why did he always have to remind her of where she came from? She was here now, wasn't she? She held out her hands in the lamplight and looked at them: clean and soft and neatly manicured by Reema; not a trace of rough skin. Tomorrow she'd wear her bonniest bracelet; and the ring the Emperor had given her on their wedding day.

Microphilus was staring at her.

She flushed. 'What are you looking at?'

'Just you, hen. I was just looking at you.' He sighed again, then squared his shoulders. 'I was thinking maybe I should go to my own quarters tonight.'

'Why?' She knew she should protest. She knew she was hurting him.

'You'll have things to be doing if you're going to the garden tomorrow.'

'Don't think I'm sending you away.'

'I don't.'

'It's just I've so much to do.' Blood was suddenly pounding in her ears. She was seeing the Emperor tomorrow. She was going to be an Empress again. She began getting to her feet.

'You'll not be wanting your tea, then.' Microphilus gave her a tight smile and got up too.

'I'm sorry.' Flustered, Helen saw Reema walking across the courtyard with the usual tea tray. 'I forgot.'

'I know, hen.' Then: 'Goodnight. Let me know when you want to see me again.' And was gone before she could say another word.

62

I have lost her. One day we are together, wriggling like two larvae in the sweet slime of our pond. Next she is rising from the water and shaking drops from her shoulders; picking off the clinging weeds, the tendrils that tied us to each other, stepping away from me on to her dry land.

She has taken out all her dragonfly silks, and had them washed, and they are drying in the sunshine: her crumpled wings, wafted by the wind, billowing and shining.

Tomorrow he will put out his finger for her to light on.

And I will return to my shell. Caddis-man, lugworm: your mayfly has metamorphosed and fled the water.

63

There had been a tense few minutes in the garden when she thought the Emperor was going to ignore her. He'd glanced towards the queens' awnings, had seen she was there, but had turned away without coming over.

Afterwards she realized he'd been afraid of seeing her; afraid the sickness might have marred her, like *Lalla* Zara, who came to the garden every week now without fail, her anxious ruined face above the rebuilt soft mounds of her body.

But Malia had tugged on his sleeve and said something which made him hesitate, then walk slowly towards where she was waiting. Feeling suddenly unsure and vulnerable. Helen had drawn the silken veil she was wearing across her face beneath her eyes. As he approached her, his expression slowly transformed from disgust to wary hope as he took in her flawless pale forehead, the escaped copper tendrils of her hair, the glowing green of her eyes.

'Aziza?' Still wary, he was bending towards her. 'Is it true what Malia tells me? That you are recovered now?' He reached out a hand to pull the veil from her face, then hesitated as disgust seeped into his eyes once again.

A sliver of ice settled in Helen's heart as she realized how much her appearance mattered to him. Was this the kind of love she wanted?

'It's been so long. I can hardly believe it.' Still he hesitated, not quite daring to pull the veil from her face.

The chilled part of Helen lifted away from her body and hovered above them. It watched her smile at the Emperor

444

over the veil, and sway gently in her green silks; it saw the glint of her emeralds rolling heavily against the skin of her chest. Saw her confidence grow: she had him again now, she was sure. Half turning away from him, she made him step nearer, forced him to follow her around, to lift his hand and wrench the veil from her fingers. The Harem's eyes were upon her as she turned slowly beneath the green awning, a green leaf on the water, pulling the white-robed Emperor after her.

The sun was low in the sky as Helen followed Malia through the Harem to the Emperor's quarters. She was washed and perfumed; hair rippling, silk blowing against her skin. Women knelt or prostrated themselves as she passed. 'It's *Lalla* Aziza,' she heard them whisper. Head high, she breathed in deeply, sucking golden air into her lungs.

She was Empress again! She fingered the thought greedily in her pocket; the coin, the sweet thing the others didn't have.

When she entered his quarters all was as it had been before: all the bonny lamps and rich carpets, the heaps of fruit, the golden cups, all flickering and gleaming like a fairytale. And him so tall, so sure, so eager for her, and her blood pounding and her body melting just as it used to.

But all the time she was gasping and straining against him, that chill wraith still floated above her, watching the Emperor and Empress glorying in each other, then drifting higher above the Harem: to find Microphilus, who loved her in sickness and in health, alone and staring out into the darkness.

64

23 May 1770

I have just come from Helen. She would not look at me. I don't mean that she would not talk to me: *au contraire*, she was rattling away fit to rival the sparrows, until the space between us was crammed full of words, like a fluttering wall, and she whisking to and fro behind it, all busy with urgent nothingness until I offer to withdraw.

So now she is all apologies, swishing more curtains of words: 'I am so confused!' and 'It was so difficult!' and 'Please try to understand.'

I do understand. Those evasive eyes spoke more eloquently than all her welter of words. She is his again.

I was delivering her allowance, hoping my fears yesterday had been groundless; hoping that she would go to him, and would pleasure him, and would return wholehearted into my arms.

She would not even let me into her chamber. Did she think I would force myself on her if we were alone? Topple and straddle her like a branded heifer? Does she not know love is worthless if not freely given?

I cannot tell whether it was anger or pain that I felt watching her bustle around with her back to me, tumbling out her flurried excuses and pretend regrets. As though she'd never kissed me, my fingers swimming and diving like seals.

I thought she loved me. So close have we been, with our chests opened and our ribs splayed like bone petals, with the

446

honey running, and our two hearts like red bees, humming and sucking together. Those weeks she battened on love and became bonny again, as though sighs were sweetmeats and laughter oil, filling her and glossing her until she is fit for an Emperor. And I am a most superlative pimp.

And so Jack is put back in his box. Poor foolish Jack: back you must go, with your spring compressed and your head bending and your lid pressed down flat.

Could she not see how he avoided her in the garden, fearing her face had been ravaged by her illness, and would have walked by had the Crone not plucked at his sleeve? How long does such love last? Until the next frown, the next illness, the first wrinkle. Helen, you wrong yourself to value yourself so cheaply.

It is evening and I am reading these lines again and hearing them spoken in Batoom's velvet voice. She was berating me as she gathered up my things, saying it was abasement to gift myself to Helen, who values me as cheaply as a bent tin coin.

I was gold in Batoom's hands: weighted like gold, solid through-and-through gold; precious to my very core.

But I did not value Batoom, and so she is spent, and so I am the poorer.

Now Helen has cast her tin coin into the poor-box. It is no more than I deserve.

24 May 1770

I washed my hair this morning. All her scents and perfumes have gone now. My clothes are clean; my face shaved; my nails manicured. Nothing remains except what there is in these pages. And these I will keep to remind Mudskipper of the mistakes he has made.

I have retrieved my button and placed it on my table, with its sheen down and its dull surface uppermost. Love is in the bone of a person. There is no pearly gleam; naught to see at all save with the mind's eye.

Batoom loved me inside out, every layer. I will not settle for less.

65

Reema wrapped a white cloth into a loose *dulbend* around Helen's wet hair, then crouched to mop the splashes from the washroom floor. 'Oh, don't worry about that now.' Helen reached for the warmed oil jar and tipped a little into the palm of her hand. 'I'll call you when I've finished.'

'Very well, *Lalla*.' Gathering damp cloths in her arms, Reema shouldered her way expertly out through the curtain and kicked it close behind her.

As soon as she was gone, Helen moved to the mirror and tugged the *dulbend* off. Her damp hair came tumbling down around her naked shoulders, thick and dark as snakes. Her breasts seemed bigger than before, almost transparent and marbled with blue veins. Perhaps she should stay out of the sun from now on, until all her freckles faded away. Until she was paler even than *Lalla* Salamatu had been. Perhaps she should start wearing white silk all the time, and pearls. So the other women would start calling her the White Empress.

'Ah. Here you are.' Malia shuffled wheezily in through the curtain. Grabbing a cloth, Helen held it over her breasts. The old hag did it on purpose, she was sure: barging in without warning, trying to catch people unawares.

'I'm not sure you'll be needing these.' Malia squatted and began tugging the usual wads of muslin out of her bag. 'It should be your time tomorrow, but when the body has been very weak, sometimes the blood does not return for many months.'

Fumbling the buckles closed again, she eased herself to her

feet and peered at Helen. 'And yet,' shuffling closer, 'you seem very –' She hesitated, narrowing her eyes. 'This colour is better. Much better. But the eyelids – this is interesting.' She reached out and wrenched away the cloth Helen was clutching. 'And the teats are darker. I wonder –' Licking a bony finger, she wiped it roughly between Helen's breasts. 'Tell me, have you had the wetness, the egg wetness this moon?' she asked, holding the finger to her droopy nose and sniffing it.

'I don't know.' Helen blushed angrily and covered herself again. She'd have to complain to the Emperor about this. The woman showed no respect at all.

Malia sniffed the finger once more, then peered again at Helen's face. 'The eyelids and the teats, these are definite signs. And the smell. So –' Sighing, the old woman began stuffing the muslin bundles back into her bag. 'What are you going to do about it?'

'What?' Helen's stomach lurched.

'The baby. Did you think I wouldn't notice?' Malia gave her a long, angry look.

What baby? What was she suggesting? 'But it can't be. I've been so ill. For months, there's been nothing. No bleeding –'

'That doesn't mean anything. If a girl is married young enough she can go her whole life without bleeding. Each time she makes a seed, whoosh, the husband's milk is there to turn it into a child.' The old woman tutted with irritation. 'Why weren't you more careful?'

Helen stared at the old woman. A baby. But not the Emperor's baby. Even she knew that was impossible. She stopped breathing. Microphilus's baby. Sometime in the last six weeks her body had produced a seed and now it had taken root inside her.

'You know I should go straight to the Emperor.' Malia was watching her.

'No! He'd have me killed. No – please, please don't say anything.' Her mind was racing. Perhaps she could pretend it was the Emperor's. She could only have been pregnant a few weeks. He'd never guess. If she could keep it a secret, perhaps she'd get away with it.

'Does Fijil suspect?' Malia asked.

'What?' How much did the old witch know?

Malia hissed with irritation. 'Does Fijil have any idea you might be carrying?'

Helen leant against the wall. This was happening too fast. 'No. I've hardly spoken to him for days. Not since the Emperor called for me again.' Her mind raced. What if the baby was a dwarf? The Emperor would know immediately she'd been with Microphilus. She'd have to give it away. Pretend it had died and get Reema to take it to some woman in the city.

'And Reema? The other slaves?'

'No. No one knows. *I* didn't know –' She tried to think what Microphilus had said about his family. His mother had sent him away, so she must have been normal. And his father too. And his brother Jamie: a man for the ladies, so he couldn't have been a dwarf. What about cousins, aunts, uncles?

'So it is not too late. We can still save the situation. I'll wash my hands and see to the slaves. You go to your chamber and get ready.'

'What are you talking about?'

'I'll get rid of it now. Before anyone suspects.' And she bustled out.

Helen stared at the swinging curtain. Get rid of it. Of course. Like last time. Hook it out like a wee cockle on a bent pin before anyone noticed. Pretend to the Emperor she was on her monthlies and in a week's time everything would be back to normal. A quick twist of agony and it would be over. No one need ever know she'd been sleeping with a dwarf. Why, then, did she want to shriek 'No!'?

She put a hand on her belly, low down, and pressed gently. A baby.

'I've told them I need to examine you.' Malia pushed back through the curtain, picked up the soap and tipped water into a bowl. 'To check you are fully recovered.'

Helen stared at the old woman's hands, at the curved claw lathered with soap. 'I can't,' she said.

'Can't?' The wet hands stopped in the air. 'What do you mean?'

'It's not the pain –'

'Are you telling me you want this baby?' Every sinew in Malia's old body spat disapproval.

'No, no. It's just so sudden. I need time to get used to the idea.'

'Very well.' Malia shrugged and dried her hands. 'But don't wait too long. In these first weeks it is easy. It comes out – poof! – just like that. Later, there can be problems.'

There was nothing to worry about. All she had to do was send for Malia and it would be out of her. She lay down and tried to rest, then got up and paced restlessly around the courtyard. She plucked a pale *ibiscos* flower and tore the big petals into strips. She felt as if she'd been found out and judged for something. As though Microphilus had sent a tiny spy to watch her and punish her.

For what? Playing sex with her own husband? How dare he be angry with her for that.

But he wasn't angry. He hadn't once reproached her. All he'd done was love her and nurse her back to health. Those weeks with him were like living in a different world, a strange wee island in the middle of the Harem. Where ugly was beautiful and wealth meaningless. And fresh bread was the most delicious food in the world. But she wasn't on that island any more. She was back in the real world.

Now there was a baby. Inside her, pulling her back to the island. Away from what she'd always wanted.

But all she had to do was send for Malia and it would be out of her. Tomorrow, she vowed through gritted teeth, bright and early, she'd get rid of it.

That evening, after she had washed and perfumed herself, she took out her pot of rouge. She felt reckless, restless, angry. Dipping her finger into the scarlet grease, she rubbed it carefully around her nipples and watched the skin shrink and pucker like silk under a hot iron. Then she brought the finger to her lips, pinching and pulling at them until they were vivid and swollen.

Dressed in shades of amber and red, with her wedding jewels like gouts of blood at her throat, she looked at herself in the long mirror. Tonight she'd be a Red Queen.

The musicians were assembled and playing when she arrived at the Emperor's quarters, but he was nowhere to be seen. She wandered over to the fruit bowl and picked out a red apple, then put it back again. A slave was lighting the lamps, working around the room with her hand cupped around a taper. It was a chilly evening and a fire was burning in the corner. Helen went over and stood in front of it, feeling tongues of heat flicker over her body.

Where was he? She wanted to feel his rough beard against her skin; his teeth, his knuckles, his bones digging into her flesh, reminding her she was his. She sat on the carpet, then rose again and pushed the door to the courtyard open, but it was too chilly to stay outside, so she closed it and went back over to the fire. After a while, she found herself moving to the music, feeling the hot silk shimmer over the front of her body.

'Aziza –'

Helen closed her eyes. At last. 'I thought you were never coming,' she said, turning to face him.

'Details, details! How I detest them. They are saying I should send emissaries to the southern border. They say the *sheikhs* need placating.' He flung off his *k'sa* and a slave whisked it away. 'Come. Tell me about your day. What have you been doing?'

'Just now, I have been dancing in front of the fire.'

'That sounds very pleasant. Show me.' He flung himself down on the carpet and a slave appeared with a bowl of water to wash his feet. 'They have nearly finished the palace at Mogador. I was thinking perhaps we would spend the summer there. Would you like that? It is so much cooler near the sea.'

Helen began dancing again, this time with the fire behind her. She'd heard him talking before about his new palace. It was to be the grandest ever built, with jade roofs and golden fountains. She put out her arms, letting the music guide her movements, feeling the heat sliding across her skin, between her thighs. What would the new queens' quarters be like, she wondered.

'I like this fire dance,' he said quietly, watching with hooded eyes. 'You seem different tonight. What is it?'

'I don't know, my Lord.' Helen looked down at him. 'Perhaps because we have been apart for so long. I feel –'

'Yes?' He was smiling, reaching for the sash of her *salwars* and tugging her closer. 'What is it that you feel?'

'I don't know. Restless. Hungry.' Hot, impatient, angry.

'Shall I call for food?'

Helen narrowed her eyes. 'It is not that kind of hunger.' She looked at his teeth, sharp and shining in the lamplight.

'I don't understand.' His eyes were smiling; his fingers

working at the knot in the sash. 'What other kind of hunger is there?'

Her red *salwars* were loosening around her hips, beginning to slip down. Suddenly she remembered the musicians. 'Please, my Lord –' Grabbing at the sliding silk, she glanced round.

'Go! All of you!' He waved his hand towards the eunuchs and they scooped up their instruments and scuttled out of the room. The door closed just as her *salwars* subsided with a whisper around her ankles.

He pulled her down on top of him, right there on the carpet before the fire, loosening his own *salwars* just enough to let his thing out. She crouched above him, like a snuffer over a candle, with her red blouse open and her rouged teats rolling against his teeth. She dug her fingers into his shoulders, wrenching his *kamise* aside so she could smell him, his liquorice and sandalwood, her teeth gritted, her breath ragged.

'Please –' It wasn't enough. She needed him on top of her.

'Please what, Aziza?' He was sliding his hand down over her buttocks, worming his fingers into the slippery pucker of her hole.

'Deeper,' she whispered, and felt a twitch deep inside her. 'Please. I want you deeper.' Again, an answering twitch, then he was tipping her on to her back and yanking her against him like a rag doll, grunting and pushing into her, hurting her, bruising where she wanted to be bruised, over and over, where the baby was, until she was gasping with pain and he was roaring above her, with his chin up and his eyes staring into the fire. She pictured his milk churning into her, like a wave around a rock, watched it breaking over the baby, swirling around it and under it, loosening it and washing it away.

Afterwards he was ravenous, clapping for food and feeding her himself, making her lick the gravy from his fingers. Calling her his red lioness, he teased her about the scratches on his back, then washed his hands quickly and hurried from the room.

'I'd forgotten all about these,' he said when he returned a moment later. 'I fetched them this morning from the Jewel Room.'

He dropped a dark blue leather pouch into her lap. 'My beautiful Aziza,' he murmured. 'I'm so glad you are better.'

'I thought, after your wounds, you might be angry,' she teased, picking up the pouch and weighing it in her hands for a moment. Jewels. Her heart hammered as she eased the pouch open and peeped inside. Something blue glinted back at her in the lamplight: sapphires. Then her blood froze. She recognized this necklace. It was the one he'd given Naseem all those months ago.

66

I am lonely. I had been wondering what this odd feeling was, where the body seems to shrink in on itself, to something hard and tight yet with a void inside. Thus I am trotting around as usual, a perky puppet with tilty head and flicking hands, blethering here and there with the women. And all the time I can feel my shell thickening. The layers crust over as I scuttle from rock to rock, from pool to pool. Soon I will be a crab again.

I believe it is the touch of human skin that keeps the Cancer at bay, that strokes light in and suffuses our souls with exuberance. And when we lack its healing light, Mother Nature must armour us, like the caddis does in its hotchpotch of a shell.

The armour protects, ay, but also repels the touches we need. So the crab becomes awkward in his movements, and barges and nips his fellow creatures, and cannot kiss without an unseemly muddle, and frights the bairns by being too rough, or irritates by maudlin softness – all, all, for the lack of Love's touch. I fancy my fingers are already stiffening to clumsy pincers. Soon I will be fumbling the simplest contacts, spilling my mint tea and clamping the Emperor's hand when I bend over it.

These last few days it has turned hot again. The sun, which has been unwonted gentle this spring, peeping coyly from her lacy cloud collars, has today revealed herself a Tyrant Queen with a fierce white ruff. We are all prostrate before her on the hot tiles, while she thunders above us. Summer stretches into the distance, as far as the mind can see. My shell is dry; my eyes dull; my pincers heavy. I am weary, so weary of this place.

Helen I haven't seen: save in the garden of a Thursday, where she sits serene under her green awning, cool as a lily in the white silks she has taken to wearing. They are calling her the White Queen, as though Salamatu never existed. How short memories are in this place.

Perhaps it is the sameness of our surroundings which encourages such forgetfulness in the women; the sameness of the weeks, with their twin peaks: market day and garden day. So they live from week to week, focusing first on the perfect scarf which may appear by magic on some side stall, that will catch the Emperor's jaded eye. And each week, when the scarf fails, is a week consigned to oblivion: for will there not be another market in a few days? So History's record is crumpled and discarded, never to stain the blank parchment of Memory.

I have heard it said that fish cannot remember. So you may catch one and discard it over and over, and from the very same pool, until its lip grows ragged where you have wrenched out your jagged hook, and splits, and grows cankerous, until your hook will hold no more and the fish must butt forever, hopelessly mouthing at the thing which would ensnare it.

Thus are these shoals of women in the Emperor's loch, ever gaping for his hook, ever thrown back to the seething water. And each, when she is discarded, sinking lower, thinking: my legs are too short, my breasts too large, or too small, my lips too wide, my *salwars* the wrong colour. And nothing else in their fishy minds save the hook, the hook ripped out, the dive back, the hook again.

So Helen is caught and hauled on to the deck. And is thrown back and caught again. When her scales lose their shine, she will be cast back again. But this time Mudskipper will not be waiting. His mouth is torn and sore. Mudskipper has found his button. He has found a way of remembering.

I have just come from the Emperor. What a rage he is in! Like a bull in the holding-stall with his nostrils red and his eyes bulging. It seems the incursions have begun along our southern border.

Batoom! Your garnets are turned to gunpowder, your malachite to muskets and spears. They have been unwinding the *dulbends* of each shrinking *sheikh* and hanging them, blood-heavy, from the minarets to flap as flags of their rebellion. Four *kasbahs* are fallen and looted, and others have sent riders galloping for help.

'Fijil, what do you know of this?' demands the Emperor when I appear. 'They say the Emperor's wealth has furnished their weapons; that Queen Batoom sent her jewels to buy arms.'

'No one knew, Master,' quoth I, explaining her rooms were always kept locked and no one allowed to venture inside.

'Jackal bitch!' shrieks he, but can find none to punish. So must flail about, and kick his slippers across the room to make a slave scramble after them, then kick the slave for looking ridiculous, and another slave for appearing shocked, and so on and so forth, until they are all cowering back against the walls with their knees trembling. But this inflames him the more until he is calling for the Royal Cutlass-bearer and would have had them beheaded like a row of thistle-tops had three thugs from the Black Guard not at that moment appeared at the door.

At which the Emperor whirls around, nostrils flaring, and sets to devising his counter-attack.

I have never seen him in the guise of General before and it is a revelation. His cruel intelligence is perfectly suited to the role. Indeed, while his Lieutenants are there, and they are discussing the placement and provisioning of the troops, he is calm, as a bairn with toothache is distracted by a favoured toy. But as soon as the soldiers are gone, up his rage wells once more.

So now he falls to scrutinizing his apartment, and discovers that furnishing he found quite adequate yesterday now seems altogether too tawdry for an Emperor of his standing. And shouts for his carpenters and goldsmiths, and when they do not miraculously materialize, grows yet more restless until his eye falls again upon me.

'So there you are, Fijil!' carps he pettishly, as though I had kept him waiting an hour or more. 'I am minded to be married again. It is not good for an Emperor to have so few wives. And don't suggest one of the harridans in the Harem. I am sick of looking at them, with their stupid smiles and dog eyes. Go, find me some fit women. And get rid of Zara. I will not have it said I have a hag for a wife.'

So I am to go on another journey, almost a year to the day when I embarked before. The thought fills me with a kind of elation. To be out in the air again! To the mountains and the sea. How I long for the taste of salt on the wind! This is just the tonic I have been needing: the jolt of travel to crack my sad shell and shake some life back into me.

If I am brisk we may set off on the morrow. I will visit the bat Malia in her cave and urge her to rustle up her wings and hoik up her sesterces. Thence to the stables to requisition the guards and check on my stallion. Perhaps this journey will cure me at last of my madness, peel its last few shreds from my mind. I will take Kath's button and my pimp's emerald. And my scribbler's tools, of course. I am John the Baptist setting off for the Wilderness.

I shall not bid Helen farewell. Let her think of me one day, and want me, and discover I have gone.

67

'How dare you! Wait until the Emperor hears about this –'
It was early morning, after breakfast. Helen had never heard Zara's voice raised in anger before. Curious, she hurried across the Queen's Courtyard towards the older queen's open gate. Inside she saw one of the senior eunuchs standing with his feet apart and a great leather-bound ledger under his arm. Zara was barring the stairway to her day room: chin high, hands on hips.

'I'm sorry, *Lalla,*' the eunuch shrugged insolently. 'But it was the Emperor himself who ordered –'

'So what is this list you are speaking of?' Zara's five slaves were standing in a silent line against the wall, watching with wary eyes.

'An inventory of the contents of these rooms, *Lalla,* so that His Majesty can decide what he will allow you to take.'

'I don't understand. Where is Fijil? Does he know about this?'

'Fijil is occupied with other business. The Emperor has put me in charge of –'

'Of what? Stealing from the Empress of Morocco?' Zara squared her shoulders and tossed her head, but the eunuch ignored her.

'These samovars, for example.' The eunuch walked over to the kitchen and peered in through the door. 'You will not need so many when you are in Tafilalt. And there are carpets. I have been informed that your store-room is half-full of carpets.'

'They're mine, bought with my own money.'

Helen stepped closer, suddenly alert. Surely she'd be allowed to keep her own things?

'And the jewellery, of course.' The eunuch jerked his head casually towards her chamber. 'The Emperor will probably allow you to keep some of the smaller items.'

Helen thought of the sapphires nestling at the bottom of her trunk; and her favourite emeralds. How many queens had worn them before?

Zara backed away and leant against the wall. 'I don't believe this,' she whispered.

'We will have to paint over these – er – markings.' He flapped a hand at the blue hands on the walls. 'But that can wait until the rooms are empty. Have you decided which two slaves you are taking? If you can let me have their names, I can begin reallocating the others.'

Opening the big book, the eunuch walked purposefully into the kitchen and began opening cupboards. Zara started to follow him, then looked up and spied Helen at the gate.

'Aziza!' She hurried over, panic twisting her features. 'Did you hear him? The insolence! He's going to take all my things. Talk to him. Make him stop.'

'He's only making a list, Zara.' Helen tried to speak calmly, but the scene had shaken her. 'The Emperor wouldn't take back everything he's given you.'

'That's what I said! It's a mistake. The Emperor loves me. He wouldn't send me away with nothing.'

Helen winced. Surely Zara didn't think the Emperor still cared for her? When had she last looked in the mirror? 'Why don't you send for Fijil?' she said, longing to escape. 'He'll sort it out.' She began walking away, though her feet wanted to run. This courtyard was a crystal ball; she was being shown her future. She didn't want to see any more.

'He said we'd grow old together.' Zara scurried after her, tripping out words. ' "We will count our white hairs together." I can hear him now. "For every white hair, I will give you a pearl." '

Helen sighed inwardly and slowed down to let the other woman catch up with her. She cursed herself for getting involved. 'Can you remember what happened when *Lalla* Salamatu moved to Tafilalt?' she asked. 'Did she take all her things with her?'

'It's because he doesn't know. He's so busy, he doesn't know half the things his slaves get up to. You talk to him, Aziza. Please. Tell him what they're trying to do to me.'

'But if the Emperor ordered it himself –' Helen breathed in through her teeth, then out again slowly. It was finished. Couldn't Zara see? Why couldn't she just accept it and go quietly?

'He didn't! That *khaleh*'s lying! He wants my things for himself.'

They were in Helen's courtyard now; Reema was rolling out the carpet and setting out a tray of tea. Helen paused, hoping Zara would take the hint and leave, but she knelt down under the jasmine and picked up the samovar.

' "A pearl for every grey hair," he said. But look –' Zara snatched off her kerchief and ran proud fingers through the tufts of chestnut fur covering her skull. 'See? Even after that illness. Not a single grey hair.'

Helen looked up reluctantly, not wanting to look too closely at the blotched skin and moth-eaten eyebrows. What she saw made her recoil: a fresh purple bruise covered one side of Zara's forehead.

'What on earth happened to your face?' she asked.

'My son –' Zara's indignation crumpled into tears. 'The elder one. Yesterday, when I saw him. He was so disappointed, you see. He'd set his heart on becoming Emperor. He blames me for – for – not looking after my appearance.' She began to sob untidily, plucking vaguely at her pockets for a kerchief.

Helen stared in alarm at Zara's red eyes and swollen nose. How much longer would she stay? For one cup of tea? Two? She didn't want to hear any of this.

'He says he'll kill me if we're despatched to Tafilalt. Please, Aziza. You're my only chance. Speak to the Emperor, please. Beg him to let me stay.'

Helen closed her eyes and let out a long breath. The poor stupid woman. She still thought she had a chance. 'All right,' she sighed. Anything to make Zara leave. 'Tonight, if he sends for me, I'll talk to him about it.'

After Zara had gone Helen felt exhausted. She felt as though she hadn't breathed properly for the whole of the visit. She was afraid of being infected by the cloud of ill luck that floated around the older woman. She didn't want to inhale it, didn't want to think of it going deep into her lungs. She was glad Zara was leaving.

An image of her bruised forehead came into her mind. What kind of son would strike his mother just for growing ugly?

She moved a hand down to her belly. She was sure her son would never –

If it was a son.

Perhaps it was a daughter, a bonny wee lass curled up.

Then she stopped herself. There would be no son or daughter this time. She had to get rid of her baby.

'If you want it done, it has to be now. I'm leaving in an hour and Allah knows when I'll be back.' Malia pulled the curtain closed behind her.

'What?' Helen stared at the old woman in dismay.

'The Emperor's asked for you again tonight, but I'll tell him you're bleeding. That will give you a few days to recover.' She dumped her bag on to the floor and crouched over it, rummaging. Helen imagined the claw hooking and prodding away inside her. Needling into her son, her daughter, and ripping it out of her.

'No.' She sat down on the divan and wrapped her arms protectively over her belly.

Malia sighed and sat back on her heels. 'So. You decide. I can do it now, and it will be over in a few minutes. Or you can drink this potion.' She thrust a tiny phial of brown liquid into Helen's hands. 'It will make you very sick, and if the baby is strong it may not work,' she warned. 'And I won't be here to help you. Mind you drink it all. In a few days you should start bleeding. Otherwise –' She shrugged, like bones shifting in a sack.

'Do you know how much in money and gifts I've given Batoom over the years?' The Emperor was pacing up and down, still in his daytime clothes, when Helen pushed open the double doors to his quarters that evening. 'I had the *Alim* total it up. Enough to keep an entire army in weapons and food for six moons.'

He unsheathed a dagger and hurled it at the wall. 'I can just imagine them laughing at me in their primitive villages: the Emperor who gave his wife money to buy guns for his enemies.'

Helen had never seen him hot angry like this before. Cool angry, yes, when someone was slow to obey. Irritated, often, at the endless fussing of his officials. But never furious like this.

'Calm yourself, my Lord,' she said, smiling. 'Will you let them intrude on your evening as well as your day? Come, sit beside me.' She put a tentative hand on his arm. His whole body was tense with anger, hard and unyielding beneath her hand. He raised his arm impatiently, shaking her off, and for a moment she thought he might hit her.

'That's what a Christian would do, isn't it? Swallow his anger like a bad oyster, then sit meekly beside his one wife, in full view of his neighbours in his stupid little house. You insult me, Aziza, to suggest the Emperor of Morocco should behave like this.'

'I'm sorry, my Lord. I didn't mean –'

His eyes narrowed. 'I know what I'll do. Send the *Bokhary* to each of their villages in turn, and steal their women from under their noses. They can rape the wives and bring the daughters back as wives. By the time they've finished no man in the province will know whether his children are his own.' He threw off his *jellabiah* and began tugging his *kamise* over his head. 'I'll show them what happens to people who laugh at the Emperor of Morocco!

'Last time I tried to be *civilized* –' he sneered at the word – 'I married the Princess Batoom to make peace with her father. I even fought her, in front of all her kinsmen, to prove I was a *worthy* husband. An Emperor fighting a woman! No wonder they're laughing. Well, this time there'll be no savage rituals. I'll take the daughters by force and make the fathers beg for peace. I'll make the *bints* slaves in my Harem.' He laughed suddenly. 'How would you like to have a princess as a slave, Aziza?' He walked towards Helen and began undoing the buttons on her *kamise*.

Helen wanted to back away from him. 'I don't know.' She looked into his eyes. They were glittering with anger and lust. Would he really send his men to rape all those women?

'Wouldn't you enjoy seeing a princess emptying your chamber-pot?' He ripped open the last few buttons, then buried his hand in her curls. 'Washing your clothes, combing this wonderful hair.'

'Zara came to see me this morning.'

'Yes, she came to me too, stupid *bint*.' He tugged off her *kamise* and threw it across the room.

'One of her sons had been beating her.'

'That would be Mahmud.' He chuckled affectionately, fingers busy on the sash of Helen's *salwars*. 'He's a good strong boy. I expect she was blubbing all over him. I felt like hitting her myself.'

'But you loved her once.' She felt cold.

'You've seen her. She has the face of a *ghoul*. What man could love a creature like that?' Tightening his fingers, he yanked her head backwards so that he could kiss her throat. Helen could feel his teeth grazing her skin. His thing was prodding at her through his *salwars*.

She could feel herself closing up, tight as a mussel when the tide goes out. An urge to push him away began building inside her, making her bite her tongue with the effort of letting him back her across the room and down on to the divan, letting him open her with his knees and knuckle into her.

'You are tight tonight, Aziza,' he grunted, pushing in. 'And dry,' pushing deeper. 'Why is that?'

'I don't know.' His thing felt huge and hot, a red fist stretching her skin. 'It makes me frightened to see you like this.'

Arms braced either side of her head, he began moving. 'Like – what –?' He was smiling, timing the words, one for each thrust.

'Angry. Cruel.'

'And – how – would – you – have – me – Aziza? – Soft – like – your – men?' His breath was coming faster. She was stinging, burning. 'Is – that – what – you – want?'

She squeezed her eyes closed. Tears burnt beneath her eyelids. 'You're hurting me,' she whispered. But he couldn't hear her. His eyes were staring, his neck-gristle sharp as two blades as he silently rammed into her.

When he had finished, he wanted her again, and made her kneel on all fours with her arse tilted up towards him. 'Is – this – deep – enough –?' he hissed through clenched teeth.

'Yes, my Lord,' she whispered into the pillow. He was a pestle pounding her. 'I – can't – hear – you – Aziza –' jerking, digging his nails into her buttocks. 'I – asked – if – this – was – deep – enough – for – you –'

'Yes!' she sobbed, biting her lip and thrusting back at him, moaning, trying to excite him, to hurry him up. But it was taking much longer this time. He was a wooden spoon digging and stirring, scraping out the last dregs of sensation. And floating separate, looking down on his pumping buttocks, the cold part of Helen thought of Microphilus's small hand cupped over the belly of the kitten, of its eggshell ribs; of the purr shaking its tiny body, its pointy chin stretching out in pleasure.

68

14 June 1770

My bahoukie is aching from a day in the saddle, as though a bag of stones had been smuggled into my *salwars*; and my thighs tender as tripe-steak, and my knees chafed, and my neb singed by the sun. Yet my determined mood has stayed with me. I am alive: these petty pains prove it. And this weariness is not the *ennui* of the Harem, where the familiarity of its tribulations saps the energy. Nay, this is the good honest tiredness of real toil; the tiredness that makes you sigh with the pleasure of simply sitting down; a mouth-watering tiredness, as of true hunger assuaged by simple food.

This, I know, is how Batoom felt at the end of her stints in her garden; this that eased open her smiles, that buried her brown fingers in her porridge and gave thanks to her ancestors.

I have been feeling her spirit as we have been travelling. We have started off southwards, along the tracks her riders would have taken as they plied back and forth with jewels stitched into the cuffs of their *salwars*; and her love with them, speeding them onwards. I would see her sometimes in her garden on tiptoe, facing south, her broad face running with sweat, her feet clotted with red mud. I thought she was interrogating the weather, checking for rain-clouds in the distance. I know now she was winging her heart homewards: keeping faith; always keeping faith.

Batoom, you kept faith with me and I betrayed you.

Thus far the weather has been kind: a light rain fell the

night before we departed and laid the dust and polished the leaves either side of the track to fresh green. And we have had a few scutty clouds and a breeze to respite us from the sun. I love the click of brown hooves on the brown track, the smell of dung and churned earth, the warm hay scent of the horses. They are frisky, all of them, with their nostrils twitching and their heads up, shying at ant-heaps, nipping and neighing at one another like colts in a spring meadow. And the mules, mostly unladen, lolloping their rabbit ears, tip-tipping cheerily along.

I had forgot how good it feels to be aloft, to see where one is going long hours before one arrives there: a tree small as a curl of parsley, meandering nearer; a distant snake-shimmer of river; even a rain-shower (there was a slight downpour yesterday afternoon), a slant grey curtain sweeping slowly towards us. In the Harem it is all walls, and one's eyes can never stray further than the next courtyard, and never think to gaze up at the sky, and contemplate what lies beyond: this banquet of Life.

A few hundred miles to our south, Batoom's kinsmen are fighting: bellying through the scrubland by night, harvesting the *sheikhs'* grain and reclaiming their herds. And the Emperor's Black Guard bearing down on them, past feuding fiefdoms and flint-eyed merchants; women with their weans under their *haiks*, the saintly beggars with their ratted hair and begging-pouches; the *kaktus* corrals and scummy watering-holes; those hyenas gorging on a carcass; the Bedouins' skin tents and rakish stallions; the mud-brick cottages and lofty *kasbahs*; all the bizarre *cuisines* and bad music, and worse singing –

How have I stayed out of the world so long?

I keep scanning the landscape for Lungile, though I know fine he is long gone. She took away his shame, that brave Berber lass. What greater gift could there be? Now he can return to Nuba a whole man.

These vistas give me perspective. Here is so much more than the small life I have been living.

Malia is leaving the Harem for good! And this is just one stone in the landslide of revelation she tumbled before me this evening. We were meandering together through our host village, snuffing up the night air and enjoying the novel feel of the uneven terrain against the soles of our slippers.

Of course, she has long schemed her retirement, but recent insults by the Emperor have spurred her to accelerate her plans. It seems she was terminally incensed by the welcome afforded to Dr Lempriere. 'As though he was the Prophet Himself (may His name be praised)!' she complains. 'Why didn't he ask me what was wrong with the women? I had worked out the cause three moons before.' Here her voice fair creaks with anger. 'All he had to do was send for me, consult me as a proper *tabib* instead of a mere madam who keeps the women clean for playing sex.'

It seems she had been testing her hypothesis on the Berber. 'She became sick, do you recall?' she asks proudly, and I must admit I had remarked a certain lack of lustre in the days before she died. 'Of course I would not have gone so far as to kill her,' she adds hurriedly.

But I'm wondering now how the Harem guards came to be patrolling the exact spot where Lungile had concealed his ladder, when a camel stampede would not normally shift them from their backgammon.

15 June 1770

A second force of the *Bokhary* thundered past us this morning. We heard them coming fully an hour before they arrived, for they fired their muskets as they came, driving herds of panicky deer before them, and flocks of those flightless giant birds the natives call *ostrich*, which fled across the plains either side of us, zigzagging between the thorn bushes and rousing the hares, which followed suit, until the whole country as far as the eye could see was a-blur with fleeing wildlife.

Their leader reined in briefly to speak to me, quizzing me on our route and casting a flinching eye over our eunuchs (I think I mentioned how one in ten of the *Bokhary* were castrated last year? The memory clearly still burns like a brand.). His stallion was bleeding at the mouth and sweat churned white on its shoulders as it trotted beside me.

It seems the Emperor is become bent on revenge and these men are his instruments. The troupe comprises the youngest members of the Black Guard: freshly trained, full-mettled, battle-hungry. Normally their graduation is rewarded by their marriage – *en masse* – to a hand-picked battalion of lofty brown wenches, with prizes promised to those who produce the first boys. But this troupe has been issued with different incentives. Instead of supplying them from his domestic stock, the Emperor has bade them capture brides in Mauritanie, with rich rewards on offer to any that can deliver the virgin daughter of a Mauritanian Chief.

The young man spurs his bloody steed to make it rear, yet keeps it reined tight as he explains his mission. His thighs are thick, his face unlined, his eyes hot with lust. The horse champs red foam and rolls its eyes. And I fear for the lassie who will be his bride, and all the women who will be consumed by this swarm of locusts – for I cannot think this troop will restrict themselves to their own virgin brides.

And I am suddenly brimming with disgust for the Emperor's cunning strategy, whereby a whole tribe is to be defiled, and betrothals ended, and alliances spoiled, and husbands cuckolded and shamed. And the women, married and unmarried, young and old, used and thrown away like dry leaves in the latrine, for it is a rare man that will embrace his wife after she has been defiled. And so a tribe of widows is made without once shedding the blood of a man.

My chest heaves with hatred for the mind that hatched this plot: for the Emperor who is so tall and so straight, whose wealth overflows his coffers; who has his choice of a thousand women, but would steal more; who has plundered the heart of my beloved.

I shall not serve him again.

Now, here is a thought. Shall I escape too? Take off like Lungile to the mountains and never return?

A slave is knocking on my door: our host would have me share a *hookah* in his house. I will ponder this more when I return to my chamber.

It is the small hours but I cannot sleep. The moon is round and milky, the sand white, the shadows sharp as axe-blades. And there is joyful cacophony everywhere, as owls yelp and dune-dogs hoot, and a caterpillar of terrible musicians perambulate the village with a retinue of dancing bairns, as all make up for the dark tedium of their long, moonless nights.

I feel as restless as a rat-flea, all a-jump with the idea of escape. To stay out here in the zinging world, and watch the moon rise and set on the long horizon: ay, and trace its circumlocution across the sky, and her sister sun too, and watch a bird jump into the air, and soar overhead on quivering wings, and dive for prey, and flap back to its nest in the mountains. And trace the whole arc, the panorama of that drama, and not the mean slices the Harem affords, its squares and alleys of sky, where every breeze is clogged with the scent of sandalwood.

I have my emerald. I am rich. I could travel anywhere and

choose my place of abode. To go where no one knows me and find –

Nay, that will not suffice. To go home, to Scotland. Now, there's a braw thought.

Excitement has me by the scruff of my neck. I can see tall grey seas and feel the flung sand in my teeth; taste a dish of vinegar-whelks on the jetty. There's a line of craw-stepped cottages, lime-washed and net-draped; with the old wifies knitting in the lee and poking snuff, cackling across the cobbles. And whisky, for God's sake, and finnan haddie, and the good fat whine of the pipers on the city wall. I will swim through the oyster bars on a tide of old claret, and Aberdeen beefsteak, and the yeastiest bread I can find.

It is dawn: at least I suppose it to be so, for day sounds are now adding themselves to the cacophony of this bright night.

Malia was just here (it seems none are sleeping tonight) and has dropped such a series of pebbles into the pond of my mind that ripples are sweeping across its surface in great arcs, obliterating all else that was there.

Helen is carrying, and the bairn is from my seed! That thing I longed for has come to pass: my seed in her womb, myself in her very core; joined by God's miracle to her own sweet spore. I could soar to Heaven on such news. Except there is more, which dashes me back to the ground, and into it, scrabbling with my mole's paws, so hard down does it cast me.

She means to rid herself of the bairn, drink some noxious potion from the cadaverous Crone that will loose his buds of fingers from their fumbling hold and flush him out of her. Even now the deed may be done – curse the Crone! The lass has had the phial since before we departed. My wee laddie may be gobbed out already: all red, all unready.

Why did she not tell me? I would scream the question

across these rutted miles and shake the answer out of her. Yet I know the answer. She will not carry a dwarf. If I were of normal height, she could pass the wean off as the Emperor's. But if the lad be a runtling, like his father –

'His father': dear God, I am a father! Oh, such a father will I be –

Yet cannot be. Yet am stillborn myself, for the wean may be dead by now.

But what if she has not drunk the potion? I know her well: she would not flinch from the pain of it. But what if she cannot? The Crone said she had already refused the talon. What if there is some true part of her that thinks of me still?

Inside the Empress Aziza, with all her ambition, are the true bones of a good woman. I know her inside and out. Day and night when she was ailing, and all her beauty stripped away, she was the more beautiful to me. I know her spit and her bile and all her stenches; the freckles livid on her pale cheeks; her square palm clammy in mine; her mossy teeth; her brave smile.

What if those true bones have captured my seed, and planted it, and will not uproot it?

Have I not always believed there was a true place inside her? When she was first enamoured of the Emperor, did I not mark the progress of weeks for her days of bleeding? And gain some calm at that time, and dub these my days of Sanity, and kneel in thanks to her bones for barring his way?

Nay, Microphilus, will you leash yourself again to the Madness that has dogged you all your life?

Where are your wits? She did not tell you about the child. She has the potion from the Crone. By the time you return, your wee lad will be scarcely a memory.

So do not return. Say, with the Crone, 'I have had enough', and find a good ship to take you back to Scotland.

Do not hope again, Microphilus. Do not rise again from the mud, and put yourself under her heel and beg her to grind you down once more: for ever repudiated; for ever Mudskipper.

I must not return. This much at least I owe to Batoom: to be a Mudskipper no more.

There is a ship waiting for me, and ports to compass; a life to live. When we reach Sallee I will find a northward-bound vessel and knock up the captain, and take out my emerald and watch his eyes gleam. Frisk aboard like a ship's cat, with salt on my whiskers –

Or shall I trail back to the Palace, faithful cur with my tail down? And a fresh flock of heedless honeys, and watch their eyes stalk out at the Harem gaudery, while the gates close and lock them away from all this glorious life. And trot off meekly to my Master for my pimp's wages, and please him and be gratified, and roll on my back, and bite my tongue, again and again, for ever. And keep watch over Helen, tethered by Love's blind umbilicus.

And one day, when he finally tires of her, and she is packing up for her journey to Tafilalt, will she accept me then? Ay, perhaps. When she is rejected again, and her true bones are showing through her skin – perhaps then she will accept me. When she wants sweetness and there is none but this crabbit apple at the bottom of the barrel.

Will you wait until then, Microphilus? Oh, Mudskipper will wait. Mudskipper will wait for ever. Microphilus, the man, deserves better.

But what of Microphilus, the father?

Your bairn, Microphilus, if she allows him to live, what kind of father does he deserve?

69

'Which of these shall I prepare, *Lalla*?' Reema stood in the doorway with a shimmering armful of silk.

Helen sighed. 'Is it Thursday already? I didn't realize. Oh, I don't know. You choose.'

'What about something blue? You haven't worn –'

'No!' Helen spoke more sharply than she intended. 'I'm sorry. No, not blue.' If she wore blue, she'd have to get out Naseem's sapphires. She didn't want to look at the sapphires. 'One of the greens. Or something white. White, yes. Something simple.' Nothing that would excite him. She didn't want to play sex with him tonight. She wanted time to think: about the little bottle Malia had given her, hidden on the shelf among her perfumed oils. She wanted to talk to Microphilus; ask him what he thought they should do.

'Can you send for Fijil, please, Reema? Tell him I want to see him before everyone goes into the garden.'

'Fijil, Lady? But he left yesterday morning.'

'What?' A cold stone settled in Helen's stomach.

'He went off with Malia. I thought you realized.'

'Of course. I didn't think.' She pictured him perched on his big white stallion last year, with Lungile pacing alongside; remembered that terrified *sheikh* grovelling on his face in the dust. How Microphilus had bent over to touch him on the shoulder, to reassure him. How he'd taken her hand in Madam Jasmine's courtyard, and kissed it, and thought it the most beautiful hand in the world. In his world it was. In his world a pebble was more valuable than an emerald. In his world she would never grow ugly.

She wandered out into the Queen's Courtyard where two big eunuchs in dusty *salwars* were whitewashing over the blue hands on Zara's walls. A green-canopied chair had come for the older woman yesterday, along with four mules for her slaves and belongings. Helen had tried to speak to her, to say she'd tried pleading with the Emperor, but Zara had pulled her *haik* tight around her face and refused to look at her.

Helen walked slowly around the cloisters, past Douvia's courtyard, with its swathes of scarlet and pink blossom, its litter of leaves and petals, the silent hooks where her twittering cages had hung. And Batoom's, bare and clean as it had always been, with its doors closed once more on their secrets. How quiet it all seemed, without the sounds of all their slaves chattering, pots clanking, water pouring.

She walked into the centre of the Queen's Courtyard, feeling the cool tiles change to hot beneath her feet as she moved from shaded cloister into blazing sunshine. Slowly she turned round: Douvia's quarters, Batoom's, Zara's. All empty. I'm the only queen now, she thought. The most important person in the Harem. The sole Empress of Morocco. I can do anything; move quarters; choose any room I like.

She walked around again, more quickly, comparing each set of rooms. Batoom's had the best trees, but the rest was so bare. Douvia's had all those wonderful flowers, but what would it be like sleeping so close to where she'd died? Zara's then, with her bonny fountain and that cool leafy bower. Once the walls were painted it would be cool and elegant again.

'It's time you were getting ready, *Lalla*,' Reema was calling her. 'The others will be gathering in the garden now.'

'I'm coming.'

rem women, waddling hurriedly along
en paths, breathless and perspiring, fanning
themselves. And the Harem itself, all in disarray, with slaves
wandering through the deserted courtyards, picking up discarded scarves and slippers; blouses, beads, kerchiefs; and the
little shaven toddlers whining for their mothers. Right now
the women would be jostling for position, eyeing the four
green canopies, wondering where the White Queen was, the
one the Emperor loved above all the others.

She could have anything she wanted. Why, then, did she
feel so empty?

In the washroom she tied back her hair and stripped off
her clothes. Pouring warm water, she began lathering herself
quickly: her feet, beneath her arms, between her legs. Then
reached for a jug of cold water and sluiced it all over herself,
gasping at the shock of it, feeling her skin shrinking and tingling.
Then suddenly there were hot tears on her cold cheeks, and she
was kneeling on the wet tiles and sobbing into her hands.

'Tell him I'm bleeding.'

'What?'

'If the Emperor asks, tell him it's my time. He'll understand.
Malia's not here or I'd ask her to do it for me.'

'Are you bleeding, *Lalla*? I didn't realize.'

'No, but Malia said that sometimes, when the body's been
weakened by illness, it can be many moons before the bleeding
returns.'

'Yes, *Lalla*. I had heard that too.' Reema made no move to
leave.

'What is it?'

'I was just wondering what you will do if the bleeding
doesn't return.' She looked steadily into Helen's eyes.

So. She knew. Helen felt a weight lift.

'There's a potion I can take. Malia left it for me.'

'But you haven't taken it.' It was a statement.

'No.'

Reema narrowed her eyes. 'Are you going to take it?'

'I don't know.' Helen put a hand on her belly. She imagined a tiny blind creature holding on somewhere deep inside her body, refusing to let go; a wee heart beating strongly; a fragment of Microphilus's world. There must be a way; all she had to do was think of one. She could get Reema to paint brown blotches on her skin like Zara, and pull her hair out to pretend she was ill again. If he sent her away soon enough, he'd never know about the baby.

If he sent her away, she'd lose her jewels.

'Have you ever been to Tafilalt, Reema?'

'No, *Lalla*. But they say it is a fine place. In a valley, with many rivers. Though they say it can be very cold in the winter.'

'Where I was born it was very cold in the winter. But our houses are built differently to the ones here. We have a fire in the middle of the house, and everyone sleeps near to it, either in the attic beside the chimney or in box beds.' Reema looked blank, so Helen started to explain. 'They're like cupboards, but with a mattress inside, and doors and thick curtains so you can close yourself in. So you only know who's sleeping inside by the shoes on the floor outside.

'When I left home I was in such a hurry I left my shoes behind. So a girl I was travelling with lent me hers. She said they hurt her feet, but I think she did it really so that we'd be friends. Her name was Betty. She was only eighteen, but she already knew she couldn't have children.'

Reema didn't say anything. Just stood in the doorway with her strong arms crossed over her chest.

'I was thinking, when Fijil comes back, he'll have some beautiful women with him.'

'Yes, *Lalla*. Last time there was Naseem and Naula, and yourself of course. And many others. All beautiful. The Emperor was very pleased.'

'And he'll probably get married again soon. So these rooms –' she waved vaguely out through the door. 'They'll all be full again soon of new queens.'

'Very likely, *Lalla* Aziza.'

'The houses in Tafilalt, do you know how big they are? The ones the queens are allocated. Zara was allowed to take two slaves, so they'd have a small courtyard, wouldn't they? And a kitchen, maybe, and a couple of other rooms? A fountain and an outhouse –' Her heart was thundering in her chest. She'd decided.

'If I'm going to speak to the Emperor, I should be going now.'

'Yes, yes. Of course.' She started smiling. A baby, she was having a baby. 'Reema –'

'Yes, *Lalla*?'

'If you wanted to find someone. A white girl who'd been sold into a whore-house in Sallee about a year ago. And you didn't know whether she was still alive. What would you do?'

The older woman pondered a moment. 'I'd sneak out of the Harem and visit a man I know. He was a slave once but now he's a free man. He knows those ports like the back of his hand. I'd ask him to look for her – but he'd want paying.'

Before she'd finished, Helen had opened her trunk. 'Would my emeralds be enough?'

Afterword

Based on a true story

I first came across a reference to Helen Gloag in a book of local history while holidaying in Perthshire. The book described a character straight out of a fairytale: a green-eyed beauty with 'the Gloag hair' (a mixture of red and gold found only in Scotland), who was captured by pirates *en route* to America in 1769 and ended up as the wife of the Emperor of Morocco.

The book gave directions to the place where she'd been born: a tiny hamlet called Mill of Steps, just outside the village of Muthill in Perthshire. I bought an Ordnance Survey map and went to investigate.

There was nothing there, of course. Just a few mossy foundations by the river where the eponymous mill must have stood, and the remains of barns and cottages nearby. But in the graveyard of Muthill Church I found the tilty old headstones of several members of the Gloag family, and the graves of a much larger family by the name of Bayne.

The guidebook made much of young Helen's dubious relationship with a wealthy local farmer named John Bayne. It also suggested that the Scottish lass might have played a part in 'civilizing' the brutal Emperor Sidi Mohammed (*à la The King and I*), who signed a treaty with Spain and established cordial trading relations with the rest of Europe and Turkey during his reign.

I tracked down the book's author, historian Archie McKerracher, who passed on some of his sources. This set me off, that sticky summer, on a long paper-chase through the archives of the Bodleian Library in Oxford and the British Library in London – and libraries in Greenock and Edinburgh – to find out more about Helen Gloag and what life might have been like in a harem in eighteenth-century Morocco.

As anyone who has ever done historical research will tell you, it's both fascinating and confusing. The problem is that authors exaggerate and pass on their prejudices. They report rumour and hearsay as the truth. They reorder events to make neat sequences. They omit items that cloud the picture they're drawing.

I discovered many references in Scotland to a red-haired beauty who became an Empress in Morocco, but they referred to dates ranging from 1618 to 1769 (*The Fourth Queen* is set in 1769). No European travelling in Morocco during this time ever actually met Helen Gloag, however – or any other red-haired woman – though someone answering to her description is mentioned again and again, as being 'Irish' or 'English', as the mysteriously absent wife, mother or grandmother of various Emperors throughout this era. And the notoriously vicious Emperor Yaseed, who reigned after the Emperor in *The Fourth Queen*, was said to have had red hair.

After a while I was forced to conclude that Helen Gloag's enslavement was just the best documented of a whole series of kidnappings that took place during this time. The earliest I came across was in 1618. This lass, too, was captured by pirates and incarcerated in the Emperor's Harem.

I suspect that this early interracial match touched a profound mythic chord in the population at that time, which resonated again and again with tales of the depredations of the swift Moroccan pirate ships which ranged up and down the West Coast in those days – sometimes even as far as Greenock – terrorizing traders and fishing communities. It's no accident,

I think, that the central characters in these archetypal stories have red hair: no one has whiter skin than a red-head. To emphasize the point, a statue carved in 1618 to commemorate 'the Emperor' in the earliest story depicts him with African features and curly hair (and so presumably very dark skin), despite the fact that Moors in those days were typically more Semitic than African in appearance.

In common with other 'true' accounts of the period, I have reordered some events to make a neat sequence, included events from preceding and succeeding Emperors' reigns because I could not resist them, and embroidered the gaps in between. If you're curious to discover to what extent I have deviated from the eighteenth- and nineteenth-century accounts, I have listed the most important books I consulted.

A Dr William Lempriere really was held under house arrest and forced to treat the wives of the Emperor – including one *Lalla* Zara, close to death from suspected poisoning. A woman named Julia Crisp really did visit Morocco, and pretend to be married as a ruse to deflect the Emperor's amorous advances. If we can believe the historical accounts, *Lalla* Douvia, the tortured child queen, really existed; *Lalla* Batoom, the head queen who wrestled with the Emperor, did too.

As for Microphilus: his voice is based on the writings of Jeffrey Hudson, the 'peppery dwarf' in the Court of Charles I. Hudson was captured by Barbary pirates and enslaved for around twenty-five years – during which time he grew in stature by eighteen inches. As he died in 1681, over seventy years before Helen was born, they could never have met. But I fell in love with him, so I thought she might have done too.

Debbie Taylor
North Shields, 2002

Further Reading

Julia Crisp, *The Female Captive: a Narrative of Facts, Which Happened in Barbary in the Year 1756.* Printed in London by C. Bathurst, with an introduction by Sir William Musgrave, 1769

Jeffrey Hudson, Lord Minimus, aka Microphilus, *The New Yeere's Gift*, 1638

Sir R. Lambert Playfair and Dr Robert Brown, *A Bibliography of Morocco from the earliest times to the end of 1891*, John Murray, London, 1892

Arthur Leared, *Morocco and the Moors* (illustrated, with an introduction by Sir Richard Burton), London, 1876

Arthur Leared, *A Visit to the Court of Morocco*, London, 1879

William Lempriere, *A Tour from Gibraltar to Tangier, Salee, Mogodor, Santa Cruz, Tarcidant and thence over Mount Atlas to Morocco: Including a particular account of the Royal Harem, etc.*, London, 1791

Archie McKerracher, *Perthshire in History and Legend*, John Donald Publishers Limited, Edinburgh, 1988

Budgett Meakin, *The Moorish Empire*, London, 1899

Nick Page, *Lord Minimus: the Extraordinary Life of Britain's Smallest Man*, HarperCollins Publishers, London, 2001

Thomas Pellow, *The Adventure of Thomas Pellow, Mariner: a Narrative of his Shipwreck and Subsequent Enslavement in Morocco*, London, 1715

Jean Louis Marie Poirot, *Travels through Barbary, in a series of letters written from the ancient Numidia in the years 1785 and*

1786 and containing an account of the customs and manners of the Moors and Bedouin Arabs, 1791

M. Russell, *The History and Present Condition of the Barbary States*, 1835

John Shearer, *Antiquities of Strathearn, with Historical and Traditionary Tales and Biographical Sketches of Celebrated Individuals belonging to the District*, 1836

Tobias Smollett, *The Adventures of Roderick Random*, originally published in 1748

Miss Tully, *Narrative of a Ten-Year Residence in Morocco*, London, 1816